D0940445

THE FIX

by

Jeff Schneider

VIVISPHERE
PUBLISHING

Without limiting the rights under copyright reserved above, no part of this publication may be reproduced, stored in or introduced into a retrieval system, or transmitted, in any form, or by any means (electronic, mechanical, photocopying, recording, or otherwise), without the prior written permission of both the copyright owner and the publisher of this book. For information address Vivisphere Publishing, a division of NetPub Corporation, 2 Neptune Road, Poughkeepsie, NY 12601.

Copyright © Jeff Schneider, 2001
All rights reserved

Author Photo by Mark Lynch

ISBN 1-58776-119-X

Library of Congress Catalogue Number 2001-087413

www.vivisphere.com

1-800-724-1100

VIVISPHERE
PUBLISHING

Dedication

Joelle, Jean Marie, Marcus Jeffrey, Elizabeth Anne—I love you.
Mom and Dad for telling me I could be anything in the world if I tried.
Tom and Joan for always treating me like one of your own.
John Dromo, I feel your hand on my shoulder, your voice in my ear. Rest in peace.

Acknowledgments

The journey and spirit of any story builds over time, including mine. My support team has been vast, including Dr. Tom Kemme, Phil Coffin, and Ray Hall in the beginning. Kathy Tronzo and Kenny Klein were also there, and always have been. Nancy Fust heard my cries, and listened. Dr. Karen Juliano and the Holy Rosary Academy family supported me when I needed it. I also leaned on the great John Grisham and Frank Karaglanis. Caroline Carney and Books Deals, Inc., opened the door. Renni and Ross Browne of The Editorial Department kept it open with their keen insights. And none of this would be worth reading without editor Betsy Tice White, a true friend and loving critic. Last but not least, it was Peter Cooper who saw something when everyone else was sleeping. Yes, I'm still thinking about that island.

And to all the mentors who ever coached me. I was listening… most of the time.

God bless. From the bottom of my heart.

Only passions, great passions, can elevate the soul to great things

— Denis Diderot

THE FIX

Prologue

Seventeen seconds showed on the clock in the corner of the television. Austin Peay led Western Kentucky by five. Western's gigantic reserve center from Greece leaned over to wipe the sweat from his hands on his socks before walking tentatively to the line for a one-and-one with the world watching his every move. He needed to make the first free throw if W.K.U. was going to have a chance to grab the rebound and attempt a three-pointer to tie.

Mike Kramer tugged his faded John Deere cap, crushed his soda can, measured the distance to the trash bin, and followed the center's arm movements, both launching simultaneously.

They both missed the shot. The center's went left off the rim, Mike's went right off the edge of the can. "Damn," Mike said, shaking his head. Peay grabbed the rebound and stalled to bleed the last seconds from the game.

Eleven. Ten. Nine. "I can't believe it," Mike said to no one. "Bunch of rednecks are actually going to win the whole thing."

Mike reached out with his foot, turned off the television set in the dayroom of his dorm. Austin Peay were the new NCAA Basketball Champions.

"Hey, Kramer, you up for a beer?" A voice from the inner hallway caught Mike's ear. For a second he considered it, but then thought about his old man.

"Nah." Mike waved as he headed for the outside door. "Think I'll do some shooting."

"Shooting? Season's over, man."

"To everyone else, not me," he said as he left, his missed shot irking him.

Outside Mike took a deep breath. The sky swirled, and the air was wet from the recent storms. Just the right amount to set the fields to sprouting. He smiled. His ma used to say a spring rain was money in the bank by end of summer. She was usually right.

Of course, it all depended on whether Fletcher, his old man, stayed out of the honky-tonks and got the fields plowed and planted in time—and that was even money every year. Good years, the family managed to stay level. Unfortunately, since Mike had come to Catholic U., there had been more bad years than good.

"You stay, Michael," Ma said, every time he suggested he should come back home to help. "The best field you can plow right now is right there in your head. God'll help us get by. Don't worry."

But he did worry, knowing she was holding back large pieces of the truth. Still, he couldn't go against her.

Mike glanced up at a cluster of dark clouds putting a zone defense on the sun. Watching others play on television always made him itchy, jumpy—a pressure system building within him that only playing could release. He knew he'd better hurry if he wanted to dribble on dry pavement.

The limestone walls separating Catholic U. from the southeastern edge of Louisville seemed to sag from the creeping decay and mild desperation that lay just on the other side. Small aging row houses were sprinkled amid tiny suburban knockoffs that seemed to be held up by their fading paint alone.

Funny how his eyes had changed. When he first arrived he only saw the college—so orderly, clean, preppie, so vastly different from the ramshackle farmhouse his family rented in the Appalachian part of the state.

That first day he was sure he had found heaven. Why shouldn't he have? His old man hadn't cussed or hit him. But three years of study and travel with the team had opened his eyes. Catholic U. was as quaint and dowdy as Louisville, though it was a drastic improvement from the mud roads back home.

Shouts from the outdoor basketball court drew his attention to a group he hadn't played against yet. He leaned against the rusting chain-link fence to watch. Five black teenage boys had separated naturally—the two best playing against the other three. All five were taller than his five foot nine, and all jumped so easily, so naturally. He wished he had their physical gifts.

He waited until the ball bounced his way, picked it up, weighed it thoughtfully. He wondered if they knew what it was like to take an elbow to the mouth. He wondered if they knew he could play circles around them—blindfolded. He wondered if they practiced day and night to get better, or if they played purely for fun. He decided to take it easy on them, though turning off his intensity was always hard to do, especially on a basketball court.

"Hey, man, that ain't no tittie," one of the taller blacks called out. "Give it up, bro."

"The way you girls play, this might as well be a big orange tittie." Mike laughed, sent a rocketing bounce to another boy under the basket, past the one who had called out.

The move brought an appreciative nod. "Hey, you play for the Knights, don't you?"

Mike turned his cap around. "Maybe."

The boys finally recognized his face. They were impressed. "We're short a man," the tallest one said. "You wanna hoop?"

"Sure."

He played at quarter speed and refrained from shooting for the first several minutes—even when he had an easy shot—measuring the boys' skills, feeling the pace of their game, not wanting to embarrass them with a quick slash to the basket.

"You guys watch the finals?" Mike asked.

"That ain't till June," one of them scoffed.

"I meant the Final Four."

"Naw, that ain't real no more, it's so watered down," one of his opponents said. "College ain't nothing now but the minor leagues for the pros."

"You right," the tall center for the other side said, huffing from a rebound and a quick scurry back to the half-court line. "Only two places the game really matters anymore."

"Yeah, where's that?" Mike lowered into a defensive crouch, waiting for the opportunity to pick the ball.

"NBA's one," the boy said, juking to catch Mike off balance.

"And the other place it's real?"

"Right here," the boy said, feinting to his right, the ball behind his back for a quick shift to the left.

But Mike stung the ball away, retrieved it, whipped a pass to his teammate, then took a position out beyond the three-point line. When the other team converged on the guy with the ball, he slid a lazy pass to Mike, who caught it, squared himself, and floated it on a perfect arc to the hoop. The ball fell silently, flipping the net over the rim.

The opposing trio turned and stared.

"You're right," Mike said with a slight smile. "This is where it matters."

Chapter 1

The killer stroked his shiny golden ponytail and waited. One more minute and the lights would go out. Finally they dimmed. He took a deep breath, relaxed. Midnight. He had measured the place for three nights in a row and knew his man was fast asleep, probably dreaming about all the sexy young coeds that had just left his room. Their bodies. What he'd like to do with them when the lights were out. He chuckled. Party was over.

This basketball player wouldn't be expecting him now, especially after all the weed and cold beer consumed at the party. The smell of the pot lingered, curling around his nose. But he had made his warning to Antoine so clear.

All in black, except for a red rubber band around the ponytail, he moved out of the shadows on the balls of his feet to silence his arrival. The only noise came from the end of the hall where the muffle of a television and some small laughter could be heard. Maybe somebody watching Leno, Letterman. The rest of the hall was quiet. College kids studying to take over the world. He was amused.

As he reached the door he was thinking the cops would make a lot of noise at first, but when they found out what the kid was doing it would all be quietly swept under the rug. Always was. He had learned over the years. Colleges hated scandals. This would be a scandal.

He felt the doorknob through his glove. His heartbeat quickened. He turned the knob slowly, then pushed gently with his left shoulder, sliding his back along the inside wall. A full moon illuminated the room, shadows of a tree falling across the ten-by-ten space. A figure rumpled the bedcovers, face turned away, blanket pulled to his shoulders. The killer wanted to wake Antoine and ask him why he didn't miss the baskets they'd asked him to miss. Why he took the ten thousand dollars, then didn't follow through with their little secret. But there was no time for questions now. He had his orders.

He slipped the gun with its silencer from the holster strapped to his right ankle, brought it quietly to Antoine's ear, then splattered the eggshell-colored wall with blood. Antoine's blood. The killer stood there for a second and watched the purple blood streak down the wall. He wondered what kind of kid would take this kind of chance. Didn't they know?

The killer shook his head, then turned and slipped a watch and some money from a wallet into his pocket. Make all this look like a robbery, give the university an out when they discovered Antoine was fixing college basketball games.

Was.

In charge of the FBI's Sports Fraud Division, Dale Cutter drove faster when he heard the news over the radio. They might have elevated him out of Homicide, but they couldn't take the job out of him. A basketball player had been found murdered at Georgetown University. That alarmed him, as it would the rest of the D.C. community later in the morning. Athletes didn't die this way. Only junkies and winos died like dogs.

He hopped out of his white Crown Victoria and walked the flight of stairs. Campus police already had the crime scene under control. Students rubbernecked to see what was going on. He flashed his I.D., then made his way to the particular dorm room.

"What do we have?" he said to his old assistant, Rudy, a wide-shouldered man with a long neck who was chewing gum at a frantic pace.

"What're you doing here, man?" Rudy propped his fists on his hipbones and stared. "You know you shouldn't be here."

"This kid is an athlete, right? I figured it fell under my jurisdiction."

"You're kind of stretching it, aren't you?"

"Only if you're into details." Dale smiled and winked. "So what's going on here? Crowd outside is getting bigger by the second."

"Shot twice in the head. Close range. Kid never had a chance. Bullets went through his brain…lodged here in the wall."

Dale winced as he followed Rudy's finger to the blood on the wall. He had never taken death as easily as others in the department. "Any motive?"

Rudy looked back from the bullet holes. "Maybe robbery. Cash missing from the wallet. Could be drugs. Could be he was fucking some professor's wife. Who knows anymore. Kids aren't like they used to be."

Dale's eyes slowly scanned the room. Things seemed in place. He had suspicions, though, especially after the recent shenanigans at Northwestern and Notre Dame. College basketball players didn't get killed in their own dorm rooms in the middle of the night once in a blue moon, not once in ten. If it were drugs, they wouldn't have come to his room and blown his brains out. Would have happened on the streets. If he were screwing some professor's wife, the murderer would have panicked and left a trail as wide as Montana. No, this was something else. Years of detective work told him so. "Anyone seen coming or going?"

Rudy scratched his head. "Not a soul. Whoever it was vanished into the night. Must have been a black cat." He looked rueful. "A cat with some real nasty hardware."

Dale walked over to a bookcase full of trophies. "Our dead ballplayer was hell on wheels, if I remember correctly." He lifted a tall trophy and inspected it. "MVP last year in the Great Alaskan Shootout. Knew I recognized his name. He was recruited out of New York a couple of years ago to play here. They all said he'd be the next Bernard King."

"Yeah, well, he ain't ever going to shoot another basketball, that's for sure." Rudy tossed a sheet over the body and shook his head slowly.

"Rudy," Dale said, putting the trophy down, "check all the kid's phone calls for the last six months."

"Hey, this ain't your deal anymore, Dale. Go back and sit in the big chair of yours and coast like they want you to. Relax, baby. Take the money and run."

"Nope, can't, I'm suddenly getting a hunch."

"A hunch, huh?" Rudy finished filling out a document and handed it to a uniformed cop. "You always got hunches. What's this one?" Sarcasm dripped from his words.

"Don't worry about that, just check the phone numbers, give me a call in the morning."

Dale stepped through the growing throng of students, made his way back to his car. The back of his neck tingled. Basketball players didn't die this way. A long-time question of his suddenly popped back into his head. Why did men become involved in games of children? It was almost always the children who got hurt. He could cite a thousand examples, including one that happened to him growing up.

"Throw it here, Dale. Hurry…hurry…hurry!"

The first baseman called for it anxiously, his outstretched glove open, one eye on him, one on the runner. Dale had the ball in his glove and knew there was time. Knew he could give the man half the baseline and still get the ball from short to first without a strain. He reached into the glove, wrapped his right hand over the seams, pulled the ball out, took it behind his ear, went to release. But something in the stands flipping in the breeze caught his eye for a split second. He turned and looked at it for some reason only a child could explain—an empty popcorn container—then directed his attention back to the game. The ball left his hand as usual, snapping through his right two fingers with authority. It sailed on a line and popped the first baseman's glove.

"Safe!"

Safe? He couldn't believe the ump's bark. No way, Dale first thought. He never missed that throw. Then he looked at Dinwitty taking the ball out of his glove, shaking his head, tossing it maddeningly back to the pitcher.

"GODDAMMIT, DALE!"

The voice was low and full of octane. Thrust from a jet you couldn't see, only feel shaking the earth. He hunched his shoulders and kicked the dirt. He knew what was coming...Coach.

"Dale, that's the third error today, son." Specks of broken blood vessels stood out in the whites of his eyes. "What the hell gives with you today?"

Before the words hit him, a stream of tobacco juice sprayed his shirt. He took a step back, then kicked the dirt again. "I'm sorry, Coach." He swiped his head with the palm of his hand. Eyes around the field were riveted to the action, you'd think he'd been caught stealing an old woman's purse.

"Sorry ain't good enough, Dale. *We're* here to win...and *you* aren't."

Coach called for the ball from the pitcher, then turned his hat around so the bill shadowed his deep red neck. He gripped it and fired it, snapping the first baseman's glove. "*That's* how you throw the ball to first, son."

The ball came back. Coach pawed it so hard his knuckles turned white. "Dale," the man screamed again, punching the air with a stiff index finger. "Get the hell off this field!"

Dale finally looked up, a sharp sun directly behind the coach's left ear. He remembered it so clearly—all he'd wanted to do was slither away. "I'm sorry, sir."

"Get...off...the field, I said. NOW!"

Dale squinted, then turned for the dugout, hearing the laughter from the crowd. Crossing third base, he suddenly felt something explode between his shoulder blades.

He fell headfirst into the dirt, sand speckling his face. For a moment he was silent, then he started to cry. The ball was the first thing he saw when he opened his eyes. The sonofabitch threw it.

Dale quickly became a basketball fan.

Rudy knocked on Dale's office door for the third time, then walked on in. "You been sleeping in here or something?"

Dale's eyes were glazed, more in the back of his head than the front. The knot in his tie fell halfway down his shirt. Whiskers peppered his face. Finally he mumbled something incoherent.

Rudy shook his head and spoke at the same time: "Bro, you look rough. Here, drink some coffee and have a doughnut." He pulled out a glaze and put it on the desk.

Dale straightened in his chair and took the coffee. A magazine fell to the floor. He coughed and cleared his throat. A clock on the wall behind his head ticked loudly.

"You fall asleep reading or something?" Rudy asked again as he picked up a copy of *The NCAA News*.

"Yeah," Dale said. "When I left you last night I came here to follow up on that hunch I was telling you about."

"Man, you're nuts, aren't you? You aren't working Homicide anymore. Can't you get that into your thick skull?"

Dale didn't even hear what Rudy was saying. "Well, I knew something was funny by what happened to the kid, so I came back here and reread some of these old issues."

"First I've heard of the NCAA dealing with murder." Rudy sat down, propped his feet on the corner of Dale's desk. He slipped another chocolate doughnut into his mouth.

"It was these gambling stories I was checking into." Dale pointed at a copy of the sports journal again.

"Gambling stories?"

"Uh-huh, gambling."

Rudy picked up immediately on what Dale was thinking. "So you think the kid may have been betting?"

"Yeah, I do."

"And he was losing and didn't pay up, and the bookie came and whacked him?"

Dale sipped the coffee, then dunked half his doughnut in the liquid. "Could be that." He took a bite before the soggy pastry dropped into the cup. "Or it could be he was involved in fixing a game."

Rudy's head jerked back. "Fixing a college game? No way."

"Why not?"

"Bro, that shit only happens in the movies."

"Fact is stranger than fiction, Rudy."

"Nah...that's nuts."

Dale bent and picked up a copy of *Sports Illustrated*. "Not really. This story is all about that deal at Northwestern where the kid was throwing games for cash. Here, check it out." He tossed the magazine into Rudy's lap. "I think I'm onto something, that's why I need you to find out all you can about the kid's phone records for me. Not just numbers...everything."

Rudy glared. "I've done you one favor already. I had to sneak this shit over here to you." He flipped the phone records onto Dale's desk. "My ass will be on the line if they know you're snooping around in something that's none of your business."

"Well, if you remember correctly, you owe me one or two."

Rudy grimaced. His old boss did have a few secrets hanging over his head, and his hunches were usually right. "Bro, this is the last one, so help me God."

Later in the day Rudy was back with an address for every phone call coming and going to Antoine Tandy over the last six months. He plopped the bulging file on Dale's desk. "Nothing, Dale. Not even one single call to get a hooker. This kid is as clean as Mary Poppins."

Dale picked the file up and scanned the contents. For fifteen minutes he didn't say a word, then finally he looked up. "Rudy, get down to that school and start asking questions. Someone must have seen something. Talk to teammates. I guarantee they'll know something. Teammates know everything. He must have said something."

Rudy shook his head. "Nope, this ain't your deal anymore, Dale. Anyhow, the boys in blue are already calling it a burglary gone bad."

Dale clasped his hands behind his head and leaned back in the chair. "I got a different hunch, Rudy. A hunch that there's a lot more gambling going on in college basketball than we all realize. And a hunch that if we don't do something about it, someone else is going to die...just like our friend Antoine. He played a hunch—"

"Yeah, and he died."

"Okay, but if you don't follow up on what I'm saying, the guilt will be on your shoulders. Can you live with that, Rudy?"

Rudy hung his head.

Chapter 2

Paul Justin tapped his ring lightly on the glass of the tall window in the World Broadcasting Company's 37th floor conference room with his 1959 Syracuse National Championship ring. Once, twice. The third time he gave the window a sharp rap, then turned and faced the five men and two women around the long gleaming tabletop.

"It just doesn't make sense, Richard," he said.

Murmurs, a few shaking heads.

"No?" The NCAA executive director's eyebrows went up. Richard Ogelsby was a political animal, a cautious man.

Justin walked to the head of the table, put his hands on it palms down, leaned forward. He frowned. "I know you think we've had the contract for the Final Four forever, but the Bird-Magic classic was the last time we reaped any significant returns. Last year's ratings were a disgrace." He waited, but no one spoke. "And do you know why?"

Herb Smithers, the alleged marketing expert, took the risk. "The Fox Network?"

Justin turned a vulture's gaze on him. "If I thought that was balls on your part...instead of sheer stupidity...I might—"

"Be fair, old chap." Peter J. McCraken, Junior, was polishing his nails on his seersucker lapel as he spoke. "You did ask if we knew why."

The salvo that rose to Justin's tongue never made it past his lips—a protective instinct arising from a promise Justin had made to the man's father, Peter "Pappy" McCraken, Senior, his own predecessor and former boss.

The great man of sports television presided over the meeting now, his portrait hanging majestically on the room's paneled wall.

"Take care of my boy for me, will you, Paulie?" Pappy had asked when he entrusted the young Boston College dropout to Paul for his first network job. "It's not right for me to train him. You're better at it, anyway."

And Paul had shown young Mac the ropes, time and time again. So much rope, more than enough for the effete, ineffectual son to hang himself many times over. But he was made of slicker Teflon than even O.J. He'd never once tasted the salt from his own sweat. By the time the old man retired, the boy had risen to the protected position of Vice President of Corporate Marketing. His only contribution—a minor one—was the recruitment of Smithers, the nerdy numbers-whiz. Between Mac and Smithers, they did the work of half a man, but at least Smithers made an attempt—occasionally.

"Yes, I certainly did ask," Paul said, stifling his inner storm, twisting the ring on his finger. He kept his tone deceptively reasonable. "You need to know that I just had my ass chewed royally by the Board of Directors, because they've concluded it would be unprofitable to bid for the contract after next year's final."

Ogelsby held his tongue. Next year he could venture away from the network and seek other bids. This year it would be suicidal to move from under WBC's umbrella.

"But what about tradition?" McCraken had gone from polishing nails to adjusting his pearl cufflinks. "Doesn't the board care about that?" He winked at Ogelsby.

"Oh, yes, the board actually had quite a lot to say about tradition." Justin moved to an easel, uncovered a graph that looked like the south slope of Mount Everest. "See, here was tradition they liked." He pointed to a slightly ragged line that built to a long, rising crest. "This was when our NCAA basketball coverage was profitable." He moved the pointer down the falling slope. "And this is the tradition since this particular group took over marketing and programming."

Ogelsby squirmed.

"I think they're overestimating our control," Smithers said. "Who would have thought Wichita State would upset Michigan last year to get to the big dance? And this year. How the hell are we supposed to market a championship game featuring a bunch of rednecks from Austin Peay? What were we supposed to use for a logo, a chamber pot?"

"Peay fans are probably still drunk and dancing in their underwear." It was a feminine whisper from the far end of the table—Carter, the graphics pro.

Before Justin could fix his glare on her, McCraken spoke up. "I, for one, was embarrassed for all of college basketball to hear them chanting during time-outs...'Let's Go Peay!' Really, I ask you."

Ogelsby chewed the end of a pencil, listening to the volleys.

Justin rubbed his temples. There was only one thing worse than this nightmare—the fact that he was awake.

"Both clubs were Cinderellas," Demsky, from Programming, said from his place at one side. "That normally makes for good television."

"The critics loved your graphics," Ogelsby said, with what he hoped was an endearing smile. "Having the coach turn into a pumpkin and then change to a basketball really got their attention."

"Come on, do you really think viewers in L.A. and New York, or even some of the folks in Europe cared?" Paul asked. "The real glass slipper is ratings, and right now we look like the ugly stepsisters."

One chuckle from the side of the table was swallowed quickly behind a false clearing of the throat. Justin ignored it, opened his briefcase instead, and handed a large stack of papers to McCraken, who took the top packet and passed the pile to his left.

"Gentlemen, ladies, here are next year's rating criteria from the board. If we reach these goals, the board may allow a bid for the new contract." Justin turned away and walked back to his vantage point by the window, biting his lower lip.

"Excuse me," Ogelsby said.

"Yes?" Justin half turned.

"These criteria call for a twenty-eight rating." Ogelsby's glasses were on the end of his nose. "The best we've ever reached is twenty-two."

"What's your point?"

"I believe his point," McCraken said, "is that the highest we've ever reached was twenty-two."

Justin ignored McCraken to zero in on Ogelsby. "What do you think the highest rating was before that high mark? Twenty-one?" He moved to the graph again, pointed to the middle of the crest. "We were stuck in the middle teens until the Bird-Magic match-up."

"Those kind of match-ups come once in a lifetime. Look at what happened to the NBA after they both retired."

"I'll tell you what happened to the NBA. Michael Jordan, Grant Hill, Shaquille O'Neal, Tim Duncan. That's what happened." Justin sputtered with disgust. "People have never given a damn about the theme songs, logos, the student-athlete facade you guys hide behind. They want players, kids they can follow and root for every chance they get."

"But the kids don't stay in college anymore," Smithers said. "They leave after their sophomore year."

"Hell, some of the little ingrates turn pro right out of high school now," Ogelsby said. "Let's see, Kobie Bryant, Kevin Garnett…"

"Moses Malone," McCraken said.

What an idiot, Justin thought, glaring at the man. Malone had entered the defunct ABA as a hardship case. Kobe Bryant's father played in the NBA, raised the boy in affluence. He eventually turned from McCraken to assume a professorial stance, chin on his fist.

"Carter, you're Catholic, right?" he said to the woman at the far end of the table.

"Yes, sir."

"Who was Notre Dame's star basketball player this year?"
Silence.

"How many of their games did you watch?"

"Uh, maybe two or three."

"Why did you watch them?"

"Well, uh, they're Notre Dame."

Paul let his finger roam the table, stopped at Demsky. "You're from L.A., right?"

"Orange County, south of L.A."

"Close enough. Watch U.C.L.A., U.S.C., Pepperdine?"

"Whenever they're on, sure."

"Where did you go to college?"

"N.Y.U."

"That's right." Paul's smile might have been a sneer. "You wanted to be a filmmaker."

Smithers waved his hand excitedly.

"Yes, Herb?"

"I just did some preliminary figuring." He held up a piece of paper filled with equations. "The latest demographics indicate that a Final Four consisting of St. John's, U.C.L.A., Notre Dame, and North Carolina would offer the best ratings from a mixture of alumni, name awareness, and regional audience."

"That's very nice."

The marketing assistant looked like he was about to launch into a long recitation of facts and figures.

Justin cut him off, turned to McCraken. "Hey…will you see that we get those teams for the Final Four this year?"

All around the table, guarded eyes suddenly became unguarded as the fantastic request sank in. Maybe Justin was serious, not sarcastic.

Smithers wouldn't be put off. "I figured it out, sir. If those four teams made it to the finals, we would realize… $112,687,450…in additional revenues."

Ogelsby grinned, shot an elbow to McCraken's side.

Justin studied him for a moment. "Can I borrow your calculator?"

"Sure," Smithers said, flushed with excitement.

"Let's see…the odds of that happening are…"

Justin punched numbers randomly into the calculator, held it up for all to see, his eyebrows raised in mock shock. "Zero. Nil. Zippo."

The blood drained from Smithers' face.

Ogelsby spoke up. His NCAA lapel pin sparkled under the lights.

"I know times have been better, but we've been together for almost a quarter of a century. You were an athlete, a good one at that. You know sometimes, no matter how hard you fight, you don't always win. And then, when you're not expecting it, you all of a sudden break out of that slump and go on a tear.

"I really have a gut feeling that something exciting is going to happen this year. We've got some outstanding teams out there in some potential hot markets. All we need is a team like U.C.L.A., Georgia Tech, Georgetown, or St. John's to get to the Final Four. And from all the research I've done, I think it can happen."

No one spoke. Justin pondered, twisted the ring on his hand, reflected on something Pappy had told him years ago:

"Search the soul, son. There the truth lies. Sometimes it's not the answer you seek, but truth nonetheless."

He was wishing for Pappy now, wishing for some of his magic again. Old Man Mac was a workhorse who brought sports to the forefront during the mid-1960s with live sporting events from Rome, Austria, Los Angeles, all around the world. A photo of Pappy with Cassius Clay after Clay knocked out Sonny Liston in the first fight still hung in Justin's office. And beyond the sports, Pappy had also directed WBC's coverage of the Vietnam War, the Apollo 11 moon landing, the shootings at Kent State. A miracle-worker, he was idolized in the industry and sorely missed at WBC.

All eyes were still fixed on the boss. He took a deep breath, exhaled, then curled his lips. "All right…it's a deal. I'm going to give the Final Four one more year…that's if I can convince the board."

Smiles filled the room. McCraken threw an arm around Richard Ogelsby, handed him a Cuban cigar.

Justin retreated to the window, whispered up at the looming portrait above him. "Pappy, looks like we'll need one of your miracles to pull this one off."

After the meeting broke, Justin nodded at McCraken to stay. "Mac, there's a certain part of me that tells me I just made a stupid decision with the NCAA." He paused, placed a hand over his mouth, paced back and forth. "The only reason I agreed on continuing this contract for one more year is because they stuck with us during our lean years...and the fact your old man would want it this way."

"I'm behind you a hundred percent. You did the right thing."

But words weren't going to solve the problem, especially words coming from the pitiful specimen in front of him.

Justin coughed hard. The heart attack again. "Mac, I'm getting too old and unfit for all the pressure of this anymore. My wife has even been urging me to retire." He paused, studied McCraken's face. "I've been thinking about this for some time. I'm putting you in charge of seeing this thing through."

McCraken winced. The last time Justin had seen such a face was back in high school when Chuck Bielefeld gave Mr. Winkler, the English teacher, a Coke laced with urine. "In...charge? Of the Final Four?"

"Right." Another deep hack. Justin eased into a chair. "I won't be around forever. It's your turn. The board wants the ratings up."

At first the idea drew a slight smile, then the reality of it hit McCraken. "But, I...I—"

"Be a man, boy." Justin's hand slammed against the conference table as shades of red inched up his neck. "I've shown you everything. I've coddled you from the day your old man brought you here. No more. Now you have to produce. The gravy train ends."

McCraken stepped back. "W-what should I do?"

Justin shook his head. "You figure it out. I'll be around if you need help, but it's time you grew up...earned your damn keep."

The bartender took a twenty and said the beer would be out as soon as he tapped a new keg.

"How about here?" Peter asked.

Ogelsby sat down at a corner table as he eyed two nude lesbians kissing on stage. "Boy, they sure don't have places like this back in Indy."

"I come here pretty often after hours to get the taste of Justin out of my mouth. He can be a mean bastard."

"He was pretty uptight today. I'm shocked he made the decision he did."

"I think it's the heart. He hasn't been normal. By the way, he just put me in charge of the Final Four, which he'd never do if he were feeling well."

A waitress with big red hair and a ring in her nose brought two frosted glasses and plunked down the pitcher in the middle of the table.

"We'll need another one in about ten minutes." Peter winked. "My friend has a long flight home."

They both took deep drinks, scanned the dance floor.

"God, I hope to hell this year's Final Four reaches an all-time high," Ogelsby said. "It would solve a lot of our problems, especially since we'll have to spend so much in the move to Indy. As a matter of fact, I think we need to take your boy Smithers up on his proposal."

"What d'you mean?"

"In the meeting. What he said."

Peter reflected. "What was that?"

"One hundred and twelve million dollars…and change."

"Come on, Ogelsby. You mean getting those four teams into the Final Four?"

"Yeah, wouldn't that be great? God, those teams would solve the ratings problem, especially the Irish."

McCraken slumped in his seat. "In point of fact, I'm not a basketball fan, but it does seem getting any two of those teams Smithers mentioned in the Final Four would be a godsend. Everybody in the world would watch U.C.L.A. and Notre Dame play."

Ogelsby filled his glass again, spilling beer down its side. "They would. The last good game between them was when the Irish stopped the eighty-eight–game winning streak. Remember?"

McCraken didn't, but he played along. "Certainly I do."

Ogelsby checked his watch. "Say, if I keep drinking like this, I'll sleep all the way home." He whistled quietly to himself when a trim blonde skirted by. "Christ, McCraken, you really know how to show a guest a good time."

Peter smiled smugly. "Stay here long enough and you'll see anybody who is anybody. I've seen Madonna in here before with Rodman."

"Yeah, I could see Dennis Rodman in here."

They both laughed.

Ogelsby loosened his tie, slammed his beer. "Maybe we could get those two to sing the national anthem at the Final Four. It'd be great pub."

They laughed again. McCraken offered a cigarette, waved for another pitcher of beer.

"No thanks, Pete."

Something on the other side of the smoke-filled room caught McCraken's eye. "Richard...see that big man over there?"

Ogelsby half turned, his wire-rimmed glasses glinting as a strobe light crossed the room. "The one with all the gorgeous women around him?"

"That's the one."

"What about him?"

"He could get Madonna to sing."

"Is that her agent or something?"

"No, that's Luca Marzzarella. They call him The Big Cheese. Mob."

"Mob? Seriously? Why do they call him The Big Cheese?"

"Think about it. Marzzarella, mozzarella. He's big-time all right. My father knew him. I remember once going with Father to the man's house on Long Island. I thought our place was super until I saw his.

He had his own bowling alley and a shark tank in his bedroom."
McCraken blew a cloud into the ceiling.

Ogelsby took another long look.

"Would you like me to introduce you?"

Ogelsby threw a fool's glance at his friend. "Yeah, right. I could just see the paparazzi popping up out of nowhere and shooting a photo of me shaking the hand of some mob creep. That would look good in the *National Enquirer*. The NCAA doing business with the mafiosi. No thanks, Pete, not tonight."

Chapter 3

F ather Charles found a parking spot on Euclid, half a block down from Vine. The bulky red-faced Jesuit wiped his fore-head with the back of his hand and checked the back seat to be sure there would be room and nothing of importance that might get crushed. He glanced in the rear-view mirror, feeling funny wearing a Hawaiian shirt—his only souvenir from a conference on alcoholism in the priesthood in Oahu four years ago. Quite appropriate for tonight's mission.

He got out of the car and walked into Clark's, a campus hangout with a trendy bar that also attracted businessmen on their way home for the evening. Pictures of past C.U. athletic teams decorated the walls. License plates from every state in the Lower Forty-Eight were nailed to the ceiling. A picture of Jimmy Buffett hung behind the bar. Thankful the place was only half-filled, he headed directly toward Bill Hopfinger who was waving to him from a rear booth. Catholic University's overweight trainer, Hopfinger could easily have passed for a young Jackie Gleason.

"Thanks for coming, Father." Bill was nervous. "I wasn't sure what to do."

"Where's Coach, Hoppy?" Father Charles scanned the tables, but he didn't see Big Eddie.

"He's in the can." Hoppy nodded toward the long hallway that led to the restrooms. "He's pretty wasted."

"What set him off this time?"

"That junior-college transfer from Chicago decided to go to DePaul." Hoppy lifted his hand for the waitress, but she didn't see him. "You want something, Father?"

"No thanks, we should probably get him out of here as soon as possible." The priest leaned across the table. "Father Callahan's been secretly talking to the board about replacing Eddie. At best he'll be on probation. If they get wind of the fact that he's on another bender…"

"It's just the preseason, Father," Hoppy said, still trying to catch the waitress's eye.

"You know, Hoppy, if they bring in a new coach, more than likely he'll bring his own staff with him." He grabbed the big man's rumpled lab-jacket sleeve. "And that might include a new trainer."

Hoppy blinked. "Damn, Father, I've been here longer than Big Eddie. I thought…"

"Guilt by association."

"Shit." Hoppy slumped hard against the booth. "He wasn't like this before Sally left him."

Father Charles folded his hands. Had he been a parish priest, having regular contact with couples, he might have been better equipped to deal with such affairs of the heart. Most of the students on campus were young, filled with the promise of their lives. Their heartbreaks usually resulted in a temporary dip in grades, not a long desperate slide into alcohol and depression.

"Let me go see how he's doing in there." Hoppy slid out of the booth.

Father Charles stared at the quarter-filled beer glass and the line of empties in front of him. Coach Eddie Cantrell was his friend, their relationship spanning the seventeen years of the coach's tenure at Catholic University. They had met before, briefly, but at C.U. the friendship bloomed. He didn't just admire and like the man, he was probably his best friend.

Both had grown up in the St. Louis area, though with vastly different experiences and results. While little Chuckie was attending Catholic schools in the suburbs, Eddie Cantrell grew up on the inner-city streets, in walking distance of Kiel Auditorium, home of the NBA's St. Louis Hawks.

As an altarboy, Chuckie had assisted Fathers Gregory and
Aloysius with morning Mass, then after school pondered the subtle-
ties of catechism and the joy of serving Christ. At the same time,
Eddie and his friends were regularly sneaking into games to see Bill
Russell, Bob Cousy, Bob Pettit and other great players. But instead
of getting autographs from the players, Eddie had waited patiently in
the cold corridors to talk with the likes of Red Auerbach, who explained his version of the fast break, and Harry Gallatin, who preached
the wisdom of a trapping defense. Cantrell soaked it all up and decided early in life he would become a coach. Father Charles soaked
up Catholicism and entered the priesthood.

The two had come to know each other from meeting at the
cathedral. Young Chuck used to take a bus there most weekends
to help Father Gregory say Mass for the city's downtrodden, and
Eddie Cantrell's mother dragged her son there regularly as well.
Eventually they both put in some time playing basketball at the
nearby Y and became good friends.

After three brief but highly successful stints coaching at a
high school and two junior colleges, Cantrell had come to Catholic
University as an assistant coach in the same year Father Charles
arrived as a young history professor fresh from St. Xavier's in
Ohio. Three years later Eddie took over as head coach and Father Charles became the team chaplain.

Two years after that, the Knights went to the school's first-
ever Final Four. The board gave Eddie a long-term contract, and
he and his wife Sally bought their first house. Father Charles was
there to help them unpack the boxes and then stayed to dinner,
toasting the couple's newfound success as they toasted their
friendship with him.

During that first decade not one coach across the country
had a win-loss percentage that rivaled Cantrell's. The Jesuits
considered themselves fortunate to keep him. Lucrative coaching offers rolled in from Georgia Tech, N.C. State, Marquette,
and others as his mighty program won eight conference titles
and reached the Sweet Sixteen every year. But Big Eddie was
loyal.

And his loyalty was rewarded with record-breaking attendance. His teams packed the house during home games, and alumni the Jesuits hadn't seen in years were returning with contributions to the program. Prime-time television games became common, advertisers were spending more money, the national media came knocking at the door. Cantrell even appeared on ESPN, where he offhandedly mentioned Father Charles's locker-room prayers as one of the ingredients of the team's success.

For several weeks after that everyone on campus—students, players, other teachers—mercilessly kidded the ever-blushing Father Charles. When the campus notoriety died down, he was relieved to return to his relative anonymity.

But there was no relief for Eddie. After he rode a decade-long crest, rumors began to filter back to Father Charles that the coach was betting heavily at the track, and worse, chasing women on recruiting trips. The chaplain knew it would be difficult to broach the delicate subject with his friend, but finally during practice he pulled Eddie into the coach's office and asked him straight out if the rumors were true. After several denials, Eddie admitted he might have let the publicity and success go to his head.

"You have to just stop it, Eddie," Father Charles told him. "If I hear these rumors, there's always the possibility Sally will hear them too."

Eddie was staggered by the possibility. In a moment of panicky realization, he asked one of his assistants to take over the rest of the practice. "Make sure they don't slack off on the wind sprints," he called over his shoulder as he raced out of the gym.

Father Charles heard the rest of the story four nights later from Hoppy, on the first of what was to become a regular mission—retrieving the drunken coach from local pubs.

Eddie had pulled into the driveway as quietly as possible to surprise Sally with flowers and champagne, sneaked around back, and entered through the back door. He tiptoed through the sprawling house, then flung open the bedroom door, announcing, "Baby, I'm home!"

Sally, his bride of twenty-three years, was carnally entwined with someone who ducked under the covers.

Eddie stood in silent shock until the simplest question arrived on his lips. "Why?"

Her laugh was bitter, and with a shake of her red head, she gave him an equally simple answer. "Because."

He pointed to the form under the sheet. "Who?"

When she didn't answer, Eddie pulled the sheet back and found himself staring at Dr. Chudwin, who had worked on his teeth for the past ten years.

"Jesus, Sally."

"Well, it is Wednesday," she said with a laugh. "Go on downstairs, will you, Eddie? Do the decent thing."

"Shit," Eddie said, and walked downstairs and poured himself a whiskey.

As he was pouring his second Sally came in, buttoning her robe. "Can I have one?"

They both heard the front door close.

He nodded, poured the drink for her. "Does this mean...?" He couldn't finish it.

"Yeah, I guess it does."

"Shit."

The divorce was uncontested. He kept the house, she got their stocks and savings and moved with Chudwin out of state.

Eddie's answer to his pain was booze, going so far as to keep a pint of Old Grand Dad in the top drawer of his office desk. When Father Charles chided him about it, Eddie claimed it was the only medicine against a toothache that couldn't be fixed. Toothache? Heartache. Father Charles hurt for his friend.

Eighteen months later, Father Charles discovered that Eddie was also deep in debt. He arranged a loan with a local bank that was collateralized by Eddie's contract with the University. The payments went directly to the bank from the school, severely cramping Eddie's lifestyle.

The coach started working the players harder than ever, the practices growing longer and longer. Their grades dipped, their performances during games were often sluggish as a result of the exhausting practices. The team's winning percentage likewise fell, and visits to the NCAA tournament became a thing of the past. In the halls of the rectory the Jesuits grieved silently as their golden boy's halo began to tarnish.

Hoppy slipped back into the booth now, interrupting Father Charles's reverie.

"Said he'll be right out," Hoppy snorted, "after he finishes an ecumenical discussion with the porcelain halo."

"Isn't there anything we can do, Hoppy?"

"Maybe if Sally would come back, but I don't think that's going to happen."

"But…all those rumors, about women on the road…hasn't he met anyone?"

"Excuse me, Father, but after he walked into the bedroom that day, he seemed to lose his…confidence in that department. Know what I mean?"

"No, I'm afraid I don't."

"Sexually."

"Ah." Father Charles leaned forward. "That takes…confidence?"

"More than you could ever imagine, Father."

The priest's eyebrows almost met as he tried to find the exact words for what he wanted to say. "Hoppy, what does it take for a man to get his confidence back?"

"Usually, the right woman."

"What does right mean?"

"Well, see, she can't be too forward, 'cause that would scare a guy. But she can't be too pure either, because…see, when a man is down…he doesn't think he deserves her…"

"I see. So, how is he ever going to meet this perfect someone…if he doesn't—"

"He ain't gonna, Father."

Father Charles sighed. "So all is lost?"

"Not necessarily."

"No?"

Hoppy grinned. "You may have just given me a great idea, Father."

"I did?"

"You did." Hoppy rose as Eddie approached the table unsteadily.

"Ah, you must be my taxi driver," Eddie pronounced his words very carefully, covering his embarrassment.

"At your service, Brother Edward," Father Charles said, as he and Hoppy each took one of the coach's arms.

"Sporting of you to come get me, Father Chuck." Eddie smiled, then tried to focus his eyes on the Hawaiian garb. "But you really need to get a new shirt."

"Sorry about losing that kid," the priest said.

"Yeah, but you know the worst part?" Eddie's voice suddenly thickened with emotion. "That transfer was gonna be my gift to Mikey, you know?"

Father Charles and Hoppy grabbed Eddie as he lurched against a table.

"A gift?" the priest said.

"Mikey's got more heart than any kid I've ever met, Father." There was a soft sob, the maudlin emotions of a drunk. "We got a good team, but we need a rebounder and an intimidator under the glass. If I do nothing else with what's left with my life..." he was starting to slur his words a little now, "...I want Mikey to go to the tournament, you know?"

"We know, Coach," Hoppy said, grim-faced.

"'Cause this year it's for him. Way too short for the NBA. But a fuckin' heart..." He spread his arms sideways, then upwards. "Biggest heart I ever seen. I used to be like him..."

"That's true," Father Charles consoled.

"And the best fuckin' jump shot in the country." Bleary-eyed, Eddie suddenly jerked around to look right at Father Charles. "Sorry, Chuckie."

"It's okay, Brother Eddie." Father Charles patted his arm. "Sometimes life isn't fair."

"No, it isn't," Eddie said. "It ain't fair at all."

Chapter 4

Clara smiled as she pulled a cigarette from its pack. "Well, unless my eyes deceive me, it's old Paulie." She stuck it in the corner of her mouth, her pink lipstick staining the filter. "How in the hell you been?"

"It's been grim, doll," Justin said as he hung up his black raincoat and lit a Marlboro. "Ever since my wife went on this health-food kick, I've eaten more carrots than a circus horse." He rubbed his hands together. "Now, how about a plate of your meat loaf and gravy with a double order of home fries?"

"Like to, Paulie, but I promised your missus I'd make sure you didn't go sneaking around behind her back." She leaned on the edge of the front counter. "She said you could have all the other women you wanted, but no fatty foods."

"Damn." He gave her a mock leer. "Then I suppose you wouldn't be interested in taking the afternoon off."

"Paulie Justin." She gave him a tap on the head with her pen. "I ain't on the menu." She pointed to the low-fat section. "Especially not there where you'll be ordering from."

"I'll get her back." He frowned as he looked at the six ways to eat tuna fish. "I'll take the scissors to her American Express Platinum card."

Clara laughed loudly, and several patrons turned to stare. "Do that and you'll never see another piece of red meat the rest of your life."

Justin had eaten lunch at Clara's nearly every weekday for thirty years, but after his doctor warned him it was time to bring down his cholesterol—in front of his wife—he was pretty much handcuffed to a bland diet of carrots, saltless soup and broccoli. The scent of fresh-baked apple pie was testing his willpower today.

"Okay, you traitor, just give me some Melba toast and vegetable soup and my regular table in the back. I've got some company today."

"Who you firing today, Paulie? Packer? Nantz? Or are you cutting some deal I'll read in the *Times* tomorrow?"

"Just business, doll-face."

Justin winked at her, wove his way through the crowd to a small table in the back corner. He looked at his Rolex, then checked the clock hanging on the wall. It was just after noon, and Peter Jr. was late. "Figures," he muttered, then opened the sports section of *USA Today*.

Ten minutes later a nervous Peter Jr. entered, looked around with disdain, then spotted Justin. He hurried over.

"Sorry, old bean." He sat still wearing his raincoat. "Traffic's all bollixed up in this rain."

Clara delivered Justin's lunch and asked Peter what he wanted.

"Just coffee." And as she started away, "In a clean cup, if you please."

Paul rolled his eyes, shook his head.

Clara stiffened, turned back. "You're doing business with him?" she asked, thumbing toward Peter.

"Actually, I'm sorry to say he works for me."

She snorted. "Must be time to sell my company stock."

Paul stubbed out his cigarette as Clara flounced away, shaking her head. "Okay, Mr. Manners, what's on your mind that can't be discussed at the office?"

"I figured out how to do it." Peter rested his hands on the table, then lifted them to check for residue.

"Figured out how to do what?"

"What you asked, at the meeting. Hit a twenty-eight rating for next year's finals."

"You have?" Paul leaned back, disbelieving.

"Actually, yes." He put his hands in his lap. "Though the original idea came from something Father did, years ago."

Paul nodded. Of course. "And what idea is that?"

"A way to ensure a Final Four consisting of St. John's, U.C.L.A., Notre Dame, and North Carolina, following Smithers's formula."

"By any chance, does this plan of yours have anything to do with the Pope?" Paul sipped a spoonful of soup to hide his distrust.

"No, although there is an Italian involved."

Paul closed his eyes. How could this schmuck not know the Pope was Polish? Another sip of soup. Then another.

"Want to hear how?"

"Oh, I surely do," Paul said.

"Ever hear of Luca Marzzarella?"

Paul pursed his lips, and his hand shook slightly. "For your father's sake, please don't tell me you're mixed up with The Big Cheese."

"I'm not mixed up with him," Peter said. "But he has agreed to help us."

Paul put a fist to his chest. He struggled to hold his tongue as Clara returned with Peter's coffee, made a big show of wiping the table in front of him, then dried it with a cloth napkin. Finally she set the coffee cup down gingerly and walked away without a word.

"You're out of your fucking mind," Paul said in a tempered whisper. "When I said full control, I didn't mean this."

Peter gave Paul a condescending look. "It's not as if this sort of thing has never been done before."

"Never since I came to the network."

"Oh, yes."

"Oh, no."

McCraken pointed to Justin's soup. "Are you almost finished?"

"No. Why?"

"Because he's waiting for us."

"Where?" Paul looked around the café.

"In the limo outside." McCraken leaned forward. "By the way, did anyone follow you?"

"Actually, half the people in here are FBI."

McCraken glanced around wildly, but Paul stopped him. "Jesus Christ. Settle down. Look, it wouldn't matter if J. Edgar Hoover was flipping burgers back in the kitchen, I'm not meeting with him anyway."

"But you have to."

"Why do I have to? No, I don't. Listen, Mac, this isn't Abbott and Costello, so cut the crap." Paul put his spoon down. "The hell you say."

"Oh, yes, because he'll be very angry if you don't."

"What can he do, except maybe save me the trouble of breaking your kneecaps for coming up with such a lame-brain idea?"

"Look, Paul, the deal's already set. We just need you to approve the terms."

"Terms." Paul shook his head. "Isn't that what they call a stretch in prison?"

A beefy man in an expensive suit walked into the café to stand warily by the doorway, staring at the two network men.

"That's his man," McCraken said, rising. "Come on."

"I'll go, but only to tell him no deal." Paul rose as well. "Aren't you forgetting something?"

"What's that?"

"Didn't your mother give you lunch money today?"

"All I had was coffee."

"Pay, and leave a big tip."

McCraken extracted a money clip from his pocket, left a ten-dollar bill on the table.

"Another one."

"For soup and coffee?" He peeled off another ten, dropped it.

"Might as well be a good day for somebody," Paul said, pushing McCraken ahead of him and waving good-bye to Clara without looking at her.

The waiting man nodded to McCraken, then walked out to the sidewalk, checking both ways. He signaled an all-clear to another man stationed across the street, then guided them to the limousine and tapped on the roof. The black-tinted window slid down halfway, and the chauffeur quickly jumped out and opened the rear door.

"Get in," came a gruff voice from the cavernous interior.

Paul glared at Peter Jr., leaned inside. "Look, there's been some kind of mistake here."

"Get in, the both of ya."

They did, taking the backward-facing seat.

Luca Marzzarella was wearing a full-length black leather coat. A big diamond set in heavy gold shone on the hand curled over a silver-knobbed cane. His gray hair was thin and slicked back, revealing a deep Arizona tan with abundant wrinkles and brown spots. None of the three looked at each other straight on.

"Petie here said he was bringing Paul Justin. Izzat you?"

"Yes." Paul settled into the facing seat, eyeing the cane.

"You wasn't too bad when you played football for the Orange."

Paul nodded. "Thanks, that was a long time ago."

"Right." The big man's mouth snapped shut, then opened again. "Let's get this wrapped up. I ain't got all day, either."

"There's nothing to wrap up," Justin said. "I told you, this is a mistake. The kid here has let a little power go to his head."

A bodyguard with shoulders wide as an ironing board settled into the seat next to his boss. His eyes were glued to the other two. Mean eyes.

"As I explained to you, sir," Peter Jr. said quickly. "Our board of directors at the network are coming down heavy. Very heavy. They want the Final Four to be as big as the Super Bowl. And that means we need to control it by having the four top-drawing teams survive the first four rounds."

Paul released a short grunt, part laughter, part terror.

"You got a problem?" the big man said.

"Yes, I'm leaving." Justin reached across Peter Jr. for the door handle. A large hand intercepted it. Mean Eyes glared.

"Siddown," Marzzarella said. He meant it.

Paul sat back, then whispered to Peter. "Your father would be ashamed of you."

Marzzarella laughed. "Saint Pappy? You think his old man never come to us?"

Paul sat back, astonished. "What are you talking about?"

"We ain't exactly breaking new ground here." Marzzarella was eyeing him, sizing him up. "More than a few well-known names in the sports field has, you might say, appreciated our help. Not unlike certain Italian singers who become fucking gazillionaires."

"I don't believe you," Paul said.

"Who do you think WBC would have made more money off of—Sonny Liston or Cassius Clay?" The big man straightened his expensive silk cuffs. "Liston was washed up. He knew it. All us *paisanos* knew it. And Pappy McCraken knew it. Clay…" he laughed dismissively, "or Ali as the big mouth calls hisself now…he was the meal ticket."

"And I suppose you made it possible for Seattle Slew to win the Triple Crown?"

"Are you kidding, horse racing we don't touch it." Marzzarella shook his head hard enough to jiggle his jowls.

Mean Eyes glared.

"Maybe one day, just not yet."

"I still don't believe it." Justin said.

"What is this? Your man asked for this meeting, not me." The big man frowned, waved his thumb toward Peter. He looked back at Justin. "You think it's all about money? It ain't. Look, pal, I grew up wanting to be a ballplayer, prolly just like you. You think mobsters' kids traded Al Capone cards or something?"

"N-no…" Justin put his hands up, a feeble protest.

"Hey…it's okay. I got no illusions." Marzzarella leaned forward again. "But sports is also business, and sometimes you got to tip the scale to keep things innaresting. Look at politics. We've had so many fucking losers in Washington, people don't even vote no more. Same thing's happening to you. When people ain't innarested in the Final Four, we lose money too. Betting goes down. Hell, you know how much money I make off the Catholics when Notre Dame loses a football game?"

"So, you're telling me it's to your benefit to fix the Final Four?"

"Naw, this is just a history lesson." Another thumb toward Peter. "Your boy here told me how much you can rake in if the right teams are in the Final Four."

Justin shot a dark glance at Peter, who shrugged. "Fine. You intend to fix the Final Four. My lips are sealed. You make your money, we make ours. End of discussion."

Marzzarella smiled. "It ain't that simple, pal."

"What else is there to discuss?" Paul was rubbing his chest.

"My people don't take no risk like we're discussing here without you sweeten the deal."

"And what would do that?"

"That's the best part." A big smile. "Next to nothing." The diamond ring gleamed.

"How much?"

"Twenty percent."

"Net, after the figures are in?"

Marzzarella flashed Paul a you-got-to-be-kidding look. "Twenty percent of anticipated gross."

"Christ! That's over twenty—"

"Million," Marzzarella finished for him. "You figured it out, congradulations. With half up front."

No one spoke for a minute.

"It ain't easy covering forty-eight teams," Marzzarella said.

"Sixty-four," Justin corrected. He turned his gaze on McCraken. "Peter, there's no way I can shake loose that kind of money, even if I was interested in such a deal. How do you imagine I could get the network to pay?"

"The network is already involved," Marzzarella said darkly. "It was your man's idea in the first place, like you ordered."

"You have no way to prove that."

Marzzarella snapped his fingers. Mean Eyes pulled out a tape recorder. Paul listened with growing horror as Peter's weaselly voice explained what the network needed from Marzzarella and his organization—and that he was acting on the instructions of his boss, Paul Justin.

"Now," Marzzarella said, fondling the knob on the cane, "if I was to decide to help the FBI do their job, my associate would deliver this tape to their offices this afternoon, and you and your bright boy here would be explaining yourselves long after the clock run out on the game."

"Go on," Paul said softly.

"Something told me you'd be stubborn." Marzzarella glanced at the dark window. "Wouldn't it be a shame to see a fine man like Pappy McCraken go down in flames?"

"He's retired," Paul said defensively. "He's got nothing to do with this."

"Not with this particular...transaction, no," Marzzarella said. "But he did do business with some of our...ah, associates, earlier in his career." He sighed. "A pity, a man like that, having a nasty little miscalculation come out to ruin his reputation. If it was me, I'd prolly blow my brains out in shame."

Paul resisted the urge to say what he thought. "I have no way of cutting you a check for ten million dollars. That ends it right there."

"A check?" Marzzarella glanced at the bodyguard. "A *check*?" A small crack formed in the man's face. Almost a smile.

"Look, pal, we're all legitimate businessmen here." Marzzarella leaned forward. "You hire one of our PR firms to handle the overflow advertising, they make the buyers a very nice price when they resell. Your problem is solved."

"I'll need time to think about this," Paul said. "But I have to tell you, I'm against it."

"You do that, Mr. Justin. You think it over. But after you've thought about it, I think you'll see things our way."

Paul shook his head, pushed Peter toward the door. Marzzarella nodded, and Mean Eyes opened it for him.

"Say, pal." The gravelly voice followed Paul to the sidewalk. "Don't forget...shame is a terrible way for a good man to die."

The door closed. The limousine pulled away from the curb.

"Well," Peter said lightly. "That was tense, but I think it went well."

"Don't talk to me, you cretin," Paul said, raising a threatening finger. "I don't want to hear one word out of your mouth. At least not until I figure a way out of this. I can't believe I was so stupid as to hand this over to you. Do you understand?"

"Yes," Peter said, blanching.

"No, you just spoke a word. Now, get out of my face!"

Justin stood motionless on the sidewalk as the other man hurried away up the street. Paul glanced at the café. Clara stared back at him through the window, holding up his raincoat. She walked to the double doors.

"Thought you might need this," she said, concern showing in her face.

"Thanks, but it stopped raining." He accepted the coat, folded it over his arm.

"There'll be other rainy days, Paulie. Lots of 'em."

"Yeah, doll-face," he said softly. "That there will."

Chapter 5

The old priest looked down into his lap for an answer, blew through his pursed lips, brushed back a lock of silver hair from his eyes. "Where do you draw the line? That's always the question with him." He looked up at Father Charles.

The younger priest studied the gleaming desktop and gulped. He hated these meetings. Why was he always the one who had to sit and listen to the grumpy old man who should have retired five years ago? Everyone on campus knew Father Callahan took naps every day after lunch and often fell asleep in board meetings.

But he had been the boss for the last twenty-five years, and no one had the nerve to stand up to him. One of these days, Father Charles thought. One of these days.

Instead of saying what he really wanted, he decided to keep quiet—and secretly hoped the old fart would fall asleep. For good. For several minutes there was only silence, except for a computer humming behind the frail old man.

"You've talked to him, I've talked to him…Bill Hopfinger has talked to him, but Eddie doesn't get it. I think it's time for something else. Have you tried A.A?"

Father Charles could tell the old man was getting upset. His right eyebrow was twitching, always the first sign. "I've mentioned it, sir, but he's afraid if he starts attending meetings someone might leak it to the media. He thinks it would hurt his recruiting."

Father Charles hesitated, arranging more thoughts. "Honestly, sir, he's actually gotten better since she divorced him. We've at least stopped him from drinking in the office."

The old priest shook his head, shot Father Charles a look. "Yeah, everyone I know drinks at his desk."

"I know that doesn't sound like much, but really, it is. She tore his heart out."

Callahan slammed his hand on the armrest of his chair. "So get him a regular piece of ass to calm him down!" The old priest's eyes blazed. "The boosters and alumni and some of the faculty are starting to get fed up with the rumors they're hearing about his drinking and carousing. I can't protect him forever, especially since he hasn't done squat for this school since...shit, I can't even remember."

Father Charles had the answer on the tip of his tongue, but he knew better than to say it.

"I've absolutely had it, and I'm this far from telling him it's his last season, regardless of his contract." His thumb and index finger were so close, a piece of paper could bridge the gap. "Our own student newspaper ranked us dead last in the conference. We can't give tickets away. We can't get anyone to donate money. Dick Vitale was even ripping us on TV last night. I wanted to puke."

Father Charles was semi-impressed. He didn't know the old priest could keep his eyes open long enough to watch ESPN. Even knew who Vitale was. "It's all going to change. We're going to have a great season this year. And that will add to his recovery, I promise."

Callahan snorted. "You say that every damn time I talk to you, Charles. Quit making me out a fool. I know more about what's going on around here than you and everyone else might think. I've heard about his little incident last year in Memphis with the flight attendant."

Father Charles gulped. A stewardess had almost pressed charges against Big Eddie for groping her when he'd gotten looped in first class. After he had promised her a C.U. sweatshirt and a couple of prime tickets she calmed down, changed her mind.

"And the professor he pointed a starter's pistol at. He almost got sued over that prank."

Charles clamped his lips tight to hold back a chuckle as he recalled Big Eddie playfully popping out of a dark corner of the arena, challenging Dr. Volney: "Hand over your money, dude, or I'm gonna blow you away."

"And—"

"I get your point, sir."

"His childish behavior…his losing…all of it is hurting the reputation of this school. What kind of example is he setting for his players…especially the booze?" Callahan rubbed his eyes.

"If you want to know the truth, I think they all love him, though I wouldn't poll them after he's had them in the gym for three hours."

"That's another thing. He can't be working his players all day and night and still expect them to achieve in the classroom. I understand he's had these kids getting up during preseason conditioning at five o'clock."

"He thinks it keeps them out of trouble. They go to bed earlier and—"

"Charles," he snapped, "what it does is keep them out of the classroom. They sleep all damn day." The old man sighed and turned in his chair, teetering back and forth.

"I'm going over to practice now. I'll talk to him about it."

Callahan leaned over the desk and wagged a stern finger at Father Charles. "This is the last conversation we're going to have on this subject. You tell him that. I'm not putting up with his crap any longer." He slumped back into his chair. "It'd be different if he were winning."

"You sick or something?" the coach hissed at his star guard.

Mike didn't look at Big Eddie. He was staring at the other end of the floor where six of his teammates were bent over in exhaustion, gasping for air, panting for water, wondering what in hell they were doing playing for Eddie Cantrell, their sadistic coach who apparently relished seeing them all in agony. He just shook his head, wordlessly.

"Then you're a big fat pussy!" The coach's voice knifed. His insults were vulgar, laced with profanities. "You should just be like the rest of the pussies in the world and quit. Go back to that little shithole you're from and grow pot like the rest of the rednecks there, Kramer.

That way I can go and recruit someone with some balls. Wanna quit, Kramer? There's the door."

Mike stared straight ahead, knowing without seeing it that a vein was throbbing in Big Eddie's forehead. "No, sir," he barked. His voice echoed off the empty bleachers in Alumni Hall. Even the managers were afraid to breathe. Big Eddie was on the war path.

"Then you better fucking start acting like the captain of this team instead of the motherfucking waterboy. Hear me, son? I think I must have been nuts to let you walk-on four years ago."

Sweat the size of jellybeans dripped from Mike's forehead to the floor. When Big Eddie turned, Mike pulled his soaked jersey off and slung it.

"Ahh, you're a little hot, are you?" Big Eddie had turned back in time to see the shirt slide down the wall. "Well, then, why don't we all just run down to the pool and jump in? You know, like all the little girls do when they get hot."

Sounded like a good idea, Mike wanted to say, but he didn't. Bastard. Go to hell.

"Would you like to do that, captain?"

"No, sir."

"Then why did you throw your shirt against the wall, Kramer? Losers throw things. Losers lose their temper. Are you losing your temper?"

Big Eddie looked at Mike and made sure everything he said had sunk in. He knew Mike was tough. Knew his old man was a drunk who couldn't keep a job. Knew there were four younger brothers back home Mike wanted to make proud. He knew the poverty gave Mike an intense desire to succeed. The kid had all As and Bs in class. Seldom slept. Had hunger written all over him. Mike was his man, but he had to get on him so the others would know what he expected. It was all part of coaching.

"RUN!"

The whistle in Big Eddie's mouth shrieked, and Mike and six others took off for another suicide. They touched the free-throw line, came back to the baseline, sprinted back to the half-court line, came back to the baseline, sprinted to the far free-throw line, again came back to the baseline, then turned for the far baseline and back again.

"Run, you girls. Run! We're not gonna lose this year, fellas. We're gonna win. Win, win, win! If any of you think you're gonna lose this year, I want you out of here!" Big Eddie stood in the middle of the floor, his gut hanging over the elastic in his shorts, a stopwatch dangling around his neck. "Now get on the free-throw line and hit ten in a row."

Mike took a ball from Q, the manager, then walked to the end of the floor.

"Q, you make sure they each hit ten in a row," Big Eddie said, walking to the water cooler, "or I'm gonna run your fat little ass. Hear me?"

Mike shook his head. Now Big Eddie was getting on Q, a nice kid with zits the size of manholes who was thirty pounds overweight, a stutterer, scared of his own shadow. He wanted to scream and tell the old man to shut up. But he didn't. He'd been in these situations before as a kid. Discipline, he told himself. Hold your tongue, or it could get worse.

Q raced to half-court and did his best to watch the shooters at the six different baskets circling the court.

After wiping his brow and drinking another glass of water, Big Eddie strolled out of the gym.

As soon as the door closed behind him, a deep voice rang out: "Fuck you, old man."

Mike smiled when he heard the voice. He wasn't sure, but it sounded like Spoon Wheatley. Spoon hated preseason conditioning almost as much as Mike. He was a skinny forward from Alabama who could jump out of the gym. Often he had to tape his shorts around his waist to keep them up. Once during their sophomore year Mike and Spoon had won a bet with a group of pickup players that Spoon could pull a quarter off the top of the banking board. He could still see their faces when Spoon took three steps, then came down with the coin.

"Hey, guys, come here," Mike said, collecting his ball and walking to Q.

The team slowly came to the center of the floor.

"What's up with that old saucehead?" Leroy Churchill said, his chin high.

Mike looked coolly at the cocky freshman not yet used to Big Eddie's practices. He wanted to tell the former Indiana Mr. Basketball selection that his press clippings didn't mean a thing in college. "This ain't shit, Leroy. Tomorrow's Saturday. Know what he does on Saturdays?"

Leroy shook his head no.

"He runs our dicks off on Saturdays, Leroy. Hope you got a big one, 'cause tomorrow he's gonna size it down. You better get some rest tonight."

Some of the upperclassmen laughed.

Leroy suddenly looked nervous. "He's tryin' to kill us, man. I shoulda went to Kentucky. Couldn't be as hard there as it is here." The kid was shadowboxing around the fact that he was basically lazy. He'd been complaining every since he stepped onto campus. His room was too small. His bed too short. The practices too long.

Mike wanted to slap him. When he was a freshman he'd never had a scholarship like Leroy's. He had to clean the cafeteria every morning before he could even go to class. Fucking pussy. Go on to Kentucky, he wanted to say. Get the hell out of here.

"He's not trying to kill us, Leroy. He's trying to get us in shape so we can win. You weren't here the last couple of years, but I was. Losing ain't fun, Leroy. This year's gonna be different, though. So if you don't want to work, you might as well go on back and complain to your high-school coach. 'Cause Big Eddie don't give a shit what you think...and neither do I."

Leroy lowered his head and mumbled something.

"Look, guys," Mike went on, "screw Big Eddie. Don't listen to him when he rants and raves. We can't let him get into our heads. We've got a hell of a team and a lot of potential. Just do what he says, and everything will work out."

Mike knew in three weeks they would be playing at Missouri in front of a hostile crowd. Keeping everyone playing together until then would be a challenge, but that's why Big Eddie had named him captain. As he sized up his teammates, the only thing he saw lacking was a big man. They would have to stay together to compensate for the lack of size. He'd seen other teams without big centers do well. Quickness and teamwork would be the keys. They would have to be.

"The only way we can lose this year is if we quit on ourselves. And as long as I'm the captain, we're never gonna quit. Got that?"

Everyone went back to the drill. The coach had spoken, and the captain had too.

"Hey, how long you gonna shoot?" Robbie Hart said. The other guard opposite Mike, Robbie was left-handed and weighed right at two hundred pounds. When he got the ball in the post, few guards could stop him from scoring. Mike was glad Robbie was on his side, because when they were freshman, Robbie used to bang him around unmercifully. He was barrel-chested and wide in the shoulders, but narrow in the waist. He could have easily played football if he wanted. And at one time when they were freshmen Mike wished he had. There wasn't a night after practice he didn't come home with bruises all over his body.

Robbie's only weakness was his ball handling, but that had improved in the four years they'd been together, thanks mainly to a drill of dribbling around chairs they both did at the end of practice. Big Eddie didn't get much credit for a lot of things, but he was the one who'd taken Robbie from the streets of South Philly and made a player out of him when no one else wanted him.

"Little while longer," Mike said, flipping another shot toward the rim.

"God, the old man has been tough. I've never seen him so...so mean and nasty. He must not be getting any is all I can say."

"I think you're right. I hear his old lady dumped him."

"That explains it, then. Why don't we go and get him some? All the guys would pitch in."

Mike could see Robbie soliciting one of the hookers from his neighborhood back home. From everything Robbie had told him over the years, his home life wasn't much better than Mike's. It was probably one of the reasons the two got along so well. Neither one of them had been raised at the local country club. Mike rebounded Robbie's shot.

"Might not be a bad idea. Son of a bitch is starting to remind me of my old man."

"Mine too."

The two seniors stared at each other, laughed, then walked off the floor cloaked in sweat, an hour after everyone else had left.

"We start winning, Robbie, you watch, Big Eddie'll change his attitude. And when we start winning, he'll be getting all he wants. Wait and see. Just wait and see."

Mike looked up into the stands. Two beautiful black girls with the tightest skirts and brightest smiles waited. "Robbie, they waiting on you?"

The guard smiled. "Uh-huh."

"Both of 'em?"

"Uh-huh, unless you want one."

Mike caught a second glance. "It's been a while, that's all I can say."

"Then come on, man. Go to the club with me. We'd rock."

Mike was still thinking about it.

"Come on. Let's go take a shower, then we'll hit the scene. You can take your pick, Mike. Or don't you like the chocolate thunder?"

Mike smiled. "Like I said, it's been a while."

"Then come with us. They're both freaks."

Mike hugged his teammate and laughed. "You're nuts, man."

"C'mon, Mike, you could use some."

It was tempting, in the end Mike turned it down. He had to concentrate as hard as he could this year, he told himself. Anything other than reaching the Final Four this season and he'd think they'd failed. He had to stay disciplined, focused, energized. His past experiences with women only made his legs weak. He couldn't be weak anymore. He wouldn't be weak. No way. The memories of his old man on the farm urged him to prove everyone wrong.

"Hoppy." Father Charles poked his head into the training room. "Are you ready?"

Hoppy smiled, tossed his jacket on, and motioned with his head. "Yep, c'mon. She'll be waiting. What about the kid?"

"Don't worry about my end of the deal. He'll be there."

Grinning conspiratorially, they left the gym at a quick pace and within minutes were walking through the front door of Clark's. Hoppy pointed at Big Eddie at the bar, vodka in hand.

"There you go, padre." Hoppy said. "It was a tough day. The J.C. player he was after couldn't get certified."

"I heard." The priest craned his neck, a question on his face. "Where is she?"

Hoppy scanned the crowd nervously, then relaxed when he spotted a slender blonde sitting in a corner booth, wearing way too much makeup. "There, in the red dress."

A short whistle filtered through Father Charles's lips. "Good job, son. What was her name again?"

"Penny North. I'm going over and sit down…bring him over in about fifteen minutes." Hoppy winked and started toward the table.

Father Charles pulled up a stool, placed a consoling arm around Big Eddie. "J.C. kid couldn't get certified, eh?"

Big Eddie didn't even bother to turn his head. "Hell, no. All that work with those tutors and counselors for nothing. This job is for lunatics. I don't know why I bother." He lifted the glass to his lips and finished his drink.

"I can sympathize. Sometimes when I feel like I've finally turned someone's life around, all of a sudden they revert back to their previous sins. But it's not the end of the world, Eddie."

They both sighed. Big Eddie ordered another vodka straight up, no olive. "Charles, kids today aren't like they were when we grew up."

"How do you mean?"

"If someone had offered me a full-ride when I was growing up, I think I would have died and gone to heaven. They couldn't have kept me away."

"Yeah, I recall."

"Remember those days at the old YMCA?"

A melancholy smile crossed the priest's face. "I recollect some of it, yes…when you had that fire in your eye."

Big Eddie turned. "What're you talking about…fire?"

"Simple…when you cared." He was treading on thin ice but really didn't care. Big Eddie couldn't fire a priest.

"Cared?" Big Eddie's gazed turned wary. "Who said I didn't—"

"Relax, no one said a thing. I'm just real keen when it comes to noticing appearances, body movements."

"Oh, so I don't project a winning…appearance anymore?"

Father Charles measured Big Eddie's mood before he went any further. Two empty glasses next to the full one. A third empty one would have made him a little more comfortable. "Not sitting here swilling vodkas, no. Father Callahan has asked me to talk to you…again—"

"Fuck Callahan. I don't need this shit from that old rumhead—" He stopped his sudden outburst as he spotted Hoppy chatting quietly in a booth with an attractive blonde. "Lookie there, will you. Hopfinger's cheating on his old lady. I don't believe it."

Father Charles mimicked concern, sniffing quickly, letting the air rush out his nose.

Big Eddie put his arm around the priest and whispered. "Chuckie, tell me what's going on with their body movements." He snickered. "I'll be right back. Looks like he needs some professional help."

Big Eddie grabbed his glass and walked to the table. "Hopfinger, what gives, son?"

Hoppy looked up with a sheepish smile. "Coach! What're you doing here?"

Big Eddie smiled at Penny North, ignoring Hoppy's question. She returned it, fluttering her lashes. He moved in next to Hoppy, keeping his eyes locked with hers.

"Coach, this is Penny, a friend of—"

He cut Hoppy off. "A pleasure to meet you, Penny." He took her many-ringed hand. "I'm Eddie Cantrell."

She giggled. "I know who you are."

Big Eddie's face swelled with pride. "Yeah?"

"Uh-huh, I've seen you doing those dopey car commercials. The checkered coat isn't you."

Hoppy smirked.

Big Eddie threw his shoulders back in defense. "Dopey or not, I get paid for 'em."

They talked for several minutes about the basketball season when Hoppy excused himself. "What goes in has to come out." He winked at Big Eddie and climbed out of the booth. "Anyone up for tequila next?"

Big Eddie gave a thumbs-up and turned back to Penny. "So, Penny, how do you know Bill?"

"Church friends," she said. "Bill and his wife helped organize a support group for divorcees. I always thought I was my husband's lucky charm, but he apparently wasn't mine." Her eyelids suddenly drooped, and she looked like she might be about to cry.

"Yeah, I know how you feel. I'm divorced myself. Caught my wife with the dentist." Big Eddie took another sip.

"My husband made it with his assistant at the animal clinic."

Big Eddie gave her a puzzled look.

"Yeah, he is a veterinarian. They were screwing like rabbits." When she laughed the tension broke.

Big Eddie joined in the laughter. "Boy, I really feel like I've known you for years," he said.

They commiserated some more about the hardships of love. She pulled a cigarette from her purse, and after he helped her light it, took a long draw that puckered her cheeks.

Hoppy returned with the tequila. "Cheers to a new season," he said.

As all three lifted the shot glasses to their lips, Big Eddie saw Father Charles heading his way with a huge Hispanic boy, at least seven feet tall.

"What the hell?"

"Coach, this is your lucky day," Father Charles announced. "Carlos here was raised in a Jesuit orphanage in Juarez, and the fathers there contacted me about him attending Catholic University. Think you can use him?"

Big Eddie looked at Carlos, then back at Penny. A big smile crossed his numb face.

Chapter 6

Mike tried to catch a nap, but the beginnings of a party were cranking up two doors down, and he never did catch a wink. Lynyrd Skynyrd seeped through the walls as Mike entered Smelly Pete's room. A keg was icing down in the back by the stereo. Six or seven guys watched the Cubs from a tattered couch. Four girls from the next dorm were busy rolling joints. Mike smiled. College was beautiful. The learning center of the world.

"Mike." A little redhead named Noele gave him an inviting look. "Want a hit?"

Mike considered the offer. He'd been around pot before but only tried it twice in his life. Once on the farm where his old man grew it, then with Robbie as a freshman at a frat party. He enjoyed its effects, but it also gave him the munchies big-time. He didn't need the added pounds right now, just before the season's start. He shook his head no.

"Sure?" She batted her eyes. "We won't tell anyone."

"Thanks, Noele, better not."

He sat and watched part of the Cubs game with the boys.

"Mikey," Smelly Pete said, "Noele wants you, dude."

The boys grinned at Mike.

"Mikey, I heard she's wild, too."

"Come on, fellas, I don't want nothing to do with her."

"You're weak, man," Smelly Pete's roommate, Victor, said. "I'd do her in a minute. She's a knockout, dude."

Suddenly Sammy Sosa busted one out of Wrigley Field. The room erupted. He was now just one behind McGuire. After a couple more innings, the party grew, flowing out the door. Pot and beer and a fixation on sex dominated the scene. Mike wanted like hell to enjoy it all, but he couldn't, not now.

Noele made several more advances, Mike turned down each one. She put her hand through his hair, then up his leg. If this had happened when he was a stupid freshman, he would have been right in the middle of it all. Noele made one last-ditch try, throwing herself into Mike's lap. She gave him a stirring kiss, then begged him to come back to her room. It was too much. He whispered in her ear, returned her kiss, then moved his hand up her leg. But something stopped him as he went inside the skirt.

Big Eddie had called him a loser in practice. But he wasn't a loser. He was a champion, and champions did the right thing. He excused himself to go to the bathroom, then just never came back. He was sure Noele could find someone else to take his place. He was sure he was out-of-his-mind crazy not to throw her beautiful body down on the bed and make love to her. No one else he knew would have passed up the opportunity.

Big Eddie ordered one of the lowly graduate assistants to dim the lights and close the office door. He fired up a cigar, put his size 11s on the edge of the desk, and eased back. He was a big man with broad shoulders who filled the chair with largeness. Since the divorce he'd gained an extra twenty pounds from the fast food and booze. His face was bloated along with his burgeoning belly. The rollers on the chair begged for relief.

"Turn it on," he said, blowing thick blue smoke and staring at a screen that dropped out of the ceiling. "This kid's got some potential, but he needs a hell of a lot of work."

Too much work. So much work, he shook his head repeatedly as he watched the video of Carlos in the last practice. Time after time he walked, tangled his feet, got knocked down going for rebounds. Once he tried to dunk the ball, but it hit the back of the rim and bounced to half-court. He wondered if Father Charles hadn't been duped. The kid was really raw.

"What do you think, Lenny?"

Lenny Klein, Big Eddie's top recruiter, didn't say anything at first. Instead he just tapped the tabletop in frustration. "Jesus, Eddie, I'm glad I didn't sign this kid, 'cause if I had, by now you'd have run my fat butt out of town."

Big Eddie took another draw on the cigar and squinted his eyes as the smoke passed. "That bad, huh?"

"Bad ain't the word. He couldn't guard Q."

The two chuckled. Q was barely five feet five, the most unathletic manager they'd ever seen. Big Eddie watched the rest of the video, then had the graduate assistant turn it off and leave the room.

"Yeah, Lenny, I know you aren't real high on the kid, and I'm not sure I am at this point, but every once in a while I see glimpses of something that's kind of special in him. He can run pretty well, he set a nice pick once back at the beginning of practice, and his arms and hands are always getting in the way of the ball."

Lenny made a face of disbelief. "You sure you ain't been drinking? That kid can't do anything right. If he's got potential, so do I. And to be honest, I think I've got a better chance of playing Division One basketball than he does."

"C'mon, Lenny, it ain't all that bad. The boy shows me something, but you'd have to have a trained eye to see it."

"Trained eye, is that what you call it? I think you'd have to have x-ray vision to spot anything there." Lenny rolled his eyes and started to get up. "Only thing I see are losses if you decide to play him, Eddie. And in case you've forgotten, the object of the game is to win. Ask Callahan about that."

Big Eddie watched his recruiter walk out of the office. He took another long draw on his cigar, then punched the remote control to watch some more of the video. Something was there. Eventually it would come to him. It always did.

The campus of Catholic University would never make the cover of one of those four-color magazines in a doctor's office, Mike thought as he tugged on his cap and walked to the basketball offices. There was really nothing to it, except for the huge stone chapel with the five-story steeple at the edge of campus. Other than the chapel and perhaps Alumni Hall, the campus was unimpressive. Actually, very depressing. No student center. No massive lawn. No row of frat houses. No Touchdown Jesus. Only entertainment was watching the bag ladies talk to themselves while feeding the flocks of pigeons everywhere you looked.

Sometimes he longed to be at one of those big state schools with all the money and all the facilities. Whenever he traveled with the team and saw the likes of Florida State, L.S.U., Ohio State and Kansas, he always shook his head and wondered why he'd come to boring C.U. Those schools always had something going on, including parties, he'd heard, that lasted for weeks at a time. Here parties were rare, except when the TKEs on his floor broke out a bottle of wine to celebrate a new pledge. Yeah, Clark's was somewhere to go, but because of the way the campus blended right in with the rest of the city, few other local businesses took the risk of opening up. They all flocked to the state schools with the big enrollments. A ghetto was only four blocks from the edge of C.U.'s tiny campus. Any night of the week gunshots could be heard if you listened long enough.

Old money and old traditions—that was C.U. BMWs and pressed shirts and sidewalks that rolled up at eight every night. Too bad none of the money went to the improvement of old buildings or the construction of new ones.

Even most of the girls were fat and ugly. And the few girls who were halfway cute had no intention of making eyes at a hillbilly from the eastern part of the state. It irked him at first, but then he figured it was for the best. He didn't need any more problems on top of trying to get through school and helping his family out back home. And most of the girls he'd met, like Noele, wanted one thing: a romp in the hay. Most guys he knew jumped at every chance. But there was something about it all that didn't sit easy with him.

He wasn't an innocent, by any stretch. He did have Darlene Smithson to brag about if he wanted, a slip of self-discipline during spring break as a freshman. And there were a few other girls always hinting, but he wanted more than quick hits. He wanted substance. He wanted toughness, honesty, integrity, patience, gentleness. He smiled. He wanted someone like his mother. Girls would have to wait.

Mike entered Alumni Hall, went into the basketball offices and stared at the shiny trophy case in the lobby, the first time in a long while he'd stopped to look at the articles of glory. Yellowed newspaper clippings of past victories and curled black-and-white photographs reminded him of the days as a kid when he'd listen to the Knights on the radio with his four brothers. He couldn't believe the hair Big Eddie had back then, how skinny he was. The old-timers at the barber shop back in London were always talking of the days when C.U. dominated college basketball, beating Kentucky three years straight until the Cats stopped scheduling them. Their voices of respect and awe were influences that brought him to the school.

Kathy, Big Eddie's secretary, snapped him from his daze. "Mike, you can go on in." She pointed to the door.

The coach was on the phone when Mike sat down. He half listened to the conversation, casually scanned the numerous Coach of The Year awards decorating the wall from *Basketball Times*, *The Sporting News*, *Associated Press*.

"Mike, thanks for coming in." Big Eddie put the phone back in its cradle and picked up a pencil, spinning it in his hands.

"No problem."

"Everything going okay?"

"Yes sir," he said, knowing that back home trouble brewed because his old man was nowhere to be found.

"Good." Big Eddie scooted back in his chair and placed his feet on the corner of the desk. "The reason I asked you to come in is that I want you to take Carlos under your wing. He's new to this school, hell, he's new to the States, and he needs some guidance. His background is a lot like yours. Can you do that for me?"

Mike shrugged his shoulders. Big Eddie sure knew how to be nice when he wanted something. "Sure, he's pretty cool."

"He's a project now, but I think he's going to be a hell of a player in time, just like you."

"Yeah, he's got the best hands on the team, and he blocked a shot of mine the other day I couldn't believe."

Big Eddie grinned. "Can I ask another favor?"

"I guess so."

"Will you let him room with you?"

Mike flinched. After three years of being on the waiting list in the dorms for his own room, he'd finally gotten one. The last three years had been spent with nothing but clods. Guys who came in at five a.m. Guys who farted. Guys who threw up. Guys who snored. Now Big Eddie was asking him to give it up. Hell no. Hell no! He stared at his feet.

"Well...I don't—"

"I would really like you to help him out, Mike. Kid needs someone to lean on, and I think you'd be a perfect role model."

There he went again with the sugary voice. Why couldn't he have asked Robbie? Spoon? Even Q? Walk out the door, now, he thought. Walk. Walk. Walk. But he didn't. He just sat there. He knew pissing Big Eddie off wasn't real smart.

"Sure, I guess so."

Big Eddie smiled. "Thanks, Mike. I appreciate it. Carlos is going to help this team out. I'll give him the word."

Mike turned and walked out. He wanted to kick himself. He should have seen it coming.

With a newspaper article resting in his lap about a girl on campus who helped football players with their footwork, Mike stared out the open window of his fourth-floor room at a pair of skinny squirrels skittering wildly through the branches of a tree. The city was so different from the landscape of home. Squirrels back on the farm were plump, a plentiful diet of nuts and wild berries filling their fat bellies. Here they were lean as greyhounds, not worth wasting a tablespoonful of buckshot on. He wondered what his Ma would say if he brought home a city squirrel. He was sure she would laugh.

The wind carried the scent of late fall through the screen, taking him back to the mountains and hunting of his youth. The chill in the air reminded him of deer season, sitting in the woods with nature and listening to the wind strum the golden leaves of the maples, his pant legs sopping up the dew from the piles of leaves already on the ground. He could see the pines and sweetgums rising silently from the soft earth, hear the whistle of a hawk, the volley of territorial birdcalls.

He'd taken his first deer when he was twelve, out behind the grove of persimmon trees. He and Paul, his younger brother, hunkered down for three hours in a pool of deep shade under a couple of majestic oaks. Paul spotted the thick-shouldered buck grazing in the tall grass along the fence row, oblivious to the sound of their beating hearts. It looked up once when a crow darted through the thicket but eventually bent back to continue its feeding.

The swirling wind flipped his hair just as he brought the rifle butt square to his shoulder. He placed the bead on the animal's left flank, then slowly, like Fletcher had taught him, squeezed the trigger gradually so as not to jiggle the barrel. The sudden discharge echoed through the pasture, then seeped into the growing wind and was gone, alerting the animal all too late. The deer froze, then dropped instantly to its knees, buckling under its great size, falling violently to one side as thick dark blood gurgled from its neck.

Paul threw his fist into the air and yelped as they scurried to the prize. Mike treasured the memory of Fletcher's grin when he and Paul dragged the deer a half mile through the woods, across the field, then up to the back porch, dogs barking in their wake, announcing their conquest. He could still feel the old man gripping him around the shoulder as if they were great friends. Everything was pure and possible that day, that one day.

Mike swiped a tear. A red-letter day.

Life back home was usually so very different from that.

"Oh, Mike, your pa loves you," Ma would say, "but he just ain't sure how to show it."

Ma was always taking up for Fletcher, but he knew even she sometimes wondered about her sanity, especially after the beatings. Mike rubbed his leg.

He thought back to the day Fletcher swung at him when he'd accidentally let Crockett, the prize boar, out of its pen. "You stupid little kid! What the hell is wrong with you?"

Fletcher's riled voice was unlike anything he had ever heard. It sent chills through him now. And his experience of it was why Big Eddie's tirades never bothered him. Ma said it was the whiskey that brought it on. Uncle Ben told him it was the fact that he wasn't good at handling pressure. Whatever, the voice always made him quiver.

Another tear swelled and inched down his face. He longed for home but was glad he wasn't there.

"Boy, what the hell you doing out here playing basketball all the time? I need you helpin' me get this tobacker in. Nobody I know of ever mounted to nothin' playin' basketball."

Mike saw Fletcher spit into the dirt, shake his head. The heavy eyes stared, ripping his heart out.

"Who the hell you think you are, wantin' to go to college and play basketball? College is for rich kids. And if you look around, you'll see we ain't rich."

Fletcher was even more animated when he was so shitfaced he couldn't hold his eyes open. "You ain't even the right color, Mike. Niggers takin' over basketball, boy. Ain't like it was when Rupp was coachin' the Cats."

The sky was darkening, faint strokes in the distance refusing to fade. Mike turned back to the newspaper, but he couldn't read. Too many thoughts cluttered his mind. Why did people always doubt him? Hadn't he constantly proven them all wrong?

When he was a freshman in high school they said he couldn't play varsity. When he started, they said it was luck, he'd never play much. When he made All-State, they said the talent level was down. When he took London High to the state tournament, they said it was because Corbin, their cross-town rival, had been decimated by injuries. When he told them he was going to play college basketball, they all laughed. He wouldn't even tell them about his goal to go to the Final Four. That was locked inside.

A hard knock at the top of the door broke his reverie. He moved from the window to open it.

He hadn't expected his roommate so soon, but he was cordial. "Hey, Carlos." Mike strained his neck looking up at the seven-footer, then down at the antiquated vacant bed. "Hope you fit."

Carlos bent his neck and walked through the door. He was all arms and legs and then some more legs. Veins in his arms swelled like the spring creeks back home, Mike thought. He had the body of a gymnast, but one that was seven feet tall.

"Here, amigo." Carlos handed Mike a small, gift-wrapped package with a green bow stuck to the top.

"I don't want any—"

"No, I insist." Carlos threw his hands up. "Coach tells me of your unselfishness. I'm deeply indebted. Please, open it."

Mike tore the bow off and carefully unwrapped the gift—a silver cross on a neck chain. "Thanks." He looked up, now embarrassed at his initial reaction when Big Eddie had made his request. "You didn't have to get me this."

"No, no. In my country it's tradition." He pointed at the cross. "Read it, on the back."

Mike flipped it over. *I am Catholic, please call a priest.* He looked back up. "Are you Catholic, Carlos?"

"Very much so. Brother is a priest, sister is a nun."

Mike slipped the necklace on. "My mom's a saint. We might have something in common."

Mike finished his shots and turned and watched Carlos struggle to sink two consecutive free throws. Each shot fetched a different technique. He eventually called out when the frustration was too much. No one could be this bad. Not even Shaq, the bricklayer of all bricklayers.

"Carlos, your feet are all screwed up. Square 'em. And keep your elbow tucked." Mike jogged across the floor, then snapped the ball from Carlos. "Look, your feet have to be under your shoulders in order to be balanced. Do you see?"

Mike was puzzled that Carlos couldn't comprehend such a simple maneuver, but he showed him what he was talking about all the same. Carlos just shrugged, his face a blank stare.

"All right, stand over there and watch me."

Carlos moved under the basket. Mike took five shots, following each one with the flick of his wrist, hitting them all without stirring the net.

"Mike, you make it look so easy. How did you learn to shoot like that?"

"Well, when I was a kid, all I did was shoot. When everybody else was watching TV, I was shooting out back on the barn. To be good you've got to practice every day, not just when you feel like it."

Carlos crossed his arms across his chest, his long limbs seemingly wrapping twice around. "Didn't that get boring?"

"Boring? Not really. It kept my mind occupied. I always pretended I was Bird or Magic or Michael, someone like that. I'd make up games and try to hit the winning shot. That's the only thing that kept me from going crazy. We lived about ten miles from town. Wasn't nothing else to do but play ball or work. And I hated working with my old man."

"How come?"

"'Cause he's a monster. Wanted everything perfect. When I didn't do something right, he'd scream. I hated working with him."

"Screamed like Coach, *si*?"

Mike shook his head. "No, Coach is a pussycat compared to my old man. No comparison."

"I would like to go see that barn. Maybe it would help me."

Mike laughed. "Dude, believe me, it's nothing special. Just an old piece of crap held together by termites." Mike hit two more. "Like I said, I didn't have anything else to do, so I just played basketball. All you need is a little coaching and more practice. Watch how my feet balance me."

The net flicked around and hung on the rim.

Carlos stretched and unhooked it. "I played soccer as a kid, but only goalie," he said. "Coaches said I was clumsy. Never played basketball until I was almost seventeen. Basketball is getting big in Mexico, but not like here in the United States. My family all thinks they'll see me in the Final Four." He gave Mike a foolish grin.

Mike stopped his shooting, insulted that Carlos took the idea so lightly. "Why's that so funny?"

"Takes a great team to get to Final Four, Mike. We are just a little school, no?"

"Yeah, but so what?"

"Underdogs seldom get to the big dance, right?"

"With your footwork, yeah." Mike let go a big smile, then did a double-take, walking to Carlos and reaching a hand up to his shoulder. "You know what, something just came to me. It gives me an idea about something I just read about. C'mon."

"Mike, tell me where we're going."

"Just follow me, Carlos, and quit asking so many questions. You can teach me how to eat tacos later on, but for now let me teach you how to play basketball so you might be able to help the team sometime."

They came to a rundown warehouse with a couple of cracked windows. Inside, fluorescent lights illuminated a huge floor with blue tumbling pads. Rattling old fans on the ceiling turned lazily, hardly making a dent in the stifling body odor that hung in the air.

"What is this place, Mike, some old factory? It reminds me of back home."

Mike pointed to the sign on the building.

"Performing Arts Division?" Carlos said. "Why did we come here?"

"Trust me, Carlos. I read in the campus newspaper about this girl here who helped some football players with their footwork."

They walked in and stood silently against the wall. Scantily clad women in leotards and tights danced to some slow music coming from a boombox in the middle of the floor.

Carlos broke into a wide smile. "Good place to come, amigo. I feel like a rooster in the chickenhouse."

"You aren't here to check out the chicks, dude."

"Can I help you?"

Mike turned and met the eyes of a cute girl with dimples and brown hair. She was five-five, maybe five-six, with coffee-brown eyes and smile lines around her mouth. Her hands were on her hips, and Mike couldn't help staring at her chest—breasts like melons under the tight-fitting exercise outfit. He tried not to stare, but his eyes kept drifting back for another look.

"Uh, I'm looking for the girl who worked with the football players," he finally got out.

"That's me." She came closer, offered a hand.

Carlos shook first.

Then Mike. She was so soft. Her hand disappeared inside his. She was so pretty, so delicate and small. Being near her sent shivers through him.

"Ah, I'm Mike Kramer, and this is Carlos Lopez."

"Hi, I'm Savannah. What can I do for you?"

He pushed away the lewd thoughts before they started. It only took him seconds to realize she was different from any other girl he'd met. The glint in her eye struck him hard. All of a sudden his tongue was tied.

"Uh, well, we play on the basketball team, and, uh, I was wondering if you could help my friend here the same way you helped those football players I read about."

She sized Carlos up. "Let me guess. He can't walk and chew gum at the same time. Are all athletes like that?"

"No," Mike said. "Well, at least I'm not."

She turned away to watch the other girls on the dance floor. "Then maybe it's just a bias I have. You know, kind of like the one about all jocks being dumb."

"Man, you're tough."

She gave him a subtle smile, mischief in her eyes. "Not as tough as the dance classes I make the football players go through."

Mike looked past her. Several other sets of jiggling melons caught his eye. "Looks kind of simple to me."

"Oh, yeah?"

"Yeah. Basketball practice puts this stuff to shame. I have to have that kind of balance with someone shoving an elbow in my face."

"Please," she sputtered. "Ten dollars says you wouldn't last one hour with me."

An hour? He thought his chances were pretty good. He'd dance for ten hours to look into her eyes. "I don't gamble. And anyhow, I came here for you to help my friend here, Carlos."

"Chicken, huh?" she said, still looking at Mike as she crooked a finger Carlos's way.

"No, I'm not a chicken. It's just that the help I need...no one but God can give it to me." After he said it he didn't know why he'd said such a serious thing.

"Well, what do you think, Carlos? Big Eddie won't be able to keep you out of the lineup if you work with her."

Carlos dabbed his face with a towel. They walked slowly to the dorms. "I'm excited, Mike. She can make me better...but she might make you go crazy."

"What are you talking about?"

"I saw."

"Saw what?"

"I saw."

"Saw what, chump?"

"Chump? What is chump?"

"Chump is someone who is out of his mind. You, you're chump."

"Oh." Carlos let it hang, then said, "So I'm a chump because I believe you want me to keep going for these lessons so you can see Savannah?"

"Get real, dude. She's not my type."

Carlos laughed. "Then if I don't go back, you don't get angry?"

"Carlos, I don't care what you do, but she can make a difference in your game."

"Yes, and by the look she gave you, and the look you gave her, she can also make a difference in *your* game."

"You're a chump, dude."

"Your friend there is awfully serious." Savannah stretched her hamstrings, gazed across the room at Mike reading a book. "Two weeks, and he hasn't said a word to me."

"I am afraid my roommate has many troubles." Carlos finished his own stretching and went through a serious of agility exercises Savannah had created to put a little spring in his cumbersome gait.

"That's it, Carlos." She smiled, turned some classical music on. "See, I told you it wouldn't take that long to get your mind and your feet thinking together."

"You're a good teacher, Savannah."

"Practice and persistence, that's what does it."

"It is funny you say that." Carlos stopped his crouched shuffling and wiped his face with a towel. "Mike says that same thing all the time. He always tells me good things will happen to me if I work hard."

"I think he's right, but I also think *he* works a little *too* hard." She pointed. Mike was now marking his book with a highlighter, his face dripping intensity. "Does he always take things so seriously?"

"A driven man, I say to him all the time."

"How come he never smiles?"

"His heart aches, I think."

"Oh?" She took Carlos's hands and the two went through a series of back-and-forth steps. "What makes his heart ache?"

"He won't tell me. But it's something serious."

Her eyes drifted back to Mike. "A girl?"

"I have never seen Mike talk to another girl." Carlos followed her lead perfectly, his feet flowing gracefully over the wood floor. "I think it comes from home." He leaned down and whispered. "His family has many troubles. Mike's father does not make enough money, he just goes out drinking."

"Oh, that's terrible."

"And I think hard work helps Mike forget."

"That's sad, Carlos. No one should work all the time."

"Mike is a good person, but I don't think he knows it." The music stopped. "He is my friend, though, and I shall continue to be by his side."

Savannah looked up. "That's so sweet, Carlos."

Carlos held a finger to his lips. "Shh, but we're having a birthday cake for him after Friday's practice. And…" He hesitated.

"What?"

"Well, would you come?"

"Come? He barely speaks to me. It's like he's afraid of me or something. I don't get it. I haven't done anything…"

"Shh," Carlos said, touching his lips again. "My friend is struck by you, I know. I see it. I feel it. He comes here with me every time. Makes sure I am never late. Right?"

"Yes, so?"

"So, would he do that if he did not like coming here?"

"I don't know…"

"Savannah, sometimes speaking means no words. Please, come, okay?"

She sighed. "Okay."

Mike hopped off the elevator and stuck a key in his mailbox. He trashed several pieces of junk mail, then tore into a letter with his mother's handwriting on the outside. He walked to the lobby of the dorms and sat down to read.

Dear Mike,

I'm sorry I haven't had time to write. Your four brothers tend to keep me busy, just like you used to. We've been waiting on a letter from you, but I know you must be busy yourself.

Mr. Matheson cornered me in town the other day and asked how you been. I told him fine. He said to say hello.

Old man Clanton lost several calves the other morning. Dr. Harris said the mother was also real sick and wasn't sure if she would make it. He said he was going to run it down to a specialist in Somerset, but only if it wasn't feeling better by Saturday. Father Jentile also told me to tell you hello. He mentioned that you've done about as well as any ball player coming out of these parts. He said he was proud.

Your brothers are getting bigger and meaner by the minute. One of these days I think this old house is going to collapse when they start wrestling. Well, that's all from here. You take care and God be with you.

Love,

Mother

P.S. Your Pa got let go, but don't worry. Everything will be just fine.

Mike pitched the letter and walked out of the dorms and across campus. He had no set destination. He just wanted to walk. Walking always helped him think. The sky was a perfect blue, but he didn't notice. There was more she wanted to say, he knew, but she didn't. He caught a bus and sat in the back and wracked his brain. Why were things the way they were? Why?

As the bus moved along, winos, businessmen, hookers, college kids came and went. He struck up a conversation with one drunk. He helped one old lady into a seat, pointed out the bridge where Muhammad Ali tossed his gold medal into the Ohio River. At first she didn't believe him, but then she smiled and started calling him sweetheart. It was dark by the time he climbed off and walked the five miles back to campus. The walking would make him so tired he'd forget. But he knew it was only temporary. Like his old man's work history.

"Q, who is that up there at the end of the top row?"

The manager stirred from his chair, pushed his glasses to the top of his nose and stared into the stands. "I d-don't know, sir."

The girl's cheekbones were high and her nose delicate. She wore a silver necklace that glinted under the lights. Her brown hair rested on her shoulders, but it was her nicely crossed, long, muscled legs that caught his eye, along with the gorgeous set under the tight navy-blue sweater.

"Jesus, Q, how do you expect me to get their attention with her sitting up there? They haven't run a play since she sat down." Big Eddie swiped at the top of the manager's head. "Get her out of here."

Carlos heard the conversation and trotted over and put a hand on Big Eddie's shoulder. "Coach...Coach," he whispered. "That's my friend who has helped me." He smiled and shuffled his feet, error-free.

Big Eddie folded his arms across his belly and chuckled. "Her? She's too beautiful for a slug like you, Carlos."

"No, no. She is not here for me, sir." He pointed across the floor at Mike, his back turned, unaware he was being observed. "She has come here because of Mike...his birthday, you know."

Big Eddie's brows lifted, then came down again in puzzlement. "Mike?"

"Yes. I see it in her eyes."

"And his?"

Carlos grinned, a gold cap on his front tooth shining under the lights. He tapped his heart with a fist. "He is not Don Juan, but the feeling is there."

"Are you serious? Mike? Super-serious Mike? I don't believe it."

"I swear, Coach."

Big Eddie looked back to his star guard, then grinned, shaking his head. "Come here, Q," he said.

Q listened intently as Big Eddie whispered in his ear, then hurried off the court and up the steps. Ten minutes later he returned and whispered back into Big Eddie's ear himself.

"Okay, fellas, bring it in."

The team huddled in a circle at Big Eddie's feet, all eyes raised to him.

"We've practiced hard for the last three weeks, really improved in a lot of areas. Two nights from tonight it'll be the real thing when we go out and play Missouri." He paused, hoping his words were sinking in. "The most important thing we can do this season is play as a team and never quit. In your team goals you said you wanted to win the conference and go to the Final Four." Another weighty pause. His eyes searched the players. "Is that right?"

"Yes sir." The voices came as one.

"Okay, then let's go out there and give everything we've got." He stopped and rubbed his eyes. "Oh, before you leave to-day, get with Q and get your bag of gear. And one other thing, who we going to beat?"

"MISSOURI!" they all barked.

Big Eddie motioned for Father Charles to join them for the team prayer. The team huddled around the priest, joining hands. He smiled mischievously at Big Eddie when the players closed their eyes. Across the way Q quietly opened a door for Savannah. Father Charles ended the prayer with a definitive "Amen."

"Hey, before you go, guys, one more thing," the priest said gently, a smile easing out. "Let's sing Mike a great big Happy Birthday!"

Savannah came through the door and walked to center court escorted by Big Eddie. She presented Mike his cake while the team gave a butchered rendition of "Happy Birthday."

She blushed at the attention, smiled, and handed over the cake. Every set of eyes was directed on those two inviting pack-ages the sweater covered but didn't conceal.

Q cut the cake and handed pieces around.

"Make a wish, Mikey," Spoon said.

"I know what he's wishing for, fellas," someone else said. The team broke into laughter.

Mike's face shone like burning candles.

"You're dead, Carlos."

Carlos giggled and kept walking.

"Dead."

"I had nothing to do with it. All I told Coach is that she was a friend."

Mike stopped and looked up at Carlos. "You embarrassed me in front of the entire team. I don't get it. I thought you were my friend."

"He had nothing to do with it." A gentle voice came from next to the soda machine. Savannah.

Mike turned. "Who did then?" His stare was stone.

She looked to Carlos for help, but he was already on his way out the arena doors. "Your coach, I think."

Mike wanted to let out a string of cusswords, but he swallowed the anger. God, she was beautiful. Something about the way she looked reminded him of his mom. "I should have figured." He took a deep breath and walked over to her. "Hey, I'm sorry for being angry, but—"

"It's okay." Her gaze was on the floor. Neither one of them spoke for a minute. A hint of her perfume drifted past his nose.

"Ah…hey…thanks for the cake."

"You're welcome."

The rest of the team filed past, snickering as they went.

"Mikey, keep your mind on Missouri."

"Looks like birthday boy got his wish."

"Eat at the Y tonight, Mikey."

"Ignore them, Savannah. They're a bunch of redneck clods."

She reached in her purse. "Carlos told me it was your birthday…I got you something small." She handed him a bag of Hershey chocolates. It was the first time since he'd met her that he actually thought he had a chance.

"Wow, thanks…I…I…don't know what to say."

"You don't have to say a thing. It's your birthday. Just smile and have fun." She turned and headed for the door, then looked back. "Yeah, that's right, smile a little more. The world is good."

He moved to follow her. "Wait…I don't understand."

"What's to understand? It's a birthday present. Plain and simple."

"I don't even know you."

She pushed her hand through her hair. Her delicate eyebrows raised. "You haven't even tried."

Mike fumbled with the zipper of his jacket. "Well, I figured a rich girl like you—"

"Rich?" She blinked incredulously.

"I saw you getting into that red BMW the other day."

"What's that got to do with anything?" She looked puzzled at first, then her face suddenly cleared. "Oh, I get it. You're a snob."

"A snob?" He tossed it off. "What're you talking about? I don't have anything."

"In reverse, Mike. You think just because I drive a BMW that I thumb my nose at the world." She walked to him and stuck a finger against his chest. "When you go up against players who are taller than you, you don't run away, you find out their game and then go get them, right?"

"Sure. I do."

"Well, maybe I have a game too."

"Maybe you do, but I don't know it."

"So, have you ever thought about scouting me out?"

"Okay," Mike said softly, liking the hint. "What's your game?"

"Come watch sometime."

Savannah fascinated Mike now. He barely slept for thinking about her. The brown eyes. The perfect legs. The smile. The smell of her perfume. He had never felt this way before and wasn't quite sure what was going on. No one else he'd ever met had the effect she was having on him. He smiled. Then he smiled again. And it wouldn't go away. He smiled at breakfast. He smiled at lunch. He smiled all afternoon. Wow. Smiling wasn't so bad.

Before he boarded the team bus at three o'clock he slipped into the viewing area above the dance class, hoping Savannah wouldn't look up and see him smiling. Or maybe hoping she would. He watched with curiosity as the choreographer put the dancers through their exercises, their first moves, astonished by the amount of pain on their faces. A young man next to him, wearing a cast, explained that learning a new dance always meant pain, each series of movements pushed the muscles in a new way. They had to work through the pain so it didn't show during a performance.

"At least," Mike said, "they don't have opposing dancers trying to stop them."

"The music is the real opponent," the boy said. "And the dance itself. I think it's easier in competitive sports, because you have someone outside you to go up against. In dance, you're constantly fighting yourself, your tiredness, your memory, the music."

He pointed to Savannah. "But she works harder than any of us. She had to, she had farther to come than most of us."

"What d'you mean? Because she grew up in a rich family?"

The young man gave Mike a funny look, shook his head. "Her family's money didn't protect her from polio."

"Polio?" Mike said faintly. "Jesus."

"*He* didn't help her either."

"I thought polio was taken care of, a thing of the past."

"Most of it is, but with her I heard the vaccine didn't work."

"Jesus."

Chapter 7

Stuck between St. Louis and Kansas City, Columbia, Missouri, was no more than a tourist stop between the state's two biggest cities. Though the Tigers had had some respectable athletic teams in the past, the university was known mainly for its outstanding journalism program, or J-School, as all the preppies in their starched button-downs called it.

Mike had never been here before, but he remembered vividly his rejection letter from the Missouri coach when he was looking to walk-on out of high school. He wondered if the coach remembered his letter. Wondered if the guy even knew his name now, four years later. Probably not. Catholic U. hadn't done anything but lose, so why would the Missouri coach know who he was?

He looked up as the fans began to take their seats and wondered what it would be like to have no pressure in his life. Sometimes he wished he could plunk down a few bucks, just go and watch a game. He was starting to get nervous. The first game of the season always made him feel this way. But in a way having the season start was a relief, even more so now that he had met Savannah. Just being around her made his heart skip a beat. Also, no more playing against his teammates who knew every one of his moves. He stretched some more as Missouri ran into their locker room. In eight minutes the season would begin. He wondered if Savannah would watch on TV.

Things hadn't gone as planned. Mike wiped his face with a towel and listened. He could have done a thousand things better during the game. His shot was off. His defense even worse. Damn, why hadn't he practiced harder during the summer? Still, there was time. Maybe it would work out. Maybe for once they could start the season with a win.

Big Eddie checked the time on the scoreboard over his head, bit his bottom lip like a nervous horse, turned back to the team.

"Here's the situation, fellas. Fifteen seconds...no more time-outs...we're down by one." He paused, wiped his forehead with a sleeve, then dropped his voice. "Listen up, here's what we're running."

He diagrammed the play, then grabbed Carlos around the wrist. "Big guy, you set the pick for Mike's man and roll to the basket just like we've practiced. Understand?"

Carlos nodded, then stared out into the rowdy crowd who were already harassing him:

"It's high noon, Carlos. Sit down and take a nap..."

"Your mama don't eat tacos, Carlos. She eats me..."

Big Eddie snapped him out of his daze. "Forget about the fucking crowd, Carlos. We're here to win. Just do what I tell you." He slapped him hard on the butt. "You can do it."

The coach turned to Mike. "Give your man a good fake and cut hard. Carlos will be open. Just like in practice."

The C.U. five broke from the huddle, ignoring the blistering catcalls. Big Eddie walked to the end of the bench for a cup of water. "Say a prayer, Chuckie. Ten to one says Carlos messes it up."

Father Charles pressed his lips together and went into a silent prayer.

"Carlos." Mike grabbed the center's jersey. "Concentrate and move your feet, just like you do in the dance practices. I'll send it down quick, so be ready."

"Okay." The crowd was still bothering Carlos as he moved under the basket to watch as Mike awaited the inbound pass at half-court. The burly white Missouri center nudged Carlos with the point of his elbow. "Hey, wetback, you guys are finished. My coach told me not even to guard you. He said you were a klutz." The guy chuckled, pricking a hair from Carlos's leg. "He also said you were a big pussy. Tell me, how do you wetbacks say pussy in Mexico?"

Carlos stood his ground, waited for a second, then broke hard to the corner of the free-throw line and caught Mike's man with his hip. He spun to the basket, feeling the Missouri defender scrambling. Mike stopped and quickly flicked the ball to him in the post. He secured the ball instinctively. Now all he had to do was turn and shoot.

With his right hand he pushed the ball to the floor, thinking the whole time about how Savannah had told him not too think.

"Just let it come naturally, Carlos…"

Big Eddie held his head and screamed. "Don't put it on the floor, Carlos!"

Carlos never felt the ball return. A roar filled the arena.

The Missouri center jogged by, laughing. "Hey, wetback, I guess my coach was right about you. You are a klutz."

Big Eddie caught Carlos before he entered the locker room, speaking softly. "Carlos, it will come. Have patience. I wouldn't have put you out there if I didn't think so."

He patted his butt and let him go. Then a realization suddenly came over him. Before meeting Penny he would have blistered the kid unmercifully. This time he hadn't. He smiled. He finally felt his heart again.

With his head down, Mike walked past Carlos and jumped onto the bus, moving quickly to the back to be alone.

"I'm sorry, Mike." From his seat halfway back Carlos's voice sounded sad.

Long windshield wipers worked overtime to keep pace with the thunderstorm filling sewers and streets with its fury. Lightning flashed, briefly illuminating the parking lot. Somber coaches, managers, and staffers quickly filled the bus.

In Mike's lap a stat sheet lay forgotten. He stared out the window, listening to nasty jeers coming from drunken hecklers swilling beer. He knew from previous losses in other seasons what they were saying. The driver switched gears and eased past the small crowd, beer cans busting against the back window as the bus moved onto a side street. Finally they were on the interstate. An eighteen-wheeler rushed by, rocking the long vehicle.

Mike stood uneasily, a dull ache pitching back and forth inside his stomach.

"Fellas." Heads slowly turned towards Mike's firm voice. "Who in here thinks they left everything out on the floor?"

There was no response.

"Who played their heart out?"

No one stirred.

"Well, then how in the world are we going to win?"

Silence.

Mike closed his eyes and took a deep breath. "We should have won that game, guys. If we would have executed, we just might have." He didn't look at Carlos, but everyone got the message.

Lightning cracked the sky.

At the front of the bus, Big Eddie leaned and whispered to Father Charles. "I like it...I like it. They'll listen to him before they will me."

"He's the most intense kid I've ever met," the priest said.

Mike finally sat down, but his words hung heavy in the gloom.

Although it was two in the morning, a small group of fans waited as the plane unloaded.

"Don't worry, we'll get 'em next time!"

"Keep your heads up, guys!"

One of the voices was Savannah's. She stood quietly in the back of the waiting area. "Good game, Carlos."

The big Mexican ignored her and kept walking, his chin deep into his chest. Mike walked up behind, following Carlos down the concourse with his eyes.

Savannah was dumbfounded. "What's wrong with—"

"Leave him alone." Mike said. "He's not very happy right now."

"It's just the first game of the year."

"I think I may have said something I shouldn't have."

"Oh?"

Mike sank his hands deep into his pockets. "I got on the team a little."

"I thought he played well."

Mike's eyes shot up. "You watched the game?"

"Of course I did."

He smiled. Even at two in the morning she was beautiful. Not just her physical features. He could feel her heart.

"I wanted to see how Carlos did."

"Oh, I thought maybe you—"

"What, watched you?"

"I don't know, I…well…I just thought—"

"Relax, I did. And…" She paused. "…I saw some places where my dance class could even help you."

Mike gave her an incredulous look. "Please…"

"Hey, everyone needs improvement, even the captain of the team. Don't be such a macho-man."

"I'm not, but I can just hear what my old man would say if he heard I was going to dance classes." He rolled his eyes, then pondered it. "But, hell, he don't have to know, and maybe you're right."

"I know I am."

"Okay, I tell you what. I'll come to one of your dance classes if you go to Hoppy's annual Thanksgiving costume party."

She held a finger to her chin. "Hmm…Thanksgiving? I'm supposed to go to my parents' house."

Mike hung his head.

"But then I don't think I have anything to do that evening."

His eyes brightened. "So you will?"

"I guess so…but only if you bring Carlos."

"Carlos? I don't know about that. He probably won't even talk to me until next Thanksgiving."

"Then apologize to him. I've got someone I want him to meet."

Mike's hair was sopping wet when he came out of the Performing Arts building after his first session with Carlos and Savannah. They walked slowly to her car. Carlos somehow folded himself into the back seat. The BMW glistened in the warm evening, and Mike could scarcely believe what was going on. Savannah, one of the smartest, prettiest girls he'd ever met, was riding him back to campus. IN A BEAMER.

He wanted everyone back home to see it. A year ago if the team had lost he wouldn't have been able to talk to anyone. Now he was in a luxury car, with a beautiful girl, his hair whipping in the wind and his mind on kissing Savannah. He thought about leaning over and planting a soft one on her cheek, but something stopped him. Instead he just stared. He wondered what Ma would think. Savannah pulled to the curb and let the two out, reminding them of the next session.

"Carlos, wait up."

Carlos ignored Mike and walked faster down the sidewalk.

"Hey, man, what's wrong? I told you I was sorry two days ago."

Carlos ducked into the Co-op, waving him off.

"C'mon, Carlos, I'm sorry. I didn't mean it."

Carlos bought a bag of chips and a soda, then spun and shoved a finger in Mike's chest. "In my country friends share adversity as well as prosperity. You are no friend." He turned abruptly, walked toward a table.

Mike followed. "Carlos, you're absolutely right. I shouldn't have said what I said. Not in public."

Carlos folded his arms across his chest. "Just because I'm this tall…" he stretched his arms up and down "…doesn't mean I don't have feelings in here." He pointed to his heart.

Mike looked at the floor. "Hey, man, I know. Please…forgive me."

Carlos popped the bag of chips open and sat down, not looking at Mike. "I don't like this place anymore. Everyone is blaming me for losing the game against Missouri."

"Who is?"

"People in my classes." He sniffled. A single tear slid down his face. "You and Savannah are the only good friends I have, and now one is against me."

Mike placed his hand on Carlos's knee. "Hey, I guess I just take things way too seriously."

The center looked up and sighed. "Yeah, and maybe I should be more serious. But back home no one takes things seriously."

"All I was trying to do was make those guys realize that if they don't play with heart, we aren't going to win." Mike balled his hand and thumped his chest. "It's all right here, Carlos. It's called passion. And if you don't have passion for what you're doing, you might as well hang it up."

"You are right about that." Carlos chewed his chips, thought about it. "I know passion, Mike."

"Yeah."

"*Sí.* I have passions for things, not just basketball."

Two girls approached Carlos for an autograph, then spun away giggling.

"Must be for women, right?" Mike said.

Carlos grinned. "Oh, no. The *muchachas* make my head spin."

"Is that why every time I spot a woman for you, you never seem interested?"

Carlos shrugged. "I don't know. Women are complicated, Mike. Think just because I'm Latino and tall that I have great powers in bed."

Mike laughed. "Sounds like a good problem to have."

"For your kind, maybe."

"My kind?" Mike arched his eyes. "What're you talking about?"

"Not a putdown toward you, but toward society."

"You're getting deep."

"When people come together…men and women, I mean…it is usually about sex, no?"

Mike thought it over. "I don't know, probably."

Carlos sighed. "Please. I have seen the look in your eyes when Savannah's around."

"Yeah, and what do my eyes say?"

"That there is a violin playing love songs in your heart."

Mike laughed heartily. "You're one crazy Mexican."

"No, that's okay, Mike. She and basketball can be your passion. Every man should have passions and seek to fulfill them."

"You're getting deeper, dude."

Carlos slumped in the chair and crossed his long legs, his knees crowding the underside of the table. "My passion, I think, is to be a priest some day. And I don't want to get involved with anyone until I know for sure."

"Hey, that's cool, but wouldn't having sex help you make the decision? I mean, how can you give up sex if you don't know whether you like it?"

Carlos laughed. "Oh, I already know I like it."

Mike blushed. End of discussion.

Savannah giggled with delight when she saw Mike tuck his hand inside his Napoleon costume and stride playfully out of the dorm. He laughed back when he climbed into her car and saw her struggling with her curly blonde wig. They had only known each other for a couple of months, but they were already becoming special to each other. Yesterday she had left him a bag of jellybeans in his locker, the day before a package of cookies. They were quickly getting to be an item on campus. He didn't really mind, either. All of a sudden basketball had taken a back seat. And since he was more relaxed, he was playing better, more confidently.

He had wanted them to go to the party as John Smith and Pocahontas, but she'd voted for Napoleon and Josephine. He didn't really care. It was nice just to get away from campus—and practice—for a while. All the heavy practice and the dance sessions made his calves ache every time he moved.

"Where's Carlos?" Savannah looked back toward the lobby of the dorms.

"He's hitching a ride with Q. I think they're going as twins."

"Twins?"

"Yeah, Arnold and Danny DeVito."

She laughed again, then slipped the car into Drive. Mike whipped off his cockaded hat and placed it in the back seat. "Man, that thing is hot!"

Savannah's eyes left the road for an instant. "Yeah, and so are you, ol' great Napoleon."

"Ha, ha."

People in passing cars turned to stare, then laughed as the two of them whizzed by. Savannah's wig filled the entire side of the car, strands of it flapping out of the crack in the window. Mike did his best to hide his face. After fifteen minutes on the interstate, they turned off into the stately neighborhoods of Prospect.

"Wow." Savannah stared at the manicured lawns and immense brick homes. "Nice neighborhood."

"That's it right there." Mike pointed at a rambling Bedford stone with a three-car garage. "I heard Hop fell into some money a few years ago. His uncle died and left him with stock, I think. That's why he's so relaxed. He don't give a hoot about anything."

He jumped out of the car, then helped Savannah out. Her blue velvet gown flowed over her heels, and she had to hitch it up to keep it from dragging on the wet ground. "I'd hate to have to wear this every day." She tiptoed over the puddles that dotted the asphalt drive.

He chuckled. "Never know. The Grand Ole Opry might need another Dolly someday, and that wig is perfect."

"No way, Mike. I don't think I'd fit the bra."

"They seemed just about perfect when we were dancing yesterday."

Savannah's attention was drawn just then by a pearl-white Lexus pulling up the driveway. After it stopped, an olive-skinned girl in a nun's costume stepped out, with a few tendrils of black hair peeking out around her face.

"Savannah?" Her voice was cautious. "Is that you?"

Savannah stepped quickly across the lawn, laughing, holding up her long dress. She threw her shoulders back. "Off with your head, madam. I'm Josephine."

They tittered like schoolgirls.

The girl curtsied. "Sorry, madam."

Savannah hugged her friend. "Monique, I'm so glad you came."

"I'm not sure this is what you wear to a Thanksgiving costume party, but it worked for Halloween."

Savannah turned and motioned for Mike. He walked over, placing his hand back inside his coat. "Monique, this is Mike Kramer. Also known as Napoleon Bonaparte."

He bowed his head. "Nice to meet you, Sister."

The trio entered the party. Hoppy was dressed as Meriwether Lewis and his wife as William Clark, as they had to explain. They handed every guest a tiny pumpkin striped like a basketball, with the person's name on it. Q had come as Thomas Jefferson, Father Charles as Christopher Columbus, Carlos as a priest. Of course.

"Mike, c'mon in." Hoppy walked across the living room to collect any jackets.

"Hoppy, you know Savannah, right?"

Hoppy nodded grinned. "Aye, aye, Captain."

"General, I'll have you know," Mike said, looking stern.

"And this is my friend Monique," Savannah said.

Hoppy feigned the sign of the cross. "Monique, no offense, but the last nun I saw was taking a belt to my backside."

"No offense taken. I guess sometimes it takes more than a gentle tap from heaven to get the message across."

Savannah and Monique shortly made their way to Carlos, who was sitting awkwardly on the piano bench.

"Hi, Savannah." Carlos stood and greeted her with a warm smile.

"Carlos, this is my friend Monique."

"Hello." The big guy looked shy.

Savannah nudged Monique. "Hey, looks like you two might have something in common."

There was an awkward silence, then small laughter as the two inspected each other's costumes.

Monique spoke first, her tone playful. "Well, Carlos, we've got it covered if someone dies." Carlos's face was very serious.

"My brother is a priest." He said it so gravely that she stopped laughing. "He does more than give last rites."

"Ahh...Carlos is on the basketball team, Monique." Savannah said, trying to move the conversation along. "He's from Mexico."

"Oh, really?"

"Yes."

"What part?"

"Juarez," he mumbled.

She cocked her head. "Where's that?"

"It's not necessary to know. Just a little hole in the wall."

Savannah had picked up on Carlos's discomfort. "Will you hear my confession, Father?" She took his arm and led him quickly into the kitchen. "Hey, relax." She patted his hand. "What's the matter?"

"Priests do more than bury the dead," he said defiantly.

"She was just kidding, Carlos."

"I know, but it makes me angry. And she's...she's so—"

"Beautiful?"

"And I'm so...clumsy. My tongue trips like my feet. I'm afraid of making a fool of myself."

"Oh, Carlos. Be nice to yourself."

He ran his hands over his shaved head. "Where I come from, men aren't refined. I'm afraid I'm the same way."

"Hey, wait a second, Carlos, this isn't the Dating Game. I didn't ask her to come by to marry you, I asked her to come by because she didn't have anything else to do over the holidays."

"Yeah?" Carlos studied Savannah's face. "You mean you aren't trying to make an arrangement?"

"Carlos!" She shot him a look. "If you want a girlfriend, I'm confident you can find your own. She's just my friend. There are no strings attached."

Carlos smiled. "I'm sorry, but Mike is always trying to arrange *muchachas* for me. You know back home they do these things."

"You're not back home! This is Kentucky, in the U.S.A."

She coaxed him back out to find Monique, who was talking with Big Eddie and Penny.

The coach stood and rubbed Carlos's belly. "Hey, Carlos, for a minute there I thought Father Charles had lost about seventy-five pounds and grown ten inches."

Carlos offered a wry smile. "I say a prayer for your vision to return, Coach. I could never fill his great shoes."

A few minutes later Big Eddie slipped away downstairs, knowing Hoppy kept the bar stocked. He filled a tall glass with ice and Coke, then splashed in a generous amount of bourbon. Before he went back upstairs he took a long drink. No one would know. He took another drink. Then another.

"Hey," Penny said, popping out of the bathroom, "what're you doing?"

Big Eddie put the drink down in a hurry. "Hey, nothing." Behind his back he wiped his hand on his shirt where the drink had spilled when he set it down.

Penny blew the whistle dangling down the front of her referee's costume. "Time-out, big fella." She peered around him and spotted the half-empty glass. "What d'you call that?" She pointed.

He walked over and gave her a big hug. "Nothing. Just something to wet my whistle."

"Don't schmooze me, Coach. You might just get a T thrown on you."

"A technical?" He glared. "What would you know about technicals?"

When she saw Big Eddie was really angry, she spoke up straightforwardly. "Oh, Eddie, this isn't about technicals...I hope you know I really like you, and I think you really like me, too. But if we're going to do anything about it...well, I want you to be sober when it happens."

As she was saying it his face brightened. "When it happens? You mean, like tonight?" He reached out tenderly and flipped a lock of hair out of her eye.

"You have anyone else to go home with after this party?"

He shook his head no.

"Well, neither do I."

His anxiety showed. "It's been a long time…for me."

"Don't worry." She laughed, patted his arm. "You'll do just fine. I'll see to that."

"I will?"

"Sure." She put the whistle in her mouth. "And if you don't, I'll just call a foul."

"A foul?"

"Right." She whispered. "I've been studying this basketball stuff. There's all kinds of things that will help."

"Like what?"

"Illegal defense. Reaching in. Hand checking. Moving pick. Goaltending." She stroked his earlobe. "And worst of all—a three-second violation."

"What—" Then he understood.

Big Eddie leaned down and gave her a deep kiss. "What are we waiting for?" he said, when they came up for air. He pointed down the hall at an open door leading to a bedroom.

"Here?" she said.

"Why not? I feel hot right now, and I don't want my stroke to cool off."

She licked her lips knowingly and led him by the hand. "A lot of people might think strange things are going on when they hear about a ref and a coach behind locked doors."

He smiled. "I'm not telling if you aren't."

Big Eddie smiled from one ear to the other watching the team snap through their drills. "That's it, Carlos, way to rebound! We work like this tomorrow night against Western Kentucky, it'll be a rout."

He was right, the party had been a good idea, for more reasons than one. It had helped everybody to relax. It also took their minds off the dreary winter campus. Depression always set in during the holidays, when the players couldn't go home. But one of the remedies was to work them hard, tiring them out, distracting them. Big Eddie was excited, hopeful again, for he was beginning to see a team—although still a loosely fitted one—evolving.

Father Charles walked into the arena and moved quietly to a chair next to Q. "Good afternoon, Q."

"Hey," the manager said, barely looking up, his nose in a chemistry book in his lap.

"How are things going after the loss?"

"Incredible, r-really. He's been as c-calm as I've ever seen him."

"Really?" Maybe his little talk had done some good. "No one's been thrown out of practice? Cussed out?" Tossing a kid out of practice never really bothered him, but the cussing was a different story.

Q shook his head no. "It's been so p-peaceful, I've actually been able to do some studying while they're on the f-floor."

Father Charles looked at the book. "Chemistry, eh?"

"Hardest class in the world, Father. Wish I didn't have to take it. Guy gives us a t-test every time I turn around. All our traveling is putting a hurt on my grade-point."

"You'll do okay, Q. And you know what?"

"What?"

"I see a lot of chemistry in this team."

Q pushed his glasses up his nose. "Why's that?"

"I don't really know, but I sense something unique with these guys, with the way everyone seems to get along and like each other."

"Yeah, they do seem to get a long a lot better than some of the other teams I've seen. Especially Carlos and Mike. Since Carlos joined the team, Mike seems more at ease, more confident. And since that girl's been hanging around Mike he seems a lot happier. They go everywhere together. Saw them in church Sunday."

"And Eddie is more laid back than I've seen him in a long, long time," Father Charles said. He suspected it had a lot to do with Penny North, though he was a tad disappointed when Hoppy told him of their little roll in the hay during the Thanksgiving party. He wished Eddie could have waited to make it legal.

"But, son, you should have seen him in the early years. He was a dandy. It was a given we'd make the tournament every year. Teams feared us, especially on the road. We rarely lost. It was awesome."

Q closed his book. "With Carlos, I think we might have a chance this year to do it again."

"Cross your fingers, Q. And say a few prayers. And I think you're right. We've got a sharpshooter, a giant down low, two seasoned forwards—and a reason to win."

Q looked oddly at the priest. "Reason to win?"

The priest pointed to an attractive blonde sitting in the stands. "Yeah, Big Eddie's lucky charm—a shiny Penny."

Luca Marzzarella blew into his manicured hands and rolled the thoughts around in his head. All he had to do was impact sixteen tournament games to ensure the right teams made it to the Final Four. Super Dave Cobb already had his first set of instructions—meet with his stable of bookies and odds-makers to pick the season's games to be influenced. That was Phase One in building the right playoff set-up. St. John's, North Carolina, Notre Dame, and U.C.L.A. couldn't stumble at all.

Notre Dame was the only one that really worried him. The Irish had found getting into the NCAA tournament almost impossible. He told Super Dave he knew why. "They ain't got enough blacks," he said. "You know and I know, them ghetto kids are made for basketball, but the monkeys can't do the bookwork. Notre Dame's too fucking hard."

And there was one more thing that didn't sit too well with him. He'd seen to it that Super Dave had whatever he needed to bribe players, but there was always the chance that some stupid kid might not accept a bribe or knuckle under to a threat. Marzzarella wouldn't take that chance.

He needed some dead-certain insurance they'd collect in the end, and so far he hadn't come up with the right thing. God, he hated it when something that important eluded his thoughts.

He rolled back in his chair and picked up the newspaper, let his cooling coffee run effortlessly down his throat as he gazed at a photo in the *Times* of a referee calling a technical on Cincinnati's Bob Huggins.

Stinking damn job, being a ref, having to put up with the likes of irate coaches. There wasn't enough money in the world to make Marzzarella take the job. He took another sip of coffee and turned the page, then suddenly it came to him.

A great smile crossed his face as he went back to the picture again. Huggins was inches from the referee, spit flying from his mouth. Jesus, this was it! He grinned wildly, pulled the paper closer and read a story about the paltry money refs made to be refs. Yes. Yes. Yes!

There wasn't enough money in the world to make him a ref, but there was more than enough money in the world to make a ref swallow his whistle every now and again.

He picked up the phone and smiled. He was a genius. A fucking genius.

Chapter 8

Dale Cutter loved college basketball. He had once played for U.N.L.V., but after an injury in his senior year he didn't get to go on to the Final Four with the rest of the Runnin' Rebs. He considered himself a perfect fit for the FBI's new Sports Fraud Division, though sometimes he still liked to dabble in homicide work. And no matter what else came up, there was one homicide he couldn't get out of his head—the baffling murder of Antoine Tandy, the basketball player at Georgetown.

Most of his work now involved touring the country, speaking with college athletes about keeping straight and avoiding any gambling involvement. Sometimes he even persuaded a former teammate to come along—Reggie Roberts, now manager of the Springs Hotel in Las Vegas.

His secretary's voice interrupted his thoughts. "Mr. Cutter, you have a phone call." She waited.

He gazed up at the ceiling, annoyed by the intrusion. "Okay, but this is the last one I'm taking. I've got to get this report done before I fly to Louisville tomorrow morning."

When Dale picked up he immediately recognized the voice.

"Every time I call you I feel like I'm being interrogated by your secretary, bro. What's up with that?"

Reggie. He should have known. Anytime he was trying to get something done, now or back in college, Reggie was around to throw a wrench into his plans. He remembered the night before his wedding, when he'd vowed to behave, but Reggie wouldn't listen, and they ended up hitting every bar on the Strip. His bride was not well pleased to see what a hard time he had walking down the aisle the next after-noon.

"You wouldn't feel like that, Reg, if you weren't so shady. When are you gonna get a wholesome family job, like mine?"

"C'mon, bro, slide me some slack. My birthday is tomor-row. Be nice to ol' Reg."

Dale couldn't help but laugh. Reggie was almost like a little brother, except for the fact he was black. "Give me the scoop, Reg. I need to hear something interesting for a change. This place is as about as exciting as watching an NBA exhibition."

"Funny you should say that."

"Why? You hate the NBA even more than I do."

"Nah, not about the NBA, but about hoops."

"Well, what about it?"

"That's why I called."

"About hoops?"

"Uh-huh."

"You called me on our 800 number to talk to me about bas-ketball?"

"Why not? Tell me if I'm wrong, your job has nothing to do with sports."

Dale sighed. He always sighed when Reggie called. "Reggie, the fucking auditors around here are gonna check this call out, and then I'll have to pay for it, they'll say it was personal."

"No, they won't. I've got something crazy you might be interested in. Real crazy, and real interesting."

Reggie called him at least three times a month with the lat-est conspiracy. A month ago it was a motorcycle gang using slugs in the slot machines. Before that he had a story about some L.A. gang members spreading counterfeit money up and down the Strip.

Dale leaned further back in his chair, propped both feet on the corner of his desk. He wished that once, just once Reggie would have something solid. If he weren't an old teammate, the guy wouldn't get past his secretary.

"What is it this time, Reg? Some old-timer using magnets on the slots?"

"Funny, dude. Real funny." Reggie sounded hurt.

"Had to, my man. Had to."

"Okay, I'm sitting with the girls at the casino one night, and this dude who looks like Homer Simpson comes walking up to the counter and lays down a ten grand bet."

"Homer Simpson, huh? Wow, that's earth-shattering, Reg. You are in Vegas, you know…where all the nuts are."

"Hang on, bro, give me a chance. This is for real. He placed a bet on what four teams would get into the Final Four."

"The Final Four? You guys take bets like that?"

"Sure, why not? We take bets on the next sighting of Elvis."

"Maybe the cuckoo has more money than he knows what to do with. So what?"

"Yeah, I thought that too, and kind of let it go. But the more I thought about it, the less sense it made. So one night when nothing was happening, I made some calls to some buddies at some other casinos and found out the same guy had made four other bets, just the same."

"Let's see, that's fifty big ones, right?"

"Uh-huh. Fifty grand…on exactly what four teams would make it in the Final Four. And if he just happened to hit it right, at two hundred to one odds, brother Dale, that would mean a return of ten million bucks."

Dale gave a slow whistle through the line. He knew college basketball was big dollars, despite the latest scandal involving Northwestern players, but ten million— Maybe Reg was onto something. He sat straight in his chair, put his feet firmly on the floor. He was suddenly hooked. For some reason Antoine Tandy's blood on the wall at Georgetown came to mind. Sick—gory as hell.

"Hey, that's only the half of it," Reggie said.

"There's more?"

"Yeah, the guy used a different Social Security number with every bet."

"No shit? The IRS might want to know about this."

"Uh-huh, and the best of it all is that one of my buddies caught the guy on video."

"No!"

"Yeah."

"That's great, Reg. I knew you were good for something."

"And if you want, I can download the guy's photo into your computer."

Dale was smiling. "You know what, Reg?"

"Nah, man, tell me."

"You ain't bad for a black guy."

"Well, somebody's got to keep you honkies on top, in your comfy offices...'cause none of you can play basketball worth a damn."

Dale waited twenty minutes, accessed his e-mail, then double-clicked the mouse button and had the man's picture in front of him within seconds. Reggie also sent the Social Security numbers the man had used. Dale studied them for fifteen minutes, but couldn't figure what they meant. He hit the intercom on his phone.

"Susan, get San Lee up here as soon as he has a minute. I need him to do something for me."

He locked his hands behind his head and studied the screen some more. San Lee was a young comer at the Bureau, eager to make his mark. Maybe he could make some sense out of it all. Dale sure couldn't.

The Georgetown murder, the bets, the various Social Security numbers—Dale couldn't let it go so he could sleep. His wife got up and moved in the guest room, he was so restless. Finally he caught a couple of hours just before dawn, then had to wake up to make his flight out of town. Sleepily, he purchased a *Blue Ribbon College Yearbook* at Dulles, figuring he could study the schedules of the four teams named in the bet on the plane to Louisville.

There was a sense of urgency in the Bureau to crack down on illegal gambling, and this might just be the case that could help him move up in the ranks. It was a hunch, but he'd learned to trust his hunches. Something told him if he followed each of the four teams' winning patterns through the season, something fishy might very well be revealed. What? He didn't know. But not even the most addicted gambler in the world would place fifty grand on a bet that seemed to be a sure loser. None he knew of, at least.

After a short nap at The Galt House, Dale caught a Yellow Cab to Alumni Hall. He had been excited about seeing the Knights and U.C.L.A. play, but now, after the game, as he studied the C.U. players' faces as they walked off the court, he knew he had picked an unlikely game to enjoy. He remembered losing, how awful it felt. This wasn't going to help his little gambling talk.

"Shake it off, guys," he said softly, sure they didn't hear a thing he was saying. "You'll get 'em next time."

The team ignored him, and he stood uneasily outside the locker room waiting for the coaching staff.

Big Eddie blew past him, then came back five minutes later smoking a cigarette. "Dale." The coach glared at him. "I would say I'm glad to see you, but you must be the one who brought the bad luck."

Dale kept quiet, not sure if he was serious or joking.

"Fuck," Big Eddie said, "I hate losing, especially here at home. U.C.L.A.'s not that good, and we're not that bad." He tossed the cigarette on the floor, then stomped it out with the heel of his shoe. "Why in the hell did I ever get into this business?"

"Because you're good at it, that's why."

"I don't know about that."

"Well, you should know. What's this, your first loss?"

"Second, we lost the opener to Mizzou."

Dale shrugged. Big Eddie rubbed his chin, then blew out the last traces of his smoke. "I'm getting too old for all of this. I need a nice comfy job...like yours. Show up, talk to a bunch of kids about something none of 'em would ever dream of doing, then fly out the next day. Tough duty."

Dale grinned. "Hey, somebody's got to do it."

Big Eddie read a stat sheet, shook his head, then wadded it up and tossed it into a garbage can. "Well, shit, let's get your little speech over with so I can tell the athletic director you did your job. I don't want to be here all night, especially after the way we just shot."

Dale patted Eddie's back. "C'mon, Coach, cheer up. The season's still young."

"No, you better cheer up, 'cause your talk is gonna go in one ear and out the other. Hey, when we lose they don't even listen to me."

"Yeah, I noticed. Your guard blew by me. He was fuming when he went in."

"Which one?"

"The white kid, Kramer."

"Yeah, he's probably in there lecturing them as we speak. Ten bucks says he is."

"Hey, no gambling, okay? That's what I'm here to try and convince them not to do."

"Oops, sorry."

Big Eddie opened the door and pulled Cutter with him behind a partition, listening.

Mike's voice filled the room. "We lost again, guys, and every one of you knows we shouldn't have. We're gutless, especially here at home...in front of our own fans."

Big Eddie winked at Dale and stepped into the open. Mike had his shirt off, pacing back and forth. A vein popped in his neck.

"He's right, fellas," Big Eddie said. "We can't win unless we play with our hearts and—"

Mike shot Big Eddie a glance that would kill. He wasn't through. "We also lost because we didn't execute. And we weren't mentally ready to play."

Big Eddie tried to interrupt Mike's speech twice more, but Mike was so angry he cut the coach off every time. Cutter and Big Eddie exchanged a humorous glance. Finally Mike realized what he had done and apologized.

The coach nodded. "Hey, there's not much I can add to what Mike just said, except to put this game behind you."

He turned and introduced the FBI agent.

The players cut tape from their ankles and half listened as Cutter went through his annual speech about staying away from gamblers.

"If any of you is approached," he wound it up, "report it immediately to the coach or athletic department." He smiled. "I don't think I need to worry about that with Mike around. He seems to be keeping everyone in line."

Chapter 9

Pain rolled through Super Dave's squat body as he held the receiver to his ear. He had spent the good part of last night in a neighborhood bar, throwing darts and chugging draft beer. Now he was paying for it. His eyes felt like cinders, his hair looked like a greasy mop. If he'd had to choose between living and dying at this moment, he would've chosen death.

God, his head hurt. "Yes, boss, I hear you." He stuck the phone between his ear and shoulder and rubbed his temples.

After twenty minutes of listening, he reached over to the bedside table and hung up. He was wide awake now, the light above his head shining directly into his blood-streaked eyes. He squinted at his watch. A little after three. Change fell on the floor as he searched his pants pockets for his wallet and pulled out a dog-eared card covered with phone numbers that only he could decipher. He called for a cab to pick him up in thirty minutes.

After a half-hour in city traffic, despite the pounding headache, Super Dave was ready to go to work. He eased out of the cab and ambled onto a sidewalk teeming with tough-looking, cigarette-smoking hoods.

"Yo, Super Dave! What's up? You got a job for us? Tell The Big Cheese we got our own hardware." A couple of the punks flashed guns. "Can't be traced."

He shooed them away. "Go to school, boys, and make something of yourself. Don't you know crime don't pay?" They all laughed. He turned the corner and entered the back door of Pera's Bakery, then climbed the stairs to an apartment on the second floor.

Five sets of eyes fell on Super Dave when he opened the door.

"See this?" Super Dave removed a 9-mm from his gray trenchcoat. "The big man says if this deal don't go off, you guys will all be swimming in the Hudson."

He sat down and placed the gun next to him, its snub barrel pointed toward the others at the table.

"All right, Vinny, what shit you got?" Vinny Vagotis was Marzzarella's trusted bookie from Queens.

Vinny loosened his tie, cleared his throat. "Yo, Supe, this here is no different than the old days, when we was all young punks and we fixed the N.I.T." He nibbled on a toothpick, unmoved by the intensity on Super Dave's face. "Your punk ass wasn't even born when we made a ton off C.C.N.Y. winning the title in '50. This here is as simple as dealing crack to the niggers and Puerto Ricans in Harlem."

Super Dave wagged a finger, shook his head. "Vinny. Don't ever underestimate."

Vinny blew through his lips. "Chickenfeed compared to the Fifties."

"Okay, give me what you got." Super Dave unconsciously stroked his snub-nosed gun.

Vinny stood up, moved to a black chalkboard and picked up a piece of chalk. He wrote the four Final Four teams at the top of the board, underscored then with thick lines. "See all these four teams? I've went over them with a fine-tooth comb, every fucking thing about 'em, and I like what I see. Big names here...and even bigger fans with plenty of dough.

"But there's just one team, now, one team I ain't so certain can win twenty games. . . nice little squeaky-clean Notre Dame." He took the chalk and circled the school name. "All them other teams pays their players plenty, but the fucking priests up there gotta be keeping all that money for theirselves."

Mild laughter traveled around the table.

"Right," Vinny went on, after his own laugh, "they gotta be. They got so much fucking Irish tradition, why else ain't they winning? Look at it this way. If Digger Phelps won there once, hell, anybody can. I don't get it, but that's another story. Anyway, I don't see no problem with getting U.C.L.A., St. John's, and Carolina in. With them, the fucking odds is in our favor. But now them Irish Micks…" His voice trailed off.

"Well," Super Dave said, leaning an elbow on the table, "we'll just send a man to every one of their games. Solve the problem. Give us the insurance we need."

"Ah, no, Supe, don't overreact," Vinny said. "Notre Dame being who they are, eighteen, maybe even seventeen wins, that's prolly good enough to get 'em in. But even that many's gonna be a hell of a struggle."

A fat man named Scotty Scallion who ran the book in Long Island spoke up from the end of the table. "If the NCAA was smart, they'd let Notre Dame in every year. Fucking Catlicks would go nuts. You guys have any idea how much money would be bet?"

"What d'you say, Scotty?" Super Dave said. "You think Notre Dame has a chance?"

"Sure. Why not? Especially if the big man is behind 'em getting there."

Super Dave drummed the table. "Who they playing?"

The fat man lifted a *Street & Smith Yearbook* from the table and went through the pages. "Well…I say they'll beat Valparaiso, St. Mary's, DePaul, St. Louis, Creighton, Hofstra, Syracuse, Manhattan and, with a little luck, maybe Indiana, with Knight gone bye-bye. Prolly they can at least break even in the Big East.

"With a couple wins in the conference tournament, that gives them right at eighteen, nineteen, maybe twenty wins. To me, that's a lock, specially since they're playing a pretty decent schedule…the NCAA looks at that hard. They also got a young coach. He might be worth two, three wins alone."

"And they got the fucking Pope on their side," Vinny snorted. "So you say odds of them having a real good season and getting in the tournament don't look too bad."

Scallion nodded.

"Give me some odds," Super Dave said.

Scotty looked across the table at Vinny. "Something like three to one."

Super Dave stretched his fingers protectively over the gun. "Hell, that's good enough for me." He licked his lips, then pinched the bridge of his nose, the headache still hammering his brain. "Okay, you already got your instructions. Just keep me posted. And remember, the boss is talking big-time bills here for everyone."

Cautious smiles appeared as the room emptied of everyone except Ricky Ridgeway, who leaned in his chair, rocking back and forth.

Super Dave stood, walked slowly down the table, then stared out a window. "What d'you think, Ricky?" Ricky pulled a cigarette and lit it, blew out the first drag's smoke. "I think them guys would be fools to give you bad information."

Super Dave nodded. He was satisfied. Cars and trucks jostled and honked in the street below.

"So now the rest of them punks is all gone," Ricky said, "fill me in on this genius other plan."

Super Dave looked at Ricky, then away. His eyes were red around the edges. Too much pot. "Refs, man. He's gonna buy four of 'em."

Ricky straightened in the chair, cocked his head forward like a turtle. "Mother Mary, how?"

Super Dave's face suddenly went blank. "Don't take this personal, but I really can't say."

Ricky jerked away, resenting the snub, then decided to let it go. "Just four?"

"One for each team."

Ricky scratched his head. "Shit, man, the refs get moved around."

Super Dave put up his palms and closed his eyes. His head really hurt. "Ricky...don't sweat the small stuff. Like I said, you're on a need-to-know basis. It's for your own good. The boss man ain't messing around."

Ricky blew a line of smoke. "So when do we start? My guys are ready to go."

"Who you got lined up?"

"Rizzio in L.A., Lucas in Chapel Hill, Little Pete in South Bend, and me here in the city with the Red Storm. That is, unless I find somebody else I trust for here."

Super Dave removed an envelope from his jacket and handed it to Ricky. "Here's the names of the clinics where they can pick up the virus."

Ricky's usually expressionless face registered surprise. "Damn! The boss wants to put AIDS in the water coolers?"

"Get with it, man." Super Dave's eyes closed to a squint. "The flu, moron. He don't want 'em dead, just throwing up and running a high fever. And he wants it done the day before the game during shooting practice, when the media is hanging around distracting everyone…or if that don't work, then we go to their hotels."

"Yeah…" Ricky was thinking it through. "That'll work. But during the tournament security's always a whole lot tighter than usual."

Super Dave gave him a look dead-on. "No shit…so that's when we might have to twist a few arms, you understand?"

Ricky grinned, the cigarette dangling out of the side of his mouth. "Got it all the way."

"Tell your guys here're the possibilities…" He ticked them off on the fingers of one hand. "The water bucket, team dinner the night before, or even breakfast before the game. And if that don't work, a little visit with a crowbar will have to be arranged."

Ricky took a last deep drag from the cigarette then flipped the butt out the window. "A broken leg? An ankle?"

Super Dave nodded yes.

Ricky Ridgeway sipped coffee in Clara's and slowly scanned the newspaper. St. John's was playing Manhattan in Madison Square Garden tomorrow night. He had already gotten Manhattan's shoot-around time by calling their sports information office, saying he was a reporter with *The Sporting News*.

He'd decided to be the first one to test the virus, even though he knew Manhattan had little chance of beating St. John's. More than anything, he just wanted to see if it worked. The virus had come two days ago from a clinic in Brooklyn, delivered by hand in plastic vials with screw-off tops—guaranteed to work after being cultured in their lab.

"You all done, buddy?" Clara came walking over with a towel draped over her hunched shoulder. She wasn't crazy about men with ponytails.

"Right, I got nothing else to do here. Good chow, by the way."

She gave him a peculiar look. "Don't I know you?"

"I don't know, do you?"

"Thought I seen you in here before." She studied his face. "But I just can't remember when. What's your name?"

"Richard," he said, standing up.

"Hmm...it'll come to me." She leaned and wiped off the table. "Know I seen you in here. Or somebody that looks like you."

He threw down two bucks, grabbed his coat, got out of the café quick, and walked the three blocks to the Garden. He entered through the service area and sat down courtside with a reporter's notepad in his lap. For several minutes he watched alone as the team went through a light workout until a manager with a pimply face skipped over to retrieve a stray ball.

"Uh, who are you?" the kid asked innocently, picking up the ball.

Ricky turned his head away from the action and looked up. "Reporter."

"Yeah, for who?" The kid could already see his name in head-lines.

"*The Sporting News.*"

The kid got real excited. Nationals rarely dropped in on Man-hattan practices. "You're with the b-baseball bible?"

"Sure, why not?" Ricky said coolly.

"I thought they only did baseball."

"Nope, we do it all."

"I'd like to be a writer some day." The kid sat down, getting chummy fast.

"Yeah?" Ricky scribbled a bogus number in his reporter's pad and ripped the page out. "Here, give me a call when you get your degree."

The kid broke into a wide smile, exposing a set of braces. "Wow."

Ricky saw his chance and thumbed at the water cooler at the end of the bench. "Hey, mind if I get a drink?"

"Hell, n-no." The kid stared at the phone number. "Get as much as you want."

Ricky waited until the kid went back to the other side of the floor, then casually twisted the top off the cooler and emptied the contents of the match-sized vial inside. He put the top back on the cooler and moved back to the bench, and when the coach called the team into a huddle, he slipped away, certain no one had seen his move.

Sheets of gray clouds hung so low Little Pete reached to see if he could touch them. If his short arms were just a little longer, he thought he could probably put a cloud in his pocket. Flakes of snow scattered in the biting breeze, dancing merrily around the outblow of his breath. Leaves cartwheeled out of piles drifted in corners of buildings. The wind whipped across the flat land and jumped anything daring to tangle. Thick smoke from the power plant seemed frozen as it lifted from a towering chimney, then took a sudden horizontal bend like a river running downstream. Little Pete wiped snot running down his numb nose, lowered his hand, and muttered to himself. "Why the hell did I get South Bend in the winter?"

The warm air splashed his face when he entered the hotel where St. Louis University's team was booked. He saw the team unload and knew it wouldn't be long before their evening meal was served. He grabbed a bellboy and asked directions to the kitchen. He was in and out in ten minutes. Hundred-dollar bills sure came in handy when he started waving them under the nose of a greedy chef, especially if the chef was one who helped himself too often to the cooking sherry. The Irish would win big tonight, that was the only warm feeling he had as he walked back out into the cold.

Rizzio had been by U.C.L.A.'s Pauley Pavilion numerous times before but he'd never entered the hallowed arena. He jiggled two or three doors, then found one unlatched. Wearing a gray janitor's uniform, he climbed the rows of seats and picked one at the top, momentarily forgetting his mission. The NCAA championship banners were so numerous he stopped counting. Down below he spotted Pepperdine's managers and trainers setting up for their shooting practice. In and out they came with bags of equipment, leaving the court empty for fifteen minutes at a time.

He decided that when they came and went again he would make his move. Pepperdine would face the Bruins the following afternoon, carried on ESPN. The early line was U.C.L.A. by two. He felt his wallet and chuckled. There was still plenty of time to get down a big bet that they'd win bigger. Much bigger.

Lucas Mahoney waited until the last call for TWA 333 before boarding. He couldn't wait to see Georgetown's players writhing in pain. He hated Georgetown, and seeing them lose to Boston College would be a sliver of revenge.

He read a newspaper in first class while the flight attendants prepared drinks. The Hoyas sat behind him in the first rows of coach. After he received his beverage, he stood and stretched outside the pilot's door.

"Feeling okay?" The stewardess was still busy making drinks.

"My legs just need a little circulation. Am I in your way?"

"Not at all. Hey, can you hold something for a quick second?" She hurried down the aisle to help an old lady stow a bag, then came back. "Sorry."

A grin crossed his face. "What was it you wanted?"

"This ice bucket…I'll be right back. This old lady is driving me batty."

His grin suddenly got much bigger as she rushed down the aisle again. "No problem, lady. I'll hold it right here in my hand. Don't worry about a thing."

Super Dave smiled, watching Marzzarella read the Sunday morning *New York Post*. Every so often the boss looked up over the sports section and gave him a wink.

"See, boss? It works."

Marzzarella put the paper down. "Damn straight." The ominous voice was more gravelly than usual, with a cold. "When I was in Germany, we done this to the platoon sergeant. Got hold of somebody's infected snot, grew it out in a can of chicken soup, put it in the bastard's food. Cocksucker was down for a whole week."

The old man huffed out a grunt meant for a laugh. He jabbed a finger against a half-page picture of the Georgetown coach puking in front of the team bench. "See? The bigger you are, the harder you fall." He tapped his buffed nails on the tabletop. "Right, this part of the plan works. Now the next part, that could turn out a little tricky."

Super Dave leaned to listen. The man sitting across the desk from him possessed unimaginable power. He was one of the few men in the world whose mere name could stop the changing of the guards at Buckingham Palace. It was he, not the Bush administration, who'd persuaded Saddam Hussein to break off the Gulf War, sending word that unless Hussein backed down, none of his oil would ever dock in the shipyards Marzzarella controlled across the world.

But today he seemed diminished by his cold, his voice weaker and crackling, his eyes reduced to half-open slits. His flesh seemed daubed with chalk, his graying hair limp as wet straw. He was even wheezing now and then.

Physically he was much different now from the awesome figure he'd been when he took Super Dave in off the streets of Brooklyn as a skinny, shivering kid with no family, no future. A stroke five years back had forced him to slow down, and a cold today—but even so Super Dave knew the man he looked at was still as ruthless as ever.

"Here." Marzzarella pushed a white business card across the desk. "This here is the man you need to see."

Super Dave picked up the card and read it, then looked a question at his boss.

Marzzarella shook his head. "This guy, you don't have to worry. He'll make sure the right officials gets with the right teams."

"And…what if he won't cooperate?"

Marzzarella looked down at the desk, gave a slow sigh. He was tired. "Be nice to him, David, point out real clear how this can benefit him. You know what to say. That's why I picked you for this job. He ain't no dummy. He'll get it the first time, if you explain it right."

Super Dave could see the guy now, laughing in his face, but he nodded anyway.

"I got you, chief, but even I think he'll balk when I tell him these officials are gonna rig the Final Four."

"David, are you giving me a hard time?"

"Oh, no, chief, just trying to figure all the angles."

"Good. I don't like people giving me a hard time." The old man relaxed a little in his chair, clasped his hands on top of the desk. "No…he ain't gonna give you no hard time. That's where you're wrong."

He stood up, went to the window, stared down into Central Park. Skaters made bright spots on the ice rink in their red and blue and green winter attire.

"Let me tell it to you again." The words seemed to come from the back of the big man's head. "You're not gonna tell him you're the one putting in the fix for the Final Four. You're gonna tell him we're all in this together. That when something benefits me, it benefits him, benefits all. Do you unnerstand?"

"Yes, boss, I do."

"Right. Then get out there next week and fix everything. Fix it nice, David. You got that?"

Super Dave bit his lip nervously. "But if for some reason he don't understand me?"

Marzzarella turned back, his narrow eyes focused as radar. "Then, David, if he still don't get it, you just tell him what really happened to young JFK."

Ricky Ridgeway pulled up in a black Lincoln, popped the trunk, then waited for Super Dave to load his luggage and climb into the car. He blew a mouth full of smoke out the window that could have gagged the entire metropolitan area and handed Super Dave the latest issue of *Sports Illustrated.*

"Check it out."

"What's that?"

"The Irish. They're fucking undefeated. Big story there. Read it."

Super Dave smiled at the front cover: "The Luck Of The Irish."

"Little Pete is doing a hell of a job out there." Then he thought about it. Maybe too good. "Oh, shit."

"What's the matter?"

"Damn! This!" Super Dave pointed at the cover.

"What? They've won six games by less than two points. There's three pages inside about it all. Read."

"Not that, dummy. The cover. It's gonna jinx 'em."

Ricky looked at him curiously. "Huh?"

How could he not know about the *S.I.* cover being a hex?

"Ricky, for years the cover has ended up being a jinx for whoever on it. It's a well-known fact. This may be very bad for us."

"That's crazy as hell. Since when have you been superstitious?"

"Since the boss told me to make sure Notre Dame is in the Final Four, that's when."

Ricky waved him off and steered the Lincoln onto the expressway toward La Guardia. "Nah, don't let it worry you. This is the best thing that could happen. Now everybody and his fucking grandma will lay bets on the game. The people who hate Notre Dame will bet against 'em, the people who love Notre Dame…all the Catlicks in the country…will bet for 'em.

"And as long as we got Scotty looking out for the team, why, hell, Supe, I'm gonna make a killing." Grinning, he let go of the steering wheel and rubbed his hands together.

"Watch it, man!" Super Dave grabbed the wheel to steady it. "Don't get cocky, Rick. I don't know about all that. Scotty told me he's taking a beating out on the Island. Said Notre Dame winning is killing his profits. Lost a hundred grand this past weekend."

"Yeah, I know, he told me the same thing, but Scotty's always saying that."

"Well, the next time you talk to him, tell him to relax. The big man guarantees a bigger pay-off when the Irish lose in the Final Four."

Super Dave took the magazine and tossed it in the back seat. "Catholics will be putting down money like it was the collection plate." He laughed. "You know them priests...they ain't nothing but bookies for God anyway."

Chapter 10

Mike spotted the small church next door to the hotel and decided to duck in for a quick prayer before the team boarded the bus to Clarksville, Tennessee, for the next game against Austin Peay. Three candles flickered on a stand in front of the altar, their shadows dancing along the dark walls. He moved into an empty pew and placed the kneeler gently on the floor, the quiet of the place a balm to the troubles he couldn't forget, the troubles back home. For ten minutes he sat in silence, then turned when he heard the door creak open.

"Mike?" Father Charles walked down the aisle and sat next to him. "We're leaving in a few minutes."

"I know," Mike said, eyes turning from the priest back to the altar.

"Something bothering you, son?"

Mike sniffed, then sighed. "Nah, just needed some time to myself. When we're on the road, these guys start getting on my nerves a little. Kind of like being home during the holidays with nowhere to go."

The priest nodded, knowing better. He prodded some more. "The loss still bothers you, doesn't it?"

"A little. We should have beat I.U. They aren't that good. We made too many mistakes."

"Yeah, we should have won, but sometimes, no matter how hard you work, you still lose. And that's the one part of God's kingdom I still don't quite understand."

Mike moved off the kneeler and slouched back into the pew, letting his eyes rove around the ceiling, then all around the church. He thought he saw Savannah's image in a mural on the side wall. "I don't understand a lot about His kingdom."

"Anything in particular?"

Mike ran all ten fingers through his hair. "Yeah, why couldn't I have grown up in a family that wasn't so cotton-picking dysfunctional?"

So that was it—the troubles back home were haunting Mike again. Some kids always took on everything that presented itself. Mike was one of the ones who always thought he could change all the wrongs in the world. "Yes, you've mentioned it many times before, but you need to stop dwelling on it and do something about correcting it."

"Okay," Mike said simply. "Then I'll quit the team and go back home and get a job to help my mom pay bills."

Father Charles raised his hands. He had heard the stories before about Mike's old man. "Whoa, whoa, whoa...Mike." He pointed at his head. "It's up here where you stop it. Get your education and help them that way."

"I am, but that doesn't pay the bills."

"Not yet, but have some patience, my son. The Lord moves in mysterious ways. There is a reason why, we just don't always know what it is. It's my guess that if you hadn't grown up the way you did, you wouldn't be sitting here with me now. You wouldn't have that great heart of yours that doesn't cave to adversity or challenge."

The priest draped his arm around Mike's shoulder and gave him an encouraging pat. "If it's any consolation, you're a lot like someone else I know."

"Yeah, who?" Mike said in disgust.

"Big Eddie. He grew up on the streets of St. Louis. He never knew his father, so I guess you at least have that going for you."

Mike wasn't consoled. "Sometimes I think it would be better for everyone if I didn't know my old man at all."

"Hey, get your head up, Mike. I'm not afraid to tell you that I love you. Time and again in the nearly four years you've been here, you've shown me that you're not poor where it counts. Take things day by day, and I can promise your tomorrows will be full of greatness."

Mike moved through the crip line at full speed thinking about what Father Charles had told him, a thick sweat already pouring through his jersey. He had tried to call Savannah before leaving the hotel, but there was no answer. Probably out with someone else. The thought angered him. His green number 33, the one he wore out of respect for his hero, Larry Bird, suddenly seemed to bleed at the edges. He had read how Bird grew up poor in French Lick, Indiana. Mike felt they had something in common, except the fact that Bird was twice the player he was.

"Way to get up, Spoon!" Mike called. "Good shot, Beezer!"

Q and Father Charles watched from the end of the bench.

"M-Mike is into it tonight," Q said, a towel over one arm and a bottle of water in the other hand.

"He better be. Big Eddie is still fuming about the loss to Indiana."

Q shook his head. He knew the Knights should have won the game, but when the Hoosiers sank a three from mid-court they were finished. "We'll get Peay tonight, I can feel it. Mike's pumped."

"There's one thing for sure," Father Charles said. "I don't know anyone who takes life more seriously than Mike." He looked over to Carlos. "Say, Carlos even looks more confident. Look, he's actually moving his feet without tripping. Maybe I should start taking those dance classes. Right, Q?"

The Austin Peay crowd stood through introductions, booing C.U. A roll of toilet paper unfurled near the C.U. bench, missing the Knight mascot by inches. Ninety-five percent of the fans were tobacco farmers, the other five percent soldiers from Fort Campbell. Bib overalls seemed to be the fashion statement of the day.

"Bunch of rednecks." Big Eddie walked over and kicked the toilet paper off the floor, then called the team into a huddle as the Peay players were introduced. "They aren't giving us any respect, guys."

Carlos looked at the crowd in amazement. "Where I come from, they don't even boo the bull this way."

The comment broke the team up. Big Eddie even smiled. Carlos had a way of putting people at ease. Maybe it was because basketball wasn't big in Mexico and he never felt the pressure. Maybe he had more important things on his mind.

"All right," Big Eddie said, "let's not try anything out of the ordinary. Remember, these guys are the defending national champs, and they won't quit without a fight. Stick to the fundamentals, keep everything simple. We can beat these guys. Forget about our record right now and get out there and play as hard as you can." He stopped and eyed each member of the team, pointed to his head. "Let's *think* out there."

The five starters—Kramer and Robbie Hart at guards, Spoon Wheatley and Beezer Miller at forwards, and Carlos at center—broke from the huddle and walked to center court where the ref stood with the ball in the crook of his right arm. Peay's five moved around the circle, and when everyone was set, the ref tossed the ball up to begin the game. Carlos leapt five inches above the Peay player, pushing the ball behind him to Spoon. The noise from the fans was deafening.

Wheatley swung the ball over to Mike. He moved it to the top of the key, took a pick from Miller, and popped in a three with a man in his face. "Take that, you bunch of rednecks!" He threw his fist into the air.

The hopped-up crowd momentarily went silent. Big Eddie and Father Charles simultaneously threw their own fists into the air. The Knights fell into a two-two-one, full-court press. Peay was caught sleeping when Hart stole the inbound pass and dumped it to Spoon, who cut to the hoop for two more.

Five to zip.

Father Charles grabbed Q's arm and leaned over and whispered. "We're going to win by twenty over the defending national champs."

Suddenly, Q jumped out of his chair. "Oh...shit!"

Mike had deflected a pass and dived for it as it was going out of bounds. He fell into a reporter at courtside, spilling soda and knocking paper everywhere. The crowd hovered above him, one fan purposely spilling beer on him. The refs and a couple of rent-a-cops moved the crowd back quickly. Hoppy sprinted across the court with his shirttail hanging out of his pants and knelt down over Mike.

"Mike…Mike…Mike…can you hear me?" Hoppy checked him over carefully. He took two fingers and pushed back the right eyelid, then the left. "Mike…can you hear me?"

No response.

Hoppy opened his bag and pulled out a tiny container wrapped in white gauze tape, then moved it under his nose.

Instantly Mike's eyes watered. The ammonia snapped his head back.

"Awwwww." Mike rubbed his eyes, squinted at the brilliant lights coming from the ceiling.

"Shit," Hoppy said to Q. "He's worse than I thought. See if you can help me get him on his feet."

With the help of one of the security guards, Hoppy and Q led him past the bench and toward the locker room.

Big Eddie approached with his hands on his hips and concern in his eyes.

"How is he?"

"K.O.ed," came the reply. "Lights out."

Big Eddie scowled. "Can he come back?"

"Doubt it. It'll be halftime before he even snaps out of the fog. He must have hit something at just the right spot for this to happen. He's awful woozy."

Big Eddie walked back to the bench and went through some revised instructions with the team, while Hoppy and Q and the security guard went on into the locker room with Mike.

"Get a bigger bag of ice, and put it right on his forehead." Hoppy pointed Q toward a cooler. "He's gonna have a hell of a shiner tomorrow."

Hoppy snapped his fingers. "Yo, Mike, you hear me?"

After five minutes, Mike slowly came to. "Where's Ma?" He pushed the words through a thick slur.

"Mike, it's me, Hoppy. You went after a loose ball…and fell."

"Huh?"

Hoppy half turned. "Q, see if you can find me a blanket. I want to keep him warm."

Q darted out of the locker room. Mike tried to sit, then fell back on the training table.

"Hey, relax, dude. You're done for the day."

Mike rubbed his neck. "What time is it?"

Hoppy laughed. "Why? You ain't going anywhere."

"Why is this table spinning?"

"It's not, Mike."

Q came back carrying a blanket.

"Thanks, Q. Now go and tell Peay's trainer I want to take him to the hospital—"

Mike grabbed his wrist. "Uh-uh, Hop, no way. I need to get back out there."

"Yeah, right. You don't even know where you are. We're going to the hospital first, pal."

Mike shook his head. "I ain't going to no hospital." He propped himself up on his elbows. Water from the bag of ice trickled down the side of his face. "One of my old man's cows hit me once like this. Kicked me right here." Mike pointed to a spot just below his eye. "Knocked the hell out of me. My old man carried me into the house and gave me a shot of moonshine. I snapped right out of it."

Hoppy leaned back and scratched his nuts. "I ain't Dr. Kramer. And I think I should take you to the hospital for a look at that noggin."

"C'mon, Hop. Please." Mike's grip tightened.

"No way."

"I'm already feeling better. It wasn't a knockout. I just kind of slipped. Let me play. We can't afford any more losses."

Hoppy studied Mike's face one more time. He did seem to be coming out of it. They did need to win. And he knew Mike would never sue. During their four years together he had come to respect the kid's desire, his toughness. If anyone was telling the truth, it was Mike. He shook his head and thought about it.

"Hell, might as well. We can't win without you, and you're so damn hardheaded I'm sure nothing is wrong." He reached into the bottom of his equipment bag and pulled out a half-empty bottle of Jack Daniels, looked over his shoulder. "This ain't moonshine, but it just might work, and if you ever tell a soul about this, I'll kick your country ass all the way back to the mountains."

He lifted the bottle and poured a hefty shot between Mike's lips.

"Ahh!" Mike sighed, shaking his head, the fire slowly trickling to his stomach. "Just what the doctor ordered."

Hoppy rolled his eyes and made the sign of the cross, then took a long drink of his own. "Now get your butt out there and make me look like a hero."

When Mike came back C.U. went on a tear, scoring fifteen unanswered points, winning the game by twelve. Ecstatic, but with his head down, Big Eddie walked to the locker room, avoiding the writers and fans. He knew his team had something special now—that intangible something every coach searches for but rarely gets. He saw it when Mike returned and the team came together, thumping a squad on the road it had no business beating. He wanted to tell someone he'd won the lottery. He wanted to tell someone he'd visited with Jesus. Instead, he told the team the bus was leaving in thirty minutes.

He took a stat sheet and turned his back to the showering players. He didn't want the win and the smile glowing inside him to go to their heads. He had bigger things in mind. Damn, finally. Finally he had another team. Oh, it felt good. Maybe the long wait was over.

Mike was tired from the game. "I'll see you later, Hoppy," he said, his head low. "Gotta get a move on it."

Hoppy looked up from a report he was writing. "Keep it in your pants, son. And put some more ice on that shiner tonight. It'll keep the swelling down."

"Yeah, Hop, I'll do that."

Mike headed out of the training room, then half-jogged to the dorms through a wet snow that crunched under his feet and made tree limbs groan. He picked up his mail, read a letter from home, crumpled it, tossed it viciously into the trash can, and headed at a determined trot toward Savannah's dorm.

Though it was dark already, he could see tiny icicles hanging from a security light at the corner of a building. Fat at their base, they tapered to a point and shimmered like the winter ponds back home on the farm. The picture of him, his brothers, and neighbors passing a flattened soda can with garden hoes across the frozen water brought a smile. Sometimes when the county road was impassable and school was closed, a few of the neighbor kids would join in the Kramer boys' homemade hockey games. They came in four-wheel drive trucks, or sometimes by horseback. They played from the time they got up until dark, often from the lights of the tractor his old man pulled close. But it was just games, not friends.

Now Mike jogged around the dorm to clear his head. Cold air filled his lungs, his fingers tingling as he remembered. He could see Canada geese overhead, honking loudly and sometimes gliding down to pick the last few grains from the tired cornfields. Behind the bare trees an orange sun rose in the distance, seemingly casting a picket fence across the fields. Smoke poured from the chimney of the house, sending a line through the sky that drifted above the pond and over the bordering treetops. The kids' excited voices darted across the farm, and every now and then brought Ma to the back porch with a sweater draped across her shoulders to make sure the big kids weren't getting too rough.

"Mike!" He could hear her voice carrying across the barren field. "You boys be careful with them young uns."

He would cup his hands around his mouth and holler an acknowledgement, but after she stepped back inside they'd use a good push or two to show the little ones how far they still needed to come. It was how he had learned. He couldn't even begin to remember how many elbows and shoves he'd taken over the years. The black eyes. The deep bruises. The mouse under his eye now was nothing.

Mike smiled and slowed to a walk. "You the man, Mike!" He looked up. Someone had yelled from a dorm window. "Kick Cincinnati's ass, bubba!"

"Will do," he hollered back, giving the guy a thumbs-up.

He went inside Savannah's dorm, hopped on the elevator, then made his way to her room at the end of the hall, getting curious looks from the other girls on the floor. He hadn't seen her for a couple of days. And he had missed her. No other girl ever had made him feel this way. He felt a smile coming on.

"Your hair's wet," she said when she opened the door.

"I wanted to get over here as soon as I could." He pushed a wet lock out of his eyes. "Are you ready?"

Savannah grabbed her keys and a small black purse that matched her black skirt. Her blouse was red with black polka dots. "You'll get sick coming out of practice with a wet head."

"You sound like my ma. She used to tell me that all the time."

"Your eye. Oh, it looks awful. Does it hurt?"

"Not when I'm with you."

She flashed a smile, and they walked quickly to Clark's. Mike was feeling better already, just being with her.

As they waited to be seated Savannah said, "Do you bring all your dates here?" She was watching some girls at the bar staring at the two of them.

"No, I hardly ever come here. I usually take dates to better places." He laughed at his own joke.

Savannah wasn't amused.

"Just kidding. Really, I don't have time for dating. Seems all I do is play basketball, go to school, and study."

A waitress named Brooke seated them at a table next to an eight-foot tall wooden Indian.

Savannah was watching him fondly. "I have a hard enough time just going to class and studying," she said. "I don't know how I'd do it if I had to go to basketball practice every day."

"It's not easy." Mike said. "Sometimes when the alarm sounds, I just want to pull the covers over my head and sleep. People don't realize how physical basketball is. Especially under Big Eddie. He works our butts off."

He mustered up his courage and came out with something he'd been wanting to say. "But you've worked hard yourself, especially with your dancing…and overcoming polio."

She looked up from the menu, surprised. "How did you know that?"

"Hey, you told me to check out your game."

"Yeah," she confessed. "It was a nightmare. I had to go through some tough physical therapy. I still can see that therapist, this guy named Joel, pushing me until I wanted to cry."

"Really?"

"Yeah, really. Hardest thing I've ever done."

Mike ordered a pizza as a provocative little blonde cheerleader brushed by the table, said hello, and gave him a comely smile. Her jeans and sweater were a size too small. A green ribbon fell from her hair.

"Never come here?"

"She's just a bimbo cheerleader."

"What about me?" Savannah said. "Am I a bimbo?"

"Nope, as a matter of fact, you seem very smart for a girl who drives a red Beamer."

The waitress returned with their drinks. Savannah twisted a lemon slice into her tea, then sprinkled in a dab of sugar. "Hm, I don't know if that's a compliment or not."

"It is, and while I'm handing out compliments, you're also one of the prettiest girls I've ever seen. I can't believe you're here with me."

She set her glass down and looked away. It was one of those odd moments, when the date could have taken a wrong turn.

Already blindly committed, Mike seized the opportunity. "What's the matter, don't you believe me?"

"I don't know. People used to make fun of me because I had polio. They said I was crippled. Now you're telling me I'm beautiful. It just doesn't make sense."

Mike reached across the table and took her hand. "Hey, I mean it. Why are you so embarrassed? I don't say things that I don't mean."

"I've never had anyone tell me that before. That's all. My dad never let me date in high school because he didn't want the boys…making fun of me."

"Ah." Mike grinned. "I like your old man already."

The waitress brought their pizza, and Mike promptly devoured a slice.

Savannah changed the subject suddenly, and the tension between them was gone. "A lot of people are saying C.U. has one of the best basketball teams in the country. They say there's a chance you'll get to the NCAA tournament."

"Boy, who have you been talking with?"

"Everybody's talking about the team."

"Well, if they'd talk to Big Eddie, he'd tell them just the opposite. Today he told us we couldn't beat Bellarmine College, a Division Two team."

"He's probably just trying to motivate you guys."

"Nah, I doubt it. Knowing him, he was serious."

"Don't you like him, Mike?"

"Sometimes I think he's one of the greatest coaches I've ever met. Other days I think he's the biggest jerk in the world. But I guess when I get out of here I'll thank him for what he's done for me. At least that's what my mom and Father Charles keep telling me."

"Do your parents ever come to games?"

Mike looked away. "Hardly."

"How come?"

He didn't really want to answer, but somehow Savannah could make him bring out private things. "My brothers have been before, when we played close to my home, but not my folks. We don't have a lot of money, and they hate to leave the farm. Never know when one of the animals might get sick or hurt." Mike's voice cracked. "Especially that damn hog."

"You mean they haven't seen you play in four years?"

He shook his head no.

"That bothers you, doesn't it?"

"Not anymore."

But she could see that it did.

He looked toward the ceiling to conceal his pain. "But your—"

"Hey, enough, I really don't want to talk about it." He slammed his hand against the table, stared at her, stood up and grabbed his jacket, then walked outside.

She paid the bill and collected her things. Every man in the bar had his eyes fixed on her tight skirt as she walked after him to the door.

"Mike." She hurried to catch up. "I didn't mean to upset you."

His hands were deep into the pockets of his team jacket. He stared at the stars. "Yeah, whatever." His face was tight.

Not knowing what to say, she just took his hand as they walked slowly to the dorms.

After a block of silence Mike spoke, his words heavy and haunting. "Savannah, not many people know this and not many people care, but my dad's an alcoholic who can't keep a job. Half the time we don't know where he is. My four younger brothers work before and after school just to help my mom meet ends. Sometimes...lots of times... I want to quit and go back home and get a job. I want to be able to buy my mom something nice. A new dress. Some perfume. Take her to a movie with my brothers. But Father Charles keeps telling me to stick it out here instead."

He wiped his eyes with his jacket sleeve. Except for Father Charles, he had never told anyone else this stuff about his father. It was odd how Savannah put him at ease. He trusted her. Other than his mother and Father Charles, he told his feelings to no one. He didn't understand what was going on, but he didn't fight it, either.

"Gosh, I'm...sorry. I didn't mean to—"

"Don't be sorry. My old man is having a hard time." He paused, pulled her close. She was so soft. He looked into her eyes. "But, dammit, I'm gonna do something with my life. I'm gonna be somebody someday. His troubles aren't gonna get me down. I'm gonna win, Savannah. Screw what everyone else thinks."

He clutched her between his strong arms, sobbed, then raised his eyes again to the stars.

"Mike, you're already somebody." She was looking up into his face, trying to give him some of her own hope. "This entire school is so proud of you. You don't realize how people talk about you and the team. Don't you understand? You've already made your mark."

"No, I haven't! I've had a goal to go to the Final Four since I was a little boy back home. I want to prove to everybody that I'm not some poor dumb country boy. I want to prove to everybody back home that Mike Kramer isn't a lazy, no-account bum. Savannah, when you're poor and wearing ragged clothes, you think about stuff like that."

"You shouldn't be so hard on yourself."

His eyes blazed. "If I'm not, who will? Nobody gives a damn whether I sink or swim. My dad sure don't."

"Mike! Don't say that! You know he does." She had taken his hands in hers.

"Then why doesn't he ever bring my ma to come see me play?" Tears ran uncontrollably down his face. "It hurt like hell when I saw all the other parents come to our Christmas tournament. Spoon and Robbie and all the rest of the seniors went out afterward with their parents. I went back to my room."

She didn't have an answer for him. She just looked sadly into his reddened eyes. "I'm just saying that you've accomplished a lot, Mike. You've done things with your life other people can't say they've ever done or even attempted. How many other people will be able to say they've played four years of college basketball and earned a degree?"

He shook his head. "Hell, I don't know."

"I do. Not many."

He gave her a fierce stare. "So what? It's not enough. How am I gonna help my family out? That's the question, Savannah. They need money…now. And I can't do anything to help them. It's killing me!"

Good morning, sir," Father Charles said. "It was a fine game you missed last night."

"I heard, I heard," Father Callahan said tersely, rubbing the corners of his eyes. "You're the second one who's said that to me this morning."

With 8 A.M. Mass just twenty minutes away, the old priest fumbled through the sacristy cabinets looking for some misplaced communion hosts. Saying Mass was about the only thing he could still do, Father Charles thought, except terrorize faculty and staff about losing their jobs.

"Never seen a crowd like last night." Father Charles flashed an I-told-you-so smile. "Gosh, Big Eddie had them ready. They were diving for loose balls, hustling for rebounds. They've been killing teams since they beat Austin Peay."

"Killing, Father?" The old priest widened his eyes.

"Oops, sorry."

"Who'd they beat?"

"Marquette."

"By how many?"

"Twenty-one."

"Hm…what's their record now?"

"Sixteen and four."

"Who have they lost to?"

"Missouri, Memphis, U.C.L.A., Indiana." Father Charles recited the names quickly. "But we should have beaten the blasted Hoosiers."

"You think they're pretty good, eh?"

"Well, I might be getting a little ahead of myself when I say this, but I think they've got a shot of at least getting to the Elite Eight…maybe the Final Four."

"Aha, I knew I had some more hidden back here." The old priest found what he was looking for, emptying the bag into a small glass plate. "Final Four, eh? Hmm… so you're the one who's been down in the wine cellar."

"I mean it, sir. Big Eddie has that team playing like they did in the early years."

The old priest fumbled in his pockets now, searching for his homily notes. "How's he doing? Has his personal life gotten any better?"

"Well, yeah, as a matter of fact." He hoped the Lord wouldn't penalize him for a little white lie. "He's seeing a real nice woman. She's straightened him out. He's even been attending pregame services with her. I think she may have even gotten him to stop drinking."

Callahan looked up. "Stopped drinking? Mother Machree. I remember his early days. He was a pistol. What about the gambling? Has she stopped that?"

"From what I've been told…"

"By who?"

"Riley."

"Riley?" Callahan said. "Do I know this person?"

"Yes, the colored janitor. Wears the earring, walks with a slight limp."

Callahan nodded, his memory jogged. "Riley notices a lot and says little. He told me all Eddie does now is bet an occasional NFL game. Not anything like before."

"That's good to hear, but keep an eye out. Like alcoholics, gamblers are never cured, just arrested. And as competitive as Eddie is, he'll not likely kick the habit with ease."

The two put on their vestments and entered the chapel, then walked slowly to the altar as an organist played softly in the background.

Dale scratched his head and read *USA Today* in a busy bagel shop down the street from his office. College basketball was his favorite sport in all the world, not just because he'd once played, but because it was so far removed from all the money and greed and disordered priorities of professional basketball. Now that he thought about it, college basketball might be the greatest sport of them all. Anything could happen.

He studied the line scores with growing concern. North Carolina beat Duke by nineteen at Duke. St. John's beat Syracuse in the Carrier Dome by twelve. U.C.L.A. upended a strong Washington team by twenty-three. Notre Dame—*Notre Dame*—beat Louisville at Freedom Hall—and was *undefeated*. Now that was real strange. Notre Dame never beat anybody outside their own Christmas tournament, and especially not Louisville.

Dale sipped his coffee and read each game story closely. According to the paper, key members of every single losing team had come down sick just before the game. He jotted a note to remind him to check with San Lee about the Social Security numbers. His hunch was getting stronger every day. College kids getting sick was nothing new. But Notre Dame going undefeated sure as hell was.

Chapter 11

Fletcher barely lifted his head off the hard cot when the pain jabbed him. Shit. The great-granddaddy of all headaches. He kicked the steel bars with the heel of his boot and called out.

"Shorty, I need some fucking water! My motherfucking head is killing me!"

He'd been here so long and the sheriff still hadn't got a plumber in to fix the goddamned sink. The galvanized pail in the corner that had held water was empty now, and as he stared at it a roach scurried around its top rim.

He closed his eyes and listened to steps clicking along the concrete floor, then a key jiggle and a door down the hall screech open.

"Is that you, Shorty? Dammit, I need some water!"

He rubbed a hand dirty with oil and gasoline across a field of silver whiskers, knowing he couldn't wipe the hangover away.

"Goddammit, Fletcher, you're gonna wake up the whole county with your damn bellyaching." Sheriff Harlan "Shorty" Stump peered grumpily through the bars, holding a cup of cold water in his hand. He breathed heavily, as if he'd just climbed a flight of stairs.

"You want some damn water, here." He drew the cup back, then tossed the water through.

Fletcher jumped, forming a fist. "Damn, Shorty! What the hell's ailing you?"

"I'm looking at what's ailing me." Shorty shook his head from one side to the other, real slow. "Fletcher, when you gonna let all your meanness go? It would do you a world of good if you would, know it?"

Fletcher didn't answer, just sat back down and stared between his legs at the floor.

"For the last month you've been nasty as a stung mule. I can't keep letting you sleep your drunks off here. What the hell is the matter, anyhow?"

Fletcher lifted a hand and waved him off.

Shorty sighed, scratched his big belly hanging way over his belt. "Fletch, you got kids at home. I know times ain't the best, but—"

"You a fucking counselor now, Shorty?"

"Nah."

Fletcher stood and hitched his pants. "Then mind your own damn business and let me the hell out of here."

Shorty checked his watch. "You've got another hour…"

Fletcher gave him a fierce stare.

"…but I guess it ain't gonna hurt anything." He put his key in the cell-door lock, turned it, opened the door wide.

Fletcher grabbed his Army jacket and slung it over his shoulder.

Before he hit the cell-block door, Shorty stopped him. "Fletch, ol' Mike and his team been kicking some ass." He pointed at the newspaper. "They keep winning, they're gonna go to the NCAA tournament. Be the first time in a long time C.U. gone to the tournament. Ain't you getting excited?"

Fletcher shrugged his shoulders, then turned away.

"Go on home, Fletch." Shorty stood in the door and watched Fletcher cross the street. "Them young uns need you. Hear me?"

Fletcher pushed the key into the ignition and turned. Strange noises most men considered trouble only caused him to shake his head. Engine again. "Fuck." He stepped out of the pickup and pushed the hood open, fiddled with the choke, then climbed back into the cab and fired up the vehicle, dark smoke clouds pouring from the rusted exhaust pipe.

A faint sun broke the gray sky for a moment as Fletcher waited for the engine to warm. Stray leaves from a heavy wind pushed across the windshield and into the bed of the truck, joining empty beer cans and whiskey bottles from several earlier drunks. After a few minutes he could feel the heater warming his toes and inside his pant legs all the way to his knees. He put the truck in Drive and followed the road out of town, suddenly feeling the dampness of his shirt from where Shorty had tossed the cup of water.

"Son of a bitch."

The top of the cab was still chilled, and his breath fogged the cracked windshield. He reached across the seat, balled his fist, and popped the glove compartment hard, searching for a rag. He found one, under a quarter-full bottle of whiskey he'd forgotten was there. His first reaction was to finish it off, but something stopped him.

Maybe it was what Shorty had said, or maybe it was the feeling of cold water thrown on him. Years ago, if a man had ever shown such disrespect, Fletcher would have run him out of the county. But now it didn't seem to matter if people pointed at him and talked behind his back. He was still studying about it as he wiped the windshield clear with the rag. Now people were proud of Mike, but nobody was proud of Mike's old man.

Fletcher's days of glory had long since passed, tilled into the earth like garden manure. Short-lived, made that way by pure and simple human biology. He'd met Mary Boggins back in high school when he was a star for the London Rockets. She was a gentle Catholic girl from a family on the other side of the county, people of even more meager finances than his own.

One night, after he had scored forty points against an all-black team from Louisville in the state tournament in Lexington, she finally succumbed to his urges. Six weeks later, just as the daffodils ushered in spring, Mary told Fletcher of her visit to the clinic in Corbin. They married on a hot day in July with only their fathers in attendance and moved in with the Kramers to live.

At first everything was great. He and Mary made love every night, sometimes two, even three times if his folks were out of the house on weekends. He found a steady job working for the Fish & Wildlife department in the Daniel Boone National Forest. He finally saved enough money to move out of his folks' place and buy a house trailer at the foot of Cooper Mountain.

Mike was four when they sold the trailer and moved to a rented farmhouse, because Mary was pregnant again. They named the new baby Paul, after her father. A year later Greg was born. Five years passed before Bobby, then Jason came two years later.

Kids cost money, and money was tight. The job in the park wasn't enough. Fletcher decided to make some extra cash farming the land where they lived. It was a great idea at first, especially with tobacco crops bringing top dollar. Then the economy plummeted. Mom-and-pop farms suddenly went belly-up. He hung on as long as he could, but no matter how many hours he worked on top of his full-time job, he still couldn't get ahead.

Then one day he walked into work and was handed a letter saying his government job was being eliminated to reduce costs. He argued, even offered to take a cut in pay, but nothing could change the decision. At the ripe old age of thirty he felt the breath of life suddenly squeezed out of him. The drinking began soon after—and hadn't ended yet.

He tossed the bottle over his shoulder and lumbered past the forestry sign:

Daniel Boone National Forest
Hunting Strictly Forbidden
Violators will be prosecuted to the full extent of the law.

Screw 'em. Jail was nothing new to him. In the snow Fletcher knew the deer had no chance, especially since he was hunting out of season and the animals weren't so wary now. If there was one thing in the world he could do better than any other man, it was placing a bullet in the body of whatever it was he hunted.

He soon found two sets of tracks cut deep into the two inches of snow. He followed them up the creek bed, certain the deer were feeding on acorns from the big oak grove on the other side of Maupins' pasture. The wind stung his bare face like aftershave, but he was glad it was coming toward him, keeping his scent from drifting toward the two animals—a doe and a buck—he now spotted fifty yards away.

Without creating so much as a ripple in the moment, Fletcher slowly crouched, his right knee oozing into the wet earth, his other steadying his left elbow and the rifle barrel. Even though the trees had shed all their foliage months before, a lone leaf drifted from above, twirling before him. He slowed his breathing, felt his grizzled whiskers rub against the barrel's stock. He needed to cough, but he held the heaviness down by swallowing. At such a short distance it was easy to predict what was about to happen. He had hunted since he was a child, bagged his first buck when he was just ten. In seconds he would have another one.

Just as he squeezed the trigger for the first shot, a barn owl dropped out of a long-limbed pin oak, startling the fat doe. Before he could draw a second bead, the doe dashed off into the white pines and up the ridge.

"Shit."

He relaxed his finger and eased off the trigger. No use wasting his ammunition. He brought the rifle to his side, barrel pointing to the ground. He'd shot one. No sense in getting greedy.

Seeing such a nice fat buck lying there, a six-pointer, its eyes not yet glazed, gave him a feeling of being a man again, a father who could provide for his kids. He heaved the buck up on his shoulders, its long legs wrapped around his neck, held by hands that could crush stones. Even though minutes earlier he had finished the last drops of the whiskey, he hardly broke a sweat walking the half-mile back to the truck. Years on the farm had conditioned his body to hard labor.

Before he stepped out into the clearing, he looked up and down the road for travelers. With no one in sight, he tossed the deer into the back of the truck and quickly covered it with a green tarp kept for occasions just like this. He stowed his rifle in the gun rack against the rear window, then slowly moved out of the snow and back onto the road.

A few miles further on he turned onto a muddy lane pocked with ruts and sparse gravel. The mailbox was crookedly lettered, RR5, 22B. On one side of the lane ran a small creek, on the other a barbed-wire fence nailed to leaning cedar posts. During spring rains the road often became part of the creek, sometimes forcing him to park and walk to the house. Today he plowed on through, his bald tires slipping badly over the snow and ice. Chickens scattered from his path, cows on the other side of the fence looked up.

Two dogs raced each other to get to him first. He shooed both as he stepped down out of the truck and stretched, but one jumped up on him anyway, placing two wet paws on his chest to lick him square in the mouth, leaving a muddy print on his Army jacket.

"Goddammit!"

He pushed the mutt off, then drew back and kicked the animal squarely in the jaw, sending it shrieking for the barn. The other dog backed away, then clipped at his heels as he carried the deer onto the back porch and slung it on a picnic table.

He opened the back door just a crack. "Boys, get out here and look at this!" he yelled.

Within seconds the four clamored around him, inspecting his prize.

Bobby was jumping up and down with excitement. "Where'd you get 'im, Pa?" Fletcher grinned and rubbed the boy's head. "Ol' bugger jumped right in the back of my truck."

"Aw, c'mon, Pa. No, it didn't."

"I swear it did, Bobby. I think it's a reindeer. Them buggers can fly."

Fletcher laughed, proud of his sons' admiration, then told them to run inside and get their mother. A few minutes later Mary appeared, her eyes concerned and questioning.

"They wondered where you'd taken off to." She caught his eye but didn't let her gaze linger.

"Out hunting," he said, grinning, pointing at the deer. "Biggest one I seen all winter."

She stared at the deer, then back at him. "But so many days, Fletcher...the rest of the time...where?"

He pulled a bag of Red Man from his coat pocket and stuck a wad in his mouth, then spat into the yard. "Went down to Corbin…heard that new factory was hiring."

Her face suddenly softened. "Anything come of it?"

"Don't know yet. Told me to call 'em back end of the week." He pulled a phone number from his coat.

She nodded her head, then lifted her nose and caught the liquor smell. "They missed you. They need a father 'round to help 'em. Not down in the honky-tonks."

"Whatever, woman."

Bobby ran back out onto the porch, carrying a long knife. "C'mon, Pa, let's cut it up."

Fletcher smiled. "All right, young un, we're gonna eat good tonight."

Before walking back into the house, Mary turned again. "Oh, Mr. Karcher came by the other day and said he wanted to talk to you."

Fletcher looked up. "Yeah, what did he want?"

"Said he'd been understanding enough." She stared straight into his eyes. "Said if he don't get some money soon, he's going to ask us to leave."

He nodded his head, then plunged the knife deep into the deer's plump belly.

Fletcher looked out at the frozen landscape and noticed a black Chevy truck bouncing down his road. He recognized it immediately and rose out of his chair and put on his coat and hat. Jefferson Karcher, their landlord, was climbing down out of the muddy 4x4 when Fletcher met him.

"Good seeing you, Mr. Karcher." Fletcher extended his hand and waited for the grim-faced old man to step around the door.

"Hello, Fletcher," the man said. "That road needs some major repair."

Fletcher looked past him at the sludge caked to his wheel wells. "Could use some gravel, yeah." Fletcher paused. "Pretty day, though, ain't it?"

"If you're a damn polar bear, yeah."

Jefferson Karcher owned half of the county, including a big coal deposit over in the far southeast corner of the state. He had leased the two hundred acres to Fletcher several years ago and never said a word when payments were late or even a little short. Fletcher usually made up with him by giving him bushels of corn, cartons of strawberries, and sometimes, after a slaughter, plenty of meat to put in his freezer. It had been an agreeable relationship, but today Fletcher sensed something different in the man.

Before Karcher said another word, Fletcher apologized for being late with his rent, told him about the job he was certain to get down in Corbin.

Karcher sighed, looked down at the ground. "Fletch, I've got some news you aren't going to like."

Fletcher set his jaw and listened.

"Some developers up in Lexington have approached me about an offer for the land. They're already developing some new subdivisions on the other side of town…and they think this land here is a prime spot for another…" The old man kicked a stone in the road. "And I'm thinking about selling it to them."

Fletcher drew still, his back stiffened. No job. Cold water tossed in his face. Now this. "You can't do that. This is my home."

"I'm sorry, Fletch, but, hell, you haven't paid me a dime in, what, four months? I'm losing money here." The old man threw his hands up. "If I thought you could ever—"

"My lease gives me a first option to buy." Fletcher's voice was firm.

"Yeah, it does." The man gave a scornful grin. "But hell, Fletch, you can't even pay me monthly. How you going to come up with a down payment of fifteen thousand dollars?"

Fletcher looked at his muddy boots. The shame was bitter. He looked up again, spat at the man's feet. "You ain't taking my house, Jefferson. I've worked this place too damn hard."

The old man saw Fletcher's disposition changing. "Hey, Fletch, don't get angry with me. It's your problem, not—"

"You old greedy son of a bitch. I've got four fucking kids in that house to support, and you're trying to sweep this place out from under my feet 'cause I can't keep up with payments, never mind that I'm out of a job." He propped his fists on his hipbones, stared down into the man's cringing eyes. "Have some compassion, for God's sake!"

"Hey, Fletch, c'mon, I've been pretty understanding..."

Fletcher was inches from his nose. "Don't fuck with me, Jefferson." He stuck his finger in the man's chest, pinned him against the truck. "Get the fuck off this property, and you tell them damn developers I better not catch 'em snooping around this place, because I'll fucking blow their heads off."

Fletcher walked over to his pickup and grabbed his rifle. Karcher saw what was happening and quickly climbed back into his truck wide-eyed, locked his door, and struggled to make the engine start.

Mary stepped out onto the front porch, no longer content to watch through the window. "Fletcher!" she screamed.

He ignored her and fumbled in his pocket for his shells.

Karcher backed the truck up slowly, keeping Fletcher in his view and glancing in the rearview mirror every few seconds as he drove.

"You better get the hell out of here, Jefferson, before I get this thing loaded!"

Karcher was halfway toward the road when he rolled the window down. "Fletcher," he yelled back, "next time I'm coming out here with Shorty!"

Fletcher laughed wildly, then fired two shots into the air that sent the truck sliding out of the mud and off the property. "You do that, Jefferson. And tell Shorty I've got one in here for him too!"

"What was that all about, Fletcher?" Mary moved to his side, watched the truck fly down the county road, its horn blowing the entire way.

Fletcher looked into the distance, then spat on the ground. "Jefferson wants to sell the farm out from under us. The old S.O.B."

Father Charles had decided long ago that Kentuckians used basketball as a way to forget all the depressing, foreboding days that seemed to run one into the next during wintertime. He reasoned that they flocked to basketball games because the gyms were warm, well-lighted, full of action. Today was one of those days that drove people inside. The soot-gray sky touched tops of buildings, a blanket that extended as far as the eye could see. Gusts of wind bent treetops with their strength, as if the trees themselves were stretching before an athletic event. Bare trees. Cold. He couldn't remember what they looked like with leaves.

He sighed and tried to put the weather out of his mind. His mission was to find Mike. He hadn't shown up for practice yesterday, and Big Eddie was worried. He had asked Carlos about him in the locker room, but the big man only shrugged his shoulders. Maybe he should give Savannah a call. She had come to him a few days ago about Mike, seeming distressed. The priest suspected a true romance was developing between the two.

He first tried the Co-op, where students hung out between classes. After ten minutes of looking with no luck, he decided to check the library across the street. He remembered Mike telling him once how much he liked reading out-of-town papers because their coverage was much better that the local rag. Father Charles said hello to a few librarians, then made his way up a flight of stairs to the card-catalog area. No Mike.

Perplexed, he made his way across the quadrangle towards the men's dorms. Spring-break flyers for Aspen and Florida papered the inside of the elevator. At the end of a hallway the priest found Mike's door closed. He knocked softly once. No answer. Maybe he was sleeping. He knocked again, much harder. Still no answer. He waited for a few minutes, then tried again. Finally he pressed his ear against the door. Not a sound. He decided it was pointless. If Mike wanted to miss practice, then that was his prerogative. He deserved a day off now and then, even though Big Eddie didn't agree.

"Morning, padre."

Father Charles turned to a voice he recognized. "Spoon, it's noon. You just getting out of bed?"

"Uh, no, I, uh, been studying. Needed to take a shower to freshen myself."

Father Charles suspected otherwise but didn't question any further. "Hey, did you see Mike this morning?"

Spoon thought about. "Yeah, he was at breakfast."

"He was?"

"Uh-huh, but I didn't talk to him."

"But he was there?"

"Well, if you call sitting all by yourself staring out a window being somewhere."

"What do you mean?"

"I mean he was acting kind of strange."

"Did he say anything?"

"No, I don't think so. Why? Is something the matter?"

The priest shook his head no. "Just curious, that's all."

Spoon yawned.

"Well, let me get going," the priest said, "so you can go back to your…ah, studies." The chaplain gave Spoon a friendly wave, then turned and walked back to the elevator.

From the dorm he moved ahead to cover the two blocks to chapel, glad of fresh air and a few minutes to collect his thoughts before evening Mass. He soon reached the sacristy, a forlorn cubbyhole behind the altar. Winter seeped through cracked walls, keeping the room from ever being comfortable. He moved across the marble floor to the thermostat hidden behind some yellowed church bulletins and cranked the knob. The furnace came on with a loud clank, and he stood over a heat vent and felt the warm air rush up his pants.

On a small oval table a Bible, plate of hosts, and bottle of wine sat undisturbed. He liked the tranquility of the place. Here he always thought clearly. He meditated for several minutes in a chair, recounting the day's events, then heard a noise coming from somewhere beyond the sanctuary. He rose to investigate.

The big chapel was dark, but he made out a figure kneeling in one of the pews. Probably just a student saying a last-minute prayer before a test. But when he heard sobs he took a second glance, this time noticing a green-and-white letterman's jacket. He stepped quickly down the altar steps and along the aisle.

"Mike, is that you?" Mike didn't answer. Even in the gloom of the place Father Charles could see that he was crying.

"Mike, talk to me."

No answer. The priest sat down and pulled out a rosary, working the beads in his hand, murmuring a prayer, hoping maybe Mike would eventually tell him what was wrong.

"Our Father, who art in Heaven…"

Father Charles went through the prayer three times before Mike responded.

"I got another letter from my mom."

"Bad, eh?" The priest handed Mike some tissues from his pocket.

"We didn't win the Powerball."

"How long have you been here, son?"

"I don't know."

"Come on, now, Mike, just relax, like I told you up in Bloomington, you've got to quit worrying about it and take care of what you can. Your dad is probably out looking for work."

"Fat chance."

"Be positive."

"Yeah, right. My family doesn't have any money. Live day to day, and you want me to be positive?"

"I'll say it again. The Lord works in mysterious ways."

Mike wasn't hearing him. "I'm gonna get a job at night."

"You could do that, but I think it would be pointless. You're here to study and play basketball. You can make money later."

The late afternoon sun broke through the stained-glass windows, brightening the chapel's gloom.

Mike threw his head back and stared. "Well, then, I guess I'll start taking some of that money the boosters are always offering."

Father Charles had heard of the secret handshakes but never witnessed one. He peered over his glasses to look hard at Mike. "That could get you into some serious difficulties."

"No, it wouldn't. Who's gonna know but me?"

"You'll know it's wrong, and it will disturb your conscience."

"No, it won't."

"Mike, there's a reason for everything that happens in your life. Taking money might seem logical now, but it's not the right thing to do. You know that."

"Hey, I'm just trying to help my family. I'm not thinking about me. Hell, if that was the case, I could be driving a fancy car like some of the guys on last year's team."

Father Charles rubbed his eyes, then looked straight ahead at the ten-foot crucifix hanging behind the altar. "Mike, I really can't tell you what's right or wrong. You must make your own decisions. But I want you to take a look at that crucifix hanging there. That man not only suffered physically and emotionally, but he died for what he believed."

Mike sighed out of the corner of his mouth. "This is getting real heavy."

"Son, I don't mean to lecture, but I'm just trying to help you. Have you told anyone else about all of this?"

"No, just you."

"Well, Big Eddie is worried about you."

Mike gave a cynical laugh. "Sure he is. Without me he'd have to start the freshman. That would give him ulcers."

"I think you're wrong about that. He's the one who asked me to find you."

"Ah, bullshit…sorry, Father." Mike pressed the heel of his hand against his temple. "I've played for him for four years, and until now he's never cared. The only reason he does now is because we have a hell of a team, and he knows he needs me."

"Mike!" the priest snapped. "That's not fair at all. If anything, he understands better than anyone. He didn't grow up with a silver spoon in his mouth either."

Mike shook his head, ballooned his cheeks in a big sigh. "Yeah, I don't know. I'm sorry. I just need some sleep. I think I'm going to my room." He stretched and yawned.

"Mike, don't do anything stupid. Get some rest, and we'll talk again. I know you want to help your family, but do it by getting your degree, like I told you earlier. Taking money from a booster would only add to your worries. Trust me."

Mike was too tired to answer. He patted the chaplain's back and got up and left.

"Is he okay?" Big Eddie folded his arms and waited for Hoppy to answer. From Father Charles Big Eddie had learned a bit more about Mike's family troubles, but tonight he was more worried about the fall the kid had taken after shooting practice earlier in the day. He'd slipped coming out of the showers, banging his head against the corner of a locker.

"It bled a little," Hoppy said, "but he was fine."

"X-rays show anything?"

"No, nothing."

Big Eddie watched Mike, mechanically going through his warmup. His usual enthusiasm wasn't there. "He seems out of it, if you ask me."

Hoppy threw his hands up, then walked to the end of the bench.

Big Eddie studied Mike some more, but he knew he really didn't have any other choice but to start him. They needed to beat U.A.B. for their twentieth win. He whistled for the team to join him on the bench, then waited for the starting five to take their seats.

"Everyone feel okay?" He was looking particularly at Mike.

Heads nodded yes. Mike's didn't move.

"How about you, Mike?"

"I'm fine." The words came out flat.

"Okay, this is our last home game of the year. Let's give our fans something to be proud of."

Big Eddie sat down to watch the tall U.A.B. squad take the court. Their players seemed to outweigh his own by ten pounds at every position. Next year he'd recruit his own beef, maybe go up to Wisconsin or Minnesota to get some big white kid who could throw an elbow or two.

The ball went up, and Carlos tipped it to Mike. He collected it and drove it hard to the corner, then pushed it over to Robbie Hart who was wide open at the top of the key. Mike got in position for a rebound under the basket, but the shot went in. He jogged down to the other end.

"Nice shot, Robbie," he said.

The lead flipped back and forth ten times in the first fifteen minutes, and with less than a minute to play, U.A.B. clung to a seven-point lead when Mike saw Carlos wide open under the basket. Immediately he rocketed the ball to him, then moved in for a rebound in case he missed.

The ball circled the rim four or five times before jumping off. Mike was in perfect position, but Carlos's cocked elbow caught him suddenly in the mouth. He crumpled to the floor and writhed in pain while the officials waited for play to end.

"He's b-bleeding bad, ref!" Q hollered. "Wake up!"

Finally they blew the whistle and waved at the C.U. bench to take a look.

Hoppy made his way across the court and bent to inspect. "Mike, Mike!"

Blood gushed from his mouth. "God," Mike groaned, "I think I lost a tooth."

Hoppy wiped blood with a towel, then pushed his lips back. "He cracked you good, Mike. Two teeth, from what I can tell. Son, you just can't keep from getting hurt, can you?"

Hoppy waved at two players to come out to help him get Mike into the locker room. The crowd watched in shocked silence, then broke into polite clapping when he left the floor. Two doctors hurried in and joined Hoppy in inspecting Mike's mouth. They both agreed he needed emergency treatment for his injury.

Sweat dripped off the team at half. Pools of it collected under Robbie. Q hurried to get more towels. Carlos and Spoon took two apiece. Big Eddie paced back and forth in the back of the locker room, studying a stat sheet. Down by five points, and without his star guard, thing weren't looking good. The players glanced around nervously, waiting for Big Eddie to bust loose any second with a string of profanities.

Instead, he talked calmly. "Mike is gone for the night."

Heads turned in his direction, surprised.

"He had a couple teeth knocked out, thanks to Carlos over here."

Carlos lowered his head. "Sorry."

"He's at the hospital, and it'll be tough winning without him."

Not a sound.

"Injuries are part of the game. It happens to every team. But don't let Mike's absence get you down. Just go out there and give it your best…the fans will understand if we lose."

Eyes darted back and forth.

"I know we all had our hopes on winning this last home game, but sometimes things just don't work out. We'll get it back together when Mike is ready for the conference tournament. All right, let's bring it up!"

Out on the court, the players went through the crip line, muttering to one another.

Carlos finally called them into a huddle at the free-throw line. "I'm sorry, guys. It's my fault Mike's not with us. Now we have to come together and make the best of the situation." He thumbed at the bench. "Coach thinks we can't win without Mike. Let's show him different."

"Damn straight! Let's do it," Robbie's eyes danced.

"I think Big Eddie's the one that got hit in the mouth," Spoon said. "Thinks we can't win without Mike. Old bastard is crazy."

Big Eddie watched the action out of the corner of his eye. They were steaming inside. His plan was already working.

Before the ref blew his whistle, Carlos walked the baseline and beckoned the fans to make noise. Within seconds the partisan crowd stood on their feet.

The U.A.B. players inbounded the ball, then passed it around the perimeter until one of their guards found an opening and went up for a wide-open lay-up. Out of nowhere came Carlos's hand. He smacked the ball three rows into the stands. The crowd went berserk. Carlos slapped high fives, then glanced at Big Eddie.

Again U.A.B. inbounded the ball, and this time, when their guard attempted a ten-footer, Carlos swatted the ball a second time. It landed at half-court, and Spoon grabbed it and slammed it at the other end. He ran up the court glaring at Big Eddie.

After that C.U. went on a tear, scoring fifteen unanswered points. Each time they scored they pointed at Big Eddie. As the clocked ticked down, the crowd stood on their feet and cheered.

"All right, Carlos, do what Savannah says without falling this time." Mike sat on the floor, still wearing his jacket, leaning back against the wall. His left cheek was swollen just below his eye. It hurt him to talk. The doctors said the swelling would go down in forty-eight hours, then he could eat solid food. He sipped on a milkshake and watched Savannah show Carlos the move one more time.

"That's it, Carlos!" Savannah exclaimed. "Get up on your toes and spin."

Carlos pirouetted and leaped like a Nutcracker ballerina. Finally he stopped, breathing hard. "I think I'm getting it. Mike, what do you think?"

Mike shrugged. "I think you're the goofiest Mexican I've ever seen. You got two left feet, son."

Savannah looked so cross, Mike started to laugh.

"I bet you can't do that!" she said.

"Sure, I could, but the doctors told me to take it easy. Anyhow, we've got a plane to catch to Memphis. Come on, Carlos, I don't want to be late."

Carlos dashed off to change.

Savannah walked across the floor to Mike. "Do you think you'll be able to play in the conference tournament?" She bent and touched his swollen face.

He flinched. "Ouch, that hurts."

"Oh, c'mon. I thought you were tough."

"Yeah, that's what I want everyone to think, but down deep I'm just another confused college kid."

"What's wrong, Mike?"

"Nothing, except the fact that I'm tired of being poor. Tired of my folks being poor. Tired of getting beat up. Tired of everything, really."

"Wow, you sound like the world's getting ready to end."

"That wouldn't be so bad. Then I wouldn't have any problems, any stress."

"Stress?"

"Yeah, stress. You think it's easy playing basketball in front of all these crowds, having people pressuring you to perform every night like you're a machine? Getting your teeth knocked out? Before games my stomach gets tied in so many knots, sometimes I have to throw up."

"Really?" She grimaced. "Yuck."

"Always been like that. Even in high school I got nervous before games because there was always so much pressure."

"Why do you feel so much pressure? It's only a game."

"What do you mean, why do I feel so much pressure?" He frowned. Why?

He shouldn't hold it against her, but she'd obviously never had to carry pig slop in the dead of winter. "God, girl, do you know what it's like to wake up Christmas morning and find your old man under the tree drunk, urine pooled on the floor from where he was too wasted to get up and go to the john? You know what it's like to see your mom and brothers get smacked around? Do you know what it's like to want something so bad you think about it every minute of every day?"

She shook her head.

"My old man used to beat the crap out of me on a regular basis, and I told myself a long time ago I was gonna make something of myself just to prove him wrong."

"Mike, relax, you're getting upset."

He wiped his face and stood, then put his arms around her waist. Her hair smelled like honeysuckle. "Savannah, we're this close from getting into the NCAA tournament. All we have to do is win the conference tournament and we're an automatic bid. Since I've was a little kid, I've dreamed of playing in it and going to the Final Four. I'm sorry if I'm so intense, but you've got to understand. I've worked hard. No one's going to get in my way."

Mike leaned and gave Savannah a long kiss. She moved close to him, putting a hand behind his head.

Catholic University beat Tulane by thirteen in the quarterfinal of the Great Lands Tournament. Mike sat out twenty minutes to protect his jaw. In the semifinal game, the Knights struggled for the first twenty minutes against Virginia Tech, then exploded in the first five minutes of the second half, winning easily in the end by nineteen. Though they were playing the best basketball of the season, with twenty-two wins, Memphis, their championship opponent and tournament host, would be the stiffest competition so far.

Mike hated playing against Memphis. He considered their fans even bigger rednecks than the ones at Austin Peay. Usually Memphis fans threw pennies (Big Eddie said that's all the poor bastards could afford) and cussed the players. Only thing he liked about Memphis was seeing Elvis's mansion. He knew Savannah wanted to see Graceland, too. She told him once her mother had a picture of Elvis on her refrigerator.

Mike knew Carlos would have to play his best game of the season in order for the C.U. team to get the automatic bid to the NCAA. The Memphis fans would be all over him, especially since he'd got dunked on three times in the regular-season game.

"Carlos, these fans down here are vicious," Mike said, walking up on the center at the bench as he tied his shoes. "They're gonna call you every name in the book. Don't let it bother you."

Carlos looked up, perplexed. "I have no enemies here."

"Carlos, it doesn't matter. These people are crazy! When I was a freshman, someone from the stands threw a knife onto the floor. Someone else flung a penny and hit Big Eddie in the neck. They're the biggest bunch of rednecks in the world. In the dictionary under armpit you'll see Memphis, Tennessee, mentioned."

"They sound like the fans back home at the bullfights."

"I've never been to a bullfight, but it can't get any worse than this place."

Carlos scanned the arena. The colors of blue and gray were everywhere. Men with sideburns and beer guts and unshaven faces pointed at him. One kid with a blue M painted on his chest grabbed his crotch and beckoned Carlos. His buddy mouthed four-letter words. An fat black woman stood and clapped her hands over her head, showing hairy armpits. In a matter of seconds another thousand joined her.

"And one other thing, Carlos," Mike said, over the growing noise.

"Yeah?"

"They hate Mexicans down here."

Carlos arched his eyebrows. "Yeah, I'm getting the hint."

"I also read where their center said he's gonna dunk on you again, like he did in the last game. In the paper this morning they called you Big Softie."

"Seriously?"

Mike saw his words taking effect. He had learned something about motivation from Big Eddie over the years. "Yep, seriously."

"Big Softie?"

"Big Softie."

"Ain't gonna be no dunks tonight, Mike." For the first time Mike saw something come over Carlos. He was actually getting angry.

"Good, 'cause this is for an automatic bid to the NCAA tournament in two weeks. If we win, we're a lock. If not, we become an at-large team. I don't want that. I want to win."

Carlos put an arm around Mike's shoulder. "No dunks tonight, Mike. I will play like never before."

Fifteen minutes before the start of the game Mike found a quiet spot under the stands away from his team. Tears wanted to swell up in his eyes, but he blinked them back. Again, no one from home. How many games had he played when no one came? Thirty? Fifty? A hundred? He'd stopped counting a long time ago.

Everyone back home had said he'd never amount to anything. "Like father, like son," they'd say. He had heard it. God, he could remember how often it was said, how it tormented him, then motivated him. The runs through the mountains, the pain in his calves when he skipped rope, the blisters on his fingertips from shooting the ball when there was snow on the ground. Dammit, he was entitled! No one else had put as much into it as he had.

"Hey, what're you doing?"

Mike just stared, stunned. "Who…Savannah? What…how did you get down here?"

"Drove down with some friends…Q snuck me a press pass. He's so nice."

"I don't believe it." Mike hugged her. "I think I'm gonna cry. I can't believe it!"

She squeezed his hand and whispered something that brought a gigantic smile. He hugged her again. Tight this time. A tear did escape.

She pushed away. "Is that okay?"

"Yeah, that's okay. I love you, too."

Just as Mike suspected, Carlos played inspired. Every shot that bounded off the rim, he snared with his great hands. He had six blocks and a thunderous dunk over three Tiger players that ignited the Knights to rally from ten down. With thirty-three seconds remaining in the game and the Knights down by two, Mike was being double-teamed, and Carlos got an inspiration to free him for a final shot.

"Coach, I've got an idea," the big Mexican said.

"What, Carlos?" Big Eddie snapped.

"I know how to get Mike open."

"You can't even get yourself open. How you gonna get Mike open?"

"When we're ready to throw the ball in, I will dance through the lane and distract them."

Big Eddie held his tongue, wanting like hell to rip into the kid for taking the moment so lightly. Finally he threw his head back, thought about it for several moments, eased out a little grin. Maybe the kid had something. "Tell me more, Carlos. What do you mean, you will dance?"

"In my dance classes there is this routine." He explained the move. "You know, like in ballet, arms over the head, spin on the toes." The team broke into grins.

Big Eddie saw the tension instantly evaporate. The one thing he had learned over the years as a coach was to listen to his players and take chances. Even if they didn't win the game, they'd still get a bid to the NCAA tournament. Hell, why not? Maybe it was time to start doing a little gambling again.

"All right, let's give it a try. Diagram this for me, Carlos."

Big Eddie handed Carlos his clipboard. Carlos took the pen and drew the play in detail. The refs blew their whistles.

Big Eddie sat back in his chair, crossed his legs, and locked his hands behind his head. "If this works," he said to Q, "I'm buying steak dinners for everyone."

The ref handed Robbie the ball. He started the play by passing it to Mike. Mike held the ball at the top of the three-point arc, then looked to Carlos.

Positioned on the blocks under the basket, Carlos reached up over his head with both hands as if he were stretching, then skipped up one side of the free-throw lane and down the other.

Just as the big Mexican had figured, every eye in the arena was riveted on him. When Mike's man turned to see what all the laughter was about, Mike took the opportunity to drain a three as the clock expired.

Big Eddie leaped off the bench. "Steaks for everyone tonight, guys! We're going to the Big Show!"

Chapter 12

San Lee fiddled with his short ponytail and studied the numbers in front of him. He sipped a warm Coke. He had taken the Social Security numbers given by the bettor and matched them up with airline travelers arriving in Las Vegas a day before the bets were placed. Now he had narrowed the list to just two men who happened to be in town on those two days. Dale studied San Lee's pensive face. "What d'you think?"

"I went back and checked some records. This guy here is a respectable car salesman in Dubuque, Iowa." He pointed to the top of the screen. "This other dude used to work for the New York City Sanitation Department. He's a drunk, a wife beater, and on disability. And, get this, he has less than five hundred bucks in the bank."

"No kidding! Really, how you'd find that out?"

"Easy. A lawyer friend of mine did some digging for me. Really, it was luck, but I'll take the credit. Thank you."

Dale patted his protege on the back. "So which one do you think placed the bet?"

"Very good question." San Lee stroked his chin, then took another sip of his Coke. "If I was a betting man, and I'm not, I'd put money down on this cat."

He pointed at the second number.

"Why him?"

"Well, because he doesn't have a dime to his name, he's on disability and…" San Lee smiled, "because ten to one he's related to this guy here."

San Lee held up a copy of *Sports Illustrated* and pointed to a story about World Broadcasting's twenty-five-year stranglehold on the NCAA tournament.

Dale didn't get it. "Related to who? What're you talking about?"

"I'm a big college basketball fan, and I was just reading this story yesterday about the Final Four's recent ratings decline."

San Lee handed Dale the magazine.

Dale glanced at a series of pictures. The first one was Pappy McCraken, the second Paul Justin, the third Peter J. McCraken Jr. "I'm not following you," he said.

"I know it's just a wild stab, but the guy I think placed the bet in Vegas is this second number. His name is Mickey McCraken. With that quirky spelling, it can't be a common name. These two guys in *Sports Illustrated* are also named McCraken, spelled the same way."

Dale read the agate print under the pictures closer, then shook his head in disappointment. "You're dreaming, San. You've been in here looking at that screen way too long." He picked up the can of soda and sniffed it. "Sure you ain't been drinking, son?"

San Lee held his ground. "Laugh if you have want, but if I were you, I'd sure look into it. You haven't got anything solid otherwise."

"You're serious, aren't you?"

"Yes, I am."

Dale saw the gravity in San Lee's eyes and backed off. "Okay, say you're right...you got any suggestions?"

San Lee smiled confidently. "Sure do. Where's that photo your buddy in Vegas sent you?"

Dale rooted through his briefcase and plucked the hard copy Reggie had sent through the computer. "Right here."

San Lee placed the color print next to his keyboard, then dialed into the web. He entered Mickey McCraken's name, waited, then watched the man's driver's license photo appear on the screen.

"God, computers are amazing," Dale said.

San Lee placed the hard copy next to the photo on the screen and nodded. "Yep, when you know some good hackers who've taught you a thing or two."

Dale was still staring at the two images wide-eyed. "Damn. It's the same guy. The eyebrows...but in the picture you're holding, he's got a mustache."

"Yeah, and if he's got a mustache here, and not there, what does that tell you?"

"Either he suddenly lost his razor when he went to Vegas...or somebody was afraid he might be recognized. Good God, I think we've just found our motive, Mr. Computer Whiz. Good job, son."

"Thanks, it was no big deal, except now I owe my hacker buddies some cold ones."

"No big deal? It sure is. This is leading somewhere huge, I know." Dale sucked in his lips. "But we can't tip our hand yet. We can't let anyone go leaking this information out."

San Lee looked around as Dale paced the room. "I'm not going to leak anything."

"I know...what I mean is that if this guy is actually related to someone inside WBC, old Pappy McCraken's son, then we need to get some wiretaps and surveillance in place as soon as possible."

"How come?"

"Because, Mister Basketball Junkie, the NCAA tournament is getting ready to start."

The Big Cheese snapped another peanut shell and grumbled at the action on the television set. The Knicks were down by six to the Celtics with ten seconds left in the game. "Look at them guys, Dave," he grumbled. "They act like they don't even care."

"Right, boss. It's a pity, ain't it? Making that kind of loot and they're a bunch of stiffs. One thing the NBA don't have to worry about is those guys throwing a fucking game for money."

"You got it." Marzzarella chuckled. "Turn it over to the ACC championship. I can't stand watching the NBA anymore."

Super Dave got up, changed the channel, and returned to his seat across from the boss's desk. He couldn't understand why such a big shot wouldn't spring for a new TV set with a remote.

"You called Pappy's boy?" Marzzarella asked.

"Right, I called the clown. God, he's an oddball. A real oddball. Probably a fucking queer."

"I don't care nothing about that. Just tell me what he said about a meeting."

"He was real nervous, but he agreed. Said he'd be here in about a half hour."

"You got a driver ready?"

Super Dave nodded.

"He don't know nothing about your other meeting, right?"

"Right. Nobody knows a thing but me and you and Mr. X."

Marzzarella brushed shells off the desk. "Yeah, right, Mr. X. What did the punk say when you told him what I want done with the refs?"

"He balked at first, like I thought he would, but then I explained things to him, just like you said. Real slow."

"Yeah?"

Super Dave smiled. "He got the message real quick. Said he'd get four guys he's known for a long time to do the job."

They both laughed. There was no way the man was going to turn down their offer. Funny how the fear of dying worked.

Marzzarella pulled a cigar from a humidor on his desk, torched the end with a stick match, then blew smoke to the ceiling. He gazed out the window at a beautiful day in the city. "Mr. X…how much is he gonna cost me?"

"At first he looked like he wanted to play hardball. Then after I did some explaining he came down."

"Down to what?" Marzzarella's eyes moved restlessly back from the window. He leaned on the desk with his elbows, his rolled-up silk sleeves baring a tattoo of a naked woman on his right forearm.

"A million and a half. He said he'd give the refs fifty grand for each game, he's taking the rest. And, get this, he wants his money wired to an account in Belize."

Super Dave waited for a string of obscenities, but none came.

"Not bad," Marzzarella said coolly. "A guy like that, I had him figured for much, much more."

Marzzarella puffed the cigar harder and fixed his attention on the television set again. "Them dark uniforms, is that Maryland?"

"Right."

"And Carolina is in the white?"

"Yes."

"Who's winning?"

They both waited for the score.

"Wow!" Super Dave said in surprise, "Maryland's up by twelve."

"Twelve? Shit!"

Super Dave jumped.

"You know them beating Carolina could fuck things up." Marzzarella scowled. "Who you got down there taking care of all of this?"

"Lucas."

"Mahoney?"

"Right. Lucas Mahoney."

Marzzarella took a deep drag, the tip of the cigar turning brilliant orange. "Who did he grease?"

Super Dave pointed at the screen. "Number forty-four there. The big black kid."

"If Carolina loses, tell me if I unnerstand this correct, it might mean a lower seed in the tournament."

Super Dave drummed the desk. "Don't worry, Carolina's got this one wrapped up. That Maryland dude's old lady is a crackhead. She got picked up last week after an anonymous tip, but Lucas was able to get the charges dropped. The kid didn't cost us a thing, only the cop."

Marzzarella grinned. "I knew there was a reason I keep you around here."

Suddenly someone knocked on the door. Marzzarella motioned with his head for Super Dave to answer it. They needed to explain some things to Peter J. McCraken.

Dale Cutter beamed when he watched young McCraken entering the plush high-rise. "God, this is happening so fast," he muttered.

Earlier San Lee had picked up records of a call made to McCracken from a PR firm in New Jersey, asking for a meeting between him and the man who lived in the building's penthouse— Luca Marzzarella, New York's most powerful mob boss.

Dale still couldn't believe what he thought was going on. This was his chance to make it big. Big!

He radioed to two men walking the street. "Just hang out and pretend nothing is going on, guys. Let him come and go. By this evening we'll have this entire building bugged."

Dale donned a pair of sunglasses and studied the basketball game being played on the portable Sony Rudy had plugged into the cigarette lighter.

"Carolina's down by eleven at half," Dale said to his partner. "But I've got a sneaky suspicion the Tar Heels will win going away. Just wait and see. And the pigeon that just walked into that building has something to do with it all. I can just feel it." He grinned with satisfaction.

"Think so, huh?" his partner grumbled.

"Of course I do, why don't you like the idea?"

"You're gonna make me miss seeing what teams make it into the NCAA tournament, that's why. I have a big party at my house every year."

Dale pointed at the wallet-sized Sony. "Watch it on this."

"Thanks," Rudy said, his face quickly drooping. "Thanks a whole lot."

Before letting McCraken enter the apartment Super Dave checked him for weapons, patting his armpits, his coat pockets, around his waist, up and down his legs. Not often did he get to run his hands up and down a silk suit. He wondered if it was from Hong Kong. Most of the thugs he usually frisked were punks from the street. Maybe he'd buy his own silk suit with the money the boss had promised if everything worked out. He liked that. A silk suit from Hong Kong.

The boss had already gone out the back way and down the service stairs.

"All right, pal, you're clean," Super Dave said. "Come with me, we're gonna take a little ride." He motioned for McCraken to follow him. They walked down a dark hall, then climbed onto a dirty service elevator that emptied into a vacant garage in the basement. Cobwebs filled the corners. Empty cardboard boxes were strewn haphazardly.

"Here, now, what's this?" McCraken said nervously. "I was under the impression Mr. Marzzarella wanted to talk with me. That's how it was presented."

Super Dave didn't respond, just motioned with his hand. What a fag. They walked down a short flight of stairs, then turned a corner to where a black limousine with illuminated running lights purred.

"You can talk to him while we take a little ride." Super Dave grinned. "Hop in."

Marzzarella was deep into watching the Carolina game. He didn't acknowledge McCraken as he climbed into the back seat. Every so often he muttered in satisfaction.

"Them Carolina...whaddya call 'em?"

"Tar Heels," Super Dave said.

"Right. Them Tar Heels, they're gonna do it," he finally said as the Tar Heels pulled away by six, then seven, then ten points with two minutes remaining. "Ain't that sweet? This one is in for sure."

"St. John's won the Big East," McCraken added cautiously.

Marzzarella turned his head. "Oh yeah?"

"Beat Georgetown by sixteen."

The limo flowed under the raised garage door and took an alley into Sunday afternoon traffic.

"What else you heard?" Marzzarella asked Dave, not bothering to look at McCraken, glancing idly at some kids outside playing pickup ball on a court with chain nets.

"U.C.L.A. was beating Washington by six when I looked last."

"What quarter?"

McCraken laughed. "Ah, they stopped playing quarters a long time ago."

Marzzarella froze, shooting him a look that could have paralyzed. "Don't patronize me, pal."

McCraken gulped. "I'm...I'm sorry. I was just making a joke—"

"I don't give a fuck what you was making. I'm not screwing around. Do I look like I'm screwing around?"

McCracken stuttered something.

Marzzarella glared. He was irritated, and irritation was not something he enjoyed. What he did enjoy was smelling McCraken's fear. He liked that smell. McCraken was the candy-ass son of one of the most powerful men in television, and Marzzarella found his fear oddly pleasing. He wasn't impressed at all with this kid. He would never have risen in the ranks of his organization.

Finally he looked away. "David. Tell me again, how's Notre Dame doing?"

"They lost to St. John's in the semifinal on a last-second shot."

"So? What then?"

"Since St. John's already clinched the automatic spot by winning the Big East, Notre Dame looks good, real good. They played the Red Storm even tougher than Georgetown did today."

"Remind me…what's Notre Dame's record."

"Twenty six to one."

Marzzarella smiled, rubbed his hands together. The Irish had a national following, and they had an international one as well. "That's enough to get 'em in, huh?"

Super Dave nodded. "But they might be a second or third seed, because I think Louisville's gonna to get a number-one, even though the Irish beat Crum's team earlier this year."

"So what?" The big man was nodding his head and smiling to himself. "All they had to do was get in."

McCraken cleared his throat. "Excuse me, but in a few seconds here, we'll know where everyone is." He pointed at the television.

After they'd circled Central Park for twenty more minutes watching the selection show, Marzzarella told the driver to slow down.

"David." He felt in his pocket for a cigar. "Look in the bar there, I got a bottle of forty-year-old cognac. Whaddya say we have a little celebration?"

Super Dave nodded, went for the bottle and some snifters. He poured two fingers into each of three snifters, then handed one to Marzzarella and one to McCraken.

"They're all in," Super Dave said. "Not bad for a bunch of amateurs."

Marzzarella frowned. He didn't like it when anyone spoke disrespectfully of his organization. He'd overlook it just this once. He took a belt of the cognac anyway.

Dale's legs needed stretching in the worst way, and he was bursting to take a leak, but he wasn't about to get out of the car and reveal himself and the stakeout. He flipped his radio on and checked with the two agents on the street.

"Hey, you guys seen anything? It's almost midnight. Surely McCraken's not spending the night."

Garbled "No"s came from the other end.

"Well, do some checking."

Dale looked at his partner, who had finally given in to watching "I Love Lucy" reruns. "What do you think, Rudy?"

"I think this little TV sucks. That's what I think."

"No, about the meeting up there."

Rudy looked at the building. "I don't know. Maybe they're having sex or something. Got me."

Dale shook his head, stared across the hood of the car, wished he was home drinking a cold beer, or in bed with his wife. There was nothing worse than being out in the streets with no agenda other than waiting. "I hope to hell this isn't all for nothing. The office will be screaming if I spent all this money for a stakeout and McCraken and the big Mafia gorilla are just queers."

Rudy was chortling. "This is a great show. I used to watch it when I was a kid."

"C'mon, Rudy, pay attention. Your mind will turn to mush watching all that crap."

"You need to relax, Dale. Worrying ain't gonna help a thing."

Dale slumped in the seat and tried to stretch his legs again. He knew what they needed—one of of those bottles with a funnel and a hose, like chauffeurs use to pee when they have to wait outside a building for hours. He made a mental note to find out where they could be bought.

Fifteen minutes later a voice came over the radio. "Dale, I think I know why our man hasn't come out yet."

Dale straightened, brought the radio to his mouth. "Yeah?"

"This place has a back entrance, and the garage door is wide open. I bet they left a long, long time ago."

Dale tossed the radio into the seat. "Dammit. Dammit!" He couldn't leave anything to the new guys any more, if he wanted things to turn out right, he had to set up every frigging aspect of the deal himself. Anybody in the Bureau—the lowliest rookie—ought to expect a back door and take that into account.

He turned slowly to his partner, his face growing pinker by the second. "Might as well hang on to that TV, Rudy. From now on we're gonna have around-the-clock surveillance on these goons. They're not slipping out of my fingers anymore."

He stepped out of the car, walked into a dark alley, and got relief.

Carlos bounded off the airplane into a sea of C.U. faithful. Fans dressed all in green surrounded him and shoved pieces of paper in his face to sign. One woman with her face painted green pushed her infant into Carlos's arms and snapped a picture. He blushed, then gave the child back.

Off to one side, Savannah grinned at Carlos's reluctance to enjoy the limelight. Four news teams came close to blows trying to be first to interview him.

Mike dodged the horde by taking a side door. "Psst!"

Savannah turned and saw him motioning to her from behind a bank of pay phones. "What're you doing, silly?"

He pointed at the cameras. "Trying to avoid those guys. C'mon."

He grabbed her hand, and the two skipped quickly through the terminal to her red BMW in the short-term lot. They climbed in, and she had it on the interstate in seconds doing sixty. He loved it.

"Why didn't you want to talk to the reporters?" Her short brown hair was whipping in front of her from the breeze through the half-open window.

"Because they're only around when something really good happens. Or when something really bad happens."

"Oh?"

"Yeah, it's kinda like when I was growing up. No one ever paid any attention to me until I started getting real good in basketball. They used to call me a punk, loser, thug, anything to put me down. But then my high-school team had a good season when I was a senior, and suddenly everyone was my friend." He shook his head. "I don't buy that. Anyhow, it's good for Carlos to get some pub. He deserves it after the game he just played."

"I couldn't believe what he did. I was so nervous, then all of a sudden Carlos did the dance I taught him. I just busted out laughing. It was a trip!"

"So did everyone else. It was probably the most incredible thing I've ever seen."

She took her eyes off the road for a second to glance over at him. "You were just as incredible, Mike. You're the one who hit the shot."

"I got lucky."

"No, you didn't. You've worked hard to get where you're at. I'm so proud of you!"

Mike stared out at the passing cityscape and wondered what was going on in his hometown. They were probably thinking he was lucky, too. His friends in high school, the coach who cut him as a sophomore, the girls who always turned up their noses as he walked down the hall. The corners of his mouth lifted ever so slightly, but that was all. He couldn't smile yet. Even though the win felt good, his team still had a long way to go.

The sun jumped off a billboard at an angle that reminded him of how that same sun used to hover over the barn after supper. The shot he hit to beat Memphis was one he'd taken thousands, perhaps millions of times growing up. It had become more instinct than conscious move. Some nights when the moon was full and a string of stars filled the sky, he'd go out and hit three after three. He could hear the ball swishing through the net again, his feet thudding off the hard dirt, the dribbles he'd taken to get back to the various spots around the circle.

When the moon's position was just right, the old oak next to the barn seemed a great octopus spreading its tentacles across the court. And at the end of each tentacle was a spot from where he positioned his shots. Every time the moon moved in the sky, his next shot would come from a different location, keeping him from practicing the same shots twice. The memories made his heart soft, his eyes wet. Memory—a refuge from reality, yet with its own bitter edge.

"Goddammit, Mike! What the hell you doing out there in the dark, boy? We can't sleep with that blasted ball bouncing."

Even now the old man's voice sent chills up his spine. Mike eventually learned to gather the ball after every shot before it hit the ground to keep Fletcher from yelling. In a lot of ways it had helped him follow his shots. Mostly, though, it just gave him the incentive he needed to make something of himself.

Savannah snapped her fingers. "Hey, Mike, you with me?"

He blinked hard and turned from the window. "Sorry, just daydreaming." He yawned, stretched an arm over her shoulder. She was so soft. So warm. So easy to be with. Where had she been his whole life?

"You deserve some credit, too," he said. "Carlos has improved so much since the beginning of the season it's scary. You had a lot to do with that."

"Thanks."

She pulled off the interstate to a McDonald's and cut the engine. "Let's go in, okay?"

"Nah, let's make it the drive-through, please. I don't feel like facing somebody who wants to talk about this game and the next one."

Indiana, it would be, a team that had already beaten C.U. once.

"You know," Savannah said, "you should really try to enjoy all this attention. It won't last forever."

"Good, I'm tired of all the reporters already. They all ask the same questions."

He wolfed down four cheeseburgers and washed them down with a jumbo Dr. Pepper.

"You were hungry."

"The plane food was terrible. And after games, I'm always starved." He chuckled.

"What's so funny?"

"My mom always said I could out eat anyone alive, especially after I've been out working."

"Your mom sounds real nice. I can't wait to meet her."

"She is. There was never a time when she wasn't there for me. She's the one who helped me get into C.U."

"Really?"

"Yep. We went to the library back home and got names and addresses. We sent a letter with all my high-school statistics to about every school in the country. I think she wanted to see me go to college even more than I did. Finally C.U. offered me a chance to walk-on. I don't think I ever saw her any happier than when I got that letter."

Savannah took an upcoming exit, then followed the tree-lined road to a secluded spot in Iroquois Park overlooking the city. She set the brake, cut the engine, and snuggled up to him. In the distance the lights of Louisville sparkled.

"What're you doing, girl?"

Her hands were on his legs, then inside his shirt. His heart started pounding. His hands started to shake. Savannah was making him nervous. She was so close. She was the reality he'd dreamed about his entire life. Her hair dangled in his face. Her lips were wet, not just sweet, but erotic. No longer a lamb, she was suddenly a lion. He put his hands on her in places he'd only dreamed about.

"Relax, Mike. Take a deep breath and try to forget about basketball for a little while."

"I can't."

"Sure you can. Let me help you."

She locked the car door, leaned into him. Her kisses were fast and deep. Her fingers unbuttoned his shirt. She fell back on the seat. He found her; she found him. Steam glazed the windows, moans filled the car. Basketball was the last thing on Mike Kramer's mind.

Mike was smiling when he mounted the steps of the dorms. He still smelled Savannah's perfume. The scent of her hair. He even felt her fingernails in his back. God, life was great. Music blared from two sets of speakers, kegs of beer lined a wall. Carlos was standing in the middle a throng of drunk students with the net from the game still hanging around his neck. Girls hung from his arms.

The happy Mexican lifted a large glass of beer that spilled over the edge. "Look, everyone, it's the great Mike Kramer."

Mike closed his eyes. Even though he wanted to celebrate some more, he couldn't believe what was going on. Spoon necked with a girl in a chair in the corner, his hands in places they shouldn't have been. Robbie played quarters, losing badly. Q slumped against one of the kegs, glass clutched firmly, passed out.

"Mike, cold beer!" Carlos yelled. "Celebrate, my man!"

Carlos did his dance again like in the game. Whistles and screams followed. A girl in a tight black dress ran her hands up and down his stomach.

"Come dance with me, Carlos," the girl said, tugging him.

Mike grabbed Carlos by the arm and gently led him down a quiet hallway, the girl still holding on.

"No, Mike, amigo! Let's party!" Carlos bellowed. The girl tugged.

Mike pushed the center against the wall. "You stupid dago. What the hell are you thinking about?"

"Hey, we won the tournament! We're going to the Big Dance like you wanted."

"No. Carlos, the season is just beginning. We've got a shot at the Final Four! Don't you understand? This is what it's all about."

Carlos closed his eyes. "C'mon, Mikey. Celebrate! You're too serious. Enjoy life for a change. You only live once, Mike."

"No, Carlos. I'm not finished yet." Mike straightened his shoulders and stared up into the big man's dark eyes. "You've worked hard, and all that shit out there can wait. I want to keep playing, and we can't keep playing by thinking we've already accomplished our goals."

"C'mon, amigo. We just won. I'll get serious tomorrow."

Mike didn't give in. Carlos finally acknowledged the logic. "Okay, okay, I'm sorry. You're right. This is stupid." He dropped his head. "I have to go now," he said to the girl, who pouted, then turned to look for someone else.

"Forget about it," Mike said. "Let's go and get Robbie and Spoon. We can party when this is all over with."

Chapter 13

Bobby Kramer couldn't contain himself. "Ma, look at this!" The excited voice shot through the open door of the house, stirring a couple of pigeons from their roost in the front-porch rafters. "Ma…Ma… Mike's on the front page! It's in color. Look at this! Mike's on the front page!"

His older brother, the blossoming pride of eastern Kentucky, was in the newspaper. He pushed the front page of the newspaper in front of his mom's face and stood by to watch her reply.

"Oh, my," she said in a slow drawl. "Mike's on the front page." She took the paper and held it in both hands, walking slowly toward the kitchen table. "Hon, go get your father. He'll want to see this. Get your boots on. Hurry…"

Bobby was out the door and down the worn path leading to the barn.

"Pa," he said, breathing hard, "you won't believe it. Mike's on the front page of the paper! The front page, Pa! Ma wants you to come in to see in. It's in color, Pa. From top to bottom!"

Bobby ran back to the house, kicking up mud as he went. Fletcher watched his son scurry across the yard and up the back porch. He tossed a couple more bales of hay above him into the loft and then walked slowly to the house, stopping to blow his nose and spit at a chicken running through the yard.

Mary Kramer and her four younger sons hovered around the table, looking at the picture and reading the story. It talked about Mike's dedication and desire; it criticized his athletic talent yet complimented his oversized heart. It also talked about the recent injury when two teeth were knocked out, his desire to graduate and his dream to go to the Final Four.

It was a story that made Mary proud, yet sad at the same time. She left the boys chattering around the table to walk into her bedroom, where she sat down on the bed and sobbed quietly into her hands. She was so proud of Mike and all his accomplishments. She just wished the writer had left out the part about her husband's unemployment and the fact they still used wood to cook and heat with.

Fletcher came in, hanging his Army jacket on a hook behind the door. The kids made space for him around the table to see the picture. He studied it without saying a word, rubbing his chin the entire time. He sat down and looked at it some more, squinting through an eye at one point.

"Where's your ma?" he snapped, looking up, inspecting the boys.

The boys looked around, wondering themselves.

"I think she's in the bedroom," Jason finally said.

"Go get her."

Mary heard her husband through the thin walls. She wiped her eyes as fast as she could and presented herself. "What do you need, Fletcher?"

"Read this to me. Did he get into trouble?"

"No, no, Mike's not in trouble. They wrote a good story about him."

"'Bout basketball?"

"Fletcher, the Knights are in the NCAAs. They've only lost four games all year."

"So why's he in here?"

"He's their best player, hon. He's done something good."

"Read it to me. Every word."

Fletcher listened intently as his wife read the thirty-inch story. He raised his eyebrows at a few comments. "Why they say he ain't got talent?"

"I don't know, Fletcher. That's just what it says. That's what you used to always tell him."

"Well, this boy here don't know what he's writing if he says that. I was just trying to make Mike tougher when I said what I did. He always took me way too seriously. What's this reporter's name?"

"Richard Zobich."

"Never heard of him. Probably some little fat guy who gets blisters on his ass instead of his hands. Mike's the only one who could ever chase down that damn wild pony we had. Remember? It took some tremendous talent to do that."

"Yeah, it did," she said, glowing inside, knowing her husband was as proud as she was.

"Go on," he ordered.

Mary skipped the part about their family problems. For once Fletcher's learning disability was a blessing. If he could read what it actually said, he'd have torn the house apart and then gone looking for the writer. She finished the story.

Fletcher's eyes were moist. "Gee, I'd say that's awful nice. What d'you boys think?"

The boys were thrilled, touching the newspaper where Mike's picture was.

"I want to play there, Pa," said Paul, the oldest of the four.

"So do I! Me too!" the other boys chimed in.

"Pa, you think we could go see Mike play? Isn't Indianapolis only a little ways from here?"

"Huh? Go see him play? Well...I don't know 'bout that."

The boys' hearts dropped. They hoped he would save some of his liquor money and take them to see Mike.

"What'd that writer say was gonna happen again, Mary? Where'd he say they'd play if they win those games in Indy?"

She scanned the article one more time. "It says they'll play in Lexington next week if they win two games this week in Indianapolis."

"Hmm...Lexington. That's right up the road."

The boys' eyes sparkled. "Can we go to Lexington to see them play, Pa?"

"We'll see, boys. They gotta win two games first, and that ain't easy. Who are they playing?"

Bobby spoke up. "Indiana Thursday and then whoever wins the Syracuse–U.T.-Chattanooga game. Pa, they can beat any of those teams. I know."

The boys were still staring at Mike's picture.

"I can't believe that's Mike," Jason said. "Look at him. He's probably taking a three-pointer right there and sticking it in somebody's face."

Mary smiled. Fletcher was staring at Mike's picture too. He carried the paper into the living room to his good chair and studied it some more, and his boys followed him as if he'd had a bag of candy.

"C'mon, Pa, let's go see Mike play," Greg said, pretending to take a jump shot. "You ain't seen him play in a long time. Remember how we used to go to games when he was in high school?"

"Let me think, son. Things have changed since then. Ain't working now, you know."

Jason, the youngest, made like he was dribbling a ball. "Pa! You know what? I want to be a basketball player, too."

His three brothers laughed.

"You ain't gonna be no ball player, boy," Paul said, rubbing his little brother's head. "You're too little and fat."

Fletcher grinned with them, then narrowed his eyes. "You uns could all be ball players if you worked as hard as Mike did."

Mary was eavesdropping from the kitchen.

"Pa, will you get us a new net?" Greg asked. "The one we got on the rim ain't nothing but threads."

"We need a new ball, too, Pa," Jason said.

Fletcher had had enough. He finally put the paper down. "Damn, boys, how in the hell am I gonna take you to Lexington if I got to get you a new ball and all that other crap you want?"

The boys yelled in unison, threw their arms around Fletcher's neck, and the five of them roughhoused on the floor. A smile unfolded across Mary's face. She hadn't seen her son for months. She would say a prayer tonight for the Knights to win two games, then start baking for him first thing in the morning.

Fletcher left the house for a walk. He held the story about Mike tight under his arm. Even with his cold, he could smell the newspaper ink. The fields were soft from an early spring rain.

Cornstalks stood like mannequins, tired from the long winter. Fletcher watched a robin searching for worms. It was a good sign, he thought. Spring was nearing.

He walked some more, over a small rise in the land to a stump in the woods he often used as a bench to get away from things. He sat down, lit a cigarette, and unfolded the paper one more time.

His boy had grown so quickly. He stared at the picture, looking deeply into Mike's eyes, and saw much of himself. He was proud and embarrassed at the same time. Proud beyond belief that Mike had grown into an honorable man, embarrassed that he, Fletcher Kramer, had not.

He stretched his legs, taking a long draw on the cigarette. Wisps of smoke curled and blew with the wind. Off in the distance he watched squirrels flipping through the branches of a big old oak. A mallard duck streaked through the sky, followed by more. The whiskey was doing him in, but he couldn't imagine getting through life without it. He shook his head, bit the inside of his lip, trying not to cry. He wondered how much Mike resented him. He hadn't been an ideal father, for sure.

The wind kicked up again, a knifing cold that made him hunch his shoulders, stinging moisture from his eyes. So many things had happened to him over the years that had shriveled his will to fight.

He knew Mike had left the farm hating him. He had been exceptionally hard at times, even cruel to the boy. There was no denying it. He regretted what had happened between him and his first-born, and he was trying, really trying, to be more even-handed with the other four.

He inhaled deeply and exhaled another stream of smoke. Clouds skittered above like rock salt on ice. It was time to do something. Once, years ago, he had had Mike's same intensity for life, but somewhere he had lost it. He stared again at the picture. His tears spilled onto the newspaper like regrets, blurring the words. If Mike could overcome the odds of being a poor country boy, so could he. Mike had his father's blood running through him. The picture he stared at told him so.

"Here's something I got for your trip." Savannah handed Mike a bag of Lemonheads. "They'll make you pucker up, so get some water when you eat 'em."

They smiled at each other, each wanting to say a hundred things that couldn't be said because of all the people gathered to see the team off. The bus was in front of the dorms, its big diesel engine rumbling. Managers worked in its belly to stow equipment. Hoppy stood in front of the bus door, tapping his watch.

"'Bout the other night," Mike whispered, "I...I wasn't taking advantage of you. You know that, right?"

She looked up. "Shh...I know, Mike. I never thought you did. But don't think I do that with everyone."

Mike wanted to lean and kiss her, but he'd never hear the end of it if he did, especially after he'd broken up the party the other night. He knew every eye on the bus was riveted on them. "You make me feel good about myself, Savannah. You make me feel like I'm important."

"That's because you are, Mike. Just look at all these people here seeing you guys off. If you weren't the person you are, none of these people would be here today. God put you here for this. For all these people. For me."

In one hand he carried his duffel bag. She took the hand that was free.

"Think we got a chance?" he asked.

"A chance at what? A chance with you and me?"

"I hope I don't have to ask that," he said. "No, I meant a chance at taking home the trophy...you know, the big win."

"I think you're going to win it all," she said confidently, squeezing his hand.

"I hope you're right. Maybe my old man will be proud of me then."

"Mike, please, your father will be proud of you either way. But forget about it. Just put everything you've got into today, and tomorrow will take care of itself. My father tells me that all the time."

"You coming to see us play?"

"Yes, my father got hold of some tickets. He's excited for you."

"I'm afraid, Savannah."

"Afraid?"

"Yep, I'm afraid I'm gonna let everyone down."

"That's stupid, Mike. Think positive. Like you did to get here."

He looked at the ground. "Yeah, I guess. Just wish my family could come."

The driver honked the horn. Hoppy called for Mike. "Let's go, Romeo."

"I love you, Mike," Savannah said, her fingers trailing reluctantly from his hand. "Win it for Mike Kramer, and no one else."

He saw that she wanted a kiss, and he wanted to give her one. But he had to settle for a wink, then turned and walked seriously to the bus. Savannah waved as the big coach pulled out of the campus gate.

"What do you think, padre?" Hoppy blew a ring of cigar smoke to the ceiling.

Father Charles followed with his own. "I think if the guy who runs this place saw us smoking cigars in the locker room, he'd be angrier than a wet noodle."

"Noodle? Don't you mean angrier than a wet hen?"

"I said noodle, son. Don't ever question a priest."

"Whatever you say, your excellency." Hoppy chuckled.

Both of them were having the time of their lives, living in the spotlight. The Indianapolis paper had already run a story about Father Charles. Later in the day Hoppy had entertained two local television crews with his half-court shooting before practice.

Now Hoppy searched Father Charles's eyes. "Think we have a chance against Indiana?"

"I don't know. Indiana has all that tradition going for it. Every fan in this place will be rooting for 'em."

"Yeah, that's true, but I think we're gonna win. I sense something. Spoon seems loose, and Carlos is playing with all kinds of confidence. Even Mike appears relaxed. I think that girl he's dating is fucking his brains out."

"Bill!"

"Sorry, Father, but I just call it like I see it. Did you see them before we got on the bus?"

A door opened to reveal an eavesdropper. "So, Hoppy, you think ol' Mike's getting some regular ass, huh?" Big Eddie leaned against a metal locker. "Whatever it is, he is playing much, much better. And if it's that girl he's dating, I admire the old boy. She's got a rack on her that won't quit." He cupped his hands in front of him. "Melons, guys. She's got melons."

"You guys are a disgrace to college athletics," Father Charles said, rolling his eyes as the other two laughed.

"C'mon, Chuckie, I'm just trying to have a laugh or two before the game to relax."

"Mike's not that kind of boy," the priest said. "Only thing he thinks about is basketball and his family. I can't see a girl wedging herself in between either one of those."

"I can," Big Eddie said, looking sage. "Once you get a piece, it changes everything."

"Not Mike. The boy is too serious."

"But that's what he's saying, Father," Hoppy said. "A little loving has loosened ol' Mike up. Guys in the dorm tell me he's in her room just about every night now. Even stays over sometimes. Father Jeremy is the RA up there, and he tells me the girl spends the night with Mike on the nights he's not in her room. And unless his legs are too tired, I suspect he's gonna go out there tonight and kick I.U.'s ass all the way back to Bloomington."

Father Charles had stopped hearing about midway through the last sentence. "Hoppy…Father Jeremy told you that?"

"I'm afraid so, Father."

"Wow, it's that good, huh?"

Big Eddie and Hoppy exchanged nods and smiles. "Yeah, Father, it's that good. Once you get some, you have a hard time not wanting more."

"Sounds like a drug."

"In some ways it's even more addicting," Hoppy said.

The priest sighed. "Well, no wonder we can't recruit priests. The good Lord made it *too* good."

A horn sounded in the arena. "Put those stogies out, fellas," Big Eddie said, straightening his tie. "Team's gonna be in here in a few minutes. The smoke will kill 'em."

Hoppy couldn't resist. "Not unless the pussy gets 'em first, Coach."

"Get going, Hopfinger. You got a dirty, one-track mind."

"Let's just hope Mike has more than that on his mind tonight," Hoppy said. "He's gonna have to be good and ready for us to beat the Hoosiers. If his legs are weak, we're in trouble."

"And if his legs are weak," Big Eddie shot back, "I'm blaming you. You're the trainer on this team, and it's your job to make sure these guys get their proper rest."

"Yeah, Coach, that's right. I'm a trainer, not a jailer. I can't keep tabs on 'em twenty-four hours a day. I just do the best I can, but you can't fight nature."

"Let's go, boys," Father Charles said. "This world needs a little more loving in it. And especially ol' Mike."

Mike was shaking as he took the pass in his hands. A minute had already ticked off the clock, and it was the first time he had touched the ball. The surface of the floor reminded him of Alumni Hall as he dribbled up the court. It had dead spots, and each time the ball left his hand he wondered if it was coming back.

"Number one," he yelled, moving to his right to pass the ball to Spoon, who was flashing up to receive it. Carlos moved up to the free-throw line and Mike cut off his pick and looked for the ball from Spoon. It came hurtling in, and Mike took it in stride and went up for a lay-up. Out of nowhere, Indiana's center whirled quickly and swatted Mike's shot out of bounds, shoving an elbow into his neck as he came down, knocking Mike to the floor.

The Indiana center stood over him and pointed. "Don't be bringing that shit in here anymore, boy." The tall guy's sweat dripped on Mike as he gave his teammate a high five.

Mike bounded up and stuck his chest against the center. "You're fucking with the wrong boy, prick."

The referees moved in as the two nearly came to blows. The I.U. fans erupted in a chorus of boos. Writers hurriedly took notes, and the TV cameras moved in.

"Get out of my face, boy," the center challenged again, despite being led away by the ref. "You're going down."

Spoon and Carlos pulled Mike away.

"Ain't nobody going down but you!" Mike yelled back.

"Mike, calm down," Carlos said. "We don't want any technicals."

Mike rubbed the back of his neck. "The prick tried to hurt me, Carlos." Mike's eyes were wild, his face flushed with anger.

The fans rubbernecked, trying to hear.

Big Eddie pulled Mike out of the game. "C'mon, Mike, we need you, dammit," the coach snapped, following Mike to his seat and kneeling in front of him. "Calm down. Don't let the guy get to you. You're smarter than that."

He knew I.U. wanted Mike out of the game. It was their best chance at winning.

"He tried to hurt me!" Mike protested.

"So, hurt him back by staying in the game."

Mike got up and walked to a seat at the end of the bench.

Father Charles waited until he cooled off, then patted his knee. "Be smart, Mike," the priest said. "They want you to get tossed out. They're trying to get under your skin."

Mike chewed on a towel. "They've done more than that."

The Knights were down by eight points when Big Eddie signaled for Mike to get back in the game. As the senior walked to the scorer's table, the Indiana faithful went berserk. A fan hurled a piece of ice that hit Mike in the back.

He turned toward the crowd and pointed at the scoreboard above him. *Kiss my ass,* he said to himself.

Mike eyeballed the Indiana center as he took the inbound pass and brought the ball up the court. He went between his legs once with the ball, then back again. He rotated the ball around the perimeter, then got it back at the top of the key, just beyond the arc. He faked left, then went up into the air. The ball rotated perfectly as it left his hand.

Swish.

The C.U. fans roared. Big Eddie clapped and muttered to no one in particular, "Bury 'em, Mike."

While he was benched, Mike had noticed the Indiana guard was uncomfortable going left. He decided to force him that way and go for the steal the next time the guy tried to go around him. As soon as the guard crossed half-court, Mike struck. The guard fumbled awkwardly as he made his crossover dribble and went left. Mike saw his opening and stripped him. He retrieved the ball and rushed to the other end for a two-on-one break. He faked a pass to Robbie the defender fell for, then scored unguarded with a right-handed lay-up.

"Mike's on fire!" Q yelled. "He's p-pissed, and now they're gonna pay! Go get 'em, Mike!"

Again, the Knights held Indiana without a basket. Robbie grabbed the rebound and dribbled to the other end. He tossed the ball down to Carlos on the left block where he was double-teamed. Carlos pivoted and found Mike wide open on the opposite side of the three-point line. He hit Mike with a pass for a wide-open jumper that flipped through the rim, causing the net to hang.

Catholic U. went on to score six more points, four by Mike, before I.U. called time-out.

The Knights jumped off the bench and the C.U. fans broke into a standing ovation when Mike came off the floor.

"They can't stop me," Mike said. "Just get me the ball."

Though they were leading, Big Eddie felt uneasy and decided to call his own time-out just minutes after the one I.U. had called. He could see that Mike's mind was on nothing but offense, he hadn't played defense the entire second half.

"Jesus, Mike, we need you at both ends. Your man has scored eight on you already. Snap out of it and guard him." Big Eddie glared. "You want to lose to these guys again?"

Mike wiped his face with a towel, then swallowed a cupful of water. "No." His voice was somber. He looked away.

Before they went back out onto the floor, Carlos pulled Mike aside. "Hey, amigo, let him drive on you from now on," the big man said with a wink. "I'm going to start helping you out."

"What? Are you nuts? Didn't you hear what he said?"

"I have a couple of fouls to give. Might as well use them wisely."

Mike stared at him crazily.

"Trust me."

Mike was leery, but he did as Carlos suggested. The first time, Mike's man avoided Carlos and banked in a nifty lay-up.

Big Eddie immediately jumped to his feet. "Mike!"

"Carlos!" Mike screamed when they went to the other end. "Big Eddie will yank me if the guy scores again."

"He won't," Carlos muttered. "I promise. Just be cool. I'm setting him up."

The second time Mike's man drove to the basket, Carlos tipped the ball and whacked a spot on the man's upper arm. When the I.U. player went to the foul line his arm was dead. Mike gave Carlos a look, but his roommate just shrugged. The I.U. player was replaced and never returned.

The Knights went on to win the game by seven, despite I.U.'s late run.

After doing an interview with ESPN, Mike pulled Carlos aside in the locker room. "Hey, what the hell did you do to that guy?"

Carlos grinned, then explained that one of the homeboys in his Juarez gang had an uncle who was a chiropractor. "He didn't believe in violence, so he taught us how to hit the other guy's nerves and stop the fight."

Mike nodded. "Thanks, big guy. But you have to promise you'll never do it again. From here on out, let's beat 'em fair and square. No more Mexican magic."

Chapter 14

A syrupy blackness painted the morning. Fletcher had gotten up extra early to wait for the newspaper, something he rarely did. He moved the curtains back in the front room, checked the clock on the wall, looked out the window for headlights coming down the road. The worn wood floor squeaked whenever he took a step. He was eager to find out how Mike and the Knights had done against Indiana. The television was broken, and the radio always came in fuzzy because of the mountains, so the family relied on the paper for news.

He pulled his chair from its regular spot, wrapped himself in an old quilt, and turned his chair toward the window so he could look out. Though he couldn't read, he could look at the pictures and tell if the Knights won.

While he sat, he thought about his first child. Mike's birth had changed him from a boy into a man and then a father. He remembered the doctor delivering Mike in the back room of his folks' house as Mary hollered with pain. They celebrated with corn whiskey from Pop Garver's still up in the holler. He remembered the first time he ever pinned a diaper. He remembered hanging the basketball goal on the barn so Mike could run off some of his boundless energy.

"Pa, someday I'm gonna play for Kentucky."

"Got to be black to be good in basketball anymore, boy. Niggers done taken the game over. Ain't like it was when Rupp coached."

"Who's Rupp?"

"Greatest coach ever lived, boy. Adolph Rupp. Your grandpa knew him personally. Used to give him a ham every Christmas. You might have been able to play for him, 'cause he hated niggers. 'Bout killed him when he had to recruit that Payne boy. And ol' Adolph was right, that nigger did end up in prison. They all should have listened to Adolph."

Fifteen minutes passed and Fletcher could see the sun peeking over the mountains. The sky slowly filled with a wash of pink. Finally he saw two headlights slowly coming up the road. He tossed off the quilt and grabbed his Army jacket, then hustled to the mailbox a hundred yards from the house. Fletcher liked the smell of morning. He could feel its power in his bones as the sun continued its quiet ascent. He watched the truck as it approached.

"Who's there?" the paperboy asked as he idled in front of the mailbox, squinting into the darkness.

"It's me, Fletch. You got my newspaper, Walt?"

"Dammit, Fletch. You 'bout scared the skin off my teeth. What in the hell you doing out here so early?"

"Sorry, Walt. Just wanted to see how Mike did. Give me the paper."

Walt reached into the back seat, grabbed a paper and handed it to Fletcher. "They did real good. How's it feel to have a star in your family, Fletch?"

Fletcher thumbed through the newspaper, back to the sports section, not hearing the question. On the front page was a black-and-white photo of Big Eddie with his arm wrapped around Mike, giving him some instructions. Fletcher stared at it, beaming.

"Walt, what does it say?"

The paperboy put the truck in neutral, keeping his foot on the brake. He took the paper and read Fletcher the first five paragraphs.

"Are you sure it said he had thirty-five points, Walt? Against Indiana? Read it again."

"Fletcher, didn't you see this on TV last night?"

"Nah, been too damn busy." He wouldn't let on that the family was without a working set.

"You mean you didn't watch the game?"

"No, dammit, we didn't!" Fletcher's voice was sharp with anger and shame.

"Those TV guys talked to Mike after the game. Mike said he got mad when that Indiana player knocked him down."

"Knocked down? Who knocked him down?"

"Some big nigger."

"Nigger knocked him to the floor? Mike kicked his ass, I hope."

"No, but I could tell he wanted to. The coach pulled him out of the game. And when he came back he went nuts scoring all those points. I think at one time Mike hit eight straight shots."

"Damn, Mike didn't kick the nigger's ass? Hmm..." Fletcher studied the paper again. "Hey, who they play next?"

"Syracuse." Walt smiled. "And two of Syracuse's better players got in a fight in their last game and are disqualified to play against C.U. Mike and them will wipe 'em out."

"Wow…they might just make it to Lexington!"

"Hey, when you talk to Mike, you tell him we're right proud of him."

"I'll tell him, Walt. Thanks."

Fletcher tucked the paper under his arm and made his way back into the house. He flopped the paper down on the kitchen table and rummaged through a drawer for the keys to the truck. Crockett, he decided, had seen his last days.

Fletcher figured the big animal would bring some serious money, so he aired the tires and readied the bed of the pickup. Crockett had last been in it when he was a mere twenty-pound piglet. Fletcher didn't know for sure, but he guessed the big hog at a little over five hundred pounds, heavy enough to test the limits of the rusted Ford.

He slipped a rope through the ring in the boar's nose and gave the animal a swift kick to get him moving off the ramp and into the truck bed. Fletcher held his breath as the bed sagged to just inches above the tires. The animal was huge, its rear end stretching from one side of the truck to the other, and with the ground mushy from all the recent rain, he might have trouble getting the truck rolling through the yard.

He hopped in the cab and revved the engine, the soft earth giving under the spinning wheels. Slowly Fletcher rocked the truck back and forth, finally freeing it. He breathed a sigh of relief, then pulled onto the gravel driveway waving at Mary as he passed the house.

"I'll be back later," he yelled through the open window.

A few yards short of the county road he had to stop. A red Lincoln Continental blocked his path.

"What the hell?"

Fletcher waited for the car to back out, thinking it was someone turning around, then when it didn't move, he put his truck in park and got out.

"Hey, mister!" Someone was getting out of the car. "I need some help."

Goddamn city slicker, Fletcher thought, eyeing the man curiously, including his blond ponytail. "Yeah, what is it?"

"Looking for a fella by the name of Fletcher Kramer. Know him?"

Fletcher squinted, the morning sun straight in his eyes, the bill of his cap casting a shadow across his face. "Who's asking?" He turned his head and spat into the grass.

The man walked within five feet of where Fletcher stood by the truck, lifting his shiny shoes pickily over the water-filled dips in the road. Fletcher towered over the man.

"My name's not important. Are you him?"

Fletcher narrowed his eyes, then spat again, this time a foot in front of the man. "You got no name, I got no name."

The man pursed his thin lips. A small breeze stirred the ponytail. Fletcher wanted to ask if he also wore a Kotex.

"You're him, I can tell. You look like this boy here in the newspaper. The kid that destroyed Indiana, all by himself." The man pointed at the newspaper photo of Mike. He seemed sincere in his praise.

But something told Fletcher not to let down his guard. Fletcher stroked his chin. "Maybe I am. What difference does it make?"

"Hey, relax." The man smiled, tried to cozy up to Fletcher. The hems of his cheap suit pants were streaked with mud. "Your son is a hell of a ball player, Mr. Kramer. Like I said, he beat Indiana all by himself, and I hate the Hoosiers."

Fletcher didn't bite. He stiffened his back and folded his arms across his chest. "What's your business, mister? You the one Karcher told me about wanting to buy this farm?"

This time the man's smile was less engaging. "I've got two deeds here. One with Karcher's name on it to me. The other with your name on it."

Fletcher grimaced. Karcher was serious this time. He wondered how much the bastard got for the place. "Mister, if you bought this farm thinking you was gonna make money selling it to me, you made a hell of a mistake. The only thing makes any money here is that fucking hog in the back of my truck."

The man threw back his head and laughed, a shade too loud. It was not a reassuring laugh. He walked to the back of the truck and inspected Crockett. "We don't deal that way, Mr. Kramer."

"Then how do you deal?" Fletcher's suspicions were building.

"Like I said, your boy's a pretty good basketball player."

"He does all right for himself."

"Does better than that, according to the news reports. They're saying he's the kind of player that can make the difference whether his team wins or loses."

"You're driving a long way 'round to make a point, mister."

"I'll simplify it for you, Mr. Kramer." The man edged a little closer, looked up. "There's lots of teams a man plays with in life. He starts out with his family, then friends, then school, and finally business. Your boy's about to graduate this year, and then it'll be time for him to start doing business. He does the right business with us, you and your family stay on this farm for a long, long time." The man mimed tearing the contract in two.

"And if he don't...do this business?"

"Let's just say there could be a whole lot more at stake here than the farm." He slid his finger across his Adam's apple.

Fletcher reached back for his rifle inside the truck.

The man put his own hand inside his jacket and kept it there. "I wouldn't do that, Mr. Kramer. Some city folk know how to hunt too."

The shiny car spewed gravel as it raced away. Fletcher watched until it rounded a bend, then walked into the house to give his wife the newspaper the visitor had left with him. He sat down and stared at the photo of Mike.

Mary walked in, still in her housecoat, placed a hand on his shoulder. "Who was that out here at such an early hour, Fletcher?"

"Just some city feller asking for directions."

"Where was he headed?"

"Couldn't quite figure it out."

"You're shaking, how come?"

"Nervous, I reckon. Or maybe cold."

"Nervous because you're taking Crockett away?"

He wagged his head no. Finally he stood. "I'll be back. I've got some thinking to do." And he walked out of the house as his wife watched him go, wondering.

"What're you doing?" Father Charles sat down next to Mike in the hotel lobby and propped his feet on a big glass-topped coffee table.

"Just trying to relax. Got bored in my room watching TV."

"Big game tomorrow making you nervous, eh?"

"Yeah, lot of people counting on us. We gotta win."

"Sure, that would be nice, but it's not imperative in the grand scheme of things."

"Maybe not to you. To me it is. It's the most important thing in the universe right now."

Father Charles sat back to listen, thinking there were a billion people in China who didn't care, knowing he wouldn't say it.

"If we win tomorrow, my family might have a chance to come see me play in Lexington. That would be a dream come true." Mike's eyes sparkled briefly, then reality set in. "Hell, what am I thinking about? My old man would probably find a reason not to come, and tickets would probably be impossible to get."

"I don't know about that."

Mike looked intently at the chaplain. Father Charles had a grin on his face. "What d'you mean?"

The priest straightened in the chair. "Well, I'd be willing to bet that if you guys win, I might be able to pull some strings."

"Seriously?"

"Like I've told you, son, the Lord moves in mysterious ways. Trust him."

"Okay, I will. And tell him to start moving, 'cause if you can get some tickets for my folks...well, I know we're gonna win."

Chapter 15

Big Eddie lay on his back in bed, studying the hotel room's ceiling, thinking about C.U.'s win over Indiana. How the team had overcome its first-game jitters, how Mike had come back like a champion when the I.U. center knocked him down. He wondered what the Jesuits thought now of the way his team responded to his coaching.

In their last meeting, Callahan had impressed on him that he needed to "move the team along a progressive path." In other words, the old priest was telling him he had to win if he wanted to continue coaching the Knights. He wondered now about the old man, what he was thinking, wondered whether the reporters would credit him with rekindling the C.U. flame. He wanted to laugh with satisfaction, but he hurt too bad.

When he sat up in bed, pangs of pain throbbed in the front of his head, reminding him of the far too many beers he'd drunk the night before with his staff. He rubbed his temples with his index fingers and tried to massage the hangover out of his throbbing skull. Back and forth his fingers worked. It didn't help, and he couldn't imagine why he'd even tried outdrinking his young assistants. He had told them not to order the extra case. It was their fault. Damn.

He sat up, kicking a dead soldier out of his way, breathing hard, badly needing water to wet his sandpaper mouth. He put his feet on the floor and stood up. Blood rushed straight away from his head, and everything dimmed. He looked and felt like hell. He didn't care.

He found the bathroom, slowly, awkwardly. His head ached, and little jackhammers were beating in his stomach. He flipped on a light and squinted. A can of Coors still bobbed in the sink—last night's makeshift cooler. He considered drinking the beer to ease the headache, but the thought of the old frat remedy made him queasy. He chugged three glasses of water instead, then wiped his mouth with a towel. Why, oh, why? It was his assistants' fault, not his.

He didn't need a hangover. He had to attend a press conference in two hours and then go to practice. He pushed back the shower curtain, stepped in, stood under the hot water for a half hour, letting the stream pound his shoulders and lower back. The heat restored some feeling. The headache was beginning to subside.

Feeling minimally better, he moved out of the shower, dried off, and sat back in bed in his jockeys. He surfed the channels idly, considering what different plays he might put in against Syracuse. He'd noticed while scouting them that they maintained an aggressive defense against the forward on the wing. A few good backdoors would cure that.

He half-listened to the television as he scribbled some plays on a legal pad, wondering what the Syracuse coach was doing. He probably didn't have a headache. Or incompetent assistants. The Orangemen were already on his mind. Coaches could never quite live in the moment. When they won, they were already planning for the next game. And when they lost, the last game wouldn't end until the next game started. It was the nature of the beast, and Big Eddie understood it.

College basketball, despite what the romantics said, was big business with many hundreds of thousands of dollars—millions, even— at stake. He often thought that if it weren't for college athletics, universities would have little identity at all. Not many people he knew would shell out twenty bucks to see two schools compete in a spelling bee, or debate the ethical considerations of using nuclear weapons.

He had all of Syracuse's games on video. They definitely had great athletes who could run and jump. But his players could also run and jump, especially Carlos, who had improved dramatically since the beginning of the season. His C.U. team would be the underdogs, a position Big Eddie liked. The Orange's tradition didn't mean squat in the tournament. It was a one-shot deal.

He was confident. When Mike went down with his cracked teeth and the C.U. team rallied to win the game, he knew he had something special cooking. Only time and a little luck would tell how good they were going to be.

He had an hour to waste. He set the alarm on his watch and lay back down. When he woke up, maybe the banging in his head would be gone.

Big Eddie sat between Mike and Carlos, a long white banner with the NCAA logo stretched above the backs of their heads. The Knights would practice after the three of them finished their press conference. Big Eddie was anxious to get it all over with so he could swallow a few more aspirin and get back to his room to watch some more video.

The moderator turned the microphone over to Big Eddie, who went through a five-minute opening statement in a practiced way.

"Coach," a skinny writer with glasses in the first row asked when he'd finished, "do you believe you have a chance to beat Syracuse?"

"No, I think we ought to go on home now," Eddie said, sending up a roar of laughter.

"What I mean…" the embarrassed writer blurted, "…is, I mean, you guys haven't done anything in a few years, and now you're here in the tournament. Isn't that kind of daunting?"

"Daunting? That's a big word, pal. I'm just a poor ignorant athalete."

Again, the crowd roared.

This time Big Eddie answered the question with a wink and a smile. The writers scribbled. When Big Eddie finished, the players were next.

"Carlos, how hard has it been to adjust to the United States?"

Carlos grinned, pulled the microphone in front of him. "No adjustment really, except that my roomie here snores all night long, and I rarely get my siesta."

Smiles and more laughter.

"Mike, how has Big Eddie gotten you guys to play so well this year?" The question came from a well-dressed woman from one of the television networks in back.

"Well, he likes to scare the hell out of us, that's how."

The room erupted. Big Eddie even chuckled, then swiped at Mike with the palm of his hand.

"How does he scare you, Mike?"

"He's got this drill called suicides. And if we don't run 'em right, he makes us feel like we should commit suicide."

The reporters all focused on Mike and began to dream up leads for their stories the next day. He was wishing he could hand over the microphone to somebody else. He was eager to play, eager to claim the prize he'd been pursuing so very long. The prize he knew was within his grasp.

Another writer asked Mike about his career at C.U. and how he started in basketball. Mike threw Big Eddie a glance. The coach nodded back at him to answer. Mike talked about walking-on. About the players who signed, then transferred. About the sparse crowds they used to play in front of. About the dirt court back home where he taught himself to shoot. But he didn't talk about his old man being a drunk. *USA Today* didn't need to be running headlines about his old man.

"Is that what motivates you, Mike?" the woman reporter pressed on. "Being from a small town and not having been offered a scholarship?"

"Well…yeah, I guess. I mean, every once in a while it pops into my head that I wasn't given a scholarship at first, but as I've gotten older I've learned that the system isn't perfect. People make mistakes. That's how I look at it."

"How does you family feel about your success?"

Mike looked into the throng and wished he knew. He didn't want to answer questions about his family. He glanced at Big Eddie again, and the coach saw the fear in his eyes.

"Hell," Big Eddie said, "he's a hero back home. More famous than the guy who started that little chicken restaurant, Colonel Sanders."

The writers all laughed again. Big Eddie had saved him. The three of them thanked the reporters and walked off the stage.

Fletcher pulled into O'Brien's Stockyards and backed the truck in. Crows feeding in a nearby hogpen squawked and flew away when the vehicle sputtered to a stop. Fletcher unlatched the truck's back gate, then led Crockett down a ramp with the rope. The big boar squealed as his feet slipped on the muddy ramp, drawing the notice of a handful of men drinking coffee inside a small building.

One opened the door a few inches and yelled out. "Hey, mister, can we help you?" Fletcher thumbed at Crockett, then hollered back across the yard. "Come take a look."

Through a dirt-caked window he could see the men putting on their caps and jackets. They ambled out with amazed looks on their faces.

When they came within earshot, Fletcher spoke confidently, taking off his hat and holding it behind him. "I'm taking offers on my hog. What'll he bring?"

The men walked around Fletcher. A couple of soft slow whistles were heard. "What's it weigh?" one of the men said, squatting behind Crockett.

"Darn hard telling," Fletcher said. "Last time I weighed him was ten years ago, when my boy let him loose, and we had to get the vet and his noose to bring him in. I think Doc Millet said then he was near three hundred pounds."

Fletcher recalled the incident like it was yesterday. Mike's basketball had bounced into the hogpen, and after he'd retrieved it, he'd failed to fasten the latch. Crockett was gone for two hours before anyone noticed him missing. "Mike!" Fletcher had hollered, hopping down off the tractor. "Where in the hell is Crockett?"

When his oldest boy came around the barn to answer, Fletcher saw that the kid's sneakers and bottoms of his jeans were caked with mud.

"Did you go in there to get your ball and leave the gate open?"

Mike was silent.

Fletcher's eyes narrowed. He walked across the yard and kicked Mike's basketball into the cowpasture. "You went in there, didn't you?"

When Mike still didn't answer, Fletcher flung out an open hand and slapped his son to the ground, splitting the corner of his mouth.

"How many times have I told you to stay the hell out of the pen, boy?"

Mike quivered in his shadow, looking up. "I...I didn't mean to, Pa..."

He picked Mike up by the scruff of his neck and pushed his head into the wet ground. "Stupid little kid. I ought to beat the tar out of you, boy."

When Mike cried, it made Fletcher even madder. "Quit that crying, boy, or I'm really gonna tear a hole in your hide."

Mike whimpered, tried his best to hold back the sobs, but he couldn't contain them. The open hand struck again, this time bringing blood from Mike's nose.

"Don't you ever cry, boy! Crying is for girls. Now get your little ass up and let's go find that damn hog you let aloose."

They finally found the boar four hours later back in the woods by Clifford's caverns, a string of small caves some old-timers said led all the way to Mammoth Cave over near Bowling Green.

And after that Mike tried never to cry.

Fletcher stood watching the stockyard regulars, waiting to see what they'd say. One man took a broom handle and poked Crockett's midsection. "Biggest one I think I ever seen."

The men spent another ten minutes inspecting Crockett before making any move to talk about price. Five more minutes passed before they were through. Fletcher could tell they were impressed—and interested.

"Give you eight hundred for him," a tall man with a salt-and-pepper beard said.

Fletcher rolled his eyes. "I ain't that big a fool."

The bearded man looked back at Crockett, stroked his beard, pulled at his nose. "Thousand."

Fletcher blew through his lips. "All right. If you uns ain't serious I'll take the hog on down to Corbin. Leastways there I'll get a fair shake." He turned and tugged on the rope.

"Hey, mister, hold on." A short man in bib overalls stepped in front of the bearded man. "Give you eleven hundred."

Fletcher shook his head and kept walking.

"Hey, wait, mister. Twelve. Cash."

Fletcher stopped and turned completely around. "Boys, I know you're just doing your job, but you know damn well this hog is worth at least fifteen. Old Man Askew sold one here last winter that was smaller than mine for eleven hundred. After slaughter, you'll double your money."

The bearded man nodded at the short man, then said, "All right, you drive a hard bargain."

The short man took Crockett's rope and led him into a stout pen, latched it securely, then beckoned Fletcher to follow him inside to close the deal.

With the cash in his jacket pocket, Fletcher climbed back into the truck. On the way home he said a short double prayer—that he'd get through town without stopping off for a drink, and that Mike would get to Lexington. He had some fatherly duties to take care of. It was about time.

"What's it like out there?" Big Eddie said.

Father Charles's eyes gleamed. It was the first time in ages that he'd seen the coach visibly nervous. Perspiration seeped in crescents under the arms of his dark-blue shirt. His face was flushed, his eyes wide with worry. "Biggest crowd I think I've ever seen, in spite of the Hoosiers losing. We must have a lot of fans here."

"Bigger than the first game?"

The chaplain nodded. "Never heard so much noise. This dome is enormous. I think some of the people at the top have telescopes."

Big Eddie gave a nostalgic chuckle as he leaned against a wall and waited for the team to come back in from warm-ups. "I wish my uncle could be here tonight, Chuckie. He loved big games. He said in big games the truth always presented itself in the players. The good ones performed, the bad ones quit when things got hard. He called big games 'nut-cutting' time."

Big Eddie sighed. "It's been a long time since we've been here, you know? It seems like forever in some ways, like only yesterday in others."

Father Charles nodded, sitting down to listen.

"I've got butterflies tonight like I haven't had in a real long time. Had diarrhea all day. Feel like I've lost about ten pounds."

Father Charles smiled, then jerked his head toward the toilets. "Me too. I'm not playing, and I'm even more nervous than you or the team."

Big Eddie picked up a piece of chalk and tossed it back and forth in his hands. "I remember when my uncle took me to play in my first game when I was just a kid. I told him I was nervous, and he said it was natural. That if I wasn't nervous, then I wasn't ready to play. All the time I remember that. And you know what?"

"What?"

"He was right. I haven't been nervous enough in the past few years…and I think that's why we haven't made it to the tournament. It's been my fault."

The chaplain shrugged, started to shake his head. "I don't know about that—"

"No, it's true. I lost my drive somewhere along the way."

"You're not the first, Eddie. Life has a way of stealing a man's soul when he's not looking. It's cruel and relentless at times, but eventually everything works itself out for the best. Just always know that God has a plan for you, even though sometimes it doesn't seem that way."

Big Eddie rubbed the back of his neck, hoping to relieve some of the mounting stress. He picked up a water bottle and took a swig, swished it in his mouth, then walked to a sink and spat it out. "I feel like I'm getting back on track, though. Penny has restored something in me that's been missing."

"Yes, you seem happier, even at peace with the world."

"I am, and it's been great. I feel fulfilled. And you know something else, I've seen something in Mike's eyes lately that used to be in mine. Confidence, grit, mental toughness...desire. His play, his singlemindedness is starting to rub off on me. Maybe it's the two new women in our lives." He smiled.

"Maybe it is. And sometimes I don't know how that kid does it myself. It's almost like he's possessed." Father Charles studied Big Eddie's eyes, then stroked his own chin. "His family is going through a rough time at home, you know?"

Big Eddie looked up. "The old man again?"

"Yep. Out of work...drunk most of the time. Couldn't find him for a while, Mike said."

Big Eddie shook his head. "Damn."

Noise from the arena suddenly engulfed the locker room as the team broke through the door, Security leading the way. The players grabbed towels and water and circled around Big Eddie. Father Charles moved to the back of the room with Q and Hoppy to listen.

After drawing some plays on a green chalkboard, Big Eddie turned to face them, pacing back and forth, fidgeting with his white-striped green necktie, working out exactly what it was he wanted to say.

"We've come a long way, fellas," he said finally, self-possessed and handsome in his gray suit. "And tonight we're not going to do anything different from what we've done all season. All I'm asking is for you guys to go out there and give it everything you've got. No one has worked harder than we have."

He paused, scanning the room. "Listen, I know every one of you is nervous, but that's only natural. Once you get out on the floor and get your blood moving, you'll be fine. Try your best to tune the crowd out and think. Remember, when we win tonight, we get to go back home to Kentucky...where the best basketball in the world is played!"

He looked straight at Mike. The senior's eyes hadn't wavered once.

Big Eddie called the team up, then Father Charles said a quiet prayer.

As they were making their way back to the arena floor, Big Eddie spoke a quiet aside to Mike. "Hey, you feeling all right?"

Mike nodded enthusiastically. "Feel great, Coach. I want to get back home, so maybe my folks can see us play."

Big Eddie waited for Mike to turn a corner, then threw an arm around Father Charles's shoulders. "Did you see Mike's eyes, Chuckie? We're gonna win. I saw it in Mikey's face."

The C.U. fans watched nervously, ready to bury their heads in their hands at any second, for the momentum of the game had seemingly fallen to Syracuse. The lead had gone back and forth all evening, but now the Knights trailed by six, with three minutes to play. One time-out remained. Big Eddie had used the other two to stop a couple of ferocious runs by the Orange. He thought about using his last to call a play for Mike to shoot a three but decided to wait, knowing a lot could still happen.

Robbie brought the ball over half-court against the Orangemen's sticky man-to-man defense. Women, grown men, little children listened and watched intently, hearts pounding with excitement and fear for the Knights. Robbie Hart didn't like the pressure. He swung his hand down to keep the defender from hand-checking him. Big Eddie had complained to the officials about this defensive infraction throughout the game, but his pleas were ignored.

"Forget about it, Robbie!" Big Eddie cried over the crowd. "Play ball!"

"Four!" Robbie yelled. "FOUR!"

He made his pass to Spoon, cutting on his left. The defender reached out and grazed the ball with his foot, sending it out of bounds.

"Shit," Robbie said. "Shit."

Big Eddie jabbed his index finger at his temple, telling Hart to think. Hart nodded in instant understanding.

Twenty-two seconds showed on the shot clock. Hart inbounded the ball to Mike. He dribbled out front, then Carlos back-picked Spoon's man and Mike lobbed the ball toward the rim. Spoon caught it for the slam.

"Do it, Mike!" Q shouted from the bench.

The C.U. fans roared approval. The clock neared the two-minute mark.

The Knights fell back to play defense. With C.U. still down four points, Mike knew Syracuse was in no hurry to put up a shot. Big Eddie would be pissed if it didn't work, but Mike decided to gamble on trapping their guard anyhow as he crossed half-court, maybe catching him off balance. He walked over to Robbie and told him to get ready. The two of them were going to push the guard into the corner. Mike knew he had to roll the dice.

Mike met the guard just before he approached half-court. He pushed him to his left, and when the guard crossed over the line, Robbie stormed in to close the corner trap. Through all his years as a player, all Mike's coaches had told him never to pick up his dribble in the corner, where the out-of-bounds line served as a third defender. But the Syracuse guard did pick up his dribble in the corner, and Mike and Robbie knew they had him.

The Syracuse guard panicked. As he tried to pivot out of the trap he stepped out of bounds. The ref blew his whistle. Big Eddie cussed, certain one of his players had fouled. He turned to get a sub in for Mike.

Instead, the official signaled the other way. C.U.'s fans went crazy.

Big Eddie turned back to see what all the cheering was about. "Damn!" he said in disbelief to the grinning players on the bench, watching the ref hand the ball to Mike. "They actually made the play!"

Immediately Robbie dribbled down the left side of the court. Left wide open by his man, who was sloughing down on Carlos, he had no choice but to shoot. He checked his feet and made sure he was behind the three-point line. He squared up and let the ball fly. The Knights' bench all stood as the ball floated through the air. It hit the backside of the rim, bounced up, fell squarely through the middle of the hoop. The ref signaled for a three. The Knights were down by one, with over a minute to play.

"Q, I can't take it," Father Charles said, clutching his heart. "I'm getting much…much too old for all this."

Big Eddie called for the team to fall back into a two-three zone. He wanted to pressure the Syracuse team to hit from outside, something they hadn't done during the entire game with any success. Father Charles bit his fingernails. Everyone in the arena stood to see if Syracuse could hold the lead. Big Eddie expected a time-out, but when the shot clock ticked down to fifteen, he knew it wouldn't happen. Syracuse was unraveling.

"Contest every shot!" he screamed. Veins popped from his neck. "Get on them, Robbie! Force 'em out!"

Despite his pleading, Syracuse got off a good shot at the top of the key, a three if it fell. The ball floated for what seemed an eternity before it came down. From where Big Eddie stood it looked perfect. He winced. It missed. Spoon rebounded. Thirty-seven seconds remained. Now Big Eddie called his last time-out.

"Look, guys, it's ours to win now." He was jotting on his clipboard as Q passed water to the players. "This is what we've worked so hard for. Keep your cool... wait for the perfect shot. I want you guys to run motion.

"Mike, the ball is going to come to you. Set your feet and take your time with the shot. Carlos, make sure you get a good pass to him. I don't want the official blowing a whistle because you threw it out of bounds. Got it?"

Carlos nodded his head. Beads of sweat trickled down his face.

Mike walked to the end of the bench and grabbed a resin bottle. He shook the powder into his hands and rubbed them together to soak up the sweat. When the huddle broke, Mike walked side by side with Carlos to the other end.

He expected Syracuse to set up in a full-court press, but it didn't happen, and he was relieved, because he was getting tired. The game had taken the spring out of his legs.

Thirty-seven seconds could seem like an eternity. If they used the entire shot clock, Syracuse would be left with just two seconds. Of course if the Knights waited until the last few seconds to shoot, getting off a second shot would be nearly impossible. He didn't like that idea. But none of it would matter if he missed the shot.

A thousand times back on the farm he'd dreamed of moments like this. Just him, the ball and the hoop. He had to concentrate and forget about the crowd, his tired legs, the magnitude of the game, the media watching, the pressure. He wondered if Savannah was watching, or covering her eyes. He had to concentrate and forget about her, too.

Robbie inbounded the ball to Mike. He crossed half-court looking at the clock above the backboard—thirty seconds left. He could run the play from either side of the floor, but he wanted to go right, more comfortable from that side. He entered the ball to Parker Gray, the other forward, who was cutting up from the block. Parker held the ball high over his head to keep the Syracuse defender from getting his hands on it. Parker passed the ball to Carlos, who pivoted around at the free-throw stripe to face the basket.

The RCA Dome crowd roared when the big center juked as if he were going to drive to the basket. But instead he flipped the ball to Mike, who waited outside the three-point line.

Mike took the pass in his hands and lifted it into the air. He let the ball fly, but it didn't feel good. He had shot millions of baskets in his life, and he knew in an instant this one was off. An empty feeling twisted his stomach. They were going to lose. His dream was over.

But the C.U. bench wasn't groaning. Instead, they were on their feet. Cheering. Screaming. Jumping up and down.

Carlos had seen that the ball was going short, and he grabbed it and put it back in. And before Mike knew what was happening the frustrated Syracuse center swung at Carlos and hit him in the side of the head. A melee might have ensued, but Carlos stood calmly and quieted his teammates.

"No revenge, no revenge," he said. "Keep calm heads. We're going to win."

The Syracuse center was ejected from the game, to a chorus of boos from the Orange fans. Carlos sank his bonus shot, then the flagrant-foul technical. When C.U. got the ball back Big Eddie called for the team to stall. But as the last second ticked off the clock Syracuse's forward pretended to stumble, falling into Carlos's left knee. The big man groaned, then rolled on the floor, clutching his leg.

"You bastard," Hoppy said, running off the bench. "You did that on purpose."

The Syracuse forward pushed Hoppy away. "Siddown, fat boy, before I kick your fat ass." He jogged off the floor, laughing to himself.

Q steamed, watching from the last seat on the bench as the players exchanged handshakes and the other members of the two teams came running onto the floor. He waited until the Syracuse forward passed him, then took a bottle of liquid heat balm and squirted it on his neck and shoulders.

"What c-c-comes around, g-goes around," Q said, beaming as the forward squirmed in pain.

The writers held their breath as Carlos clambered onto the stage with an ice pack wrapped around his knee. Mike helped Carlos into the chair, then placed a cup of Gatorade next to him. While the moderator introduced them, Big Eddie skipped up the steps, beaming.

After he sat down, he whispered to Carlos. "Don't tell the truth about your knee, okay? Let them think and write what they want." He winked, then took the first flood of questions.

"Coach, did you expect to go this far?" a reporter in the first row asked.

"Of course I did. And I think we have plenty of fight left in us."

A voice from the back. "What about your center? Can he play?"

Big Eddie shook his head. "I don't know. It don't look good."

Carlos shot the coach a disbelieving look. The only thing hurting his knee was that it was getting colder by the second. He'd had far worse injuries back home in Mexico.

"Carlos, what's your opinion on what happened at the end of the game? Think it was bad luck?"

Carlos shook his head at the reporter in the middle of the pack. "Like Father Charles is always saying, The Lord moves in mysterious ways."

Pens flew. Laptops popped open to get the quotes.

"Why didn't you swing back at the Syracuse guy?"

Carlos gulped the Gatorade, then answered. "The fathers back in Mexico, the ones that taught me, they always told me, 'Thou shalt not hit'…and I also knew Coach would make me run if I did."

Heavy laughter filled the room.

"Mike, you think now you guys have a chance of going to the Final Four?"

Mike was silent for a long moment, then spoke confidently. "I've always thought I'd make it to the Final Four. It's everyone else who didn't believe."

Super Dave studied *USA Today* while sipping coffee, flipping from one page to another, jotting results onto his NCAA bracket with a small pencil, nodding and smiling as he wrote down the results.

"You doing pretty good?" Clara leaned over his shoulder and inspected his picks. "Darn, I should have talked with you before this thing started."

Super Dave straightened up and gave her a look meaning "Don't you have anything else to do?" She pulled back and folded her arms. "What's the matter? Yours top secret or something? Hell, you act like I just stole gold fillings out of your teeth."

"It's none of your business who I pick," he said, flipping his sheet over.

"Ah, hell," she said, wiping the table with a wet rag. "You ain't no fun. Get your own coffee, guy."

He shook his head and waited for her to leave. As soon as she got behind the counter, Luca Marzzarella strolled in with two men at his sides. Super Dave stood and waited for him to sit.

"Fool," Marzzarella said under his breath. "Sit…sit! Don't draw no attention. Fucking paparazzi already tried getting my picture, but Louie lost 'em coming over the bridge."

"Sorry, boss." Super Dave sat back down and pushed his picks across the table. He offered a great smile. "Going like clockwork. Every one of our teams made it to the Sweet Sixteen. I watched the Notre Dame game last night, and I swear I could never tell a thing. And my boys say the refs are delirious, knowing they're gonna make an easy two hundred Gs when it's all over. Poor slobs."

Marzzarella winked. "Money talks, David. Don't ever let nobody tell you money ain't the most powerful force on earth."

He looked over Super Dave's picks, then motioned for the newspaper. Super Dave refolded it and handed it to him with the front page of the sports section showing. Marzzarella read the feature article on C.U. in less than two minutes.

"Our friend Mister Justin's gonna be pissed now that Syracuse is out of it." He nodded at the headline and C.U.'s victory.

"Yeah, that Mexican boy there..." Super Dave pointed to a color picture of Mike assisting Carlos into the locker room. "He won the game for that freaking school in Kentucky. My only bad pick so far."

Marzzarella drummed the table, nodded in satisfaction. "Something about this headline, I like. 'Shall The Meek Inherit The Title?' It's got a ring to it. Nice. Religious, like. Too bad only two Catholic teams making it to the Final Four...Notre Dame and St. John's."

Super Dave and his employer were still sharing a satisfied laugh as Peter J. McCraken walked in the door and headed their way.

Dale Cutter found it hard to believe, but he now had pictures to prove it. One of WBC's top executives sipping coffee and eating bagels with New York's biggest racketeer. He stared for several minutes at the black-and-white photo his man in the van had taken.

He thought about Antoine Tandy—the bullets exploding his head, the blood streaking the wall. He might never be able to prove it, but he was sure there was a connection here.

What he really needed was some audio, although chances were slim considering they hadn't had enough time to plant a bug.

A clipped voice crackled over the radio. "Sorry, Dale. No luck today. Too many people making way too much noise to get anything."

"Shit." Dale tossed the photos in the seat next to him. "Nothing at all?"

"Not this time."

Dale stared through the tinted window at the front of the café. Notre Dame, U.C.L.A., North Carolina, and St. John's...all four of the Vegas bettor's picks had moved on to the Sweet Sixteen, just like clockwork, like Reggie said. But how?

He'd watched as many games as possible and hadn't detected the slightest bit of chicanery from a soul. Every single player seemed to be playing all out, and none of them, not even once, appeared to be taking a dive. Even his men stationed with the four teams said no player had been approached with a bribe that they knew of. He shook his head, rubbed his eyes.

Maybe all four teams had won fairly, unbelievable as that might seem. Maybe his imagination was getting the best of him. Maybe Reggie was mistaken. Maybe the bettor was just some kook with nothing else to do but throw his money down the drain. Or maybe the guy really had ESP. And maybe Dale Cutter ought to reserve himself a place at the funny farm.

He studied the people coming and going through the café some more. But why else would a top WBC executive be having brunch with The Big Cheese? The question nagged at him as he waited for McCraken to emerge. Soon his break would come. It always did. Virtue always prevailed—and evil always failed. He had to believe that.

Chapter 16

Mike walked out of the locker room with a glow on his face. Savannah had left a note in his locker, probably put there by Q, that said she loved him and would be waiting for him at Clark's when he got back to campus. The trip home was quick, and ten minutes after the team had arrived in town Mike was walking into the place, looking around for her.

Fans poured out of their seats when they saw him. A tanned blonde with shoulder-length hair clutched Mike and kissed him passionately on the lips. The crowd went wild. She handed him her phone number and batted her eyes. This was definitely not Mike's style. Embarrassed, he scanned the elbow-to-elbow crowd again.

When he finally spotted Savannah, he saw that she was steaming. He sat down and leaned to kiss her, but she moved away.

"I'm not second to anyone."

He rolled his eyes. "Savannah, I don't even know her…"

"She seemed to know you!" Her eyes were knives.

"She's drunk. Everyone in here is drunk."

Suddenly Savannah's face changed, softened. "I'm sorry, Mike. You…you're right. But all of a sudden everything is moving so fast."

Mike took her hand and held it.

"You guys were great today."

He just nodded. A couple of students from his dorm started doing a little dance across the room. "This place is getting crazy, Savannah."

"No crazier than I am for you."

Mike had felt it, but he'd never known for sure. The romp in the park was one thing, could be a sure sign, but these days sex never meant complete commitment. For him now it was confirmed. He leaned and gave her a strong, deep, passionate kiss. The crowd went berserk.

"C'mon, Savannah, let's get out of here. I know a quieter spot."

She looked at him suspiciously. "You haven't taken that blonde over there before, have you?"

"No, darlin', I've saved this one just for you. I go there to think all the time."

Cheers and toasts were called out as the two walked through the bar and out the door.

"When I was little my ma always made sure we went to Mass at least once a week, sometimes twice."

Savannah and Mike were sitting in the massive C.U. chapel, the only two people in any of the long wooden pews. Crosses and candles and stained glass were all around them. The looming space was darkish, warm, comforting.

"So you say you come here, when?"

"When things in my head are out of control, I talk to God. He's the only one that listens to my stories."

"You were pretty lonely as a kid, weren't you?"

"In some ways, yeah."

"I mean, you had your family around, but no one to express your emotions to. Is that close to being right?"

"Yeah, never could express my emotions." His eyes were on the altar and the crucifix. "Old man would have kicked my butt, told me only girls cry. Ma would listen when she had time, but she never had much time. So I went to the court...hoops, I mean. I went there when everything was bad. I went there to get away. I went there to change my life."

He was deep into his memories. "You know, sometimes I can't believe how much I used to play. Every day, all day, half the night. I could make that basketball talk if I wanted. Pitiful, ain't it? Never went anywhere in my life until I came to C.U. I mean anywhere. So I went to the court. Didn't know any better."

"I'm glad you did, Mike."

"Why?"

"'Cause now I know you weren't messing around with other girls."

"Other girls?" He gave a short rueful laugh. "No, back on the farm there weren't many of them around."

"You're so…so different, Mike."

"Different how?"

"Most guys just don't have the drive you've got. All most guys want to do is party and chase girls."

His eyes shifted from the altar to her face. "Most guys have choices, Savannah. I don't. That's all. I've got to be the example for my brothers. I've got to make something of myself."

She smiled. He smiled.

"I'd like it if we could pray together," Mike said.

"I'd like that too."

So they put the kneeler down and said a prayer together.

Afterward, when they had slid back into their seats, Savannah said, "I can't believe I'm here with you, Mike. I can't believe I've met someone as wonderful as you. When I had polio, no one would dare speak to me, the handicapped little girl. Now I think I've met Clark Kent and Robin Hood all rolled into one. God moves in mysterious ways."

He nodded, mocking a straight face. "Yeah, right. Superman and Robin Hood. That's what Father Charles is always telling me."

The arena was thoroughly barricaded, the doors securely locked. Any cracks or gaps were covered with big sheets. Big Eddie had closed the workout to the media and general public and worked the team for three hours, even had them run suicides despite the fact they were by far the best-conditioned team still in the tournament.

He could tell now that their cockiness had subsided. His practice had been brutal, the toughest he had put them through since Christmas break. He knew they had a great chance of getting into the Final Four, despite having to play Kansas next, then the winner of the Michigan–Notre Dame game.

Though it might have been in a previous life, he *had* been to the Final Four, and he knew what it took to get there again. Work. Hard work. Lots of it.

And getting to it one more time would silence all his critics, especially the ones in the C.U. Administration Building. No one would fire him if he got past the next two games. And even if they did, he wasn't worried. His new prestige would attract other offers.

His whistle blowing to stop practice shrieked like a boiling teakettle. He finally had extracted from the team what he wanted. He called them to the middle of the floor.

"Good workout, guys. We play Kansas the way we practiced today, and we're going to be in great shape. I appreciate your hard work today. Everyone concentrated and gave great effort." He looked around. "Any questions?"

No one answered. They were all bent over, panting heavily, sweating profusely, towels working hard to absorb the moisture.

"Okay, then get on the free-throw line," he ordered. "Free throws and turnovers will decide our future…and I don't want either one of them coming into play. Concentrate!"

He clapped his hands and walked to the water cooler, twirling the cord of the whistle around his finger, then sat down in a chair and crossed his legs. Players paired up around the various baskets. One player in each pair took two shots, then the rebounder took his turn. As Mike had requested earlier, before practice, he was working with Carlos.

"Carlos, concentrate," Mike snapped, watching both the center's shots bounce off the front of the rim. "Do like I told you…get balanced."

Carlos frowned, struggling to settle into any consistent rhythm. "I'm trying, amigo. This isn't natural to me like it is to you."

Mike snapped the net over the rim with both his shots, then moved under the basket again to rebound. "It isn't natural to me, either," he said. "It comes from practice…years of practice.

"Now take your time," he said softly. "Forget about everything going on around you, and concentrate on the front of the rim. Just put the ball over its edge."

Carlos screwed his face into a mask of intense concentration. He bounced the ball three times, brought the ball to his waist, then lifted it and flicked his wrist. The ball careened off the side of the rim, hit the banking board hard, then angled toward the sideline. Mike sprinted to get it, then fired a bullet back to Carlos.

"Hey, that isn't gonna get it. You've got to relax on your shots. Basketball is a simple game if you don't get in a hurry. This time, take a deep breath, and count to three before you let the ball go. Trust me. It'll steady your shot."

Carlos placed his feet an inch from the line, then bent at the knees. He bounced the ball three times, brought it to his waist again, then took a long, deep breath. This shot bounced off the other side of the rim.

"Goofball," Mike said, chuckling, "you've got to let your breath out *before* you shoot. Try it again...and breathe. In and out."

Carlos went through the routine again, this time exhaling before he shot. The ball fell perfectly through the rim, barely rippling the net. He smiled like he'd just won a million-dollar lottery.

"That's it, roomie. Do it like that every time, and Big Eddie might not be afraid to have you in the game at crunch time. Now I'll drop out, and you keep shooting."

Mike stood by to watch Carlos hit ten in a row. "That's the way to shoot 'em, Carlos. You'd make Rick Barry proud."

Carlos looked puzzled. "Rick who?"

The greatest free-throw shooter of all time—well, they didn't play basketball in Mexico. Mike let it pass, he didn't know who the best bullfighter ever was.

"Nothing, man. Just keep shooting."

The ball ripped through the net again.

By Tuesday evening Big Eddie had figured out a way to beat Kansas. Stacks of videos scattered the floor, along with three or four empty pizza boxes. He had three phones at his desk, all of them off the hook. A two-day beard sandpapered his face. His tattered C.U. sweatshirt was splashed with tomato sauce. Crinkled newspapers spread across his desk were all turned to stories about the Knights.

Tomorrow he would practice the team hard again, then on Thursday bus the seventy miles to Lexington, run a practice, attend a press conference, and start worrying about their game against Kansas on Friday evening.

He sat in the darkness of his office and thought. The sports complex was empty, except for a distant ponk in a racquetball court. His desk chair was hurting his back, but he didn't care. Somehow they had to make Kansas pay for playing a full-court press. In the earlier contest, Mike and Robbie had rushed their passes and got rattled by the Kansas crowd.

He hoped it would be different now. They'd be playing on a neutral court at Rupp Arena, which could be in their favor since it was so close to home that plenty of C.U. fans would be able to attend. And beyond that Mike and Robbie would surely be seeking retribution.

But he had doubts about Carlos. The Jayhawk center was a rough, white seven-footer who'd made Carlos look silly in the first meeting. During the first game the guy had scored at will and pushed Carlos all over the court. But in Kansas's press the big plodding center was an albatross.

And Big Eddie reasoned that there was no way he would be able to cover the quicker Carlos if Robbie and Mike lobbed the ball over the press to Carlos by the basket. Even if Carlos didn't score every time, the slower center was either going to foul out or tire out from running so much. It seemed logical, but so did all theories in the planning stages.

The coach decided to watch a little television before going home and flipped the remote control. A segment about a tornado in Oklahoma caught his attention. House roofs twirled in the twister—something you had to watch, like a car fire or a wreck on the side of the road.

Eventually a noise coming through the offices turned him from the screen. "Hey, who is it?" Big Eddie peered through the blackness.

"Me."

Father Charles stood in the doorway smiling, wearing all black except for a dark-blue windbreaker. "Just came by to tell you you've hit the big time." The chaplain walked over to the desk and plopped a fresh copy of *USA Today* on the desk.

"What is it?"

Big Eddie was staring at a color photo of himself. "Damn."

"Can I get your autograph on that when you're finished?"

"Very funny." Big Eddie put the paper back on the desk and rolled back in his chair, placing his shoeless feet on the desk.

"They're calling us a Cinderella team, Eddie."

"Yeah, and if we lose to Kansas, they'll be calling us something else. Don't pay attention to all the hype, Chuckie. When you start believing what the newspaper says, you're in big trouble. Schmucks don't know a thing about what it takes to win at this level."

"Yeah, but the publicity is good…especially since you deserve it. You've worked hard this year. I'm proud of the kids, proud of you."

"Puh-lease. If we get beat Friday night, I'm just another stiff on the streets. Ol' Callahan won't even give me the weekend to clean out my desk."

"You'd be surprised. He's actually quite giddy at the thought of going to Lexington to watch us play."

"Yeah, well, tell him not to get too close to the team. I don't want any negative vibes around those guys."

Father Charles sighed. "You look like hell, Eddie. When's the last time you slept?"

Big Eddie glanced idly back to the television. The anchor was talking about cheap air fares to Florida for spring break. "I don't know. What day is it?"

"Tuesday night."

"Sunday…I slept for four hours. Been here ever since. Can't lose this game, Chuckie. I've got that fire in my belly again. I'm ready to play right now. I think we're gonna kick Kansas up and down the floor."

He was quiet for a moment, then allowed himself a sly grin. "But if someone asks, tell 'em I'm worried to death. I want everyone thinking we don't have a prayer."

Mike and Carlos staked out their territory in the back of the bus that would carry the team to Lexington for the regional semi-final game. The big coach rolled slowly leaving the campus, as a crowd gathered to cheer the team off. Another throng of fans wearing green and white waved from a corner across from McDonald's. Before the driver could make it to the interstate three hundred others were lining the road.

"Good luck, guys!"

"Beat Kansas this time, fellas!"

"Hey, Carlos…dance like a butterfly and sting like a bee!"

"Pretty cool, Mike, *si*?" Carlos was waving back at the fans.

Mike turned from the window and looked back at Carlos. "You know what I dreamed of when I was a kid?"

"Girls, maybe?"

"No, I dreamed of days just like this. This kind of reminds me of the ticker-tape parades the Yankees used to get. I think I've seen 'The Pride of the Yankees' a hundred times. "

"To me it is like the big soccer games back home. Fans in Mexico are crazy about soccer. Entire towns would close when matches were going on." Carlos had borrowed a compact disc player from Q, and he plugged in a CD and put on the phones. His head bobbed up and down to the beat.

Mike turned away, stared back out the window. His uncle had left a message in the basketball offices for him to call him, collect, as soon as he got to Lexington. He wondered what that was about. Maybe his uncle needed tickets to the game. Or maybe he was calling to say his old man was back on a binge again.

Mike knew from the sky's heavy gray stillness that a spring snow was on its way. Nothing stirred, not even the topmost branches of the trees they passed at seventy miles an hour. Feeling snow getting ready to bust loose brought back a bad memory. He closed his eyes and tried to let it go, but the memory had him in its clinches and hung on, ruthless as a hungry shark.

Fletcher had gotten in a hurry one winter day, and he couldn't hear what Ma said from the front porch, so he jumped out of the truck without applying the emergency brake. Mike, who had just come in from practicing his shots, saw the truck slipping backward down the driveway. He was in the wrong place at the wrong time.

Fletcher turned just in time to see the truck slide down the hill, helpless to stop it from slamming through a barbed-wire fence and into the creek a hundred yards away. He let out a string of cusswords, but then he saw that Mike had snickered when the truck splashed.

"Oh, so you think that's funny?" Demons danced in Fletcher's eyes. Mike tensed and wanted to run, but he couldn't. His legs felt like concrete.

"I'm not laughing at you, Pa. Honest. I was just thinking it was about time we got us a new truck."

Fletcher spat into the snow, then spotted a rusted chain tossed against a barrel. He picked it up, slung it over his shoulder, started walking toward Mike.

"No, Pa, I wasn't—"

The first swing missed, but the second one caught Mike's leg and ripped it open. He fell to the ground, clutching the wound. Blood gurgled through his fingers, staining the snow a sudden, violent red.

"Don't you ever laugh at me again, boy!"

Mike clenched his teeth as he waited for the next lash. But for some reason Fletcher didn't swing again. He just stood there with evil on his tongue, nothing more coming out. He turned and dropped the chain fifteen yards from where he picked it up, then hunched his shoulders and made his way down to the creek.

Mike shook his head to clear the painful reminders, then reached back and tapped Carlos on the shoulder.

The big center removed his headphones. "What's up?"

"I need a answer for a question I got."

"All right. What?"

"Do you know what the greatest disease in the world is?"

Carlos pondered, then gave in. "No, what?"

"The lack of love, dude. The lack of love."

Mike turned his eyes back to the window, studied the brooding sky. He hoped his family would be able to get to Lexington, but something deep inside told him not to get excited. Told him not even to hope.

Big Eddie chewed a worn piece of gum and stared past the curtain. The media was waiting for him. The cutthroat bastards had been on his ass for the last several years, now all of a sudden they were his best friends.

He saw a writer with *Sports Illustrated* in the front row. Next to him were others with *The New York Times* and *The Sporting News*. On an elevated platform in the back of the room, CBS, NBC, ABC, WBC, and ESPN whirled their cameras. Across the way he spotted Louisville's local writers, including Ronnie Reid, the most obnoxious man in the business. He remembered Reid's story from the start of the season saying Big Eddie Cantrell was washed up, still dreaming about the great teams he'd had during the Eighties.

Each time Eddie had seen Reid since then he'd deliberately avoided him so as not to punch out the rail-thin jerk and suffer even more at the hands of *The Post-Standard*, the newspaper Reid worked for. Reid criticized him then for his lack of cooperation, but he didn't care. His ego wouldn't let him forgive.

But this was no time to air his grievances about the media, how much power they wielded in getting coaches fired. He might as well play it safe. After the Final Four, well, then he could speak his mind.

His Sports Information Director, Patsy Elbert, a capable redhead with an hourglass figure, walked toward him smiling, carrying a briefcase. "Coach." She patted him softly on the back. "Any time you're ready to go on up, they're waiting."

Big Eddie chewed his gum some more. "Let 'em stew for a while. Especially Reid over there. Sometimes I wish I could—"

"Coach, forget him. He's eating crow 'cause we're here."

"I know, but I'd still like to take my foot and shove it down his throat, or up someplace else. He's never played an hour of basketball in his life, probably never even started a sweat, and they consider him an expert. What a joke. The newspaper business is a farce."

He rubbed his flat eyes. "When I first started in this business, the media could be trusted. Some of the old writers used to be friends. Now it's who can outsensationalize the other. Nowadays we've even got to close practices to get any privacy for the players."

He looked around, waved his hands. "Oh, hell. Enough lecturing from me. So how's the hotel?"

Her smile broadened. "Perfect. The players have their own rooms. The city police are providing security to keep unwanted visitors off our floor. Just like you requested."

"Father Charles get taken care of? I don't want him on my ass if his room isn't perfect."

"He's between Mike and Carlos. He'll sleep like a baby between those two party animals."

"Party animals. Right!" The coach laughed, and Patsy joined in. They both knew better.

"You got my room key?"

She searched her briefcase, handed him a small envelope. "Here it is. Two keys. They gave you a suite. Sitting room, refrigerator, kitchenette, king-size bed, the works."

Big Eddie tore the envelope open, took out one of the keys, and handed the envelope back. "When you see Penny at practice, give this to her for me. I'm planning to stop off on the way back to the hotel and see an old coaching buddy at Transylvania. But tell her I won't be long."

"Okay, I will." Patsy nodded toward the curtain. "Uh, Coach...I think they've waited long enough now."

He turned his head, still working the gum diligently in his jaws. "Yeah...I guess so."

"Good luck," Patsy said.

He disappeared through the curtain and walked to the stage.

"Coach, was there ever a time in C.U.'s slump when you thought you'd chuck it all and retire?"

Big Eddie sat silently with his elbows on the table, just staring at the reporter. How many times were they going to ask him this? The same exact question had been asked in Indianapolis. A writer for the

Indianapolis Star had just done a two-page story last week. Times like this he wanted to just stand up, walk out, and never come back. If he had been as lazy in his preparation as most of the members of the media he dealt with, he'd have been fired a long time ago. Frustrating. Very frustrating.

He took a sip of water, rubbed his chin, ran his hands through his hair and, instead of embarrassing the guy, patiently went through the same answer he'd given a week ago. After ten minutes he stopped talking.

A hand lifted in the back of the big room.

"Yes, go ahead," Big Eddie said, pointing.

The reporter took a hand-held microphone. "Coach, you said last week that Mike and Carlos were the two hardest-working players you've ever coached. Now that you've advanced to the Sweet Sixteen, can you talk more about them?"

Big Eddie smiled. No more questions about his personal problems. "Two of the most enjoyable kids I've ever been around in my entire life. Both of them are from modest backgrounds, and both of them have overcome tremendous odds."

"In what way?" the reporter asked, scribbling into his notepad.

"Well," he said, scrutinizing the guy, "Carlos is from an orphanage in Juarez. It was almost pure luck that he ever picked up a basketball at all. Where he's from, the sport everyone plays is soccer. He was a goalie on one of the regional teams there and didn't pick up a basketball until he was almost out of high school.

"Our team chaplain, Father Charles Lichtenfield, is actually the one who pulled the strings to bring him to C.U. I'll admit Carlos has been a project of sorts, but he learns quickly and is the most improved player on the team."

"Is it true he took dance classes to help his balance?"

"Three times a week after practice he does ballet for an hour. I can't tell you how much it's helped him. It was a dance routine of his that helped us beat Memphis, as you probably recall."

Big Eddie stood up and mimicked Carlos's now-famous routine. The writers roared. Strobes lit up the room. After everyone quit laughing, he went on to talk about Mike.

"I think everyone in this room at one time or another has known someone in their life who has been an inspiration. Well, for me, Mike Kramer is the kid who has helped me more than anyone knows. Too be honest with you, I don't know where his desire comes from, but he is the most driven kid I've ever been around, and I've been around a few in my day. I've even tried to emulate him in some ways.

"Mike came here as a walk-on, as most of you know now. He's not tremendously gifted with great athletic talent, but his heart makes up for it. I never thought he would play when he first got here, but through hard work and determination he's become probably the greatest player I've ever coached."

"Who can you compare Mike to?"

Big Eddie wrinkled his brow. "Hmm…that's a tough question. Pete Rose comes to mind…so does Larry Bird."

"Pete Rose? That's not because he likes to gamble, is it?"

The writers broke into laughter.

"No, it's because every day Mike has the same look in his eye that Rose had barreling down the third-base line during that All-Star game when he knocked Ray Fosse into next week. Nothing stops Mike."

A great comparison, he thought, as he watched the reporters flip their pads over. He took a drink of water and went on. "Honestly, both Carlos and Mike are dreams to coach. In an age when the headlines are always filled with stories of sports figures doing drugs and getting arrested for beating up their girlfriends or carrying guns, it's refreshing to find players who epitomize the spirit of the NCAA."

Birds sang in the bare tree limbs. A nearby creek gurgled and dashed around a cascade of rocks worn smooth over the years by the water's constant flow. A snowplow in the distance billowed black smoke, then backfired and spun its tires across a brilliant parking lot. Thick white powder was still falling fast and furious, caking limbs, parked cars, walls, and roads. Carlos just stared, his eyes wide as hubcaps. He moved out from under the canopy at the hotel's side door to stand slack-jawed in just a pair of gym shorts and a warmup jacket, catching flakes with his outstretched tongue, like a puppy with steam rising off its body.

"Knucklehead," Mike said, leaning over to roll a snowball in his hands, "what the hell are you doing out here? Big Eddie sees you out here like this, he's gonna kick your butt all the way back to Juarez."

"Mike...I have never seen such beauty in all my life. I think Kentucky is the prettiest place in the world."

Snow covered the ground like thick cake frosting. Trees picked barren of leaves could have been great candles rising into the low gray sky.

"Wait until the heavy stuff starts coming down!" Mike was enjoying kidding his friend. "With the way the weather changes around here, we might have ten inches before morning."

"Ten inches?" Carlos's eyes got even bigger. "It's almost time for the flowers to come out, isn't it?"

"Well, yes. But in Kentucky, you never can tell. When I was a kid, we had fifteen inches one Easter."

Carlos turned his back to Mike, providing a perfect target for the wet snowball. Mike drew back and let fly. It thudded against Carlos's nylon jacket then fell to the ground, leaving splotches of white stuck to his back.

"Hey!" Carlos crowed, turning with a pleased grin.

He reached down to make his own snowball, but when he was ready to make his throw, Mike had already darted behind the team bus. Carlos put the snowball he had made inside his warmup jacket and shaped another, holding it in his huge hand.

"My roommate is a coward, I see," Carlos said loudly. "Where I come from, a man doesn't dodge the bull. He faces it head on."

Mike moved from behind the bus grinning, now in perfect view of Carlos. "Where I come from a man knows how to use his weapons. Ten bucks says you can't hit me from where you're standing."

Carlos smiled. "You're on."

The big center went into a baseball windup from twenty feet away, then fired. Mike stood rigid waiting for the sphere to land, but Carlos's aim was way off.

"See, that's why you miss so many free throws, you don't concentrate." Mike walked toward Carlos with his open palm out. "Pay up, dude."

Carlos jutted his chin in defiance, then slowly pulled two wrinkled ten-dollar bills from his sock.

Mike took the per-diem, then carefully folded the bills and tucked them into the band of Carlos's shorts. "I don't want your money, roommate. Your lesson is to start concentrating from now on. We're gonna need you big time when we play Kansas. Especially at the free-throw line and on defense."

Carlos stared down at Mike and smiled. "I will cover the baskets tomorrow night like the snow covering the ground today. Just wait and see."

When Mike turned to walk back toward the entrance of the hotel, Carlos took out his second snowball, threw it, and hit Mike solidly in the back. Mike turned with a surprised look on his face.

"Your lesson today is to never assume anything, Mikey. Not everyone in life plays fair."

Mike winked. "I'll try and remember that."

Big Eddie plugged three quarters into a vending machine and waited for his Dr. Pepper to drop. The interview room had emptied, except for one last reporter who was approaching him wearing an ugly lime-green sport coat with canary-yellow trousers.

"All that talking would make me thirsty, too."

The reporter smiled as the coach popped the soda open and took a long drink.

"You guys don't know when to quit," Big Eddie said when he came up for air. "I could drink two or three of these after sessions like that one."

"You've just got a real interesting story that'll pique people's interest and sell newspapers. That's what my job is all about, keep the presses humming."

Big Eddie nodded and started walking slowly down a long, empty hallway. "Yeah, and mine's to win basketball games. And I guess the reason my story is so interesting is that I've just been through a lot of bullshit in my coaching career."

"Here's something you can add to your list."

Something in the man's voice alarmed Big Eddie. "Yeah, what's that?"

The reporter handed the coach a large manila envelope. "Go ahead, open it up. It's another human-interest story a lot of people might be interested in reading."

Big Eddie ripped open the envelope's flap and examined its contents. It was Penny's purported arrest record for prostitution in New York, several photos of him with her at Catholic University functions, another photo of the two of them at Clark's. He scanned it quickly, then glared at the reporter. "Where'd you get this?"

"Sorry." The guy grinned. "The Fourth Amendment protects me from revealing my sources."

You motherfucker, Eddie wanted to say, but he knew he couldn't. With a massive effort he controlled himself. "Somehow I get the feeling you're not a real reporter. What newspaper did you say you worked for?"

"Never said, Coach. Anyhow, this is more of a free-lance assignment. The story will probably go to the highest bidder. You know…for big bucks. Real big."

"What kind of story are we talking about here?"

The reporter shrugged. "Not everything in life is about money, Coach."

Big Eddie knew he couldn't screw around with this guy. "I take it you'll be in contact?"

"You take it right, Coach. So long. And by the way, have a good one." The man turned and evaporated into the vastness of the building before the coach could collect his wits.

Big Eddie stared out coldly across the dance floor. Four empty martini glasses cluttered the small table. He was quickly working on his fifth when Hoppy strolled through the crowd and back to the booth where he sat.

"Everyone made curfew, Coach." Hoppy looked unusually cheerful, even for him. "Now we can unwind a little bit." He waved at the waitress, and when she came, ordered a draft beer.

Within minutes she was back with it. He took a long drink and watched the students gyrating on the dance floor. "Some serious ass out there tonight." He was watching a girl in tight jeans and a yellow sweater rubbing against her boyfriend. "Wouldn't mind being in that guy's shoes, would you, Coach?"

Hoppy turned and offered Big Eddie a sly smile, but the coach didn't respond. Instead, he chugged the rest of his drink, then waved at the waitress to bring him another. "Go on, Hop, get out of here. I don't need anyone telling me where I should and shouldn't be."

Suddenly Hoppy was paying attention, checking the coach out. He'd been in such a good mood himself, he hadn't noticed the shape Big Eddie was in. For several minutes he waited for Big Eddie to say something else, and when he didn't, he risked asking what was wrong.

"Nothing's the matter, just leave me the fuck alone."

"Those writers say something that's pissing you off?"

Big Eddie glared. The waitress returned with his drink. He quickly downed half.

"Coach, hey, slow down."

Big Eddie ignored him. Hoppy sat on in silence, feeling helpless, scared to think where this might end up. To his relief, ten minutes later Father Charles came strolling through the crowd to where they sat.

"Lively crowd tonight, guys," the chaplain said with a smile. "Believe it or not, I can remember when I used to dance like that. But it was way before I grew this big ol' belly."

When no one laughed, the priest grasped the tension at the table. He gave Hoppy a look. The trainer shrugged his shoulders, then stared back at the dance floor, not saying a word.

"Eddie, how many of those you planning to put away?" Father Charles asked light heartedly. "Got a game coming up, don't we?"

The coach looked up, glaring at the priest. "As many as I want, that's how many."

Father Charles got the message. He waited for Big Eddie to tell him what was the matter, but the coach wasn't forthcoming. He finally decided to clear the air. "Hey, what the hell is wrong with you tonight? You let those reporters get you this angry?"

Big Eddie didn't respond.

Hoppy motioned to Father Charles to follow him into the hall. "That's what I asked, too. He wouldn't answer. He's pissed at something, big time."

They agreed the best strategy was just to try to wait him out. Hoppy left for the head, came back, and after the second half of the martini Big Eddie finally spilled his guts.

"I think...I think...Mother of God, Chuckie," a strangled sob escaped his throat. "I think I'm being blackmailed."

"Huh?" Hoppy and the priest said at the same time.

"Yeah...take a look."

Eddie placed the manila envelope on the table and pulled out its contents. Hoppy stared at the pictures, then the police report, handed them to Father Charles.

Big Eddie wasn't too drunk to see that both of them were embarrassed and appalled. Embarrassed, why? Why not enraged? Suddenly he was suspicious. "So...Chuckie...Hoppy...you knew about this?" he said, pronouncing his words very, very carefully.

The chaplain pushed the papers back inside the envelope. "Don't blame us, Eddie. You've been feeling fulfilled, you said so yourself. Hoppy, were you afraid something like this might happen?"

Eddie was really angry now. "Something like this, something like what?" He closed his eyes, slammed his fist on the table. "The hell with this. Is this some kind of a setup? You fix it up so Penny gets me through the season, then leaves when she's finished her job?"

"I can't believe she could fake that kind of emotion," the priest said.

"You ever been with a hooker, Chuckie?" Eddie's face was purplish-red.

"No, but I've listened to more phony confessions than I like to remember."

"You know…" Now in the carelessness of anger Big Eddie was slurring his words. "When we use't win all those games, before…Sally lef' me, I thought there was nothin' more important than getting to play in the NCAA tournament every year. But I made a goddamn commitment to myself…this time…that I would rather be with Penny than win a hunnerd tournament titles."

Father Charles held up the packet. "So, you think this changes that commitment to yourself?"

Big Eddie looked at him, shook his head. His poor innocent friend. "Don't try that Mary Magdalene stuff on me, padre."

"Actually, I wasn't thinking of her at all, but you."

"Me?"

"Whoever did this wasn't trying to get money from you, he wanted something else. He's trying to stop this team by upsetting you, throwing you off balance. I think you need to talk to her."

"Wha' for? It's all here, in black and white."

"Her past, yes. Not her present or future. Or yours, for that matter."

He gave a sick laugh. "What kind of future can I have with a hooker?" He turned up his glass to finish off the last drops. "If this gets out, I'll be the laughingstock of the coachin' profession."

"Maybe. Maybe not." Father Charles took the glass gently from his hand. "But what if things aren't how you think? After all, when your wife left, you were surprised, never thought she'd ever cheat on you…even though you were cheating on her."

When Big Eddie didn't answer, Father Charles went on. "What if Penny really does love you, and all of this is just a mistake…and you let her and your chance at the title slip away? Obviously that's what the blackmailer wants. What will you have then?"

"Booze, and plenty of it."

"Come on, Eddie, you know that doesn't solve a thing. But if it means that much to you, I'll even buy you the first round at the end of the season.

"Right now, though, all those kids and all those fans are depending on you. I don't care if you go on a binge for the rest of your life, but it's not starting until this season ends, one way or the other."

The coach laughed in spite of himself, struggling to get Father Charles's face into focus. "Is 'at a papal edict?"

"As far as you're concerned, yes."

"Oh, hell." Big Eddie slowly lifted himself out of the booth. "I guess we might as well try to get to the Final Four and win the whole damn thing."

Chapter 17

S uper Dave arranged the speakerphone so his boss wouldn't have to strain to hear the upcoming conversation. He was totally convinced the four teams named would make it into the Final Four, but the boss wanted everyone on the same page. Mistakes at this late date could be disastrous. How disastrous? Very—you screw up, you die. Super Dave had never seen his boss so keyed up.

The games began again tonight, Thursday evening. He checked his watch: high noon. The Darome Connection operator said there were four participants waiting to join the conference call. He took a seat and waited. Ten minutes later the elevator door popped open and Marzzarella strolled in, leaning hard on his silver-headed cane.

When he saw Super Dave reclining in a chair, feet on the conference table, his reaction was sharp and quick. "Very nice, David, very comfortable. Can I get you something? A drink, coffee, anything?"

Super Dave leapt out of the chair and raced to take charge of his boss's gray overcoat and black fedora.

Marzzarella's face was taut, grim. "You got everybody on the line, David?"

"Right, boss. All four are on hold." Super Dave tried to look busy, embarrassed at being caught out.

Marzzarella eased into the big-backed chair, and when he started to pour himself a glass of iced water from a silver thermos pitcher, Super Dave jumped to do it for him. He motioned impatiently for Super Dave to sit back in a chair across from the desk.

When the boss hit a large black button on a speaker the co-ordinating operator's voice came through, soft, female. "All participants are ready to go, sir. If you need any assistance, please call my name at any time while you're in conference. I'll be monitoring the event, and, if anyone else joins in, I will notify you."

Marzzarella cleared his throat. "Good." He motioned for Super Dave to close a door, then began. "All you guys with me?"

Confirmations came over the line.

"Give me a roll call," he said, jiggling the ice in his glass.

Rizzio, Lucas, Little Pete, and Ricky Ridgeway identified themselves as Marzzarella listened and sipped from his glass.

"Right," he said. "Now, I don't have to tell you guys we got a big deal working here. We ain't got room for screw-ups. Everybody better be on the same page. David and the others, they've done too much work to see this go down the drain. You got that?"

Four voices answered: "Right," "Yes sir," "Got it," "Yep."

"Okay. We got two teams playing tonight, two tomorrow night. I don't want no screw-ups. None. Are we ready?"

"Done deal," Rizzio said. Marzzarella knew he was in Tempe, where U.C.L.A. faced New Mexico in the West Regional.

"I got no problem here," Lucas said, in St. Louis for the Midwest Regional. "Florida don't stand a chance against the Tar Heels, especially since three of their players had an unfortunate visit to the hospital last night with a mysterious virus."

"Yeah?" Marzzarella said.

"Yeah," said Lucas. "If I was a betting man, I'd say Carolina by at least twenty."

Marzzarella grunted with satisfaction.

"Same here, boss," Ricky Ridgeway spoke up from East Rutherford, where St. John's was playing Duke in the East Regional. "Not a thing to worry about. It's a cinch...Duke's players ain't all they're cracked up to be." He chuckled. "And tomorrow morning I'm flying back to Kentucky to take care of another little matter."

Marzzarella grunted again, motioned for Super Dave to bring him a cigar, then waited for him to light it. "Little Pete...we ain't heard from you."

"Right," Little Pete said from Lexington and the South Regional. "You know Michigan…once they was called the Fab Five—"

"Is that a fact," Marzzarella said.

"Yeah, the Fab Five." Little Pete sounded smug. "But Friday, tomorrow, after they play Notre Dame, nobody's gonna call 'em the Fab Five any more. The Fuck-Up Five will be more like it. Whole starting lineup's either down with the flu or on the take." He laughed. "Beats me. I just can't figure it out."

Marzzarella took a long pleasurable drag on the cigar, blew out the smoke, and smiled at Super Dave, then at the speakerphone. "You guys seem to unnerstand the kind of work I want. A few more days, just a few, and after that it's all gravy."

None of the other four said anything, waiting.

"One thing you can count on," the powerful gravelly voice came over the wires. "You ain't gonna regret doing this job right. I reward good work, that's how I stay in business. Just remember, no screw-ups. None. Stay low, don't take no unnecessary risks. If anything comes up, you know how to reach Super Dave. That's it."

He clicked the speakerphone, disconnecting the call.

Super Dave motioned to another phone at the corner of the table. "Mr. X is waiting for you."

Marzzarella rolled in his chair, picked up the receiver, held it to his ear. Ten minutes later when he hung up, a great smile bisected his face. His cigar had gone out, and he relit it, picked up a newspaper and studied it, then turned to face Super Dave.

"David…I don't know but what you said a little too much when you talked to that rummie coach at Catholic U. Maybe he don't need to know. They're coming up against Kansas…and if I recall, a few months back Kansas ripped 'em a new asshole."

"That was early in the season," Super Dave said. "Don't worry about it, chief. Besides, the coach is already back on the sauce. As far as he knows, it was just some smart-ass reporter that gave him the dope on his girlfriend."

Marzzarella listened intently, his eyes like two augers.

Super Dave went on talking, fast, to keep from losing his confidence. "Yeah, I know Catholic U. is a wild card, and we can't take no chances with them. But if by any chance they do happen to beat Kansas, we still got two days to arrange things."

"Yeah," Marzzarella said, "arrange things." He gave a short nasty laugh. "Are you ready?"

"My middle name is ready, boss. If the coach don't take our bait, we got another card to play. And if that don't fly, we still got an ace in the hole."

"David, you fucking better have. That's all I'll say."

Dale Cutter had listened intently to the entire exchange. Some of the conversation was garbled, and he made a note to ask the technicians why the bugs weren't working any better. But he had heard names and recognized most of them. Rizzio, Little Pete, Lucas, and Ricky Ridgeway were well-known mob operatives. Every one of them had a rap sheet as long as his arm.

But he was stumped when it came to Mr. X. He'd never heard anyone called that. He racked his brain for several minutes, still couldn't come up with a face. Maybe the guy was new. Or maybe he was fresh out of the joint. Who knew. The Big Cheese had an unlimited supply of goons. Whoever he was, Dale hoped his boys had a trace on the line. Even getting a location would be a big step ahead.

He hit the intercom on his phone, waited impatiently for someone to pick up.

"You guys get a read on that last call?" His voice was sharp. "Don't tell me you didn't."

"Chill, man. We sure did. Came from Kansas."

"Kansas? What the hell is in Kansas?"

"Dorothy, I think…" The voice laughed. "…and a hell of a lot of tornadoes."

Dale studied the address for the number Mr. X had used to phone The Big Cheese: 12224 Farley, Overland Park, Kansas. He had already told San Lee to get busy and find out what was at that address—a business, a residence, whatever. The way his luck was running, it was probably a pay phone outside a liquor store.

He leaned back into his desk chair and scanned the newspaper one more time. Even though he had men watching each of the four teams named in the jumbo bets, FBI agents couldn't follow the players everywhere without arousing suspicion. Restaurants and hotel lobbies were easy enough to cover, but when the players went to their rooms and moved back and forth from hotel to arena using back entrances and service elevators, his agents were hard pressed to tail them without being noticed, and he didn't want that to happen. Not yet.

And cash was so hard to trace. Unless a player came forward to report being approached with a bribe, Dale knew he'd never crack this case. Now he wondered why he even bothered visiting campuses every year. Money was too powerful an influence to overcome. Especially to kids who were usually broke, poor kids whose only ticket of admission was playing ball, kids who'd never had much and wanted so much more than they'd had, kids who'd run their legs off playing basketball and believed they deserved a few rewards in return.

What the hell was Mr. X's connection to all this? Was he the money man? Was he just an acquaintance of Marzzarella's who happened to call? Or was he the person responsible for the entire scheme? Maybe he was bigger than The Big Cheese. But who could that be? The Big Cheese was, in Dale's mind at least, the man pulling all the strings. Dale knew one thing for sure—Mr. X wasn't Peter J. McCraken. A tail followed him everywhere he went. He couldn't take a leak without the FBI knowing about it, and any phone calls he made were now being taped.

Frustrated, Dale tossed the newspaper onto a pile of files. His break had to come soon—his window of opportunity was slowly slipping away.

"Hey, can I come in?"

Rudy's familiar face appeared in the doorway, and he walked in before Dale could invite him, eating a jelly doughnut. He sat down, unfolded his own newspaper, and started to read. "What's up?"

"What the hell does my office look like, a freaking hotel lobby?" Dare glared at Rudy, but the agent didn't notice. His head was buried in the newspaper.

"Is that all you do…eat and read sports?"

"Nah, man, I do more than that." Rudy looked up from the paper with a smile. "Every now and then my old lady has sex with me."

"You're a piece of work, man." Dale was unable to resist a grin.

"Yeah, and so is this kid here."

Dale craned his neck. "What kid?"

"This kid here. I was down the street getting doughnuts, and while I was waiting, I picked up this sports section somebody had left behind. It's an old paper, but the story's right on time. He is one tough little sucker. Listen to this."

Rudy read three paragraphs about Mike Kramer and his rise from unknown walk-on to star, then he read the part about Fletcher being out of work.

"I know that kid," Dale said, reflecting on his earlier visit to Louisville. "He is one intense player. And a damn good ball player, too, from what I recall."

Rudy licked his fingers. "Man, I feel sorry for the kid. Old man's out of work and his four younger brothers have to work before and after school. Kids, little kids. Damn, that's rough."

"Really?" Dale suddenly took interest.

"Yeah, says here he even thought about quitting during the season to go home and get a job to help out."

"They're in the tournament, aren't they?" Dale asked.

"Who?"

"Catholic University."

"Think so. Why?"

Dale rubbed his chin, studied Rudy's face. "When was that story printed?"

Rudy unfolded it, then found the date. "Couple weeks ago. Why?"

"Let me see it. I wonder why it's still floating around now."

Rudy tossed it across the desk, then extracted another doughnut from his bag. He held the bag toward Dale. "Want one?"

Dale ignored him and read the story. After several minutes, he looked back up. "If you were out to get a player to take a bribe, who would you go after?"

Rudy chewed the doughnut and pondered. "I dunno…some poor black kid, I guess."

"Or how about a poor ambitious white kid whose old man is out of work?" Dale flipped to the second page and the NCAA Tournament information. "Rudy, this is great. C.U. is in the tournament and they play Kansas, but not until tomorrow night. Get your suitcase packed. We're flying to Lexington."

When Mike answered the knock at the door of his hotel room he couldn't believe his eyes. His mother stood there—the last person on earth he expected.

"Ma…?"

She smiled. "Just wanted to see my boy take his team to the Final Four like he promised me when he was this high." Her face looked pretty, she even had on a little soft lipstick.

"I can't believe it!" He reached out, grabbed her up in his arms, and squeezed. She was in her best blue dress. She wore a green ribbon in her hair and a button on her chest with his number on it. She smelled like lilacs. He could see the bushes now, blooming every year at the side of the farmhouse.

She looked up at him and swiped a tear. "Here, take this bag. It's full of goodies. Looks like you need to add a few pounds anyhow." She put two fingers inside the waistband of his jeans and yanked. "You're getting plain skinny on me." He took the grocery bag, then looked at her in disbelief. "How in the world did you get here?"

"Your pa brought us."

"Pa came? No."

"Yes."

"I don't believe it."

"I swear. He's downstairs with your brothers."

"Gosh, Ma, the boys, too?"

"Everybody came, Mike. The entire state is talking about you."

"I can't believe it. I just can't believe it!"

"You've gone and done everything you ever told me you was going to do. Remember this?"

From out of her purse she pulled an old envelope, then unfolded a letter. She walked to a light, cleared her throat and read:

Dear God,

Someday I want to get good enough to play college basket-ball. Hopefully you can help me be as good as Michael Jordan. I promise I'll play every day. Thanks for your help.

Mike

She looked up, holding the memory in her head. "Remember when you wrote that?"

Mike couldn't answer at first. Eventually he nodded. "Yeah, I remember."

"You wrote it that night after Jordan hit that shot against the Cetics. Remember? We had gone into town to watch the game. When you came home you couldn't sleep. I had to put you on the couch to sleep, 'cause you fell asleep at the kitchen table. Next morning I found this on the table. You were so excited you forgot you even wrote it. I never did say a thing to you about the letter, because I wanted to keep it for myself. It was so cute." She gave a little laugh. "But I never could figure how you was going to mail it."

"Ma, I can't believe you. Here, let me have it back." He reached for it, but she shoved it behind her back.

"Now, now, no one but me has ever seen this."

He put his hands on his hips and let out a laugh. "Ma, even though you're so quiet, you know everything, don't you?"

She lowered her eyes, smiled, tucked the letter back in her purse. "Just the important things."

A few minutes later Carlos came in from visiting some of their other teammates.

"Ma," Mike said, "this is my friend, Carlos. He's from Mexico."

Carlos grinned, then bent at the waist. "A pleasure to meet you, Mrs. Kramer."

Her eyes inspected Carlos, jumped back to Mike. "He's so tall!"

"He's our center, Ma. They're supposed to be tall. He gets all the shots I miss."

"Nice to meet you, Carlos."

Carlos shook her hand courteously, but when he saw that she and Mike wanted to be alone he excused himself on the pretext of going to the lobby for a newspaper.

"He seems like a nice boy, Mike."

"He is. And the second best friend I've got now."

"Oh?" Her eyes questioned. "Who's your first best?"

Mike hadn't meant to let his secret slip. "Ahh, nobody. Just someone from school."

She peered over her glasses. "Just someone?"

"Yeah, just someone."

"Mike…you can't keep a secret from me. It's all over your face."

He worked hard to hold back a grin. He could never keep a secret, especially from his mother. She always read his mind.

"It's a girl, isn't it?"

"No."

"Yes, it is. I see it in your eye. Tell me her name."

He reached into the bag and took a cookie. "All right, but you can't tell anybody else, okay? Specially them four brats downstairs. Promise?"

She smiled, nodded her head.

"Her name is Savannah."

"Oh, that's such a pretty name. I like her already."

"Yep, and when you meet her, you'll like her even more. She's helped me so much."

"I'm so proud of you, Mike." She reached out and pinched his cheek. "Everyone is so proud of you back home. Every time I go into town, it takes me twice the time to get back home, 'cause everybody has to know how you are."

Mike dropped his head. "Yeah, everybody but Pa." Just knowing his old man was down in the lobby made him nervous.

"Mike…he just sold Crockett to come see you play."

"No he didn't!"

"I swear."

"I can't believe it. I used to hate the dumb hog. I can still see Pa's eyes when I accidentally let that hog get out of the pen."

Poor old Crockett, it wasn't his fault. After the old man had hit Mike with the chain, after they got Crockett back, when Mike passed by the pen heading for the house he took a handful of rocks and threw them at the animal. He was ashamed of it now.

His mother grimaced at the memory, crow's-feet deepening at the corners of her eyes. "Let it go, Mike. Your pa's—"

"Yeah, I know. His temper got the best of him, right? If I've heard you say that once, I've heard you say it a thousand times."

She shrugged her shoulders. She had no control over her husband. Only thing that ever stopped him were the times when he would drink until he passed out.

"Ma, why was Pa so mean?" He knew she wouldn't have an answer. She never did.

She closed her eyes, then walked to a chair by the window and sat down. "Honey, please, you've got to let it go." She was tired of the memories herself.

"I can't let it go, Ma. I try, but it won't go. Sometimes I wake up at nights and see him coming after me in the snow with that chain. Remember that? He hates me, I know. And all I've ever wanted was to prove to him I wasn't bad, Ma. That's why we have to win. I want Pa to be happy about me. Not always so angry."

Mike's voice cracked. For the first time, he realized that everything—all his struggles—was about trying to make his old man proud.

"Oh, honey, he's better. He's changed. In the last couple of weeks he's been the man I married. He went to Corbin looking for work, he's been out getting the garden ready and he's even…stopped drinking."

"Stopped drinking? No way."

"Yes…and I'm just as amazed as you are."

Mike sat on the edge of the bed studying her face. "Has Uncle Ben been talking to him or something?"

"Not that I know of. It just came about all of a sudden." She snapped her fingers. "And I pray it lasts."

Mike stared out between the window curtains. "Ma, I just want Pa to be happy…to once in his life tell me he loves me. How hard is that?"

"He does, Mike." She took his hand. "Whether you know it or not, you're his pride and joy. He loves you so much. Life is so strange, son. I don't know how to explain it, but your father is so, so proud of you.

"He's got demons, I know, but you aren't the cause. It's something that goes way back. Way back to when we first met and he had this dream of playing college basketball. And then you came along. And things changed. He had to work. We didn't have anything. But we had you. You, Michael. And he loves you so much. Please, believe me. You should have seen him when that big story came out about you."

Mike gritted his teeth.

"How come he never tells *me*?"

"I don't know why it's the way it is, but I know, somewhere down inside him, he would rather kill himself than to ever see you in pain. Trust me, Michael. I know it to be true."

Mike sat on the edge of the bed. "Ma, I just don't understand anything right now. When we was growing up, no one ever paid any attention to me. Remember how everyone used to make fun of me and the boys when we was in school? I do. I remember it all. Now, everybody wants to be my friend because my name is in the paper every day. I don't get it. I'm no different now than I was then."

"You have to let it all go. I know it hurts, but you're bigger than everyone else. You're different, Mike. God made you special, and he wanted something special from you in return. He's tested you all these years, and I really believe it was because he wanted you to show people that no matter who you are or where you come from, you can live your life with honor and dignity."

Mike took a deep breath, then cupped his mother's face. "I love you so much, Ma. If it wasn't for you, I wouldn't be sitting here today. And somehow, I'm gonna get us out of this mess we're in."

Most of the year Lexington was a quiet town, but when basketball season began, it became the basketball capital of the world. Bloomington, Indiana, and Chapel Hill, North Carolina, always tried to lay claim as the hoops mecca, but they were pretenders. In Kentucky loving the game of basketball was a gene implanted at birth. And during the NCAA tournament being in Lexington was like visiting Jerusalem at Easter.

Mike knew of basketball's importance to the economy of the state, but he also understood the spiritual implications as well. His aunt had her barn painted orange like a basketball. His uncle had his entire house decorated in blue and white, the colors of the Kentucky Wildcats. For months he'd been trying to explain to Carlos the importance of the game to Kentuckians, but he finally saw it wasn't something he could teach. Carlos would have to learn it. It was the only way.

Carlos and Mike got up early and walked the four blocks to Rupp Arena. Shooting practice wasn't for another hour, but they hoped getting out in the air to walk might help ease their pregame jitters. Mike saw the nervousness in Carlos's eyes; his own stomach was doing flips as well. They entered by a side door, walked through the silent concourse, then onto the court and took seats in the stands.

"You probably never heard of this place, have you?" Mike asked, scanning the banners suspended from the ceiling.

"No, Mike. I have seen more basketball courts this one year than I ever saw in my whole life in Mexico."

"Dude, this ain't your average basketball court. Some people call this place Basketball Heaven. It seats around twenty-three thousand people, and it'll be nuts tonight, believe me."

Carlos looked up and down the ranks of seats, some of them seemingly in the clouds. "Glad we don't have to sit up there." He pointed.

"It's steep," Mike said, looking up. "But it'll be a sellout. Tonight every seat in the place will be filled. In case you haven't noticed, people here in Kentucky are nuts about basketball." He stretched his legs over the seat in front of him. "This place is named after Adolph Rupp."

"Who's that?"

Mike laughed. "Don't say that too loud around the Catheads. You might get shot."

"Catheads?"

"Kentucky Wildcat fans. Get it?"

"Yeah, I guess."

"Rupp was a Kentucky coach a long time ago…he won four national championships."

"He must have been an outstanding coach to have this place named after him."

"Yeah, I think he was, at least according to my old man and my uncle. They swear by the guy. Sometimes they tell me they wish he was still around."

"Why?"

"'Cause he hated blacks. And everyone from where I come from hates blacks."

"Wow, I didn't know that." Carlos studied Mike for a moment. "Do you hate blacks?"

Mike looked at him. "Carlos, I try my best to be as different from my old man as I can. He's the most prejudiced person on the planet, so I've vowed to go the opposite direction."

"Why do you think he is like that?"

"He's ignorant, mainly. But more than anything, I think, is that he was taught to think that way. I don't really know, but I can't do anything about it, except not be that way myself."

"You're smart, Mike."

Mike closed his eyes and flicked his wrist, pretending to shoot.

"What are you doing?" Carlos was watching.

"Visualizing what it's going to be like tonight when we play Kansas."

"Does it help?"

"Yeah, at least for me it does. When I was growing up, and when my old man used to get pissed at me about something, I'd go out and shoot and visualize about being in a place like this with people screaming. It would take me away from the farm, and I'd forget about everything that was bothering me."

"Hmm…maybe it'll help me with my free throws."

Mike chuckled. "I don't know, big guy. But it's worth a try."

Carlos closed his eyes and went through the routine. "Hey, I'm getting a good feeling. I see my shots going in. I see you hitting every shot you take."

"Good, 'cause we've got a fight on our hands tonight. It'll be the toughest game so far."

Big Eddie wrote on a chalkboard. He did his best to still his shaking hand, but it was impossible. Robbie and Spoon tied and retied their shoestrings. Carlos had just returned from the toilet for the third time. Father Charles sat alone in the back of the room fingering a rosary. Mike had Hoppy retape his ankles. Q folded towels and made sure the water bottles were filled.

Two minutes remained in the Notre Dame game. The Irish were now up by thirteen. Michigan was doomed unless a miracle took place.

Big Eddie cleared his throat. "Okay guys, let's get up here. The first game is about over."

The team members, scattered throughout the big locker room, got up and moved away from the lockers to sit in chairs facing their coach. The odors of stale shoes and heat balm floated in the air. Piles of towels were stacked on a training table. Three orange Gatorade coolers sat against one wall. Father Charles sipped a cup of the liquid and paced nervously behind everyone else.

"There's not much I can tell you that you don't already know," Big Eddie said. "We've played Kansas already, so you know what to expect. They're going to play hard and try to intimidate us from the very start. So be ready. Don't do anything stupid if someone says something to you or hits you with an elbow. Be cool, let the officials handle things."

He looked around at all his players, took a deep breath. "Remember, fellas, they beat us once. Let's go out there tonight and pay 'em back. You deserve it. You've worked harder than they ever have."

The buzzer ending the current game sounded. The team stood and listened while Father Charles said a prayer. Q tossed two balls to Mike, who opened the door and led the team out to the court.

"Shit," Dale said as he shoved his cell phone into his coat pocket, kicking at the floor in a bar at the Dulles terminal. Their flight had been delayed, and that wasn't the only thing that was wrong.

"What's the matter, man?" Rudy was watching the Knights play Kansas on an overhead television set.

"That was San Lee. That number in Kansas came from a Texaco station next to some Wal-Mart. Shit. We'll never get a break in this thing."

"We might not be getting any breaks, but C.U. sure is getting a ton of them." Rudy pointed at the screen. Carlos was taking another foul shot. "Their big center has only hit twenty-five percent from the free throw line all season long, but tonight he's perfect. Check him out."

Dale turned to the screen and watched Carlos go through a torturous routine at the free-throw line, closing his eyes, flicking his wrist, and taking a deep breath before every shot.

"He looks like he's in pain."

"Kansas is the one in pain. Him and their guards are unstoppable. It's not even halftime yet, and Catholic is up by nineteen."

"Nineteen? Wow, that's unbelievable! Didn't Kansas beat them earlier in the season?"

"They did."

Dale walked closer to the screen and watched the game for several minutes. The half ended with C.U. leading by twenty-one. He walked back to Rudy, sat down, reached for some pretzels from a bowl. "What's the score of the Michigan–Notre Dame game?"

"Notre Dame romped."

"Hmm…and if C.U. wins, that means—"

"They'll play the Irish," Rudy said.

"Yeah, and an All-Catholic Regional final." Dale tossed a few more pretzels into his mouth and watched the studio host run down a list of scores. "Make sure we get a couple people watching C.U. after this game ends. Notre Dame is the team the bettor put his money on. If I know my ass from a hole in the ground, sometime between now and Sunday, one of these C.U. guys will be asked to take a dive."

St. John's and North Carolina cruised. The U.C.L.A. Bruins struggled, but won in the last two minutes. Super Dave toasted his own successes as he and his boss watched C.U. take the floor against Kansas. Super Dave studied the coach closely. The man didn't look hung-over. In fact, he looked sharp and intense.

Marzzarella had noticed it too. "Thought you said this Big Eddie clown was a boozer."

"He is, boss."

"He don't look like no boozer to me. He looks as sober as a judge."

Super Dave laughed, eager to put his boss at ease. "A judge, sober, chief? Most of 'em...well...in my experience, most judges is boozers. But it's a funny thing...how many you ever hear of getting a DUI driving home from the country club?" He laughed again, watching the powerful man's response. "Like you always say, boss, money talks."

Marzzarella just grunted.

The C.U. team matched Big Eddie's intensity, diving for loose balls, getting all the rebounds. Every time the Kansas coach inserted a player or a new tactic, Big Eddie countered with a stifling strategy. With less than two minutes left, C.U. led by ten.

Marzzarella turned to Super Dave. "Sure you ain't waited a little to late to pull them cards out of your sleeve, David? Looks like to me you're gonna need 'em quick, and need 'em bad. These C.U. pricks, they got spoiler written all over."

Super Dave swallowed, hard.

Chapter 18

"I can't believe it. Snow? In March?"

Dale was livid. An unexpected snowstorm had swept in and blanketed all of Kentucky, West Virginia, portions of Ohio, and the entire Northeast. They couldn't get into Lexington by air. Now he and Rudy had to fly into a small airport outside Cincinnati and make the rest of the trip by car.

"Want a cupcake?" Rudy asked.

"Jesus, son, is that all you do, eat?"

"No, I read sports, remember?" Rudy grinned. "Hey, c'mon, might as well eat something, Dale. We sure as hell aren't going anywhere fast in this shit."

Dale gritted his teeth. Maybe if they hurried they could get to Lexington in three hours—providing the roads were cleared. And if they didn't slide off the side of the road dodging stranded vehicles, maybe he could get to the bottom of his hunch.

As it was, he was already behind schedule. He was as sure as he had ever been of anything that the rats had done their work well. The fix was in. All the signs were there. He just didn't have the goods on the one big particular rat behind it all. And as he stared through the window at the snowflakes darting past the windshield, he knew he couldn't do a damn thing about it. A snowstorm at the end of March. What else could go wrong?

Mike pushed the covers off to get up to go to the bathroom. He stepped gingerly to the floor, then quickly fell back into bed when a cramp seized his right calf.

"Owww!"

The muscles locked up, squeezing painfully where he'd been kicked while going for a rebound. He stretched and rubbed at the ache, then waited several minutes. Finally he put his foot down again, then his other foot, and limped from bed to the bathroom like an arthritic old man.

As he relieved himself, he felt every bang and bruise he'd taken in the Kansas game. His right arm was sore. His lower back throbbed. Even his jaw was tight from a glancing elbow in the second half. But he was happy. Only one more game—just one—to get to the Final Four.

Flushing the toilet and walking back to his bed, he saw that Carlos's bed was empty. He turned to the nightstand and checked the clock. Not even eight, breakfast wasn't for another half hour. What was up with that? Carlos never got out of bed until the last minute.

Mike let it go, rummaged in his suitcase for a clean pair of socks, sat on the bed to put them on. The sun slanted through the curtains onto the black television screen, revealing a thick layer of dust. He stared at a mirror and wondered what was to come. Beating Kansas had put him just one game away from his goal. He shook his head, astonished that they'd actually gotten this far. Little ol' Catholic U. He wondered what everyone was thinking now.

He put his warmup pants on, then a gray C.U. sweatshirt over the white T-shirt he slept in. He ran his fingers through his hair, tied his shoes, then stuffed the room key into a pocket and headed downstairs. Maybe Carlos was in the lobby reading. Maybe he had gone for another walk to the small pond in the park across from the hotel. Yesterday he couldn't shut up about the ducks that he got such a kick out of feeding. That was it. He had probably saved some food from last night's Burger King and gone over to feed the ducks. Oh, well, whatever floated his boat.

The hallway was empty. Quiet. He and some other man rode the elevator down without speaking. The guy was short, with a round head and a shiny golden ponytail. His pinstripe suit looked about a size too small. Mike halfway wanted to make some remark about how sore he was, but why would a stranger care? They guy didn't even seem to notice him. Mike let the guy get off first, then followed behind, looking past a group of businessmen in suits at a lounge full of couches and stuffed chairs. When he didn't see Carlos there or in the restaurant, he checked the gift shop, then a row of pay phones next to the bathrooms. Nothing. Nowhere.

He looked around, then noticed the man from the elevator watching him over a newspaper. When he walked past the guy to go outside, the man lowered the paper and spoke. "Hey, good game last night, pal."

Mike turned and looked at the guy. "Thanks."

"Think you'll beat the Irish?" The ponytail guy smiled in a casual, friendly way.

"If we play hard." Mike turned away to head outside into the cold day.

"Hey, Mike, what's your hurry?" the man said, following.

Now Mike was suspicious. Who was this joker? The guy seemed nice enough, but why would he be following him outside?

"No hurry, man. Just looking for a friend of mine." Mike peered across the road into the park, but he didn't see Carlos on the bench where he'd sat the day before. He walked on across the street anyhow. Maybe Carlos had picked some other place today.

"Hey, Mike, slow down."

Mike kept walking until he felt the man's hand on his shoulder. He turned. "Hey, dude, think you could let it rest? I don't know who you are, and I wish you'd quit following me."

This had no effect at all. "Aw, Mike, don't you know you need your fans? Anyhow, I've got a message from your folks."

Mike halted suddenly and turned to face the guy. "A message from my folks?"

"Yeah, seems like they've come into a bit of luck. You probably heard, their landlord was about to sell the farm out from under them, but a real-estate firm has offered to help them out."

Mike was getting real bad feelings about this guy—his eyes big as tennis balls, one long eyebrow running above those big eyes. His stomach twisted with concern. Who was this ponytail clown? And if there was good news about the farm, why wouldn't Ma have told him straight up?

"Who in the hell are you, anyhow? And what do you want with me?"

"Who I am is not important. What is important is whether or not you play along."

"Play along?"

"That's right."

"Listen, dude, what the fuck are you talking about?"

"I'm talking about your future, that's what." The man had assumed an air of understanding, sympathy. A fake look, Mike knew. "Look, kid, when this tournament is over, you're gonna find yourself in some shitty job, and your parents are gonna be shuffling around, looking for a place to live. This is your chance to do something good for them."

Mike blew through his pursed lips and turned and walked away.

"Don't be stupid, kid. Why should you lose out? Why should your folks? Don't you know that everybody makes money off this tournament except the players?"

Mike stopped, but didn't turn around. He shoved his hands deep into his pockets.

"It's not only your family you'll be helping, but others are involved. A bunch of others."

Mike's stomach jumped to his throat. His heart was racing. "What others?"

"Look, don't worry about that. Just make sure your team don't win against Notre Dame, and you won't have to worry about nothing...the rest of your life."

"What others, I said?"

"Everyone, anyone who's important to you, kid. Think about it."

"There's nothing to think about." Mike stopped himself from spitting in the man's face. "You've rattled the wrong cage, dude. I'm not throwing no game, not for you or anyone. I'm gonna call the cops."

"Do that and your mother dies. You can bury her in that nice blue dress she was wearing yesterday. Look, you really don't have no choice. Think of it as wartime and you've just been drafted. You either take care of this little opportunity—"

"You bastard."

The guy was shorter than Mike, but heavier. He looked like he could throw a punch or two.

"You stay away from my family," Mike said.

"You got no say-so here, kid. I didn't fight this damn snow getting here to hear you tell me that. You will do this, like I tell you, or your family is just the starting place." The ponytailed man smiled congenially. "Think of the outstanding TV movie they can make out of your girlfriend's story. You know, she beats polio to become a wonderful ballet dancer, only to have her kneecaps shot out because her boyfriend loves basketball more than her. Touching, huh?"

Mike balled his fists, and the ponytail man reached inside his coat. "Or I can save you the trouble and just put a bullet in your shoulder. Then the NCAA will discover that there was a deed of sale out in your name for your family's farm, and the money came from a bank in South Bend. Your family loses the farm, your team's gonna lose anyway, and it's all gonna look like you tried to go back on a deal and got shot for your trouble. You're already part of this, Mikey. Sorry."

Mike tried to swallow, but a knot in his throat wouldn't let him. "I'll get the FBI after you."

"Go ahead, kid, but the investigation will still point to you...and in a few months your girlfriend will be in a terrible accident, probably never walk again. It's all gonna be your fault."

The man went on talking in a calm, low, friendly tone. "And after that, one by one, your family's gonna have the worst luck. Your mom, your old man, those kid brothers of yours. No matter where they are, they ain't never gonna know when...and you'll get to see it all.

"Oh, don't worry about yourself, now. Nothing's gonna happen to you, Mikey. Nothing but the fact that for the rest of your life, you know you could have prevented it all, just by not being such a hotshot against Notre Dame."

A hundred crazy ideas rolled through Mike's head. He wanted Fletcher to tug his rifle from the truck. He wanted Carlos to appear from somewhere and club the man over the head. He stared at the man, tried to memorize his face until the sick awareness washed over him that he couldn't forget it if he tried.

He moved to a park bench and sat down, watching the ducks in the water. "You bastard. I don't know why you're doing this to me. My whole life, all I ever wanted was to play in the Final Four. C'mon. Why me?"

"Hey, I sympathize with you, kid. If it was up to me, I'd love to see you little guys beat some of those big schools, honest...specially Notre Dame. But this is strictly business. And nothing personal. Really."

"If you don't hate me, then I guess there must be a lot of money at stake."

The ponytail man laughed. "That's what makes the world go round, kid."

Mike suddenly saw some light, a mere sliver. "Since this is strictly business, like you say, and not personal..." Mike finally was able to clear his throat, blowing small frosty clouds into the cold air. "I'd like a raise."

The man blinked. His ponytail jerked. "What?"

"Hell, the only thing I ever looked forward to in life was the Final Four. Now you tell me I have to give it up, for a shitty little farm and some insurance. Hell, what do I wind up with...nothing? A little old hill farm like that, it's not worth more than twenty or thirty thousand, even with the rattrap of a house where my folks live. Make it worth my while, and you won't have to worry about a thing this weekend."

"You're negotiating with me?" Ponytail squinted in the cold.

"Just business, right?" Mike offered a false smile. "The way I see it, you can hurt my whole family, break my girlfriend's kneecaps, but there's always the chance that someone might get caught. Authorities would ask questions. With the kind of money you obviously stand to gain, sweetening my end of it won't bust you."

"Ain't that a bitch." Ponytail scoffed. Several cars rushed by on the street.

"Yeah, apparently life's a bitch." Mike nodded, the smile on his face as sharp as the wind. "But that ain't no reason not to enjoy it. I figure my dream is worth, say, about eighty, ninety, maybe a hundred grand."

The man whistled. "You got balls, kid."

Mike shrugged. "Like you said, I really don't have any choice. So I might as well make a little profit myself."

"That's a big hunk of money."

"Yeah…and this is a big hunk of my life."

"I'll get back with you, kid." The man stood and raised a finger. "Remember, you fuck with me, you go down. Got it?"

Mike didn't answer. He didn't even turn to see the man leave. He just sat in the cold and watched the ducks paddle around the pond.

Complacency. Big Eddie could feel it as soon as he walked from the press conference to the arena where the team had two hours for a closed practice. Complacency, the archenemy of every successful team he'd ever known. Still giddy from the win over Kansas, his team had started believing what the fans were whispering in their ears.

Carlos was stretched out on the floor, his arm draped over his eyes as if he were asleep. Hoppy was at one end of the court conducting his own three-point shooting clinic, taking bets from anyone with cash. Spoon sat in a chair and listened to music through his headphones, bobbing his head, snapping his fingers to the beat.

"Jesus Christ," Big Eddie mumbled. He watched for a moment longer, then jumped onto the court, sticking two fingers in his mouth and whistling to get their attention, try to galvanize them back to a winning stance.

"Let's get down to business. And Hoppy, pull up your pants, the crack in your big ass is showing."

Everyone broke into laughter except for Hoppy, who slunk off the court, red-faced.

"Quit your damn laughing and let's get after it. Just because we beat Kansas doesn't mean shit. We've got another game tomorrow afternoon, and by God, we're not going to take it for granted. Notre Dame will kick our ass if we aren't ready." His eyes swept the court.

"Sonofabitch," Hoppy whispered to Father Charles. "He could at least congratulate these guys for once in his life." Hoppy walked to the end of the court and punted a ball into the stands.

"Hop, he's just trying to get them ready for tomorrow," Father Charles said, watching the ball bounce through the seats. "That's all."

"I don't care. He embarrassed me in front of the team. I'd never do that to him."

Father Charles turned away and wondered sometimes why he committed so much of his time to the team. Wasn't there something better he could be doing with his vocation, with his life? He was always everyone's sounding board—like a plaster saint, not regarded as a human being at all. He almost wished the season were over.

He sat down and watched the team go through passing and shooting drills. Mike's passes had all the crackle of limp lettuce. Carlos couldn't hit a shot. Neither could Spoon. The chaplain stared out to the middle of the court where Big Eddie stood—fuming, he could see. It could only be a matter of seconds before Mount Eddie would erupt.

"Hoppy!" Big Eddie yelled. "What in the hell did you feed these guys last night after the game? Quaaludes? Every one of 'em is in another world."

Hoppy stood at the end of the court not saying a word.

"Did you tape their ankles too tight or something?"

"No sir," Hoppy replied meekly.

"I've never seen such pussies in my life. We got a game to play, and they're acting like they're already national champs. I don't like it. I don't like it at all."

Big Eddie's attention zeroed in on Mike. During the ten minutes he'd been watching him, the kid hadn't hit a shot, hadn't done anything to rev up the team. Normally Mike would have been the one jumping everyone and telling them to get moving, but today something was different. His eyes were flat. His face was drawn, as if he hadn't rested. He even had his shirttail hanging out. Something rarely seen with Mike.

A ball rolled toward the coach. He picked it up and met Carlos at the out-of-bounds line. "Carlos…what's wrong with everybody?"

"Tired," the big man said.

"Tired? How can you guys be tired? We're this far from going to the Final Four!" His fingers were spread an inch apart. "Back when I was playing I'd have given my left nut to get this far."

Carlos didn't respond.

"Do me a favor, Carlos. Find out what's eating Mike, and I'll take care of the others. We can't be messing around. I want to win. Don't you?"

Carlos nodded, then turned with a jump when Big Eddie blew his whistle and yelled.

Mike strolled off the floor slowly, studying the ground as he walked. His entire life he'd dreamed of playing in the Final Four, yet now, with his golden opportunity before him, he wouldn't be able to do it. He walked into the locker room without saying a word, then sat alone while the rest of the team showered down.

When everyone but Carlos was done and had dressed and gone out, Mike undressed too, walked into the shower, let the water pour over him trying not to think. Ten minutes later he was out and sat back down, then decided to shave. Carlos was still futzing around over in front of his locker, reorganizing his gym bag, tieing his shoes, fooling with his belt.

When Mike reached into his own locker for his shaving kit, the weight of it felt funny. He opened it, wondering if someone had played a joke on him and stuffed a wet towel in it. If so, not funny today. Guys were always playing stupid jokes. Especially Hoppy. He was the king of practical jokers.

"Jesus Christ." His eyes opened big, real big. So big they almost hurt.

He was staring at a plastic-wrapped bundle of $500 bills. There were so many he started to shiver.

"Hey, Mike," Carlos said across the way, "get dressed and we can go back and feed those ducks again. I think it's good luck."

Good luck? Luck was the last thing going for him. Mike quickly closed the shaving kit and ducked with it into a toilet stall. He counted the money as fast as he could, recounted it when he couldn't comprehend the amount.

Fifty $500 bills—twenty-five thousand dollars. The most money he'd ever seen in his life. And a note was tucked inside a rubber band around the stack of bills:

Mike — You'll get more when you follow through.
Have a good day, pal.

"Oh shit, oh shit, oh shit." A bead of sweat popped on his forehead. Then another. And another. This was really happening.

He started to sweat under his arms. On his forehead. Even his feet. What was he going to do? He had just been messing with the guy. Oh shit, oh shit, oh shit. The police were going to get him. The NCAA would suspend him. Big Eddie, oh God, Big Eddie would kill him. And then he would have to face…Fletcher.

"Hey, amigo, c'mon." Carlos tapped on the stall. "I'm ready to go. You okay in there? The ducks are waiting."

"Yeah, give me a second," Mike answered, wishing he could wiggle through the drain in the floor.

He rewrapped the bills in the plastic, leaned back against the wall, then hit the flush knob. He watched the water swirl, thinking maybe he should have flushed the money he still held in his hands.

Oh shit, oh shit, oh shit.

"You okay, Mike?" Carlos asked again, as the two walked back to the hotel.

Mike's face was white as the snow, his eyes stones. He coughed, then again and again. "Must've just had something last night after the game that didn't settle, that's all. I'll be okay once I get back to the room." Could Carlos tell he was scared? Scared to death?

Nearing the park Carlos was acting like a kid just before Christmas. "Mike…you want to come with me?" He jerked a thumb toward the pond where the ducks were gabbling excitedly.

They'd already come to connect the big guy with food, and he wouldn't disappoint them. Before the game, he'd bought a loaf of bread at a quick mart across the street from the arena.

But when Mike looked at the park he saw that blond ponytail again, heard the guy's threats against his family and friends. Saw that awful long eyebrow. "No, Carlos, you go on. I'll head back to the room."

Carlos watched Mike turn and walk toward the hotel. "I'll get you some medicine from Hoppy as soon as I'm finished, okay?"

Mike waved, but he didn't turn around. He entered the hotel through a side door and scanned the lobby for the ponytail, hoping to hell the guy was just a bad dream, knowing he was not.

After eating a meal and watching video of Notre Dame with the team, Big Eddie decided to avoid the party atmosphere in the lobby. He had the beginnings of a headache. Though in practice the team hadn't shown all the signs of being ready to play the Irish, he had a hunch that was changing now. Feeling just a shade more confident, he took the elevator to his room. He'd watch a movie or catch an NBA game. Anything to distract him and help calm his growing nerves.

Twenty minutes into a Bruce Lee movie somebody knocked on his door. He sighed, hoping it wasn't some television crew wanting one last interview, and rose slowly to answer. But it was Penny, wearing a tight black knit dress that stopped well above her knees and made Big Eddie's eyes bulge. A referee's whistle dangled in a strategic spot on her chest. She really knew how to dress to suit her figure. Voluptuous as hell. Damn!

"Want to buy some Girl Scout cookies?" she said sweetly, her blonde hair falling over one eye.

"Oh, hi." He was still hung up on her chest. "Cookies, is that what you call 'em?"

She noticed everything he'd tried not to show. "It's that bad, huh?"

He didn't answer.

"You want to talk about it?"

He raised his eyes to hers. "Do you?"

"Will it make a difference about whether we stay together?"

"Is that something you're interested in?" His voice cracked from tiredness and anxiety.

She gave him a puzzled look. "I thought that's what we were doing all along."

He nodded. "Would you like to come in for a drink? Got Bruce Lee on the tube."

She smiled. The tawny lipstick gleamed against her pale skin. "How about coffee instead?"

"You know…that does sound better."

Penny could help him feel better, he knew she could. From a chair next to the bed she watched him get the coffeepot going in the kitchenette. He looked up once while she was focused on the television, checking out her legs. All kinds of things were being thought in the quiet of the moment.

"Here you go. Freshly brewed. Just like back home."

She sipped the coffee and smiled. "Mm…very well done. I didn't know you were so talented."

"Hell yes. Besides coaching, making coffee is one thing I know how to do. My grandmother lived with us when I was growing up. She was a coffee fiend, and she showed me how to make it right."

He went over to lounge on the bed again.

"Penny…I hate to ask you this, but I feel like I have to…This scumbag reporter, the one who's threatening to reveal…you know, everything from the past…"

"Yes, what about it?"

"Well, I just need to know how you feel about it, that's all."

She was quiet for a few minutes, then finally pulled her shoulders back. "I think there's only one way to turn this around."

He looked over his cup. "Yeah, how's that?"

"Well, you know how some reporters are, right?"

He rolled his eyes. "Unfortunately, yeah. Most of 'em are jerks."

"What if we go to a respected reporter together, you know, with one of the big papers…then just tell him or her the story." She hesitated. "Unless you want to try and ride this out quietly."

He raised his eyebrows, shrugged. "Hey, this is your call, honey." Big Eddie reached for her hand. "But if we do this, seems to me we'll have to stick together from now on."

A hint of a smile flitted over her face. "Is that a proposal, Coach?"

He got up from the bed and walked to her. She expected a kiss. Instead, he picked up the whistle hanging around her neck, blew it softly, and grinned. "It's been a long day. Time for the team to hit the showers. What do you think?"

"Anything you say, Coach. I'm a team player."

The black knit dress slid silently onto the floor.

Chapter 19

Dale kicked snow off his boots as he entered the Hyatt Regency. His drive had taken longer than the anticipated three hours. Fog, snow, heavy wind—and Rudy's incessant talking and eating. If anyone had asked him how he was doing right now, he would have screamed until he was blue in the face. Luckily no one asked.

Rudy followed behind, already chewing on some fudge he'd picked up in the gift shop. Dale couldn't figure why the guy didn't weigh three hundred pounds.

"Good golly Miss Molly," Rudy said, blinking at all the commotion in the lobby. "Reporters and TV crews thick as liars at a lawyers convention. Hey, check out the babe in the green dress by the phones."

Dale shook his head. The desk clerk, some college student no doubt, had just informed him that since he was late arriving, they had moved someone else into his room. He tried to explain the snow delay, unavoidable. She wasn't listening. But there was a single room next to the kitchen if he wanted it.

"I'm with the FBI...and there's two people." Dale offered his sincerest smile.

The desk clerk smiled back just as sincerely. "Would you like me to call another hotel...in Louisville?"

He and Rudy jammed into the single room with one bed, one pillow, one blanket, and one big window that leaked cold air like hell.

After unpacking, Dale sat staring at a list of all the schools playing in the tournament. The four teams from what he now thought of as The Bet were highlighted in yellow. He shook his head, hardly able to believe this was college sports, and specially not basketball. The sport was so clean, so wide-open. Out there in the court everything was in plain view. How could this be?

"What d'you know, Rudy...looks like all four of the teams are gonna get in. This is really happening. I still can't believe it."

Rudy popped his knuckles and stretched out on the bed, nibbled on the rest of his fudge. "What do I know? I know it's happening, man."

"Rudy...it was just a figure of speech."

"Figure of speech hell. Injuries, crazy sicknesses...you've read the stories. It's gotta be, man. You're right, just like always."

They went back over what they knew. Several minor injuries had slowed secondary but important players in three of the games. Key turnovers at crucial moments turned the tide in others. Even a couple of officials' calls were questionable, but Dale knew that was like grasping at the wind. Refs wouldn't throw games. No way.

He thought about it for a moment, then dismissed it to leaf through the postgame interviews. Even now, with all the signs pointing to go, he still didn't have anything that would hold up in court. He was operating primarily on intuition, and what little information he did have was so volatile, so ephemeral, he hadn't even gone to the NCAA yet. He knew how they would take it if Dale was wrong—accuse him of ruining the sport for years to come.

But what if he was right? What if? He knew the rules—do nothing until you have absolute proof you're right.

The newspaper Rudy had shown him with Mike Kramer's picture caught his attention again. It was vertical in a back pocket of his briefcase. Its corners were as tattered as his tired mind. Catholic University was the perfect media dark horse—an overachieving point guard and an underskilled big man with a huge heart. A Damon Runyon story if there was one. If the barracudas among the reporters were going after any team, it had to be this one. His instincts told him so.

"C'mon, Rudy," Dale said, his dark eyes snapping back to life. "Let's go downstairs to the lobby. Maybe we can make a difference somewhere, somehow."

Through the double-paned window Carlos watched, palms resting gently on his knees, as a light snowfall began again. The sun had been down for hours, but against the white landscape a moon just past being full painted the night almost as bright as day. He could see ripples on the pond where the ducks were diving for something below the surface, a few kids on sleds enjoying the last moments of a long winter, a white mist floating above the warming earth as far as he could see.

Juarez was never this beautiful, even on a perfect spring morning when the blooms of desert wildflowers sprinkled the land. For that matter, nothing in his past was as awesome or as splendid as what he was watching now. He thought about the orphanage, the *barrio*, the bums on the corner. He was glad he had left home.

With the parking lines covered by snow, cars in the hotel lot were angled any old way—BMWs, Mercedes, Saabs. Rich people's cars. Carlos still found the attention given to the game of basketball in the States bewildering. When he was told he had a chance to attend college and play basketball, he had never dreamed people took the game so seriously.

When they handed him a free pair of Nikes and all the other practice gear he needed, then came back and gave him a place to sleep and eat, plus books for class, he had to pinch himself. It all made him feel guilty, especially since no one back home had such treasures. People here—young people, college students— didn't know how lucky they were. He felt like telling Mike that right now. But he held his tongue. Mike wasn't the one to tell, considering his background and the odd mood he'd been in the past couple of days.

Carlos devoured the remains of the Domino's pizza he'd brought in, then turned away from the window and started surfing the channels. He was sad, feeling distance between him and Mike that he'd never felt before. He wondered whether it was something he'd done, although he couldn't recall anything. Whatever it was, he decided to try and penetrate the shield.

"Hey, hombre, what do you want to watch?"

Mike didn't answer, just stared blankly at a book in his hands, his chest rising and falling steadily. Not even a tremor in his hands revealed the slightest thing.

"What book are you reading?" Carlos asked.

"Grisham," Mike mumbled.

"Any good?"

Mike shrugged. "Yeah, but I can't concentrate."

Carlos stared at his friend. Perhaps the stress of tomorrow's game was already eating at him. Probably. Only an athlete understood the agony of sitting in a hotel room bored stiff, knowing you would soon have to go out and perform in front of twenty thousand people whose only connection to you was a ticket. They never saw the tension that made a man throw up before a game. Pressure could get to a player before game time.

Carlos knew, for in the last weeks it had got to him. His stomach flipped and rumbled, and his guts turned to water, sending him to the toilet every ten minutes. Each person handled it a little differently. Spoon always sat alone and concentrated. Robbie cracked jokes. Big Eddie chewed gum, going through two packs before the ball was ever tipped off. Mike chewed his nails, then went out to the court to get a feel for the environment and the baskets.

Carlos found a wrestling match on TV, knowing Mike loved its action. "Look, Mike, this will wake you up. It's so fake, it's funny." Carlos guffawed as one wrestler slammed the other into a turnbuckle.

Mike didn't laugh. His eyes were still fixed on the pages of the book.

Carlos tried a few more questions without getting any answers until finally he had had enough of the weirdness. "What the hell is the matter with you, amigo? You act like you've seen a ghost or something. You and Savannah have a fight? What's wrong, my friend?"

Mike yawned, picked something out of his teeth, turned his head. "Nothing's the matter with me." His voice came out testy. "What's the matter with you?"

"*Nada*, roommate, nothing at all. But there is something the matter with you. I know, I have lived with you for almost a year. You act like you're on another planet."

Mike turned his back.

Carlos tried another tack. "Say, amigo, did I ever tell you about my life at home, before the orphanage? My mother, she was always asleep or drunk, and one day I walked in on her and one of her boyfriends. The guy beat me up. He didn't like me disturbing his pleasure."

Mike said nothing.

Carlos went on. "I just went and sat out behind the little shack where we lived, crying. Another boy, shorter than me but older, he came and asked me what happened. I was too ashamed to tell him, but the kid understood. And you know what, Mike?"

No answer.

"This older kid comes back and gives me a jacket to keep warm for the night. True kindness, no? The next morning, when the man came stumbling out of our house, still drunk, five boys jumped him and beat him up."

He hoped he was getting through, yet Mike said nothing.

"The kid who gave me the jacket, he told me that now I was one of them. None of those kids had a real home or family, they had to be a family for each other. He was a tough kid, tougher than I would ever be. But he remembered what it was like."

Finally Mike spoke. "What happened to him?"

"Dead." Sadness colored Carlos's voice. "A group from the next district came into ours, and there was a big fight. I was across the alley from him, too far away, when two older guys knifed him. After that was when the priest saw me in court and arranged for me to go to the orphanage."

Mike laid down his book. "That's tough."

Carlos shrugged. "The way I see it, a basketball team is not much different from a gang. We got no parents here most of the time, and yeah, we're older, but we have to stick together."

"I appreciate that."

"Do you?" Carlos stood over him. "I'm not on the other side of the alley now, hermano. Tell me what is going on."

Mike turned back over and stared at the ceiling. Not even Fletcher made him feel as sick at heart, as scared as he felt now. "If you had a dream in life, Carlos, and someone told you that you couldn't pursue that dream, what would you do?"

Carlos hit the mute button on the remote and turned his full attention to Mike. "Before I met you, I probably would have settled for whatever came. Now that I know you, I would fight until I die. Why are you asking this?"

Mike took a deep breath and rolled over on his side. "Somebody…maybe several somebodies…don't want me to fulfill my dream."

"What are you talking about? Who would do that?"

"I don't know if I should tell you."

Carlos frowned, hurt that Mike was afraid to trust him. "Hey, I thought—"

"This could get you killed, friend."

"You sure you are not sick, Mike? You're talking crazy."

Mike threw his feet over the side of the bed. "I'm not sick, and I'm not crazy, man. Someone…a stranger…a short guy with a blond ponytail…came to me and asked me to…throw our game against Notre Dame." The last words came out through gut-wrenching pain.

Carlos cocked his head to one side. "You mean lose…on purpose?"

Mike nodded, his voice hollow. "Here, take a look."

"*Jesu María!*" Carlos crossed himself, then stared with disbelief at the shaving kit full of money. No way. No way there was this much money in the world.

He was quiet for several minutes. Finally he patted Mike on the shoulder. "Come."

"Come? Where?"

"This is not something we can fight alone. You need more help than I can give you."

"No, are you crazy?" Mike shook off his hand. "This isn't some *barrio* where you can go one-on-one with someone. These guys are like wolves…you never know when they will come at you."

"So you will let us lose?"

"What else can I do?"

"Take yourself out of the game."

"It's the same thing, isn't it?"

"No." Carlos's eyes were piercing. "We will at least have a chance—five on five. With you trying to make us lose, that makes it four against six."

Mike waved him off. "I don't know, Carlos. Hell, do you know how much money the college makes off of games like this?" Mike walked to the window and looked out. "Do we owe them so much?"

"Yes. Without Father Francisco, I would be dead like my friend." He walked over and took Mike's arm. "Come on, Mike, please, there is one person I know we can talk to about this."

"Who?"

"Father Charles."

Mike groaned.

Carlos walked to the door and opened it. "Are you coming?"

"Good God Almighty," Mike said, turning from the window and walking after him. He carried the shaving kit in his hand.

Carlos's knock barely brushed the door—soft, as if he didn't really want to disturb anyone. Mike lowered his head and stared at the carpet between his feet. Why hadn't he just run from the man in the park? Run—run—run!

"Who is it?"

"It's Carlos, and Mike."

"Hold on, I'll be right with you."

Father Charles answered the door in a T-shirt. Carlos asked the priest if he could hear Mike's confession.

"Isn't it kind of late?"

"Trust me, padre, it's very important," Carlos said.

"All right, then, come on in."

Carlos waited at the door until Mike was inside the room, then eased out and left.

"Never can find anything when I pack," Father Charles fussed, rummaging through his suitcase. "Ah, here it is."

He unfolded his stole and moved to the small table against the window where Mike had already taken a seat. The priest arranged the stole around his neck, then turned to Mike. He saw the dark rings under the heavy eyes, the unshaven face.

"You look like the devil."

Mike gazed out the window. "I feel like his brother."

"So, what is it, son? The Lord is all ears."

Mike took a deep breath. "Are we going to do it here?"

"Do you have a better place in mind?"

"No, I guess not." At least no one else could hear what he was getting ready to say.

Mike crossed himself. "Bless me, Father, for I have sinned." Quickly he told the priest of his predicament. Father Charles closed his eyes and asked Mike to repeat a Hail Mary with him. Then he removed his stole and laid it on the table.

"I don't think you're the one who's sinned, Mike. But someone else certainly has, and it looks like we've got a big, big problem."

"You won't tell anyone, will you, Father?" Mike asked, searching the priest's face.

"I can't promise you that yet, Mike. We have to find a way out of this."

"There is no way. If we go to the police, Savannah and my family will get hurt—bad."

"Just because he says that, Mike, we really don't know for sure." Father Charles looked out the window. "It could be a bluff, one powerful enough to mess up your game. Think about it...this character could be an alumnus from Notre Dame. This stuff happens all the time. I read recently where someone once called during a Bulls game and said Michael Jordan's mom was in the hospital. The other team won, because Jordan was so worried the entire second half."

"This guy scared me, Father. I can't say why, exactly, but I know he meant what he said. Can you guarantee my family won't get hurt?"

"No."

"Then you agree that I have to do this?"

"No."

Mike sighed. "Oh, and there is one other minor problem, Father."

"What's that?"

Mike handed him the shaving kit. The priest opened it and pulled out the money, turned over the stack of bills in his hands, then handed it all back to Mike.

"Son," Father Charles said slowly, "For once in my life I feel completely at a loss. I've studied the Bible, the lives and examples of hundreds of martyrs and saints. I wish I could pull out one specific example that would guide you. But at the moment my mind is blank."

He tried a laugh, but it didn't work. "And the blessed saints know there's no mention of the NCAA tournament in the catechism."

"Maybe this is a secular question, not a religious one."

Father Charles shook his head. "One of the mistakes priests make is to think everything is religious, and one of the mistakes most laity make is to believe everything is secular. But our religion is meant to bind together all the parts of our lives."

"So what's the answer?"

"Everything in life has spirit. Find the real spirit of this question—for you and your family—and you will find your answer."

He put his hand on Mike's shoulder. It was soft and comforting. "I also believe that if you pray for guidance tonight, an answer will arrive tomorrow."

After three hours of sitting in his room and flicking the channels back and forth, Mike threw on his jeans and headed for the hotel lobby, then hailed a cab. He had to do something to get his mind back where it needed to be: on basketball, not prayer. He asked the cab driver where he could find a good pickup game. The Jamaican cabbie nodded and drove him to a small YMCA in the black section of town. When they got there, Mike jumped out and threw the man twenty of his pier diem. Mr. Ponytail would never miss it. Anyhow, it wouldn't matter. Tomorrow he would probably be dead.

Inside the Y a game was going on, just as the cabbie had said. Mike moved up into the bleachers and watched the action from a splintered bench. Two fat women in awful Lycra tights waddled by every five minutes on the oval track. He feared the track might collapse, until he remembered that was the least of his worries.

He studied the basketball action carefully, contrived possible plays the players never saw, never even thought about. When the game stopped, he ambled down to the floor and picked up a lopsided stray ball. In spite of the shape it was in, he had no trouble controlling it. Putting it through the round hole ten feet above his head was even less trouble. He found the three-point line and hit five shots in a row, missed one, then hit ten consecutive. The game was so natural to him now. So easy to play. So easy to see.

"Hey, closing time, my friend."

A dark-skinned janitor in overalls stood in the door leaning on a wide dry mop. Mike tossed five more threes through the rim. The janitor flicked the lights on and off.

"That's it, Pistol Pete."

"Can I shoot while you work, please?"

The janitor shrugged and began to push the mop around the edges of the gym floor. "Sure, I guess so. Why not."

For twenty minutes Mike continued shooting, missing only two threes the entire time.

The janitor had been watching. Finally he stopped pushing, walked over, smiled. "I thought I recognized you. You're that kid who plays for C.U., ain't you?"

Mike pretended not to hear. Two more threes ripped through the net.

"You got a hell of a stroke, boy. I used to shoot like that."

Mike tossed him the ball and took the mop. "Let me see, Gramps."

The janitor arched a shot that fell a foot short.

"Here, take the mop back. You're all talk."

"No, wait, let me get loose." The janitor's next shot missed again, but he followed with five consecutive darts through the center of the rim. "See, I still got it, son. Once you got the stroke, you always got the stroke."

"That's pretty good," Mike said, impressed. "Who'd you play for?"

The janitor wiped a thick sweat from his forehead. "Played for a small school up in Ohio years ago called Rio Grande. Look it up, we were undefeated."

"What year?"

"Seventy-one, beat 'em all."

The guy was for real. "Yeah, how many did you average?"

"Seventeen my senior season."

"Did you do anything after that? NBA? Europe?"

The janitor only shook his head. "Nope, just went back home and drank beer with my brother."

"How come?"

"I don't know. Just did. Never really had any guidance, I guess. Never listened to anyone. Never even got my degree." He laughed, the embarrassment of it all forgotten a long time ago. "Always thought playing hoops would take care of me forever. But, son, I was so wrong."

Mike took the ball back and held it under his arm. "What would you do if you could do it over?"

"I don't know, really. Guess I would have taken my homework a little more serious…and I think I would have dove for every loose ball."

"Dove for every loose ball, really?"

"Hell yeah. That's how you win. You work just a little harder than the next guy. I let too many loose balls go. Should have gotten my knees scratched up a little more."

The man was remembering, tugging at a scraggly beard. "Oh, and I think I would have just played the game."

"Played the game?"

"Yeah, I think I would have just gone out and had fun. Enjoyed the game a little more, listened to everyone tell me how to do things a little less. Basketball is such a simple game. It's everyone else who makes it so damn difficult."

Mike nodded, understanding exactly what he was saying. They talked for another half hour. Before they were through, basketball was only a backdrop for the real lessons the man had to share.

"Listen, son, let old Jackson here tell you one final thing."

"Yeah, what?"

"Tomorrow, when you get out on that floor, think of all the great lessons, the great friends, the great people you've met along the way.

Understand?" The man's left eye closed, and he glared at Mike out of his right, like Long John Silver.

Mike nodded. "Okay."

"Good, then I want you to forget about all of that crap and remember what first attracted you to the game. What made you keep coming back day after day, year after year. Go out there and play the game for that reason, and for that reason alone. And no matter what happens, you'll never go wrong."

Mike chewed his lip. "Thanks, Jackson. You've helped me a lot tonight, if you didn't know it." He handed the man his mop back, shook his hand, rolled the ball softly to the wall.

"Any time, son. Stop by any time you're in town."

Mike went out into the night, wondering if he'd be able to find another cab that late in that side of town. But one came along, to his relief, and he flagged it for his ride back to the hotel.

"Your luck must be running good tonight," the soft-spoken black driver said. "I was on my way home, going off duty, but when I seen you come out of the Y something said to me a decent-looking white kid's got no business this side of town this time of night. That's how come I stopped. You one of them basketball boys here for the tournament?"

"You got it," Mike said. "I appreciate you stopping. All of a sudden I'm plumb worn out. Hyatt Regency, that's where I'm headed."

Two friends in one night, two strangers who became friends. Something in both men's simple words struck a chord. He suddenly felt at peace with himself. Before the driver got to the hotel Mike had dozed off.

In his jeans and sweatshirt, Dale looked like any other basketball fan in town for the tournament. The only thing lacking was a cold beer, and as he searched the lobby for Rudy he saw his partner walking toward him holding two sixteen-ounce cups of suds, splashing a good bit onto the hotel carpet.

"For crying out loud, Rudy! What in the hell are you doing?"

"Hey," he whispered, handing Dale his cup, "if we're going to do a little surveillance, we've got to look the part, right? And after what we went through today to get here, we deserve it."

Rudy tossed his beer back within minutes. Well, maybe he had a point. The trip had been the bitch from hell, their room at the hotel running a close second. The crowd was made up of college kids and alumni, all dressed in green and white, having a good time getting real loud and real drunk. Two girls, all of twenty, sat at the bar and sang the school's fight song. Soon the entire crowd followed their lead.

"Check it out," Dale said, nodding at a group standing around Eddie Cantrell. "Recognize those guys over there with Big Eddie?"

Rudy wiped the suds from one side of his mouth. "I'll be damned...that's Dick Vitale and Bill Walton. Wonder what they're talking about?"

"Vitale's doing all the talking," Dale said.

"That's the problem with the dude. He talks when he should be listening."

A group of autograph seekers moved around the group. Flash-bulbs went off. Big Eddie somehow escaped the growing horde as the group drew in around the other two.

"C'mon, Rudy," Dale said. "Let's go over and see the coach while we've got a chance. Maybe he's seen something funny that could help us."

"Get real, Dale. If he did, you think he'd tell us?"

"Maybe, it's worth a try."

Dale crammed his cup into a big plant tub, then walked straight to the coach before he could get away. "Coach Cantrell." He extended his hand, flashed a big smile. "Dale Cutter."

Big Eddie threw his hands back like a hold-up victim. "Hey, Dale, you can't arrest me! Now Vitale over there—he's the one impersonating a basketball expert."

Dale chuckled. "No arrest, sir. Just thought I'd say hey and wish you luck tomorrow against Notre Dame."

The coach sighed. "Well, thanks, because we're gonna need it. Notre Dame's got everything going their way right now. They beat a damn good Michigan team, and I think we're gonna have our hands full, for sure."

Dale wanted to come right out and ask him if he'd noticed anything strange with his team or any others, but he eased into the question instead. "You've done a good job since I last saw you guys."

"I've worked their asses off, that's for sure."

"Everyone healthy?"

"Physically, yeah." Big Eddie sighed again. "Mentally, we'll wait and see about that."

"Players giving you fits, huh?"

"Nah, not really. Nerves, I guess. Not surprising with all the tension building up to the Final Four."

The strained tone in Big Eddie's voice told Dale something was definitely not right. "How d'you mean?"

"It's nothing, I'm sure. Boys are just a little bit rattled. They'll settle down when the game starts tomorrow."

"Anyone in particular?"

"Well, I can tell you, seeing as you aren't one of these reporter jerks. It's my guard, Kramer. He's walking around like a whore in church. I think it's just all the commotion, the newspapers, the TV. They're driving us all nuts."

"Wouldn't be anything else, would it?"

Big Eddie stared straight at Dale, working a piece of gum in his mouth. "Like what?"

Dale shrugged, playing it casual. "I don't know. Has he got a girlfriend? That would do it."

Big Eddie let out a bellylaugh. "Ain't that the truth...ain't that the truth! Not only do women weaken the legs, they make shit of the brain."

More autograph seekers suddenly gathered around Big Eddie, ending any kind of conversation. Dale was quickly pushed to the side.

"Good luck, Coach," Dale said, winking, giving him a thumbs-up. "Love to see you in the Big Dance next weekend."

"Did he tell you anything?" Rudy asked when Dale came back.

"Maybe, just maybe…I'm not sure. He said the Kramer kid seemed spooked, but that could be for a lot of reasons. Let's keep on it. Something will give soon. I can feel it."

Big Eddie took the elevator alone to his floor, relieved to get away from all the fans. He wiped the sweat from his forehead, got off, then decided to stop in for a word with Father Charles. The door was cracked, so he walked in without knocking. The chaplain was sitting up in bed in a red flannel nightshirt with a light over his shoulder, reading an Andrew Greeley mystery.

"Hey, got a minute? I like your nightie, by the way."

Father Charles looked up from a deep fix. "Sure. Can't sleep either, eh?"

"You got that right. My stomach feels like ten Tasmanian Devils on speed."

Big Eddie flipped the curtains back and watched the snow whipping, felt the wind rattling the window. "Snow's coming down harder now. Can't even see the moon anymore. Can you believe the weather? Snow. In March. I guess this is one reason they call it March Madness."

He let the curtains drop, then sank into on one side of a loveseat, resting his feet on the end of the bed.

"Maybe it's an omen, Eddie," the priest said, folding his arms across his belly.

"What, that we're gonna get buried by a blizzard of threes tomorrow?"

"No, maybe the other way around."

"I don't know. The team seems worried as hell. Especially Mike. He's been out to lunch."

The priest closed his book, wondering when he'd ever get to the solution of the crime. He considered telling Big Eddie about the man who gave Mike the money, but the bags under Big Eddie's eyes told him the coach didn't need any more burdens right now.

"You're just thinking too hard, that's all. Mike'll be fine tomorrow. He always rises to the occasion. Remember when he was a freshman and Henderson knocked him down and called him a punk?"

Big Eddie grinned. "Yeah, I do. He went nuts the rest of the practice and scored on everyone."

Big Eddie took a deep breath, then ran his hand slowly through his hair. "I need a stiff drink, Chuckie. That might help. Got one around?"

"Just a tiny bit of church wine, for emergency communions."

Father Charles took his glasses off, stuck the earpieces in his mouth. "You don't need a drink. It's just been a long time since we've been here. Nerves, that's all it is Eddie. Nerves."

"Yeah, maybe you're right."

"I know I am." Father Charles smiled. "Not many people gave us a shot in hell to get here, you know. Most of 'em said we wouldn't win fifteen games. Remember?"

Big Eddie nodded.

"Be proud of what you've accomplished. Enjoy the moment. Might not ever come again."

The coach closed his eyes, then yawned. "You're absolutely right about that. Lately we've come this far 'bout as often as a snow in March." Big Eddie stood and stared out the window again, watching the fat flakes fall, caking the tops of cars. He turned and headed for the door. "Say a long and loud prayer for us tonight, Chuckie. Something tells me we're gonna need a miracle to win tomorrow."

Father Charles waited until the coach left the room, then said, "Amen."

Chapter 20

Mike came out a little late, after Q had finished taping his ankles. He stepped onto the court for shooting practice as nervous as a long-tailed cat in a room full of rocking chairs. He thought about what the janitor had told him, but it wasn't working right now. Almost time to play. He checked the corners of Rupp Arena, sure Ponytail was watching him from a dark corner somewhere.

The rest of the team was split up at the two different baskets, working on shots from different angles. Mike did a couple of laps around the perimeter of the court to shake out his nervousness, then grabbed a ball off the rack at half court. He fell into a crip-line at the top of the key and took a couple of shots that clanged viciously off the back of the rim.

"Say, amigo," Carlos said after Mike had missed every one, "are you okay?"

Mike nodded. "Don't worry, I'm saving 'em."

Mike looked around again. He didn't see any ominous faces. Just the same, he would keep his eyes open. Wide open.

Big Eddie ran the team up and down the floor until they broke a sweat, then had the scout team run through Notre Dame's offense and defense. Before the allotted ninety minutes of practice were up, he had them shoot free throws.

After that the buzzer sounded and Big Eddie called the team together. He stared at the floor for a minute, thinking about what he was going to say.

"I'm proud of you guys," he began. "We've been through a lot this year. You guys have done everything I've asked of you and more. It's been a privilege to coach this team. Everyone sitting around me knows what we have to do. I don't think I even need to say it. We've had a nice practice here. All of you concentrated."

He paused. "I've been in your shoes before, and I understand the pressure involved. You all want to do well for your families, your girlfriends, your friends. That's great. But tonight, do me a favor and block that all out of your minds. Let's play the game for ourselves. For the team.

"Okay, that's it! Let's get a shower and get out of here."

Mike walked slowly to the dressing room, his feet moving like two hunks of lead.

Father Charles had sat alone on the sidelines and studied Mike closely during the shoot-around. No doubt about it, the boy's mind was millions of miles away. No intensity, no spirit, no nothing. Like a sleeping congregation, his eyes were glazed and distant.

When the session ended and Big Eddie finished talking, the chaplain stood and waited for Mike. "Hey, you doing okay?" He checked the eyes closer now. His suspicions were right. He folded his arms across his belly.

Mike wiped his face with a towel, then looked away. "I'll be all right."

"Come with me." The priest led Mike through a tunnel and down a hallway, into the main lobby of the arena.

"Oh, my God." A great smile inched across Mike's face as his four brothers ran to him.

"Mike…Mike…Mike!"

"How'd you guys get in here?"

"We been waiting for you, Mike."

Mike took hugs from his brothers, then looked up and saw his father approaching. His long arms hung close to his body. His fists were clenched. Mike had seen the walk a million times before. Fletcher didn't walk like anyone else. He walked with purpose, all the years of working the farm having seeped into the core of his bones.

The man was scary. Even Fletcher's shadow sent chills through Mike as his dad came closer. The usual leathery stare was fixed on his face, conjuring up old memories that Mike didn't want to revisit. But no matter how hard he tried, they came just the same, leaving him with only a sinking feeling in the pit of his stomach.

Bastard. Bastard! Why were you so damn mean?

Fletcher wore a hunting jacket, a green flannel shirt, and blue jeans faded at the knees and thighs. His boots and belt were the color of whiskey. A hank of gray hair eased out from under a brand-new green C.U. ball cap, the letters underscored with the NCAA logo. His hands were callused and sun-blistered, and his clothes smelled powerfully of field sweat. Thick sinews stood out in his neck above the collar. He would have looked more comfortable standing in a ditch.

Mike stood taut and took his old man's hard hand, shook it, then backed away staring at the floor. For a long moment neither of them moved. Mike's muscles felt frozen. He had thought it would be easier. He felt something deep and old twitch inside. His head flooded with things to say, but instead he just stood.

It was almost funny how he had lived so long with his old man, yet had nothing worth sharing with him. They had never bonded. How could they now? The thought circled relentlessly through his mind. What a shame.

Fletcher finally spoke, uneasily. "Boy, you getting skinny." He studied Mike's narrow, gangly frame. His voice echoed with a distance, an uneasiness that kept him from offering any kind of smile. "They not feeding you or something?"

Mike looked up, but not straight ahead. "Yeah…but not like home."

Fletcher scratched his neck and didn't say anything more.

Mary stepped up and stood behind her husband, concern on her face. "You do look awful peaked, Mike. Is something ailing you?"

Yes, something was ailing him, but he sure wasn't telling them. No way to know where Ponytail lurked. "No, Ma, I'm doing just fine. I've still got some of that cake you brought."

"We was going to stop by your room last night, but there was too many cars parked in the lot, and the snow was falling."

"That's okay, Ma. Boys would've probably made too much noise and gotten us all kicked out of the hotel."

Mike turned and watched his four brothers pass a small basketball back and forth. He longed to share their energy and enthusiasm. He knew it was what he needed for tonight's game, but it wouldn't come, no matter how many times he told himself to forget about the man and his threats.

Watching the reunion cheerfully, Father Charles spoke up. "Mike, I got better tickets for them this game. They'll be sitting closer to the floor this time, not in the rafters."

Mike turned to the priest. "How'd you pull that off?"

"The Lord moves in mysterious ways, son." He winked at Fletcher and then put an arm around Mike. "Don't you know that by now?"

"You ready for 'em tonight, Mike?" Fletcher asked, rubbing his whiskers, working a cud of tobacco inside his cheek.

"I don't know, Pa." Mike grew tight-lipped, glared at the priest, and shied away from his younger brothers' adulation. "Notre Dame is real good. Don't know how well we're gonna do tonight."

"Don't know?" Fletcher turned halfway around and looked at his wife curiously. "Is this the same Mike?"

She took Mike's chin and lifted it. "Sweetie, you sure you're feeling okay?"

He nodded his head. "I'll be all right. It's just my stomach doing flips. Just not used to all the attention."

Mike turned and walked back to the dressing room. In less than three days two things had happened to him he couldn't explain. A stranger had given him a shitload of money to fix a game and, out of nowhere, his old man had finally brought the family to see him play. Father Charles was right when he said the Lord moved in mysterious ways. On the other hand, so did the devil.

"Something's wrong with that boy," Fletcher said. He watched his son walk back to the locker room. "He looks like he's fixing to face a firing squad."

Mary Kramer followed Mike's droopy shoulders until he walked under the bleachers. "He's just real nervous about the game...and you being here."

Fletcher didn't dispute the effect of his presence. He knew Mike held hard feelings. But something else about the boy didn't sit well with him tonight. His kid had spunk, had get-up-and-go. Seeing Mike like this tonight unnerved him. Only other living thing he remembered acting so was one of the hound bitches back home who'd lost her whole litter one night when some coyotes got hungry.

"Nah, ain't that. It's something else. I can feel it."

So far in the tournament the C.U. team had dressed for the games in their rooms. For good luck, they did it again.

Medical equipment and the aroma of Ben-Gay filled Hoppy's cluttered confines. He had enough supplies for a small war. He carried five bags on the road, only one of them to hold his rumpled clothes. The rest were filled with tape, medicine, ice packs, splints, heat pads, powdered Gatorade, toilet paper, Kleenex, Band-Aids, a few decks of cards and maybe a warm six-pack if there was room. After Mike's head injury he'd even started lugging along a big blanket. Hoppy didn't like depending on anyone else for supplies. The student managers and Q thought he was a pain in the ass, since they had to tote the extra weight.

Hoppy's room was always the place where everyone played cards the night before the game. The tradition had started in Hoppy's first year as head trainer, when the team was snowed into their Connecticut hotel during a freakishly heavy winter storm. After they won the Christmas tournament, the tradition carried on.

The poker table was usually limited to Big Eddie, the coaching staff, managers, and the cops who provided security on the road, but anyone inside the inner circle with a wad of money could usually play as long as they could stand tobacco smoke, spilled beer, and obscenities. After the one time when Father Charles sat in on a game and lost all his per diem in one sitting, he'd begged off forever.

Another time the famed card game and all its smoke set off sprinklers in a hotel in Tulsa—an establishment that did not invite them back. Once in his wilder days, on a trip to Virginia Tech, Big Eddie had talked two of his female friends into joining the game. The women thought it was strip poker, and no one enlightened them. Of late, though, the game had grown more innocent and tame, with a limit of no more than a hundred dollars in the pot.

It was the day after the poker game now, the middle of the afternoon before the crucial ball game, and Hoppy was sitting Indian style in the middle of his bed, wearing nothing but a tattered T-shirt and boxers dotted with little flowers. His hair looked like he'd just stepped out of a wind tunnel. Two beer cans sat perilously near the edge of the nightstand. Others were piled along the wall, pitched there by the late-night partiers. An ashtray on the card table was chock-full of ashes and tiny white stubs. A deck of cards lay in a pool of warm beer.

Dehydrated, with a mouth that felt like the bottom of a birdcage, Hoppy stared blankly at the TV. A slow, relentless thud pounded away inside his head. He'd already taken three Extra-Strength Tylenol with a bottle of Gatorade, and he was thinking about eating three more when someone knocked.

"Unless it's a maid, come on in," he yelled, rubbing his temples with the heels of his hands.

"I ain't a maid," Mike said, viewing the chaos.

"Damn maids have been knocking on my door all morning. Tell them bitches to leave me alone."

Mike laughed, gently, momentarily forgetting his problem.

"What the hell is so funny?"

"It's almost three, and you weren't at shooting practice. We play in a few hours."

"Fuck that. I ain't playing." Hoppy stared at the TV.

Mike pushed some clothes out of the way and sat down in one of the chairs still sitting upright. "You guys had a hell of a time last night, didn't you?"

"Damn cops got me drunk, left, then came back and rolled me. I'm gonna kick Lampkin's ass when I see him today."

"You look like I feel, Hop. You'd better get moving. I came in here to beat the crowd."

"Fuck it. I ain't taping nobody's ankle today. Tell Big Eddie I ain't doing no taping."

"He'll fire your drunk butt in a hurry, and I'm not letting Q tape me again. He about cut off my circulation this morning."

"He ain't firing shit. I own that mother. I know more shit about him than anyone."

Hoppy slowly climbed out of bed and stumbled into the bathroom. He ran some water over his face then urinated, splashing the sides of the commode. He brushed his teeth and shaved, still muttering, then tossed on a golf shirt he found wadded up in the bottom of his closet. Finally he threw some empty pizza boxes out of a chair and pulled it up to where Mike sat.

"All right, fuckhead, put your leg up here."

Mike knew better than to mess with Hoppy when he was on a hangover. Bad moods produced tight tape jobs. He was quiet as Hoppy rolled on the prewrap and started crisscrossing the tape around the ball of his ankle.

"Not too tight, is it?" Hoppy asked.

"Feels great."

"Good, we need a great game out of you tonight. I hate Notre Dame. Fucking Irish pricks think their shit don't stink."

Hoppy snapped the tape off around the lower shin with his thick hands. He started working on the other.

"My family's here, Hop."

"Really? That's unusual, isn't it?"

"They haven't seen me play but once, I think, since I've been here. My old man hasn't seen me play since high school."

"Then you'll have to introduce them to your new gal, right?"

"I don't know."

"What's wrong, you not seeing her anymore?"

"No, we're still dating, but that ain't it."

"All right, you're through. Get the hell out of my face and cheer up."

Mike pulled on his white socks as Hoppy fell face down in the bed.

'I'm getting too old for all this. When I was your age, I used to be able to handle it. But now my old fat body just don't cooperate like it used to. Someday you'll be in my shoes."

Mike half listened. He'd heard the line a hundred times before. "What do you think about tonight? Think we can do it?"

"Better. I've got a hundred bet that we will."

"Seriously?"

"Yeah," Hoppy said, rolling onto his side, his pale gut spilling over his pants. "I don't think Notre Dame is all that good."

Mike looked away, then into his lap. "I don't know. I'm kind of worried."

"Worried?"

"A little, yeah."

"Hey, that's natural. Big Eddie was in here a little while ago for some Pepto-Bismol. I gave him the whole bottle."

The two grinned.

"You guys win tonight, and we're in the big show, pal."

"Yeah, I know."

"Hey," Hoppy added, more seriously, "all you have to do is go out there tonight and play your best. This team has already done more than anyone ever expected. At the beginning of the year no one gave us a shot in hell to be one game from the Final Four. Me included."

"I know. But—" Mike longed desperately to unload his burdens, but he didn't want to risk involving his friend.

"But what?"

"Oh, nothing. I'm gone. See you on the bus." Mike grabbed his shoes and opened the door.

"Hey, Mike," Hoppy said, before the door closed behind him.

"Yeah?"

"Just do your best, and give it all you've got. Then you won't have to worry about a thing."

Mr. X. waited nervously outside Rupp Arena as thousands of fans began arriving for the game. He smoked a cigarette, holding his hand close against his mouth, and kept his coat collar and muffler turned up and the brim of his hat as far down over his face as as possible. Too many top officials were entering the building. Being recognized by one person could blow it all. Finally, after fifteen minutes, he spotted the man he was looking for.

"This'll get you anywhere you want to go," Mr. X said anxiously, handing a plastic badge on a chain to Ricky Ridgeway, turning his head every five seconds to see if anyone was watching. "You got the cash for my official?"

Ricky Ridgeway nodded, his ponytail bouncing, took the press pass, then removed a hefty envelope from his coat pocket and handed it over. "Tell your boy not to spend this all in one place. He'll get the other half if the Irish win. Got it?"

Mr. X showed part of a smile. "I get my other half after the game, too, right?"

"Wired exactly as you instructed…as long as all four are in. No screw-ups."

They separated, then Ricky Ridgeway slipped the press pass over his head.

Though he was watching from a distance through binoculars, and the photograph he held in his hand was two years old, Rudy still recognized the ponytailed man's face. It was the same guy who'd placed the bet in Las Vegas, Mickey McCraken, if you went by the name on his Social Security card.

The other guy, he wasn't sure. The coat collar, hand held to his mouth, the pulled-down hat brim concealed most of his face. But something about the way he held himself, the way he moved, told Rudy the guy was someone he had seen many times before. There was some connection there, something about a sports setting that clicked.

"Dale," he whispered into the small radio in his hand. "I think we got our point man. I think Mr. X just came and went."

Fans were already lining up to get in the arena as the bus pulled around to the players' entrance. The team had been quiet on the ride over. Most listened to music, others stared out the window or tried to read.

The brakes whined as the big bus came to a stop. The players slowly moved from their seats, filed out past the security guard, and entered the arena, which was buzzing with activity from the technical people preparing WBC's broadcast. A tiny bald man in a navy-blue blazer with a walkie-talkie escorted the team down a hallway to the dressing room. He gave Hoppy instructions on how to get ice and towels, then wished the team well before heading back to his post. The perfect sentry, Mike thought. No little kids could sneak past him to get into the game.

Big Eddie held the door open as each one of his players entered the locker room, studying their moods. Over the years he'd become an expert at predicting how a player would perform by looking into his eyes before the game.

"Get dressed," he said, "then get out and loosen up."

Mike was eager to get out on the court. He was sick to death from worrying about Ponytail, his moon face, the one long hideous brow. A quick sweat would work everything out. He prayed it would.

He dressed, grabbed a ball, and walked down the corridor alone, bouncing the ball between his legs. He walked past another security guard, and as he passed, the guard spoke to him.

"Break a leg, Mike," the man said.

What the hell—you said that to actors, not to a ball player. He looked up from his dribbling. At first he didn't recognize the man, but then he looked harder. It was Ponytail. The moon face and the long brow were shadowed by a cheap security hat with a badge pinned to it.

Shit. He thought it, didn't say it. The knot in his gut tightened. He wanted to puke. His throat went dry. Run, he thought. Run! Run!

"Everything okay for the game, son?" Ponytail asked, a hyena's smile unfolding across his face.

Mike stood perfectly still and whispered. "Yeah." He was afraid his knees might buckle.

"Good, because I'll be keeping an eye on you. And remember, there's lots more candy for you when it's over. Your folks'll be fine. Your girl will be fine. You will be fine. Just don't fuck up."

Mike walked on, looking over his shoulder as he went. His stomach churned. He began to sweat. He ran past a door, then ducked into a bathroom off the hallway, vomiting violently as he ran, leaving a slimy trail across the floor. Inside the stall he bent over, hands on his knees, filling the toilet with his pregame meal. The way he felt now there was no way they could win. No way. He wanted to go home.

After a few minutes and two more heaves, he collected himself. He'd been under pressure before and knew its effects. He took a deep breath, then exhaled slowly—the good old relaxation trick coaches over the years had preached to him before shooting free throws. He did it again. Four, five, six times.

He checked himself in the mirror, rinsed his mouth, splashed some cold water on his face, then walked out of the bathroom, breathing and exhaling as he went. As he walked from under the bleachers the bright lights in the ceiling blinded him. He was hot before he stepped onto the court. He wondered if anyone could tell how nervous he was. How scared.

He looked around as he shot jumpers. The cameramen were checking light meters, the writers casually chatting and laughing on Press Row. Cheerleaders stretched. Only the ball boys paid him any attention. Each time his sweat hit the floor, they hurried to the spot and wiped it up. No one else had noticed, he was sure. No one knew he had just thrown up. No one knew he was about to risk his life for the good of his family. No one knew he was scared to death.

The Notre Dame band started up. Noise filled the arena. Father Charles walked to the corner of the court and nodded his head. "Just relax, Mike."

Mike suddenly turned white then slumped over, hands on his knees. If he'd had anything left in his stomach, it would have all come right up. "I want to go home, Father," he said, his voice muffled, not able to raise up. "I want to go home and curl up in my bed and pull the covers over my head. I can't believe this is happening."

Mike doubled over. Before he hit the floor, Father Charles broke his fall.

Chapter 21

Hoppy took an ice pack and placed it gently on Mike's forehead. Big Eddie paced the room impatiently. "Is he okay, Hop?"

"He looks fine to me, Coach. I think it was just a case of the nerves. Stress can really play tricks on people."

"I've been around a long time, Hop, but I've never seen a player faint before a game. Never."

"Neither have I. Maybe he's worried because his parents are here. God, that's it. His parents and brothers are here at the game. Mike said it's the first time his old man has seen him play since high school."

"Yeah, you might be right. Do you know where they're sitting?"

"No, but Father Charles does. Mike said he got them some tickets. Why?"

"Maybe his old man could come in here and snap him out of it. Go tell Father Charles to find him and bring him down here."

"Where is he?"

"On the bench…praying."

Fletcher followed Father Charles back to the locker room, drawing scornful looks from Security at each checkpoint. Maybe the uniformed guards weren't used to seeing somebody dressed for a cornfield. The hell with 'em. Some of 'em weren't too long out of a cornfield themselves.

Big Eddie smoked a cigarette in the hall, stuck out a hand when Fletcher walked up. "Good to see you again, sir."

Fletcher whipped off his hat and got straight to the point. "Priest here says there's a problem with my boy. What about it?" He looked hard at the coach, at a man he knew understood candor.

"Mike fainted. He'll be okay, but I thought you needed to know."

"Fainted?" A scowl worked across Fletcher's leathery face. His eyes were slits. "Where's he at?"

Big Eddie led Fletcher to a small room. Mike was resting on a padded examining table, attended by Hoppy, who looked up and said, "He's coming around, sir."

Fletcher touched Mike's arm. "Hey, Mike, it's me."

Mike opened his eyes quickly.

"They asked me to come and look at you." Fletcher wrung his hat in his thick hands. "Your mother's worried stiff."

Mike lifted the ice pack, then looked at his father incredulously. He stared blankly, tried to sit, fell back. Everything suddenly went quiet. Hoppy moved into another room, closed the door behind him.

Mike sat up again. He had never been able to speak his feelings to his father, but suddenly now things had changed. It was Savannah, she had given him confidence.

"I just don't get it. Why now, Pa? Why'd you come now? You haven't been to a game in four years, but now that we're this close, you come."

Fletcher chewed on the question, walked over and picked up a paper cup and spat into it. He wiped the spittle from the corner of his mouth with his jacket sleeve, shrugged his shoulders, lifted his square chin.

"I reckon I just wanted to see the toughest fucking kid I've ever known play ball again. A kid who reminds me of someone I used to know."

Mike stared hard at Fletcher, his jaw set. He couldn't believe he'd spoken to his old man the way he just did. But he didn't care anymore. "But what about...all the other games?"

Fletcher was slow to respond. He shuffled his feet, spat in the cup again. "Goddammit, Mike...I guess I didn't think I'd measure up with all the other rich folk around here." His eyes bore down.

Mike jerked back. The words were ominous, the sudden contrition. A tornado had just passed through without touching down. What the hell?

"That's bullshit. You could've come if you wanted. It was the drinking, and you know it."

Fletcher looked at the floor. "Maybe, maybe not, but when I seen your picture in the paper, I seen something I used to have in me. Something inside me flickered again. You made me proud and this entire state proud."

Mike saw moisture glistening in Fletcher's eyes. How strange. Never in all his life had he seen his old man tear up.

Mike sat up, tossing the ice pack off his head. He'd heard his father speak with powerful emotion before—rage and anger, but never tenderness. He felt his own chest swelling, felt his lips quiver. He wanted to hug Fletcher and tell him he loved him, but something stopped him. All those years of hatred blocking the path. But God, yes—the love for his old man was there. Hidden deep, but it was there.

Fletcher put his hand on Mike's leg. "Forgive me, son. That's all I can ask. If you don't, I understand, too." He hesitated. "You okay?"

Mike wanted to tell him everything. He knew no one could lick his old man. No one he knew ever had. He thought back to the three men who'd called Fletcher a drunk one day in town. Little Mike had been sitting in the front seat of the pickup, watching through the back window, when his old man took an ax handle from the truck bed and laid out every one of them before Shorty came running out of the sheriff's office to break it up.

"Nerves is all. I'll be okay."

Fletcher peered into Mike's face. "Your brothers are excited to be here. They want to see you at your best."

"Yeah, I bet."

"Bobby's been bouncing off the walls. Says he wants to be a Knight someday."

Mike smiled, didn't say anything for a moment. And then he asked his dad: "What do you think, Pa? Can we win?"

Fletcher took a step back, rubbed his whiskered chin. "Ain't up to me, Mike. It's up to you boys. Always has been and always will be. I can't play for you. Neither can your coach. And as long as you're sitting in here worrying, nothing's gonna happen, that's for sure."

"You ever get nervous, Pa?"

Fletched closed his eyes for a moment. "Hell yes. Ain't a man alive don't get nervous. It's only natural. I've been nervous every day lately, trying to figure out how I'm gonna straighten out the mess I've made of my life and take care of my family."

Hoppy walked in and softly cleared his throat. "You feeling better now, Mike?"

"Yeah."

A roar went up from the crowd out in the arena. Both teams had returned to the court. Fletcher threw an arm around his son, squeezing hard, staring straight into his eyes. His strong fingers on Mike's shoulder gave Mike the second most wonderful feeling he'd ever known.

"Look, Mike, you've gotta go," Fletcher said. "You do your damn best, all right? Just be a man and walk tall, that's all anyone can ever ask. You hear me?"

Mike rejoined the team as they went through warmups. His old man's presence, his plea for forgiveness, had changed everything. Mike wasn't as scared. He looked into the stands, searched the C.U. section. Everywhere he looked, fans waved pompoms. He took the ball, dribbled three times, and hit the lay-up. He eyed another section as he walked to the back of the rebounding line. No luck finding his family. He put his hands on his hips, then bent down and grabbed his toes with both hands to stretch his hamstrings and lower back.

Damn, where were his mom and his brothers?

He took the rebound, then skipped it out to Spoon, who caught it with his left hand and ran on past. Again he looked, but the fans were as thick as the squirrels in the woods back home. The band charged into the fight song. He hummed along as he waited. A couple of cheerleaders ran by and slapped his hands. He was still looking their way when the ball was thrown to him, hitting the side of his face.

"C'mon, Mike, pay attention!" Big Eddie yelled across the floor.

Mike nodded. He grabbed the ball, hit the lay-up and looked back into the stands. All he wanted to do was wave once at his brothers and his mom. The fight song ended, and when the band sat down, there they were. And after a few seconds they spotted him. He smiled quickly, not wanting to lose his concentration.

But he had to scan the crowd for Ponytail. Where was that moon face? The prick. He could still smell his discount aftershave—nasty musky-smelling stuff. Although he couldn't find him among the thousands in the arena, he could feel him. He knew with every nerve in his body that the creep and God knows how many others were watching his every move.

Before the game started Mike went to the bench to collect his thoughts and grab some cold water. He rolled the liquid around the inside of his mouth with his tongue, then spat it back into the cup. Too much water would give him cramps.

While he was sitting, Father Charles walked over, still concerned. "How's it going?"

"I'm all right. My old man came down to see me."

"I've been saying a lot of prayers for you, son. I'm sure the good Lord is listening."

"Right now I don't even feel like I need God, padre. My old man came to see me play, that's enough."

Mike stood as the rest of the team came to the bench. The announcer introduced the starting fives, with Mike being the last one called. He slapped hands with his teammates, encouraged them to play their hardest. Walking back to the bench, he spotted his dad and pointed at him. Fletcher pointed back. Mike thought about all the things his family had gone through. He thought about all the things he, and they, had sacrificed. His heart felt like it wanted to cry.

"He's nervous as hell," Dale said, sticking an elbow in Rudy's side. "He just pointed to someone up in the stands. Get over there. There might be some more bad actors up there we don't know about."

As the fans stood and hollered, the ref tossed the ball up for the opening tip. Dale pulled out a notepad and drew a line down the middle. Since C.U. was working from his right to left, he scribbled C.U. on the left, Notre Dame on the right. He clung to a desperate hope that his play-by-play wouldn't end up as evidence against Mike.

Big Eddie was as nervous as he had ever been during a game, but he hid it well as he studied the Notre Dame defense intensely. He wondered what John Wooden would do. The Irish used three defenses during most games. The two-three zone was their most effective, the one they used the majority of the time. In order to win, the Knights would have to knock in an occasional three-pointer to loosen up the middle.

"Penetrate and reverse the ball!" he yelled at Robbie, who was bringing the ball up the court.

Big Eddie watched as the ball was passed around the perimeter three times without one pass or penetration to Carlos in the middle. Mike put up a three-point attempt as the shot clock wound down to four seconds. It clanged off the back of the rim.

"Damn," Big Eddie said. If they had to rely on the three to win, they were probably about to get beat.

Notre Dame grabbed the rebound and came down to the other end, took a quick shot, scored. Spoon fouled the shooter. The arena filled with noise. Mike positioned himself to psych out the shooter while he concentrated on his free throw. He waved his hands ever so discreetly to try and disturb him. It didn't work. The shot went through, barely rippling the net.

Mike took the inbound pass, cut to his right as he crossed half-court, then picked up his dribble. Two Notre Dame defenders moved in, trapping him in the corner. Mike panicked, lost the ball off the side of his shoe.

Big Eddie stomped his own foot down hard. "What the hell is he thinking about?" he said, to no one in particular. "He's sleeping out there."

Notre Dame took advantage of the mistake, hitting a three-pointer for a quick 6-0 lead. The Irish fans stood as Mike again crossed half-court, sensing a quick run for their team.

Big Eddie pointed to his head. "Think, Mike!" He called for an alley-oop to Carlos. "Run Marquette, Mike!" He had seen Louisville run this play for years. Denny Crum had learned from John Wooden. They were both his idols.

Mike called the play, watched Carlos cut off a pick set by Spoon. The pick worked just like always, and Carlos, sensing an easy score, soared toward the basket.

Q rose from his seat. He had seen the play run a hundred times over the year. He was ready to celebrate the Knights' first score until he watched Mike's pass sail too high for Carlos to reach.

Q sat back down, puzzled. "He never does that. I can't believe that didn't work," he said to Father Charles. "Mike threw it too high."

Father Charles sat quietly as Notre Dame grabbed the rebound and scored on a lay-in.

Big Eddie was furious. Just four minutes into the game and his senior guard—his star guard—had already turned the ball over twice and missed a wide-open three-point shot. He was seething as the officials called a TV time-out at the sixteen-minute mark.

"What in the holy hell is going on?" Big Eddie screamed. "We're down by eight points. Mike, get your head out of your ass! You've already got two turnovers."

Then something stopped Big Eddie. He had to temper his rage. Getting upset at this early stage would be a mistake. What would Crum do? He scratched his head and thought.

"Guys, forget about all the bullshit surrounding this game. It ain't gonna mean nothing if we lose. Mike, I don't want to ever see you pick the ball up in the corner again, got it?"

"Yeah," Mike said quietly, swirling some Gatorade around in his mouth. It was all he could do not to turn and look around again for Ponytail. Surely the guy could tell that he wasn't trying to win the game.

"Okay, get back out there and relax. No more mistakes."

The game started again, and Carlos suddenly came alive, covering for Mike's inconsistencies. Six times he put back Mike's misses to score. Even so, Notre Dame led by nine at the half.

Fletcher sat silently, studying Mike's game. Though he hadn't seen his son play in over four years, he could sense something terribly wrong. Having watched him every day of his teenage years at the barn, Fletcher knew exactly what his boy could do.

Tonight Mike was missing the cutter with passes, shooting off balance, getting beat on defense. To Fletcher, it looked like Mike just wasn't thinking. There was no passion. When he missed a shot, he didn't seem to care. He was simply going through the motions.

Fletcher excused himself, telling his wife he was going to the restroom. But in fact he had made up his mind to work his way around Security and get a courtside seat. Guards were everywhere, but he would try anyhow. Something was wrong with Mike, and he had to get closer to figure it out.

As he walked down the steps he overheard a comment that lacerated him:

"Get Kramer out of the game! He's choking."

Fletcher held his tongue and ducked in between some band members sitting close to the court, crossed behind the blue security curtain, and moved into an empty seat along Press Row. He tucked his hat inside his shirt, then removed his hunting jacket and placed it at his feet. He spent the remaining minutes of the first half watching Mike. His view was much better. Now he could really see from Mike's eyes what was going on.

He watched closely, and all doubts disappeared. Something was horribly, hideously wrong. As the buzzer sounded, he grabbed a notepad and pencil off the press table and walked into the crowd of coaches, players, and media people. He moved into the tunnel under the stands and watched his son and the team walk off the floor.

As he watched, a reporter in a green blazer suddenly appeared and whispered something into Mike's ear, freezing Mike like a deer caught in headlights. Fletcher had seen the look too many times before. It was the way Mike looked when his own father had flown into a rage for no reason at all.

Ricky Ridgeway smiled, watching the team walk off the floor. He stood just off the court now in a green blazer with a press pass dangling around his neck.

"Hey, Kramer," he said, walking up to Mike.

Mike's head turned to the voice.

"Keep up the good work," he whispered coolly. "You're Notre Dame's best player tonight."

The team was in the locker room now, with the door closed. It was a big room, with plenty of space for everyone to relax. Only the team was allowed access. The players took seats in chairbacks, and those who had played wiped themselves with towels and drank water and Gatorade. Big Eddie took a towel Q handed him and wiped his face.

They had fifteen minutes to get back on track, or the season was over. He'd used every trick in his bag to get the team this far, and now he didn't know what else to do. He searched his mind for something stimulating, something the team hadn't heard before. He stopped his pacing as the room grew very quiet. Finally he decided to rely on sheer honesty and grit.

"There's two things you boys should know," Big Eddie said softly, his eyes glued to the floor, not really wanting to open his heart, but unable to keep it closed. "First off, something is going to come out in the papers, but I wanted to tell you myself."

The team looked around, confused. Big Eddie struggled to say what was on his mind. He explained about the reporter who threatened to expose Penny's past, how she decided to go public herself, rather than hurt the team in any way.

"As far as I'm concerned, this game is for her." He finally looked up. "It'll all come out in the newspaper pretty soon."

"And secondly, I want to tell a story no one has heard before. When I was a senior in high school, we went to the state tournament. We had this team down by thirteen points with two minutes to play." He raised two fingers. "Next thing I know, our point guard fouls out, and I'm told to bring the ball up the floor. Anyone want to take a guess at what happened?"

His eyes scanned the room. "Yeah, you don't need to raise your hand, you probably can figure it out." He waited. "We lost the game, fellas. I turned the ball over so many times, I don't even remember now how many it was.

"A guy hit a last-second shot to beat us. I had my hand in his face. I did everything I could to stop him...but the ball dropped. We lost. My coach wouldn't talk to me. My teammates turned away. Every day until I graduated, people pointed fingers. And since then I've thought about that game every day of my life. It hurt. It'll never go away. We were so close." Tears were shining in his eyes.

"But you know what? When I got a little older I realized what had happened wasn't my fault. Us losing was meant to be. God has a way of throwing obstacles at us to test us, and that was one of my tests. I finally realized that I had done my best. And no matter what happens out there tonight…win or lose…if you can walk off that floor knowing you've given it your all, then that's all any man or God can ever ask."

He stared over their heads, the pains of the past and present flowing through his mind. The team stared back wide-eyed. Suddenly a deep electricity filled the room. The players stood united. Seeing the hurt on their coach's face imbued them with a new energy.

"Let's go, guys," Spoon said.

"Win it for Coach," Robbie barked.

"Fuck Notre Dame," Carlos said. "They might have the best Catholic team in the world, but we have the best one in Kentucky."

Mike was the last one to leave the locker room for the floor. He stared at the ground as he walked. Fletcher stepped away from the wall and blocked his path.

"I saw that man whisper to you, Mike," he said. "I seen him before."

The jackhammers started again in Mike's stomach. His throat went dry. He should have known he couldn't fool his old man. Never could before. "You have?"

"He came to the farm. He wanted you to do poorly, I expect." Fletcher nodded encouragement. "You go play your game, son. Let me worry about us."

Mike didn't know what to say.

"Make you a deal, Mikey." Fletcher put his arm around Mike's shoulder and walked him to the runway. "You do your best, and I'll never take another drink…as long as I live."

"Seriously?"

Fletcher nodded. "Yeah, and something else."

"What?"

"Remember all those people who said you couldn't get here today?"

Mike shook his head. "Yeah, like you."

"Yeah, like me."

"What about it?"

"Take those hurtful feelings out there with you now…and win it for your ma. She's the only one who believed."

Mike grabbed Fletcher's shoulders and held him tight. "I will."

Ricky Ridgeway moved into the first row of the Notre Dame student section, at the end of the court. While the teams were out he had gone to the lobby and had his face painted green and gold, then bought himself a Styrofoam hand making the Number One gesture. He'd carried that into a stall in the men's room and dug out a channel in it so he could aim a gun through the pointed finger if the need arose.

Marzzarella had ordered a win for the Irish, no matter what it cost. If they lost, Ricky Ridgeway/Mickey McCraken knew it would cost him his life.

When Mike emerged from the runway, Ridgeway tapped him on the head with the large hand. "Very convenient, Mikey…having the whole family here."

"Fuck you, asshole," Mike snarled, then walked onto the court.

Ridgeway watched Mike through the warmups, then turned to watch the Kramer family. He noticed that the old man was gone.

Chapter 22

Five minutes before the second half began, Mike sat at the end of the bench to collect his thoughts. He had just twenty minutes of basketball left to realize his dream. He closed his eyes for a few seconds to create some privacy, going back home to find his soul. It was where all this pain had been conceived.

A soft rain dropped through the canopy of trees, beating against the tin roof of the barn, its echoes ping, ping, pinging, then dissipating into the dense forest surrounding the farm like fringes of smoke. He felt the earth under him vibrate as the ball bounced at his side. Up and down. Up and down. The net flipped around the iron rim. The old Rawlings basketball grazed off the side of the barn, skittered up against the fence and stopped, folding over a shock of grass. He walked over and picked it up, dribbled again, shot. As old as the routine was, each time he went through it, it brought dreams, brought freedom, brought manhood.

He squatted under some branches when the rain picked up. The bark of the tree was dark brown, like his water-soaked ball. His hair hung wet in his eyes. Water dripped beneath his shirt. He looked to the back porch and through the door, watched his ma working in the kitchen. He turned to the field and saw Fletcher on the tractor, its grooved wheels churning mud as it went. He looked to the road and saw the neighbors' kids racing by in their dad's pickup, blowing a horn. How he'd wished they'd stop and talk, but they never did. How he wished he was back there again. No coaches, no teammates, no fans, no pressure. The ball, the rim. . .his imagination. His dreams.

Always he tried to figure out why he was the one, and not someone else, who came to the court each day to be in solitude. After a
while he got so tired of thinking about it that he decided it was God's
calling, and that he shouldn't meddle. The loneliness of being a basketball player eventually seeped into his soul, common as the dirt
under his nails. Yes, he was a loner, but all artists were, he always told
himself.

And that's what he was, pure and simple: an artist. Every
time he took a shot, he imagined a different scene for the canvas.
One day it was winning the NCAA title, the next shaking hands
with the U.C.L.A. players after his team had won. At other moments he was Larry Bird hitting a last-second shot in Boston Garden
against the Lakers, or even Michael Jordan swooping down the lane
for a ferocious slam-dunk that brought the fans out of their seats.

The sky hung low and x-ray gray, boxing the court off and giving
him his own pretend indoor gymnasium. His feet were wet and cold,
his right big toe pushing through the hole in his shoe like a groundhog
boring from its winter bed. The ball went up again, splattering the
banking board with streaks of water and mud that bled like stalag-
tites. His fingers throbbed, the tips red from the bracing cold. Snot ran
from his nose, thick as jam.

Was he crazy? Always by himself. Always trying to go somewhere else. He used to ask himself that often. Maybe, but there was
nothing else to do. The only way off the farm was to shoot and shoot
and shoot—and dream about where those shots could take him. Even
if the odds were against it, miracles did happen.

He felt his middle finger and remembered the fingernail he'd
snagged in the rim one day, trying to dunk the basketball. He screamed
and screamed, but no one heard him. He found an old rag in the barn
and stopped the bleeding, then ripped the nail away in one quick jerk.

Because it took a month to heal, he taught himself to shoot with
his left hand. The great ones could use both hands, he knew. Pete Rose
could. Mickey Mantle. Barry and Bird and Magic. So instead of taking
the time off, he got better. Soon the left hand became natural. Now he had
weapons on both sides of his body.

He took a swig of water from a cup Q handed him. "Thanks,
bud," he said, slowly opening his eyes, watching the photographers at

the end of the basket checking their cameras. He wondered if they knew how many nights and days he had dreamed of this moment. No, they couldn't know. No one did. They weren't there with him. No one was. Except Ma. He always felt her smile.

"You okay, Mike?"

Mike winked. Q didn't talk much because of his stutter, but he was the one member of the team Mike understood best. They both knew what it felt like when people laughed behind their backs.

"Yeah, man. I'm fine now. We're gonna win, bud. Just wait and see."

He stood and stretched, easily touching the palms of his hands on the floor. He rolled his neck, then jogged in place for several moments. He looked into the stands where Fletcher watched, nodded his head. The old man didn't respond, just stared. A muscle in his jaw jerked. His eyes fixed in a beam.

"Let's go, fellas." Carlos turned and waved for Mike to join them.

Mike came to the huddle hearing his old man's voice again: *You do your best, and I'll never take another drink…as long as I live.*

He filled his lungs with air, turned toward the C.U. fans, then motioned with his arms for them to make noise. Suddenly half the arena was engulfed, and then, just as quickly, the other half exploded.

Ricky Ridgeway muttered between clenched teeth. "Better not, country boy. Better not."

Savannah crossed Mike's mind. He loved her. How strange life was moving. He couldn't let her down, or go against his morals. The ref signaled for the game to begin. Mike took the pass from Robbie. Finally—the ball felt good in his hands. Soft, controllable, an extension of his arm. He dribbled left. The Irish defender went with him, but he was too far away. Mike gave a head-and-shoulder fake right, then popped a sweet fall-away jumper that arched perfectly and touched nothing but the net when it swished. The C.U. fans roared, but Mike didn't hear a thing. He studied his man's dribbling habits. Every time the guy made a cut, he'd yo-yo the ball. Mike told himself that the next time he did it, he was going to strip the guy. The only way to win was to take a few chances. This was one of them.

The guard crossed half-court, and, when he made his move, Mike cleanly picked the ball before the Notre Dame guard could react. He'd heard people say he had the quickest pair of hands in the country, but being a good defender also involved letting a man get comfortable and careless with the ball, then moving in for the kill. He'd read in high school about how Bill Russell used the same ploy in blocking shots. He liked the idea and often used it afterward to his advantage.

"God, Q, he's back!" Father Charles said, nudging the manager, watching Mike score uncontested. "Whatever his old man said to him, it's working!"

The Knights and Notre Dame battled back and forth. Spoon had foul trouble and sat for ten minutes. Big Eddie went to his bench to buy time. Down by five with two minutes remaining, he used his second time-out. Sweating profusely, he squatted to talk to the team, gently and slowly, as if trying to talk a would-be jumper down from a ledge.

"We've probably got two possessions left." He held up two fingers. "We need a score both times and we need to stop them both times. Got it?"

The players nodded as they drank water.

"On the first possession, let's take the best shot available, regardless of how much time is on the clock." Big Eddie squeezed Mike's leg. "And I want the ball in your hands. It's up to you now."

Mike gazed at the exhausted faces of his teammates, nodded.

"Mike, you get the ball and dump it down to Carlos. Carlos, if the shot is there, put it in. Don't worry about drawing a foul. Just score. Got it?"

Carlos nodded, then finished his cup of water.

"But if it's not there," Big Eddie continued, "get the ball back to Mike. I want good shots. Mike, if the play isn't there, Robbie is going to come and set a pick for you at the top of the key. Take the shot if you're open. Remember, we only need a three and a basket to tie. Also, we've only got one time-out left. After that, nothing. You hear me?"

Everybody nodded that they understood. The huddle broke. Mike wiped the dust from his shoes with his palm. He took the inbound pass, and as Big Eddie directed, quickly dumped it down inside to Carlos. Carlos's man was playing behind him, so the entry was clean. Carlos dribbled once, backing up as he did so, and turned to square up to the basket. The ball went up but hit short of the rim, kicked off left, and bounced around a few times before it fell out of bounds.

The ref under the basket was blocked off, and before he made his call, to the agony of the crowd and teams, he conferred with the two other officials. Finally he motioned his arm in favor of the Knights.

"Mike!" Big Eddie screamed, motioning. "Come here!" Mike ran quickly to the coach's side. "Do it again! They won't be expecting it."

Mike had seen Big Eddie gamble before, but not run the exact same play twice. It was a roll of the dice, but he liked the call. He did as instructed, and when the ball was popped out to him from under the basket, he dumped it back to Carlos again, who was wide open this time. He slammed the ball through the rim. No one was calling him soft now, Mike thought. The guy had come so far, so quickly. He wondered what Ponytail thought of the slam.

The emotions in the arena were at fever pitch as C.U. cut the lead to just three. The cameramen for the NCAA production crew squirmed in their roll-away chairs, positioning themselves for the best angle. The C.U. cheerleaders had the fans standing and screaming. Notre Dame called time-out.

During the time-out, Fletcher followed the C.U. mascot as he hurried to the bathroom. He was grateful the kid was so big—big enough for football. Fletcher couldn't figure why he didn't play. Once inside, Fletcher locked the door and waited for the kid to leave the stall. When he finished, Fletcher tapped him on the shoulder as he was about to put the headgear back on. "Hey, buddy, I'm sorry."

Fletcher made a hard fist and cold-cocked the big kid, knocking him out in the middle of the floor. He quickly stripped the kid's uniform off and yanked it on over his own clothes, holding the sword on his shoulder like his trusty rifle. After making a fool of himself in a routine with the cheerleaders, Fletcher looked for the ponytail, and after a minute he spotted it. He picked a point not ten feet away from the bastard and settled in, watching his every move. Ponytail was focusing too intently on the court to even notice he was there.

When the action began, Notre Dame worked the ball around the perimeter of the three-point line. The shot clock ticked down to seven—six—five—then a forced shot went up from the forward just five feet from the right side of the basket. Spoon had a hand up but failed to block the shot. Mike turned quickly and watched the trajectory of the ball. From all his years playing the game he knew the five-foot shot was the hardest one to hit. It was the in-between shot every player dreaded, never knowing whether to shoot it hard or soft. And indecisiveness was usually the reason they missed.

The ball drew the front of the rim, then circled once before slowly rolling off. Carlos leapt high, stretching his arms as long as they could go, and pulled the errant shot into his large hands.

Down by three points with thirty-four seconds remaining, Mike raced to the official on the baseline and called time-out—C.U.'s last.

Amid the thunder of the crowd's applause, a hollow voice rang out as Mike stood under the basket. He recognized it immediately. "You better hope it works out, Mikey."

He turned and saw Ponytail sitting smugly, unaffected by the electricity in the building, indifferent to the blood Mike had spilt during his childhood to get to this moment.

Ponytail held the Number One finger up and pointed it at Mike. "You better hope it works out."

The jackhammers started again in Mike's stomach. He stared at the man for a second longer, then turned away as his old man's voice echoed in his head:

You do your best, and I'll never take another drink…as long as I live.

Mike walked to the end of the bench and looked into the stands. The C.U. fans were up on their feet, applauding, whistling, slapping hands, crossing fingers, biting fingernails, praying that the fairy-tale game would have a happy ending.

His eyes were wet. He saw the drunks lobbing beer cans at the bus, heard his old man's ridicule, listened one more time to his schoolmates laughing and pointing at him.

In the stands his brothers clapped. His mom covered her face with her hands, too afraid to watch. Finally he saw Savannah, wearing his number on a green jersey. They locked eyes. She mouthed "I love you" from her seat.

Mike turned away, Big Eddie wanted him. "Mike…Mike…get down here!"

He walked to the huddle. Big Eddie reached him before he got to the rest of the players. "Are you okay?"

"Yep, sure am."

"We need a three to tie. Got it? Do it. You're a winner, son. The greatest competitor I've ever had the pleasure to coach, and I love you. You do it, do it for nobody but you."

Mike swallowed hard as he listened to the coach call his number, knowing that this was exactly what he had always wanted. The ball in his hands. The moment of truth. A chance to do what they said he couldn't do.

When the huddle broke, Father Charles whispered into his ear. "May the Lord be with you, Mike."

Mike waited for the official to hand him the ball. The noise had actually grown louder. The drums, the flutes, the trumpets in both bands increased tenfold. Thirty-four seconds, and one way or another his future would be decided. Closing his eyes wouldn't even make it all go away.

Rudy worked on a box of popcorn and watched the action from where Dale had told him to sit. He hadn't noticed anything out of the ordinary, except for a few students getting drunk off beer, and one girl with the biggest set of tits he'd ever seen. But right before halftime he almost swallowed his tongue, because the man outside the arena before the game with Ricky Ridgeway was now sitting on Press Row— smiling and slapping backs.

Now Rudy knew who he was. "Jesus Christ," he said to himself, ashen-faced. "Jesus Christ…Jesus H. Christ."

He clicked his radio, then spoke frantically into it.

Dale slid out of the seat and followed several steps behind so he wouldn't be detected. Rudy was already inside the media room just in case their man went in there. Every time he thought about it, his body felt like jelly. It couldn't be. No way.

The man stopped and waited for the final seconds of the first half to end, standing confidently against the wall of the runway that led the teams and the officials to their lockers. When the officials passed by, the man followed behind, slapping the back of the third ref, grinning far too familiarly as they both made their way inside and secure behind a locked door.

Dale closed his eyes, hoping he wouldn't hurl right there in front of everybody. He held it back, then whispered into his radio.

"Rudy, as soon as they're out of there, I want that area wired…and that official and his buddy followed when this game is over with. If this is what I think it is, college sports will never be the same again. God…it's a sick world we live in."

Mike took the inbound pass and eyed the Rupp Arena scoreboard. Everything suddenly slowed down. His old man was splitting wood, Ma was hanging clothes on the line, his brothers were wrestling in the yard. He felt the ball spinning in his hands, to the floor, back again.

Carlos was bent over, stretching his shorts. Father Charles clutched his rosary. Q couldn't bear to watch. Hoppy screamed something Mike couldn't make out.

He felt his defender's breath, smelled his sweat. With his shoulders he jerked, sending the Irish guard to his heels. "Get back, chump," he said.

He heard his friends telling him he would never amount to anything. He heard Big Eddie screaming that he was a redneck from the hills. He heard Ponytail telling him to give up his life-long dream.

"Fuck 'em," he said under his breath. "Fuck 'em all."

"Motherfucker," Ricky Ridgeway muttered. "Motherfucker is trying to win this game."

Ridgeway licked his lips, swallowed, brought the barrel into position. Notre Dame was still three up. Wait, he thought. No need to get excited—yet.

Fletcher followed the action on and off the court, coming down on one knee just in front of where Ponytail stood with the Irish fans. He was dying for a drink.

Moving over the half-court line, Mike screamed over the noise in the arena. "Call out the picks, fellas. We're going to The Show!"

His teammates nodded and received their men. Mike gave the clock a quick glance: twenty-five seconds remained. Father Charles had said to look deep and to find the spirit. He wasn't sure where it had gone, but he was ecstatic that he finally had it back.

In the split second that Mike looked at the bench, the Irish defender leapt at the ball.

"Son of a bitch." Ricky Ridgeway stomped as Mike whirled away from the defender, narrowly escaping a turnover.

Fletcher, watching out of the corner of his eye, felt it. The little man's body movements were giving him away. Fletcher stood and waved his knight's sword at the Notre Dame crowd, then went down to his knee again, edging ever closer to Ponytail.

The Notre Dame defense hugged the three-point line just as Mike expected. A three would tie the game. But Mike had come too far to let the Irish leave the arena with a victory.

He called what Big Eddie wanted, raising two fingers over his head to signal the start of the play. Carlos hesitated, then moved into position to set the pick on Mike's defender.

Twelve. Eleven. Ten.

Carlos set up on Mike's left. Mike motioned right. Carlos moved over, catching Mike's man with his butt and a portion of his leg, closing off any chance he might climb through the pick. Bedlam rocked the arena as Mike planted his toes outside the three-point line, then squared his shoulders. The defender made a desperate move toward him, but Mike shifted his feet and jumped.

Ricky Ridgeway cursed, then lowered the Number One finger. A puff of acrid smoke poured from the end of the foam hand.

The ball rotated perfectly as the Notre Dame defender slammed Mike to the ground. He clutched his arm. Couldn't see. The ball bounced off the rim, hit the backboard, rolled around. The crowd erupted as the ref threw his arms into the air signaling a three—and a foul.

Two seconds showed on the clock as the C.U. bench exploded into chaos.

"He did it!…He did it!…He did it!" Q hugged Father Charles. "He did it!…He did it!…He did it!"

"He's hurt, Q!" Father Charles couldn't rejoice, because he saw Mike writhing on the floor. "He's hurt!"

Carlos waved for Hoppy. Hoppy scurried out with a towel draped over his shoulder and a smile as wide as the Ohio River on his face. "Mike, goddammit, you…" But suddenly Hoppy stopped hollering when he saw the blood pouring from Mike's arm.

"What's the matter with him, Hop?" Carlos hovered over Mike like the shadow of a blimp.

Big Eddie rushed onto the floor. "Is he okay?"

Hoppy looked up in disbelief. "I'm no damn detective, but I think he's…been fucking shot."

The ref moved in, frowning at a supposed attempt to delay the game. "Can he go to the line?"

Big Eddie whispered into his ear. "He's been shot."

"What? The hell you say!" The ref bent over and inspected Mike's left arm. He suddenly looked up and scanned the arena floor. "Security!" he yelled, pointing at C.U.'s team mascot with his sword at the throat of a green-and-gold-painted, ponytailed Irish fan. Two men in suits and a couple of security guards were quickly moving to the scene.

"Hey, looks like it's already under control," one of the refs said to Big Eddie, nodding. "We'll have a damn riot if I go over to the scorer's table and tell TV and the rest of the media this kid has been shot."

Out on the floor, Mike was shaking his head and gritting his teeth. "Patch me up. My old man's whippings used to hurt more than this. Just stop the bleeding...and let me finish this game."

Hoppy looked at Big Eddie, who nodded. "Is it possible, Hoppy?"

"From what I can tell, the bullet went right through his flesh. He's lucky as hell it didn't hit any bone."

"You sure, Mike?" Big Eddie asked, down on one knee.

Mike squeezed his hand. "They've been telling me my whole life I couldn't do this," Mike said softly. "Winners don't quit, no matter what. You told me that."

Big Eddie choked back a smile, but it leaked out any way. "Son, you are one tough bastard. I take back everything I ever said about rednecks and hillbillies. I wish the hell I could bottle what you've got."

The ref stepped in. "Let's get going, or I'm going to call an official time-out and he can't shoot."

Quickly, Hoppy bandaged Mike's arm, then helped him to his feet. The confused crowd watched the ponytailed man being led from the court by the police, and when they spotted Mike get up, a volcano of cheers almost took off the roof.

As Mike toed the free-throw line, Carlos walked by and whispered in his ear. "Hey, I told you playing on a basketball team was like being in a gang."

Mike nodded, then took the ball from the ref. His dream was one shot away.

Luca Marzzarella set his drink down and straightened up in his chair, stroking an automatic pistol that lay in his lap. A closeup of Mike's face and the bandage around his arm came up on the television screen.

"Make this, and I'll kill you myself, kid."

Mike dribbled three times, took a deep breath, tried his best to block out the arms being waved behind the basket by the Notre Dame fans, then let the ball go. As soon as it left his hand he turned and pointed at his old man. The ball swished through the net. Notre Dame took the ball and heaved it the length of the floor, but the shot dropped short. The wildest of wild celebrations broke out on the C.U. bench, then fans stormed the floor to cut down the nets.

Carlos scurried to Mike, wrapping him up in his long arms. "We did it, Mike! We did it!"

Mike closed his eyes and cried. "I can't believe it, Carlos. I can't believe it."

Cameramen suddenly raced to Mike and Carlos, their embrace shown in homes all across the nation.

Marzzarella shook his head, pointed his gun at the set, and fired.

Chapter 23

Dale Cutter watched the ambulance move out of the arena and the media scramble to figure out what had just happened. He spotted Father Charles walking away from the wailing vehicle, then grabbed his arm and pulled the priest away from the commotion.

"Father, you remember me, right?" Dale asked, his hand firmly around the priest's biceps.

Father Charles pulled back and stared strangely at the agent. "You're the—"

"I'm the guy who comes and talks to the team every year about gambling. Remember?"

Father Charles pulled at his double chin. "And you were the one with that man who—"

"Yeah, shot Mike."

The priest buried his face in his hands. "I knew I should have come to you from the beginning. Where are you going to take me?"

"You're not in trouble, Father. Just tell me what you know."

In minutes Father Charles confessed to Dale all that Mike had told him. "Mr. Cutter, I'm so dreadfully sorry. I didn't know what to do. What could I have done? Mike feared for his life."

"With good reason, obviously," Dale said. "It's not over yet. You know now they're going to come after Mike, don't you?"

The priest looked up, wiping his eyes with a tissue he pulled from his pocket. "Surely not. Even though you're holding their man?"

"All the more so."

Dale put his hand on the priest's shoulder and guided him away from the crowd. He told him everything he knew—the bet, the wiretaps, his well-founded suspicions that referees and players had been paid off or interfered with in other ways. The priest couldn't believe what he was hearing. These kids, innocent kids, caught up in something so vile.

"And one other thing, Father," Dale said.

"Don't tell me…the Holy Father is involved, too?"

Dale shook his head. "No, Father, not His Holiness." He pressed his lips together, hating what he was going to say. "Just the NCAA tournament director of officials."

Father Charles shook his head in disbelief. Dale nodded a yes.

"We saw him taking a package before the game from the man who fired at Mike. We've got it on film."

"Do you know what was in the package?"

"Not for certain, no. But it had to be money, and I think he gave it to one of the referees, because we checked the officials' and the players' locker rooms and haven't found a thing. My partner even had the area wired, but these guys were too slick. We got nothing on them except what we saw."

"This goes beyond all logic," Father Charles said. "The director of officials of the NCAA tournament? I don't believe it. Why would someone of his stature get involved with something like this?"

"Money, Father. Big money. I know it's all true, but I can't prove it unless I can break down the slimeball who fired on Mike."

The priest rolled it all around inside his head. "Maybe I can do something."

"Yeah, like what?"

Father Charles told Dale his plan.

"I like it. C'mon, now that the snow has finally melted a little, I can get a jet down here in two hours. We can be there first thing tomorrow morning."

Savannah's face above the hospital bed was a mask of anxiety. "I can't believe what you've just told me, Mike. I'm starting to get real, real scared." She looked around nervously, even though two policemen were stationed just outside Mike's room.

"It's true, Savannah. All of it. Father Charles has the money. Go ask him."

"I'm not asking him anything. This…this is plain crazy. Oh, Mike, why did you ever let someone convince you to take that money?"

"I didn't take it, they planted it in my locker." Mike sat straight up in the bed. "But I would have taken it," he said, "because they were going to hurt you."

She was clutching his hand firmly as the door of the room opened and Fletcher walked in.

"Mike, how you doin'?"

"I'll be fine. Just a scratch on my arm, that's all."

Fletcher's gaze fell on Savannah.

"Pa, this is Savannah. I told Ma about her."

"Hello. Nice to meet you."

Savannah shook Fletcher's hand. For only the second time in far too many years Mike felt very close to his old man.

"Pa, thanks for all your help back there. I wouldn't have won that game if you hadn't told me to."

"You did what was right, Mike. I'm real proud of you. So is your ma and your brothers. Hell, the whole state for that matter. Mayor stopped me coming out of the arena and said he was gonna push to have a park named after you back in London."

Savannah squeezed Mike's unhurt arm. "That's unbelievable, Mike."

"Really?" Mike said smiling, looking at Fletcher. Somehow things were starting to fall into place. His eyes watered.

"Yep. He was as serious as a man gets."

A news flash raced across the television screen, interrupting the regular program. Mike and Carlos were shown hugging, then the picture turned to Mike being taken away in the ambulance. Finally the announcer came on and said that sources close to the FBI were saying that a top official within the NCAA was being linked to a possible fix of the NCAA tournament, and that members of a powerful underworld organization were thought to be involved.

"Good God," Fletcher said, watching the newscast. "A man inside the NCAA fooling with a kids' game. Greed is the root of all evil. Don't you kids ever forget that."

"Well, all I know is that we're gonna to have to be careful for a long, long time," Mike said. "Our whole family, Savannah too. I shouldn't have—"

"Yes, you should have," both Fletcher and Savannah said in unison.

Mike looked at the two of them, never expecting to see them both in the same room, and surely not agreeing on anything.

Luca Marzzarella was in his office when the secretary buzzed him and told him a priest was waiting to see him. Incredulous, Marzzarella told her to let him in. He struck up a cigar and waited, wondering what church wanted a donation this time.

"Come on in, Father," Marzzarella said smoothly, standing up, offering a cigar.

"No, thanks," the priest said. "That stuff'll kill you."

Marzzarella laughed. "Sometimes a little wickedness does us good, padre. Have a seat."

Father Charles sat down. "A little wickedness, perhaps. Everyone is human. But most people can't leave it there. Give wickedness an inch, and it'll take a thousand miles."

"Hey, I like that. Mind if I use it?"

Father Charles shook his head. "No, I don't mind, provided you leave my friend Mike Kramer alone."

Marzzarella's brow furrowed. He clinched the cigar tight between his teeth. "Ah…excuse me, Father, but you'll have to explain yourself."

He offered his hands, palms up. "You're talking a riddle here. I'm just an ordinary businessman, trying to make an honest living in this wicked world we live in."

"Don't bullshit me," the priest said. "You *will* leave him alone."

"Who the hell are you, anyway?" Marzzarella said sharply, twisting the heavy diamond ring.

"Just a priest, a nobody. Have a look." Father Charles stood and unbuttoned his shirt. "No wire. Just to let you know I'm on the up-and-up."

Marzzarella studied the priest for long moments, holding the cigar between his fingers, every now and then tapping ashes into a glass tray on his desk.

"Mike Kramer, eh? He the kid I read about here in *The Times*, the one that got shot?" Marzzarella lifted a copy of the newspaper and pointed to the front page.

"That's the one."

"Ah, you can't believe nothing you read in the papers. Them reporters, they come up with a lot of wild stuff. Even said he took money from a looney-toons Notre Dame fan." He laughed, a mean little laugh.

"I don't suppose you'd know anything about where he might have put that money, would you, padre?"

"It was donated to the church."

"To the church? Now, there's a real racket for you." Marzzarella made another laughing sound, but there was no humor in it. "The way I see it, that kid oughta give it back to the guy the FBI picked up… poor bastard's gonna need every cent for his fucking attorney."

Even though he was inwardly quaking, Father Charles appeared cool on the outside. "The offer we have to make may be a lot more valuable to you than that."

"We? Who's this we? You got a rat in your pocket, padre?"

"No, no rat. Just me and the FBI."

"Ha…nice company you keep, padre. A religious man like yourself, I'd of thought you'd know better than to hang around with them punks."

Marzzarella sucked smoke deep into his lungs, took a drink from a glass of water, then folded his arms across his chest. "Okay, let's hear it…this fantastic offer."

Father Charles swallowed hard, cleared his throat. On the plane flying up Dale had filled him in on all the details of the fix. And he'd told him to take it easy, that if anything got out of line, he'd be waiting in the car. If Father Charles didn't show after thirty minutes, Cutter would come looking for him.

"Well," the priest said, "seems to us this whole thing is a wash."

Marzzarella snorted. "Sorry, padre, I don't follow you. A wash? It don't look like that from where I sit."

"Since Mike got shot, the network ratings have rocketed through the roof. Everybody and his brother will be watching C.U. play North Carolina next week. Whatever deal you made, well, they'll get their money's worth."

"A deal? You think I had a deal with WBC about the ratings?" His fabled control was breaking. "I don't think so. I think you been drinking way too much of that cheap church wine."

"Forgive me for getting it all wrong." Father Charles managed a wink. "But just in case you did…"

"Right, padre. Just in case." Marzzarella paced, caged.

"So, when you look at it that way, really there's only two losers. The man who shot Mike…"

Marzzarella's eyes narrowed. "Yeah, who else?"

"Who else? The man in Las Vegas who bet fifty thousand dollars on the exact Final Four teams."

Marzzarella puffed hard on his cigar, his mouth working. "Another riddle, padre…you amaze me. And just who might that have been?"

"I'll tell you, but you have to promise me one thing."

"Me, promise? Promise what?"

"The man's father is dying. If you plan on speaking to him, please wait until after the funeral."

"Oh, yeah? I can't make no promise if I don't know who you're talking about." Marzzarella lifted the newspaper again. "What about this NCAA dope here the paper says was involved? Even money says he'll tell the world anything to save his sorry ass."

Father Charles held up his hands. "You guarantee Mike his and his family's safety, and I think I can persuade the FBI to…how do you guys say it?…deep-six the case in a pair of cement shoes."

Marzzarella grinned the first time for real. "I like your style, padre. I'm gonna think your offer over. Who knows, things just might work out."

Chapter 24

Savannah gripped Mike's hand as the two walked down the aisle, then slipped into a pew close to the altar. Sun splashed through the great stained-glass windows as the chapel began to fill up with guests.

"Big Eddie's shaking," Mike whispered into Savannah's ear.

"He's handsome in that tux." She turned and smiled. "You'd look good in a tux like that, you know?"

"Think so, huh?"

"Yeah, think so."

They locked eyes for a long moment until organ music suddenly filled the chapel. The doors at the end of the long aisle opened. Penny North appeared, in a gown of all white.

"She's beautiful," Savannah said.

"You'd look beautiful in something like that."

Savannah blushed, then gave Mike a quick kiss. "I think I'm going to cry. Weddings always make me cry."

Ten minutes latter Penny became Big Eddie's bride. They walked hand-in-hand down the aisle and out the chapel doors, greeted by a large group of fans. The crowd sang the C.U. fight song and pelted the newly-weds with rice before they drove off in a limousine.

Father Charles walked up behind Mike and Savannah as the couple stood with the other smiling, waving guests. "You kids wouldn't be thinking about doing this, would you?"

They both turned and stared at the priest as if caught with their hands in the cookie jar, then looked at each other.

"Ah...well...um," Mike said.

Savannah just giggled.

"I didn't think so. Not yet, anyway." The priest gazed down the road after his friend's departure. "Big Eddie looks pretty content right now, even though we didn't beat U.C.L.A. to win the title."

"Yeah, he does," Mike said. "I think Penny's gonna be real good for him."

Father Charles waved at Carlos, who was escorting his date to the parking lot.

"Hey, Father!" Carlos yelled, keeping one arm around his date's shoulders tight.

"Darn," the priest said, snapping his fingers. "Looks like we've lost another potential priest."

Mike chuckled, watching Carlos lean and kiss the girl. "Yeah, I think he's made some important decision in his life."

Father Charles sighed. "Mike…before you go…can I have a minute?"

Mike shrugged. "Sure. I won't be long," he said to Savannah. "Wait here."

Mike and the chaplain walked back into the chapel and sat down together in a back pew.

"How's that arm of yours?"

Mike rubbed where he'd been shot. "Don't feel a thing anymore. Hoppy and the doctors did a great job."

"And how's everything at home?"

"Awesome, my mom says. My old man got that job in Corbin…and he's quit drinking. For real."

Father Charles smiled. "I'm so happy, Mike. See, the Lord was watching over you."

Mike thumped his chest. "Sometimes I used to wonder where He was at, but now I know."

"Yeah, where?"

"Right here in my heart."

The priest reached and hugged Mike. "I'm so proud of you. Don't ever forget that, son."

"I won't, Father Charles. I won't. Anyone who could stop my father from drinking is very powerful. I'm just afraid someday that man…you know the one…I'm afraid he'll come back for revenge against me and my family, like he said."

"You don't need to worry about your little problem, Mike. It's been taken care of."

"Huh?" Mike looked strangely at the priest. "You mean the people who—"

"Yeah, those guys."

Mike's eyes lit up. "Come on, Father. Give it up. What're you talking about?"

"Someday I'll tell you the entire story, but not here."

"Hmm…" Mike moved to stand up, but he had one more question. "Whatever happened to that money?"

"Like I said, the good Lord was watching over you. It's been set aside." The priest broke into a wide grin. "In a scholarship in your name…so your brothers can use it when they want to come here."

"No way." Mike stood, staring. "You mean…?"

"Yep, free ride, Mike."

"No way."

Father Charles nodded. "Good things happen to good people, Mike. Now get out of here, go be with your future wife."

Mike smudged a knuckle across his cheek. "I don't understand life at all, Father. All this just doesn't make sense."

"That's the beauty of it, Mike. You didn't understand, but you still had faith. Our friend upstairs appreciates that."

Mike hugged the priest. "Thanks for being there. I love you."

"No, Mike, thank you," Father Charles responded, swiping at a tear of his own. "It's kids like you that keep me hanging in this job, make life worth living."

Savannah stood alone at the top of the steps, a faint breeze stirring the pink ribbon in her hair. "What was that all about, Mike?"

"Oh, nothing. He just wanted to tell me that he took care of that little fix I was in, that's all."

She stood on her tiptoes and reached up for a long kiss.

"Wow, what was that for?" He took hold of her waist, wanting another.

"For being exactly who you are, that's what." They clung together, laughing. "I love you," she said, "and I'm so proud of what you've done. C'mon."

She took his hand and led him through campus. When they passed some kids playing basketball they had to stop after a couple of them came sprinting over to Mike.

"Mike, come on, hoop with us for a little while!" they begged. "Show us those moves you used in the Final Four. We need somebody who can really play the game."

Mike smiled, still gripping Savannah's hand.

"Guys," he said softly, "once you learn the key to the game, you'll be able to play it in your sleep."

The kids looked puzzled. A fat boy wearing a Louisville tank top cocked his head. "Key? What's the key, bro?"

"The heart, dude. And if you want something bad enough, don't ever let anyone tell you you can't do it. Hear me?"

"Yeah, man. Yeah. We hear you."

"I mean nobody!"

"All right, Mike. We hear you."

"Good, now get back out there and keep playing. That's where it all begins."

Paul Justin sat at the counter, waiting, until Clara came back with his coffee.

"You need to quit smoking those cigarettes, doll-face," he said. "They're going to kill you someday."

"Yeah, big deal. We all gotta die. Might as well go out the way I want."

Justin smiled. "You got a good point there, I have to admit."

He read the newspaper, then looked up over his coffee. "You know something, Clara? I probably won't be coming in here much anymore."

She turned from the coffeemaker she was cleaning. "Why's that?"

"Retiring, doll. I'm fed up, sick to death of all the bullshit."

"You mean they're still on your butt? Even after the ratings were so high for the Final Four?"

"Yeah, it's always something."

"It was a great tournament, though. One of the best."

"It was, but I wish Catholic University had won the whole thing, instead of U.C.L.A.," Justin said. "I'd have liked to see that kid who got shot holding up the trophy."

Clara put her hand on his shoulder. "From all I hear about it, that kid won more than a trophy. He kept his self-respect."

Justin sipped his coffee. "Self-respect…right, I guess he did have that."

"Listen, Paulie, if you're retiring, who's taking your place at the network? Don't tell me that stuck-up moron you had lunch with last fall."

"No," Justin said, "it won't be him. As a matter of fact I haven't seen him since his father's funeral."

"Yeah, I was sorry to hear about the old man's passing. He was one of the good ones. You always talked highly of him."

"The end of an era, Clara. The end of an era. And you know what, Clara?"

"No, Paulie, what?"

"I think today I'm going to have a piece of that apple pie. After all that has happened, I deserve it."

"Yeah, you do. And so does that Mike Kramer kid. Maybe I'll send a slice his way. He does seem like the All-American kid."

Jeff Schneider is a Development Director at a high school in Kentucky. He played Division I basketball at St. Louis U. and worked 10 years with two national championship coaches as a Sports Information Director at the University of Louisville. A graduate of Bellarmine University and Western Kentucky University, he coaches his own basketball team and is presently working on his next novel. For more information on Jeff, please visit: www.readthefix.com or communicate directly with the author at: thefix01@hotmail.com.

For other fine titles from Vivisphere
please visit:

www.vivisphere.com

or call for a catalogue:

1-800-724-1100